JACKALS' REVENGE

IAIN GALE

Jackals' Revenge

HarperCollins*Publishers*

HarperCollins*Publishers*
77–85 Fulham Palace Road,
Hammersmith, London W6 8JB

www.harpercollins.co.uk

Published by HarperCollins*Publishers* 2012
1

A catalogue record for this book
is available from the British Library

ISBN: 978 0 00 727870 1

This novel is entirely a work of fiction.
The incidents and some of the characters portrayed in it,
while based on real historical events and figures,
are the work of the author's imagination.

Set in Sabon by Palimpsest Book Production Ltd,
Falkirk, Stirlingshire

Printed and bound in Great Britain by
Clays Ltd, St Ives plc

MIX
Paper from
responsible sources
FSC
www.fsc.org **FSC C007454**

FSC™ is a non-profit international organisation established to promote
the responsible management of the world's forests. Products carrying the
FSC label are independently certified to assure consumers that they come
from forests that are managed to meet the social, economic and
ecological needs of present and future generations.

Find out more about HarperCollins and the environment at
www.harpercollins.co.uk/green

1

Dawn rose over the pass of Thermopylae as it had since the beginning of time. As it had on that day 2,000 years ago, when Leonidas' Spartans had died to the last man holding this great natural strongpoint against the invading Persian hordes. This morning, though, something was different, for with the dawn came a new sound on the air, drowning out the bees and the birdsong and shattering the peace of an Attic morning. It was a high-pitched whine, descending earthwards out of the sky. The sound of modern war. The clarion call of a new and terrible barbarism which had laid claim to the civilised world.

Captain Peter Lamb heard the sound and looked up in alarm. He knew it only too well. Had become familiar with it in the fields and on the roads of France less than a year ago, and it made his blood run cold. Without a second glance he yelled across the pass to where his men were sitting pulling through their guns. They had been on stand-to all night, waiting for the German attack that was sure to come. Their faces were drawn with exhaustion, but for all their fatigue they had already heard the sound. The younger men, the new recruits and replacements, were still looking skywards, not certain what they heard, although it was not new to them. The old hands, though, were already on their feet as the words left Lamb's lips.

'Stukas. Take cover.'

The first bombs fell seconds later as the whine of the sirens fixed beneath the wings of the hated aircraft reached its crescendo. The men cowered in their funk holes and in any space they could find in the unforgiving rocky landscape, their hands over their ears and their tin hats, their mouths open to lessen the shock of the blast, their bodies tucked up into tight balls. As the bombs hit, their hammer-blow explosions dug deep into the baked white rock, sending lethal shards in all directions, and the men, even though they had not been hit, mouthed their oaths. They shut their eyes tight and two of the younger ones tried to push themselves into gaps in the rocks.

Tucked into his own tiny slit-trench, Company Sergeant-Major Jim Bennett saw them and ran across to them at a crouch, before speaking through the din, hard into their faces. 'Now then, Dawlish, Carter, you don't want the captain to see you hiding like that, do you?'

'No, Sergeant-Major.'

'No, Sergeant-Major. I should bloody well think not. Now bloody well brace yourselves and look like soldiers. They'll be gone soon enough.'

Bennett swore quietly. It was bravado, of course. But sometimes, he thought, keeping up morale was more like being a wet-nurse. He thought of the old platoon, of the men they had left behind in the fields of France last year and the few they had led out and who were still with them, and he wished for the impossible. Bennett knew they would just have to make do with what they had. But he had confidence in Lamb. If any officer could lick them into shape he knew it would be his. Hadn't most of them already come through Egypt together? He knew

To Patrick Barty
and
the people of Crete

that some of them at least had the makings of good soldiers. Still, though, he longed for his fallen friends and prayed that these new lads would prove themselves capable of avenging them.

Bennett had been right about the raid. Within minutes it was over. Two bombs each, and that was it for the six-plane squadron. The dive-bombers veered away like hawks up into the azure sky and the men crawled out from their holes into the dusty air of the balmy April morning, coughing and cursing.

Lamb and his men, C Company, the North Kents, or the Black Jackals as they were known to the army, had been given simple orders. 'Hold the pass. Do not allow the enemy through.'

His CO, Colonel George de Russet, had made it plain enough to them at the last Order Group. 'Gentlemen, here we are and here we bloody well stay.'

Lamb knew that the Stukas had only been a taster and prepared himself for what he knew was to come. This would be as hard a battle as he had yet fought, and perhaps his last.

He shouted across to Bennett: 'Sarnt-Major. Any casualties?'

'Two, sir. One's a goner. Spencer.'

Poor bugger, thought Lamb. He's the first then. How many more today? He turned towards the young lieutenant in command of Number 1 platoon, Charles Eadie. 'Charles, see if you can make those slit-trenches any deeper. This rock's bloody stuff but we'll have to do better than that before their big guns open up or we'll all be goners.'

As the lieutenant scuttled away across the rocks, Lamb considered their position. He had led eighty men into Greece just under a month ago. Now he commanded something over half that number. They were still in their

3

three platoons and of the three junior officers he had lost only one, the young lieutenant of Number 3 platoon, who had been replaced with a transfer from Battalion HQ. There were now forty-eight men plus himself. And, whatever their orders, whatever position they were told to hold, it was now his ultimate task to get them away and back to Alexandria. Two days ago the Greeks had surrendered, and now the British and Commonwealth troops who had been sent to defend them were on their own.

Lamb's immediate orders were to cover the withdrawal of the New Zealand 6th Division. So now here they sat, the Jackals, in the pass of Thermopylae. The bloody rearguard. Again.

The Greek campaign had been a hard schooling, and of the casualties in his company two were now in hospital in Athens with nervous exhaustion, their minds as shattered as the bodies of those who had died. In a previous war – his father's war – they would have been shot as cowards. Now Lamb thanked God, at least they were only labelled insane. It did not surprise him. Although they had seen action in Egypt, they had only caught the last of the fighting in Cyrenaica before the Italian surrender in February. Greece had been very different. They had seen and felt the full might of the German war machine. Worst of all, the Germans held the skies. There seemed to be no end of their planes. Surely they would just bomb Greece into submission?

Eadie was back with him now. 'I've got all the platoon sergeants on the case, sir. I've told them to get the men to dig down another foot.'

'They'll be lucky if they manage six inches.'

Charles Eadie was a curious-looking man, with a large head sitting on huge, broad shoulders and a naturally nut-brown complexion which suggested that at some point one of his ancestors might have been born the wrong side of the counterpane, as his mother would have put it. His movements too seemed awkward, but strangely he managed to be quite dexterous and was always perfectly turned out, even now in this dustbowl. His green eyes shone like emeralds from the dark skin and as usual he was wearing a smile, but it did not disguise his nervousness.

After a few moments he spoke. 'We can't really hold them here, sir, can we?'

'No, Charles. I don't think we can. But we can try, can't we?'

There was a pause. 'D'you think we'll make it out of here, sir?'

'I would say we had a fighting chance. Wouldn't you?'

'Of course, sir. We're the Jackals, after all. And it's a pretty good position.'

'Yes, pretty good.' Lamb smiled. 'Although it didn't do the Spartans much good.'

'Sir?'

'Thermopylae, Eadie. Where are your Classics?'

'Oh, I wasn't very good at Classics, sir. I was more of a mathematician at school. But I do know that there was a battle here before. In history.'

Lamb nodded. 'And we, Charles, are standing in the footsteps of heroes.'

The man who had been standing to their right, a sergeant, now spoke and Lamb realised unsettlingly that he had been there all the time. He had a curious accent, clipped and cultured, yet somehow not of the establishment, as if behind everything he said there might be an element of sarcasm. 'Actually, sir, there have been six battles here. The Spartans, of course, the famous one against the Persians in 480 BC, but then there was another in 353 BC, one in 279 BC when the Gauls attacked, then

the Romans came here in 190 BC, and then they themselves were attacked by the German tribes in AD 267, and
then of course there was the Greek revolution in 1821.
Byron and all that.'

Lamb shook his head. 'Is there any end to your knowledge, Valentine?'

The sergeant shrugged. 'Couldn't say, sir. I was just
praying that we'd get out of here alive. And that we aren't
captured.'

'I share your sentiments.'

'But I really do mean it, sir. You know that when the
Greek revolutionary hero Diakos was captured here by
the Turks in 1821 they impaled him and roasted him
alive on a spit.'

Eadie blanched. Lamb laughed. 'Valentine, I hardly
think that the Germans will do that if they capture us,
do you?'

Valentine shrugged and smiled. 'Who knows, sir.
Anything can happen in this war. Permission to brew up,
sir.'

Lamb nodded, and as Valentine wandered off he shook
his head and wondered to what god or gods that conun-
drum of a man had been making his prayers.

They had been through France together, and Valentine
had saved Lamb's life. Twice. They had come through
the chaos of the Dunkirk retreat and had made it back
home. But they had also witnessed atrocities in France
and he knew that similar massacres were already happening
in Greece. But roasted alive? He hardly thought so. Not
even the Nazis.

Lamb sat on a rock, took the map from his pocket and
wiped the sweat off his forehead. Above him on a high
rock a goat moved, loosening stones and jangling up the
hill pursued by a small boy who was shouting something
in Greek. Life goes on, he thought. For a while at least.

He wondered what lay in store for the Greeks once they too had fallen under the Nazi boot. The same fate as France? Stories had come out that in that country where he had fought so recently the population was being systematically brutalised.

He had brought out a French girl, Madeleine, and he thanked God that he had. They had become very close. Lovers. But he had left her back in London when the battalion had shipped out to Egypt with 1st Armoured Brigade in January and he wondered how far she had got with her efforts to join the Free French army that had formed in London under de Gaulle. He had no love for the man, not after what had happened to the Highlanders temporarily under his command on the Somme last year. But they said that his presence now as the leader of the Free French in London had given his countrymen fresh hope, and that, Lamb knew, was what really mattered.

He was not sure, though, what hope there was for him and Madeleine. Although he had written to her several times, he had received only one letter from her since Egypt and that of course had been censored. He wondered if he would ever see her again. It seemed to him at this moment that he would either die here or be taken prisoner and he wondered how long the war might last. Hitler must be stopped, of course. But now Britain stood entirely alone against the might of the Nazis.

He looked over at his men as they recovered from the air attack, lighting up cigarettes and making tea. They were new faces, most of them, and a precious few of the die-hards of his old platoon that he had brought out of France. Apart from Valentine and Bennett there was Private Smart, his batman and the newly promoted signals operator at Company HQ. He watched as Corporal Mays, now made up to sergeant of Number 2 platoon, cadged a Woodbine from one of the new intake, and looked across at the group of Butterworth, Hughes, Perkins and Wilkinson, corporals now, all of them. Stubbs, the heavy weapons expert, was a corporal too and had been given command of the company mortars. And Private Hale, who had been wounded at the Dyle and whom they had all given up for dead or captured, had miraculously appeared again at the depot at Tonbridge and now he too had a stripe.

Lamb counted himself particularly lucky to have managed to hold on to Jim Bennett. The army had wanted the tough cockney sergeant as a drill instructor for officer training. But Lamb had insisted and, although the Sergeant-Major didn't know it, he had made it a condition of accepting his own promotion to captain and the company that went with it that Bennett should stay with him. A little string-pulling had done it. But then what were connections for, if not for that? He and Bennett knew each other in the way that only a junior officer and his sergeant can. They were a close team, each reading the other's thoughts at any crucial moment. He could not afford to lose him. And he knew too that while Bennett might be one of the bravest men he had ever met, at present his mind was filled with more than the battle that lay ahead. Bennett had left a young wife back at home in London and she was due to give birth in seven weeks. And they had all heard what was happening to London. He cursed the Luftwaffe and reminded himself to keep a close watch on the Sergeant-Major.

The power of his connections in the higher echelons of the army had taken Lamb a little by surprise. He knew that he had managed to turn a few heads on the Staff and raise a few eyebrows with his unorthodox behaviour in France. But his promotion had been faster than he might have supposed. It had been suggested to him that he might be interested in joining a new unit, as yet unnamed, that was forming in Scotland. Some sort of elite force drawn from various regiments. Lamb had refused. He was an infantry officer, as loyal to his regiment as he was to King and country. He loved the Jackals. They were his home. And he wasn't sure either about his exact views on an 'elite unit'.

He also wondered whether the regiment hadn't been chosen for the Greek expeditionary force on account of his belonging to it. Lamb had glimpsed the signature on the battalion's movement order and recognised it as that of a certain colonel on the staff whom he knew to be keeping an eye on him. The same man had earlier suggested joining the new unit. The posting had certainly puzzled the battalion CO. 'Greece? Us? With the tanks?' de Russet had said. 'Good grief! Flattered, of course. Honoured. The Jackals are always spoiling for a fight.'

He was wondering how long the war might last, when Britain might defeat Germany, when around the edge of the gully came a British major wearing red tabs on his collar. He was escorted by two armed riflemen.

The staff officer saw Lamb and smiled. 'You the Jackals?'

'Yes. The rearguard. C Company. Captain Lamb.'

'Well, you're to fall back. The rest of your battalion's doing the same. Making for the Peloponnese. We're all pulling out. Your battalion transports are in a field to the west of the village. Take the Brallos pass. Head south. You'd better be quick about it, Jerry's almost here.'

'Sorry, sir. I was told we were holding the pass.'

'Well, you're not holding it any more, Captain, are you? We're leaving it to the Anzacs. This is their party now.' He frowned. 'You don't actually mean you want to stay?'

Lamb shrugged. 'Well, I want to do what's right, sir. At least we'll do what we're ordered to, sir. I thought we might hold them up for a few hours.'

'Or get blown to pieces in the process, Captain. Come on. Ten minutes. That's all.' And with that he was gone.

Lamb turned to Bennett. 'I don't believe it, Sarnt-Major. Do you?'

'Just like in France, sir, if you ask me. No one knows what the blazes is going on. Not ours to question, though, sir. Eh? We'll leave it to the Kiwis.'

'Yes, you're right, Bennett. It's just that I can't help feeling as if we've been given a last-minute reprieve. And desperately sorry for those poor bastards in the pass.'

Bennett was right, he thought. It was just like France. There too they had been told to pull out after having first been ordered to hold on. There, though, Lamb had disobeyed the order and it had damn near killed him. The wound in his back still gave him the occasional pain. This time he would do as he was told. This was no time for heroics. Not yet. He wondered, though, when the army would really stop retreating. They had won a victory in Egypt against the Italians, but it seemed that wherever they met the Germans in battle it was the British who did the running. They looked down into the pass towards where the New Zealanders had their forward positions.

'They're damn good fighters, sir. They'll hold Jerry up for a while.'

Lamb nodded his head. 'Yes, Sarnt-Major. I'm sure they will. We'd better get moving if we're going. Get the chaps together, will you. We've only got ten minutes.'

There was a whine from north of the pass followed by a huge explosion.

Lamb stared at the rising cloud of dust. 'Christ, those are 88s. Come on.'

The promised transports laid on for their withdrawal were a motley collection. According to the major, the Battalion HQ, along with A and B Companies, had gone on ahead, leaving Lamb with the last pickings. They amounted to two 3-ton trucks, a Bren carrier and a couple of fuel bowsers. Somehow, though, they managed to cram themselves in with all their equipment, and at last, with more rounds from the German anti-tank guns crashing into the emplacements behind them around the pass, they set off south west. Lamb took the lone carrier in front, and led the way along the road away from Thermopylae.

Their path was surprisingly clear. They rattled along through the morning heat, the distinctive scent of thyme and the baking, parched earth rising from the countryside. From time to time they passed evidence of German air attack: a shot-up vehicle or a peasant cart and the bodies of a horse or a team of oxen. They drove on for two hours, climbing steadily until the poplar-clad mountains enveloped them on both sides. The lower slopes of the hills, where the trees had been taken, were dotted with scrub. Beyond this was thick foliage: oaks and beeches and, as Lamb remarked to Bennett, pear trees. Ahead of them they could see the dust from the column, and occasionally, where the road took a twist and doubled back on itself, they saw their comrades below them, in a long trail of carriers and trucks.

Near the village of Brallos, through the pass that guarded the left flank of the Allied army, the countryside opened out and they found themselves on a high plain looking across to a vast mountain range. It was breathtakingly beautiful. They passed into a lush valley dotted with red-roofed farms and olive groves. But now Lamb began to worry, for apart from a few old men playing cards outside a bar, a few villages back, they had not seen any people. Not one.

On the outskirts of the little town of Levadia they turned a corner and came to an abrupt halt behind a cart. It was moving, but only just, and was piled high

11

with belongings – a chest of drawers balanced on a table sat next to battered leather suitcases and two gilt-framed pictures. Perched amid and on top of the whole pile was an old crone dressed in black from head to foot. She was sitting facing them, travelling backwards, rocking back and forth and wailing quietly. Beyond the cart lay what looked to Lamb like an endless line of other carts and trucks of all descriptions. There were donkeys, too, and a horde of civilians. He swore. 'Damn. This is what I feared. Those villages back there were much too quiet. This is why. They've heard the Germans are coming and they're not staying to welcome them.'

Smart spoke. 'Perhaps it's just a bottleneck, sir. Maybe someone'll pull the plug.'

'Maybe, Smart.'

But ten minutes later they came to a halt and ten minutes after that they had still not moved. Lamb spoke to his runner, Bill Turner, seated behind him in the carrier, who had been chosen for the post as the fastest man in the company. 'Turner, go ahead and see what's going on.'

Five minutes later the man returned, breathless. 'It's a real jam up ahead, sir. Trucks and carts and all sorts.'

'No idea what's causing it?'

'Could be anything, sir. Just goes on for about a mile. I didn't get to the front. Shall I go back, sir?'

'No, don't bother. Any sign of the rest of the battalion?'

'No, sir. There's no Brits up there. A few Greek soldiers, but aside from that it's all civvies.'

'Damn. This lot must have cut in between us and them at that last junction. Well, there's no other route and Jerry's too close on our tail. We'll just have to get out here and hoof it.'

Lamb looked around at the countryside. It was hard terrain off the road, with steep drops and vineyards and olive groves, which would make the going hard. But how

12

the devil could they get past the mass of humanity on the road? He climbed out of the carrier. 'I'm going to take a look. Sarnt-Major, Turner, you come with me. The rest of you wait here. Charles, tell the others what's going on.'

The three of them pushed through the crowd of civilians along the road and Lamb marvelled at their composure. For the most part they passed through the crowd without comment. But soon Lamb became aware of an overwhelming atmosphere of grief. While children wailed and mothers chided, some of the refugees seemed almost catatonic, staring at the ground or away into the distance. Occasionally someone, usually a Greek soldier, would notice the three Englishmen and smile or give a thumbs-up. Civilians were mixed in with the military, and looking at them Lamb thought how war had become a great leveller, possibly more than it had ever been. Over to his left a woman in a fur coat and an ornate hat was stumbling along the road on high heels accompanied by her ageing and still neatly besuited husband. Who was he? he wondered. A lawyer, a doctor? Groups of civilians stayed close together, presumably families and neighbours from the same villages. What had they left behind, and what did they have now? And where were they going? To stay with relatives in the safety of the mountains? He supposed that more than a few of them might not have any idea.

The trail of people and vehicles seemed endless. At last, after what Lamb reckoned might have been the best part of a mile, they found what they had been looking for – a huge truck, old, with peeling black paintwork and of uncertain age and make, was slewed across the road and around it stood a cluster of Greek men of all ages: old men and boys, farm hands and soldiers in filthy and incomplete battledress. The men were talking and gesticulating towards the truck. Lamb had no Greek save the little he had learnt at school and he had quickly discovered how different that was from the local patois. It was clear to anyone, though, that the thing was stuck. He pushed through the men and stared at the truck as a Newmarket trainer might look at a horse, assessing its pedigree, its probable strengths and weaknesses, for one of the traits which marked Lamb out among his fellow officers was his knowledge of mechanics. Before the war, while he had thrown himself into the Territorial Army, his first love had been motors. When not employed as manager of a garage in his home town of Sevenoaks, when not in the drill hall or on manoeuvres, he had spent his evenings tinkering with his beloved BSA. There was little about engines that Lamb did not know or could not work out. He could of course take the easy option. They could take the brake off and push the thing off the road. But he looked around him at the empty, anxious faces and knew that it was not really an option. To destroy this precious means of transport might mean the end of all hope for a good dozen of these people if not more – old women and young children incapable, try as they might, of making it through the mountains to the safety of some hilltop village. The truck was their only chance of salvation.

He walked over to the truck and lifted the bonnet. A man beside him muttered something in Greek and Lamb smiled at him and shrugged. Then, propping open the bonnet, he removed his battledress top, tucked his tie into his shirt and rolled up his shirtsleeves before getting to work.

The Greeks stood staring, fascinated, as this British officer worked away at the engine. After a few minutes Lamb raised his head from inside the bonnet and yelled at Bennett. 'Sarnt-Major, turn her over, will you.'

14

Bennett climbed into the cab and, finding the starter, switched it on. There was a deep roar, a thump and a chug and the Greeks gave a cheer. But after three revolutions the noise stopped. Lamb swore and dived back into the oily mess that was the engine.

Half an hour and two further attempts later, despairing, Lamb again raised his head. 'Right, Bennett. One more time.' The Sergeant-Major, patient as ever, turned the starter and the machine burst into life. The Greeks, who had not stopped watching, reserved their applause this time, but now the motor continued to turn over and after a few minutes they began to cheer. Lamb emerged from the bonnet wearing a huge grin, his face covered in grime and his hands caked in oil and grease. One of the Greeks offered him a torn sheet and he wiped himself down gratefully. 'I thought we'd never get it,' he said to no one in particular. A priest standing close by nodded and smiled at him and several of the men clapped him on the back. 'Whose truck is it, anyway?' asked Lamb, gesticulating. But, to judge from the shrugs, no one knew. Perhaps, he thought, the owner had given up and abandoned it. He called to Turner. 'Get it moving. Get as many on board as it'll take.' Returning the handshakes of the Greeks, Lamb smiled and accompanied by Bennett made his way back to the carrier.

'You know, sir, you could just have ditched it. Pushed it off the edge, like.'

'Yes. But did you see them? How could I do that? It would have been like a death sentence.'

Bennett nodded and said nothing. He knew that Lamb was haunted by something that had happened in France. A bridge that they had been ordered to demolish with high explosive. A bridge that had been packed not just with the advancing enemy, but with Belgian and French civilians – men, women and children. And he knew that

15

Lamb would never forgive himself and would take any chance to atone.

They reached the carrier. 'Smart, see if you can raise Battalion on that crystal set. Tell them we've been held up. Get their direction, can you.'

While the radio operator began to tinker with the unreliable field wireless, Bennett started up the carrier. Ahead of them the convoy was beginning to move.

After a few miles they reached a junction in the road and were soon caught up in a massive column. While the refugees remained in front, they were no longer the bulk of the column. From a road to their left, the road from Thermopylae by way of the coast, lorries were filtering on to the main highway, filled to bursting with British, Greek and Commonwealth troops. Lamb looked at the men in the trucks. He saw grim, unshaven faces, tattered uniforms, and noticed the shortage of weapons. This is an army in retreat, he thought. The same army, in fact in many cases the same soldiers that he had witnessed pulling back in France almost exactly a year ago. A year that seemed a lifetime away.

It took them another five hours to get to the outskirts of Thebes. Lamb looked down at his watch. It was close to 4 p.m. As they drove on, he looked to either side of the road and saw that they were in a bivouac area, bounded on either side by slit-trenches and laagers of trucks covered in camouflage netting. To the right on a slight rise in the ground stood a lone 25-pounder. Everywhere, in the olive groves that lined the road, men were sitting, shattered by exhaustion. Most of them were asleep, quite oblivious to the cacophony of the column pouring past their billets. He wondered which enlightened officer would have chosen to make camp there. It was not a position that he would have chosen – open, exposed and with little natural cover. He was wondering where they should stop when there was a cry from the roadside. 'Aircraft. Take cover.' Instantly, Bennett killed the motor on the carrier and the other drivers followed suit. The men slapped open the tailboards and, jumping down, ran to the sides of the road and threw themselves forward into the foliage, disappearing amid the scrub. Lamb followed them and landed hard on his back, reawakening the pain from the old wound. Sitting up he found himself beside two New Zealanders, their heads buried in their hands. One of them spoke, without bothering to see if he was addressing an officer. 'Hide yer face, fer Chrissake, mate. The Jerries can spot anything down here.'

Lamb silently ignored the man's lack of deference, took the advice and pushed his head between his knees. As he did so, he heard the whine of engines in the sky and waited for the bombs.

2

There was nothing at first, just the shrill noise of a single-engined aircraft. Lamb did not dare to look up. Spotter plane, he thought. Then he heard it wheeling away and a few seconds later it was replaced by the deeper drone that he had dreaded. The bombers came in low and dropped their sticks in no particular way on the road. He heard the bombs fall almost rhythmically and thought, There really is no point in worrying. If one of them has my name on it then that's it. This is war. Random and unforgiving. There was a huge explosion and then another and another as the stick of bombs fell in their orderly row along the road. Another, different explosion told him that one of them had found a target, a truck of some sort. He prayed that there had been no men left inside. They were so powerless here, utterly unable to fight back. Perhaps the politicians had been right after all before the war. Perhaps the battle for the skies was what would win. Hadn't the Battle of Britain proved that? But from where he was sitting this was an infantry war as well. These rocks, these hills, he knew would never be taken until the Wehrmacht had pushed the last Allied soldier back into the sea. And even then, when the Germans were in

18

Athens, he knew the Greeks would not give up their country. Another stick of bombs crashed through the earth and Lamb, pushing his tin hat down on his head, heard the big New Zealander next to him let out an oath and sensed the man pushing himself into the ground. He thought of Bennett and knew that his thoughts must be going out to his wife as she sat cowering, as they were now, beneath the stairs in the Sergeant-Major's house in Islington. And just as he waited for the next bombs to fall, Lamb heard the engines fading.

As the planes wheeled away he raised his head and turned to the New Zealanders. 'Who are you?'

'20th Battalion, 5th Brigade, sir. We've come down from Molos. Never seen anything like it, sir.'

His mate joined in, stony-faced. 'Hundreds of our lads were killed. Hundreds of them, some in a bayonet charge. We was shelled all morning and as we were pulling out too, shells everywhere. Didn't even know if we'd get out or not.'

Lamb said nothing but shook his head, hoping that would be enough. He stood up and looked for the company. Called out. 'Sarnt-Major, Lieutenant Eadie, Mister Whitworth, Mister Sugden. To me. Sarnt-Major, casualty report.'

'Sir.'

'Gentlemen, I think that we had better get on before Jerry makes the road impassable. Get your men together and mount up. We leave in ten, casualties notwithstanding.' He turned away and raised his voice. 'Sarnt-Major, casualties?'

'None, sir. It's a bloody miracle.'

'Well, saddle up then. Ten minutes.'

Leaving the New Zealanders to manage as best they could down the pot-holed road, they carried on. Thebes itself was deserted. The German bombers had done their work here. It was hard for the untutored eye to tell what was an ancient ruin and what more recent damage. Through the town they began to gain height as they went until the sides of the hills became steeper and they entered a pass, thickly wooded on both flanks.

Lamb turned to Bennett. 'Keep your wits about you, Sarnt-Major. If the Jerries have managed to get round the flank this would be the perfect spot for an ambush. Smart, have you managed to raise Battalion on that thing yet?'

'No, sir. Sorry, sir.'

'Don't worry, not your fault. I just wish we knew where they were.'

He looked at the tattered map that he had taken from the canvas map case at his feet. 'Once we get through this pass there's a village and then a fork in the road. We take the right, towards Corinth. Once we get over the bridge there we are in the Peloponnese. Then it's a straight run to the sea.'

Bennett smiled. 'I do like to be beside the seaside.'

'Home in time for tea, sir?'

'Not quite, Turner. But we'll give it a try.'

The mood of optimism was short lived. As they drove on, the pass became ever narrower. Lamb scanned right and left. 'Be alert. Keep your eyes open.'

They rounded a bend in the road and Bennett slammed on both brakes, bringing the carrier to an abrupt halt. Lamb jolted forward, knocking his chest against the front of the carrier and dropping the map. 'Christ, Bennett, have a care . . .' Then he saw that ahead of them to the left lay a defensive barrier of stones made into a chest-high wall – a sangar, which was matched on the opposite side of the road by another, leaving a narrow gap only just wide enough for a lorry to negotiate. The top of each wall was lined with Lewis guns and riflemen, while a heavy machine-gun had been set up in the middle of the road. As they looked on a sergeant appeared from behind the right-hand sangar, his Thompson gun held at waist level and fixed directly on Bennett.

The man spoke in a broad New Zealand accent. 'Who goes there?'

'Friend,' said Lamb, quickly. 'North Kents. We're trying to get to Corinth.'

The sergeant whistled and within seconds they were surrounded by his men, rifles at the ready. The sergeant advanced to the carrier and peered at Lamb. 'North Kents? What the bloody blazes are you lot doing here? We thought you were Jerries. Almost let you have it.' He paused. 'Maybe you *are* Jerries . . .'

Lamb shook his head. 'Good God, not again. Listen, Sergeant, I went through all this in France a year ago. How many times? I don't know. What d'you want to know? Who won the Cup last year? The length of Don Bradman's inside leg? The name of the King's dog? Where Winston Churchill gets his bloody cigars?'

The sergeant peered at him. 'Nah, sir. You're kosher. No bloody fifth columnist would ever have said that. Sorry, sir, can't be too careful. We're the rearguard, see. Jerry can't be far behind you. Haven't you heard, sir? They've taken Corinth. Yesterday. Only took them two hours. Paratroops. We blew the bridge, though.'

Lamb felt as though he had been punched in the stomach. If the Germans had taken the Corinth canal then that meant the whole of the Peloponnese was cut off. He was aware that the New Zealand sergeant was still talking. '. . . I said why don't you go through there, sir. The pass broadens out again there, sir. You'll find yourself a billet if you need one.'

Thanking the sergeant, they drove on and Bennett

summed up Lamb's thoughts. 'I wonder if the battalion got across before the Jerries took it.'

'Well one thing's for sure, Sarnt-Major. If they did, we can't follow them now. There's only one way out for us and that's through Athens.'

There was no point in trying to make Athens by nightfall, and if they carried on along the road in daylight they would just be more sitting targets for the Luftwaffe. Better to stand here and set off again in the early hours of the morning under cover of darkness. 'We'll stop here, Sarnt-Major. Pull up over there.'

They parked the trucks and Lamb walked across to one of a number of the sangars which dotted the area. The pass, as the sergeant had told them, had broadened out and given way to olive groves and a landscape of cultivated fields and vineyards. He found a corporal. 'Is your officer anywhere?'

A voice spoke from behind a wall of rocks. 'Actually I'm over here. Who wants to know?' A tall New Zealand captain walked forward. 'Captain Nichols. And you are?'

'Lamb. North Kents.'

'The Jackals. Didn't know you were here.'

'I'm trying to get my company through to Corinth, but there's no hope of that now.'

'You heard, then. About Corinth.'

'Yes. Paratroops.'

'Well, we knew they'd do it one day. So what now?'

Lamb shrugged. 'Well, I reckon that the battalion must have got through, but wherever they are it's Athens for us.'

The captain nodded. 'Yes. Look, I'd get your heads down, if I were you. No point in leaving till the morning, before sun-up, of course, or you'll be strafed to bits by Jerry. You'll find a free olive grove over there somewhere,

22

near my boys. Help yourself. And you're welcome to join the mess, Captain, what there is of it. Boiled eggs and sardines last time I looked – by the crateful. And the CO's still got a bottle of whisky, if the old man hasn't drunk it all already. Reckon you could use a glass. Your men can scrounge a bit of bully off our cook if they like. I think we've got enough to go round. Found a wrecked rations convoy back in the pass.'

Lamb smiled at the unexpected generosity. 'Thanks. I'll see that they're fed.'

Nichols explained the position to him. 'The road here twists its way up a gorge, with a wonderful view down towards Kriekouki. That's the road Jerry will take. D Company's over on the left, then A Company, and C Company's over there, away out on the right. They're right up on a knoll, with a sort of ravine between them and A. They're all linked in to Battalion headquarters by lines. The Aussies did that for us this morning. Not that it'll do anyone much good at the moment, of course. Complete wireless silence. Not a peep, or Jerry'll throw the lot at us. Worst thing is that if we get bombed there's bugger all we can do but sit it out. Those Aussie gunners have been told not to fire at any planes unless they see us.'

'But if we're getting bombed they'll have seen us anyway, won't they?'

Nichols shrugged. 'Don't ask me, I just know the orders. I don't have to make them, thank God.' He smiled, indicating an opinion of the High Command, and then carried on. 'So the Bren carriers from 20 Battalion are on the left flank, and the others and the machine-gun company are out on the right, just in case Jerry decides to drop any more paratroops. Oh, and we've got part of an Aussie field ambulance unit in the village. You might need them.'

Lamb nodded and looked across to the left flank, where

the Bren carriers were, but saw nothing. Their camouflage was good. The ground too was in their favour. The lower slopes of the mountain were covered with a sort of short scrub, rather like broom; then farther up was bare rock. As far as Lamb could see most of the hills on the north side were wooded, right down to the edge of the valley. It was dense cover: pine, holly and oaks. On the whole he felt more secure here than he had at Thermopylae.

Eadie, Wentworth and Sugden saw to the men before handing over to their sergeants and joining Lamb at the 'mess', which consisted of two groundsheets and some camouflage netting slung between some olive trees. An orderly had managed to find enough crates to act as a table, so there it was that they sat, sipping warm beer that the quartermaster sergeant had found in a taverna in Levadia, while Lamb accepted a measure of the colonel's precious scotch.

The New Zealand captain talked to Lamb about the Greek landscape. 'Terrible country here, you know. God knows how they farm it. Nothing but blasted rock. The only thing that'll grow are blasted olive trees. Hardly surprising there's nothing but bloody goats. Christ, who the hell would farm bloody goats? Now you want to come and see New Zealand, old man. You haven't seen grass till you see our fields. And our farms. I'll show you what real farming is. Honestly, Lamb. If you want a new start after this is all over, come and see me. I'm not kidding.'

Lamb smiled. He had never contemplated emigrating. Never would. What, he reasoned, could he possibly find on the other side of the world that he could not have in England? He respected the New Zealanders and the Aussies. Had fought alongside them in the desert. They were good fighters, tough as they came, and they made his own men, most of them, seem puny with their physique. But he would never get used to the extraordinary relationship both nationalities had with their officers. Never. Of course his own relationship with Bennett, and even with the unfathomable Valentine, come to that, was something special, but about the Antipodeans there was a lack of respect, a lack of deference that would never be part of what Lamb knew to be at the heart of the British army. So he smiled sweetly at Captain Nichols and raised his glass. 'Love to, old man. After all this.'

He was just wondering whether the colonel might offer them another whisky when there was a commotion from the sentries. No shots, just raised voices, one of which sounded to Lamb distinctly patrician. The colonel looked around and nodded at one of the junior officers. 'Frank. Be a good chap and see what that's all about, will you.' He paused and smiled, weakly, like a man resigned to his fate. 'The rest of you might like another. We'd better make the most of it, don't you think? God knows where we'll be tomorrow, after Jerry gets here.'

The mess steward, a hairy former sheep-shearer from Auckland, moved around silently through the group of officers dispensing from the whisky bottle until it was drained and then, as the soda water followed from a syphon that bizarrely had made it to Greece across 8,000 miles of ocean, there was a roar from the road and as they watched, still clutching their drinks, a long black limousine, a Citroën, Lamb thought, sped past their improvised mess, along the road, in the direction of Athens.

It was preceded by two exhausted-looking motorcyclists and followed by several other vehicles, brimming with troops.

Lamb looked at the occupants and recognised General 'Jumbo' Wilson, commander of the Allied forces in Greece, in the front seat beside the driver. Behind him, alongside a woman wearing an elaborate hat, was a tanned and callow youth wearing the uniform of a general in the Greek army, his face set in a stern expression. The vehicles drove past them throwing up dust and rock. Lamb turned to the Kiwi CO, Colonel Robertson. 'Was that who I think it was, sir?'

The colonel nodded. 'Yes, I think it was.' He called to the gawky lieutenant, who had come hurrying back from the sentries. 'Frank, who the devil was that?'

'The Prince of Greece, sir, Prince Peter, and General Wilson.'

Captain Nichols spoke. 'Blimey, sir. Jumbo himself. They weren't half in a hurry. Didn't even stop for a drink.'

There was laughter from the officers. Colonel Robertson smiled. 'They're on their way to the sea. Getting away. And I daresay that's where we should be headed now ourselves, gentlemen. But for the moment we've got to stay here and fight.'

It was the signal for the end of their little party, and Lamb returned to the men. He found Bennett. 'Sarnt-Major, get the men together. I need to talk to them.'

They assembled quickly. He would not say much, he thought. No 'St Crispin's Day' oratory. Just a few words to steady their nerves. Lamb climbed on to a rock to address them; looked around and saw some familiar faces, those few of the men who had come with him out of France the year before, and many more of those whom he had led through Egypt and into Greece. Men whom he knew he would now trust with his life. He coughed and smiled.

'Good evening. I hope that you've been fed and that the Sarnt-Major has looked after you all.' There was laughter and someone called out, 'Like me own mother, sir.'

Lamb nodded and went on. 'You know what we've got to do. We came here to stop the Jerries taking Greece

26

and we haven't quite managed it. It's no fault of yours. But now we've got a different job to do. If we can't save Greece then at least we can save our own men and let them get away to Egypt. The command don't expect the Kiwis here to hold this place. What they have got to do is slow Jerry up and give him a bloody nose. And we're going to help them.'

One of the men spoke. One of the new ones, Hay, a good-looking East End lad on whom Lamb was keeping his eye for a future NCO. 'Like the Guards at Dunkirk did, sir. Didn't they?'

'Yes, Smith. Just like the Guards did at Dunkirk.'

The boy can't have been long out of school when that happened, he thought. But they all knew about Dunkirk, about the miracle, Churchill's miracle. They didn't know, of course, about the other evacuation, down in Normandy, at a place called St Valery, where Lamb and his few survivors had got away. That had been no miracle. Far from it, and not spoken of now. Nor were the 8,000 men of the Highland Division whom they had had to abandon there to be taken prisoner with their general. And Lamb knew that for the present, at least, that must stay in the past. There was another battle to fight now and the enemy were pressing ever closer. He spoke again.

'You've met the Kiwis here. They're good men. Good fighters. There's a battery of 25-pounders up on that ridge to our right. Aussies. So while the gunners fire at the tanks and trucks, it's our job to take out the advancing infantry who'll be following on behind. Some of you have fought with me before. You lucky few.' More laughter. 'The others will have heard all about that and they will know as well as you veterans do that I'm not a man to give up. So we'll stand here with the Kiwis and do what we can, and then when we're given our orders we'll make our escape. And one more thing. I don't want to leave anyone behind. Got that? Now, get what rest you can and good luck.'

There were a few murmurs of 'Good luck to you, sir', and the men drifted away to find shelter in the olive grove.

Lamb stepped down from the stone. One of the men had hung back. Spencer.

'Sir, just one thing.'

'Yes, Spencer.'

'Sir, what exactly are we doing here? I mean, sir, I know what you just told us, about saving the Greeks and all that, but why are we here?'

'We're sent here, Spencer. By the generals. To try to stop Hitler. And to try to stop him without getting ourselves killed. That's all you need to know, lad. Now off you go.'

Lamb himself wondered what they were doing in Greece. What relevance it had to Britain. France he could see. That was obvious. But he was sure they were in Greece for purely political reasons and he wondered if that was a good enough reason to die. The more he saw of those reasons in this war, the less he liked it.

Two of the lieutenants were standing beside him, and a short distance away the old lags of the company including Bennett, Valentine and Mays.

Wentworth spoke. 'Must seem a bit strange for you, sir. A year after we get out of France we're doing the same thing again. Retreating, I mean.'

Lamb shrugged. 'Well, yes, you're right, Hugh. I didn't expect to be doing this again, not so soon. But the main thing is that, whatever happens in war, you must never stop believing. The trouble with the Jerries out there is they believe they can't be beaten. But I tell you they can. We can beat them, and we will. If not here, then we'll beat them soon enough.'

'We can't really beat them here, though, sir, can we?'

'No, if you want me to be honest. But as I told the men, as far as I can see all that we can do is hold up the German advance and then get away with whatever we can.' He looked across to Bennett and Valentine. 'Sarnt-Major, come and tell the lieutenant how easy it is to beat the Nazis.'

Bennett grinned and walked over.

'Tell Lieutenant Wentworth what we did to the enemy in France, Sarnt-Major.'

'Well, sir. Gave him a right bloody nose. Blew up an air base, we did, and captured a colonel. Had them chasing around all over after us. And then we got all those men away off the beach, sir, didn't we. And before that, up north, Mister Lamb – sorry, the Captain – well, he just walked out with a sack of grenades and took out two enemy positions and . . .'

Lamb cut him short. 'All right, Bennett. That's enough, I think.'

Wentworth looked at him. 'Sir? Did you do that?'

'Some other time, Lieutenant. It'll have to wait. Thank you, Sarnt-Major. The main point is that the Hun can be beaten. He's not some bogey-man. He's human like you and me. We beat the Ities in Egypt and we can beat the bloody Jerries too. But maybe not just yet, if you see what I mean. So get back to your platoons and when they come make sure you don't do anything silly. I want all of you, all of you, with me when we get aboard that boat to Alex.'

They saluted and left Lamb with Bennett, Valentine and Mays. It was the best that Lamb could manage to keep Wentworth's spirits up. But he had seen the boy's face. He knew, they all knew, that their position was hopeless. Not just here at the pass, but in a global sense. It was perhaps even more hopeless than it had been a year ago, even though Britain itself was no longer under threat of direct invasion. The RAF had seen to that back in September. Nevertheless, with Greece under the jack-boot, Egypt was threatened. And if Egypt fell then the way would be open for Hitler to walk into India. And then the end of the Empire and no more men from Down Under. Then they really would have their backs to the wall, and he wondered whether they would survive. Lamb caught himself. Mustn't think like that. Defeatist talk. This war was all about morale. Wasn't that what he had just told the men? If they believed in themselves they would come through as victors.

Valentine spoke. 'Of course you know why we're really here, sir?'

'No, Valentine. You tell me, because I'm sure you're going to.'

'Well, sir, we're here because those chaps in the High Command all studied Greek at Eton and Harrow and they're a little sentimental about this old place. Can't stand the idea of Nazis jack-booting about all over their precious temples.'

'I thought you were a Classical scholar yourself, Valentine.'

'In a way, sir, but not in the way they are. It's Greece for the Greeks, sir, in my book. With them it's personal. You see they all have ancestors who came over here in the eighteenth century and pinched the statues to smarten up their stately homes. And now they just can't bear the idea that the Jerries will do the same.'

Lamb slept fitfully and had strange and disturbing dreams about Greek statues and the General Staff, in the last of which the New Zealand captain dropped from the sky by parachute, shouting 'eggs and whisky'. He could still hear the words in his head as he was awoken by the sound of two explosions, jolting him into semi-consciousness. Coming to, he realised that they came from the direction of Thebes. He found his watch.

It was 3 a.m. Lamb got to his feet and, stumbling through his prostrate men in the olive grove, bumped into a Kiwi corporal.

'What the hell's happening? Any idea?'

'There's an enemy column advancing towards us, sir. A hundred vehicles at least. Tanks too.' The word sent a chill through Lamb. He had a secret phobia of tanks. Of being crushed beneath their tracks. He had seen in France what that could do to a human being. He had noticed earlier, though, while talking to Nichols, that the country to their immediate flank was almost certainly tank proof. Nichols had told him that there was a track through the village of Villia up to Kriekouki, but it too was steep and easily covered. There would be no option for the German armour but to advance along the road.

There was a crash from the front and then the whoosh and thud of artillery rounds followed by several explosions. Lamb raced towards the forward sangars and saw in the valley below them that the fire from the Australian artillery had already set fire to two trucks from which, in a vision of hell, enemy infantrymen were leaping, their clothes ablaze. The sound of their screams mingled with that of gunfire and echoed across the hills. He looked along the road and saw, behind an advance guard of motorcycle troops, three more lorries outlined against the night and in front of them the unmistakable shape of a tank.

'Here they come. Stand to.'

As the tank slowly climbed up the pass towards them, Lamb yelled again. 'Wait for the tanks. Fire at the infantry.'

They were only 1,000 yards away now. He felt the

31

knot tighten in his stomach as it always did when they went into action, and the dry mouth that came with it. He checked his Thompson gun, the weapon he now favoured above a pistol. One full magazine and three more in his pockets. That would do for now. The tank reversed briefly, shoving the burning trucks off the road to allow those following to pass through. Again the artillery crashed out, hitting another truck, but the rest of them lumbered on, jammed tailboard to radiator on the narrow road. The motorcyclists had halted now and had established themselves in cover on either side of the road. Within moments their heavy machine-guns were spitting death at the New Zealanders. More Germans were spilling from the backs of the trucks now, diving for cover in the scrub.

Lamb yelled. 'Now. Open fire. Fire at the infantry.'

The three platoons opened up, and as they did so the New Zealanders around them joined in, turning the pass ahead of them into a killing ground filled with a horizontal rain of burning lead. He watched as the German infantry tried to burrow deeper into the ground to avoid the fire and as the rounds hit home, sending the young stormtroopers hurtling back like marionettes in a ghastly dance of death. Lamb squeezed the trigger of the Thompson and it kicked into life, spraying the scrub before him. He heard Bennett shout, 'Keep it up, boys. Don't let them get away.' All the frustration of the past few weeks, the anger at dead friends and comrades and the knowledge that they were an army in retreat, was released in an instant. For a moment Lamb's men forgot that they could not win this battle, that no matter how many Germans fell to their bullets they would eventually be forced to pull back. All that mattered for this moment was the fact that they were winning. They were killing the Germans in the pass, cutting through Hitler's finest with round after deadly round of small-arms fire that had in minutes transformed a peaceful Greek hillside into an inferno. One man from Number 2 platoon stood up and, shouting some inaudible war cry, fired his rifle from the hip. Eadie yelled at him to stay down, but it was too late. He fell, almost cut in two by a hail of bullets from the machine-gun. This was no pheasant shoot. There were men out there firing at his lads.

Lamb called out, 'Stay down. Stay in cover.' A burst of automatic fire ripped through the night air just above his head. There was a cry from his left as another burst of German fire hit home. But it was paid back twofold. The rifles and machine-guns spewed bursts of flame into the night, the bullets ricocheting off the stones and tearing at the trees and bushes.

And then it was over. As quickly as they had come the Germans were running away across the scrub and through the vineyards, climbing back into the trucks, limping into the undergrowth and crawling through the short vines away from the stream of bullets. Still the artillery on the heights fired into the column, and more trucks burst into flames. Those that were still intact began to reverse down the hill, and the tank, which, pinned down by the gunners and blind in the dark, had showed itself powerless in such a situation, followed as fast as it could go.

Lamb gave the command. 'Cease firing.' The Jackals held their fire, all but three men who, elated by their unexpected success, carried on shooting at shadows until their platoon sergeants had shouted themselves nearly hoarse.

Lamb surveyed the road and hills before them. Counted eight lorries and two motorcycles burning on the highway.

He saw Nichols. 'Well, that sent them packing. I wonder how long before they try again.'

'Not long, I should say. If they do.'

'They won't try to bomb you out, will they? They need the road intact.'

'Don't be too sure. They don't care how they get rid of us. Then they'll just fix the road, or build a new one. They're already building a new bridge at Corinth.'

Mays found him. 'Sir. Two wounded. One bad, Marks. Hit in the thigh. He'll need to be treated, sir.'

Nichols spoke. 'Our MO's somewhere by the command post to the rear. Take him there, Sergeant. I'd better see to my own men.'

Lamb walked across to the left as they were helping Marks back to the aid post and gave him a smile. 'Well done, Marks. You'll be fine.' He looked around at the others, sitting in the moonlight on the rocks, wiping down their weapons and sensed not just exhaustion now but a sense of achievement. 'Well done, all of you. That showed them. Sarnt-Major, make sure they're ready in case Jerry tries it again. And be ready for air attack too. They know where we are now.'

It only took a few minutes before the recce planes came over. They flew close to the ground, like hawks hovering over a wheat field, swooping and climbing in their search for prey. There was no point in trying to hide. It was too late for that, and no sooner had the planes gone than others appeared over the mountains. Dorniers, lumbering in. The heavy stuff. Lamb saw them and joined in the warning shouts.

'Aircraft. Take cover. Take cover.'

The aircraft were not as low as the Stukas. There was no frantic, screaming dive, but looking up he could see the bomb doors open and watched as the black sticks fell from the belly of the plane. He ran to one of the stone sangars and found himself crouching next to Bennett, Eadie and Smart, and it crossed his mind that this sort

34

of thing was really of no use as cover against air attack. He prayed that the order forbidding anti-aircraft fire would be lifted, but it was a full ten minutes before he heard the crump of the Australian batteries as they tried to down the bombers. He looked up and saw little puffs of smoke appear in the sky around the planes, but by then it was too late.

'Just in time,' scoffed Eadie. Some distance over to their left another sangar filled with Kiwis had taken a hit and its useless stones lay scattered across the valley, along with the remains of its occupants. Lamb looked away as the Dorniers turned for home.

As the dust settled and the post came to life, with desperate medics searching for signs of life, Nichols came up to him, smiling broadly. 'Haven't you heard? We're pulling out. Being relieved by 1st Armoured and the Rangers. You'd best get ahead of us and make time. No point in waiting – you'll just get caught up in our undertow, and there's nothing else you can do here. Our sappers are going to blow the pass anyway. Jerry will have to make a new way through.'

The adjutant, it seemed, had established a control post at the Villia crossroads to check out the brigade and the hangers-on, while the Kiwis' CO, again in charge of the rear party, supervised the blowing of demolitions in the pass. After the excitement of the raid, Lamb again felt the cold of the night and shivered. 'Charles, find the others and get the men together. We're moving out.'

'Can you say where to, sir?'

'Athens, as far as I can see. Then a boat to Alex. After that it's anyone's guess.'

Bennett found them. 'Sir, no casualties from that last lot. We were lucky, sir.'

'Yes, damned lucky. Let's hope it holds out.'

They watched as stretcher-bearers passed them

carrying what had once been a man. Galvanised, Lamb spoke. 'Right. Let's get moving.' Eadie sped off with Bennett and within minutes the men had assembled, rubbing their hands together and blowing on them against the cold. They lined up in platoons and sections and Lamb looked them over. There was no denying it, they were hardly fit for Horse Guards, as scruffy a bunch of soldiers as he had ever seen. But they were alive, and that was what mattered to him. And they were going to stay that way.

Before the German attack the transports, including their own carrier and lorries, had been moved a few miles to the rear and they made their way on foot at first.

As they passed through, Lamb heard the explosions as the first charges went off, bringing what sounded like half the old mountain down on to the road.

'Jerry'll never get through that lot, sir,' said Bennett. 'Leastways, when he does we'll be long gone.'

Lamb heard Valentine speak, to no one in particular.

'A thousand years scarce serve to form a state;

An hour may lay it in the dust.

That's Byron. Lord Byron, if you will. You walk, gentlemen, in the cradle of civilisation.'

On their arrival at the transport area they were met by the unexpected and welcome sight of four Australian corporals and a handful of Australian nurses handing out tots of rum. Bennett held out his tin mug. 'Blimey, this is a turn-up for the books.'

Valentine piped up. 'I thought this went out with Wellington.' He smiled at a nurse. 'I'll have a double please, my dear. Just like a Friday night at the Bag o' Nails.'

An Australian sergeant approached them. 'You got transport here, sir?'

'Yes. One carrier, two lorries. Where did you leave them, Sarnt-Major?'

'Over to the right there, sir. In those olive trees.'

The sergeant nodded at Lamb. 'Very good, sir. But you'll have to wait your turn with the others. There is a queue.'

'Naturally,' said Valentine, taking a short nip of rum.

They found the trucks and Lamb produced the distributors which he had had the foresight to remove, carefully replacing each one. As they waited and slowly sipped at the acrid spirit, they watched other units depart, queuing up for their turn to get away to freedom.

At last the sergeant nodded them on, saluting Lamb, and the three vehicles rumbled out on to the road. As they hit the track an Aussie redcap, standing at the roadside, yelled across. 'Put your foot down, mate. We don't want to hold up the ones coming behind.'

Bennett shook his head. 'He's got some hope, sir. No headlights. That's the order. Isn't it?'

'Yes, that's the order, Sarnt-Major. Stop the Jerry planes from seeing us in the dark. Better do as he says, though. Quick as you can then.'

'Whatever you say, sir.' Bennett pushed gingerly on the accelerator and soon they were doing a comfortable 15 miles an hour along the narrow road, just able to see the rear of the truck in front, by the light of the moon.

'Just as well we can't see a blind thing, sir.' Turner said. 'Reckon there must be a sheer drop over there.'

At that moment, Bennett pushed the carrier round a turning and Lamb was suddenly aware in the moonlight of a yawning ravine directly under their tracks. 'Good God, man. Be careful.'

'Christ, sir. Sorry, that was a bit close.'

'Too bloody close, Sarnt-Major. Let's try and get there in one piece.'

*   *   *

Lamb wondered whether the rest of the battalion had made it across the Corinth canal before the German attack. He prayed that they had and would get away from the Peloponnese. But that was of no immediate concern to him and his men. From what Nichols had said, the Germans were advancing from two directions now. He had no doubt that they would soon complete their bridge across the canal.

He turned to Smart. 'Have another go at raising Battalion on the wireless, Smart, will you?'

"I tried an hour ago, sir. There's just no signal in the mountains.'

'Well, have another go. You never know, do you?'

There was a click in the darkness and then the familiar hum of the set in its blackout cover as Smart began to talk into the hand-piece. After ten minutes he gave up. 'Nothing, sir. I told you, it's the mountains.'

Lamb nodded and pushed himself deeper into the seat, his hands tucked under his armpits for warmth. The next thing he knew, he was lifting his head, aware that he must have fallen asleep. He quickly took in their surroundings as one vine-covered hillside succeeded another. He looked at his watch. For almost half an hour, it seemed, he had been drifting in and out of sleep. They were all exhausted, of course, but he knew that they would have to find that extra ounce of strength if they were to get away.

Here the road to Athens was no more than a tiny, winding, dusty track crammed with refugees and soldiers: Greeks, Brits, Kiwis, Australians. Most were on foot and only the lucky few, like the Jackals, in trucks. Lamb and his men, scarves over their mouths and noses against the dust, drove on without lights, as ordered, their road lit only by the stars and the moon. Even so, they could barely see thirty yards in front of them. After Bennett's

38

near miss with the cliff edge, they drove at a tortuously slow pace over the next few miles of curling roads and ragged hills.

Lamb swore. 'Damn this. Switch on the lights, Sarnt-Major, or the Jerries'll be on our tails before we ever get to Athens.'

'You sure, sir? We were ordered to . . .'

'I know what the orders were. Switch the damn things on. They'll see us in the daylight soon enough.'

Bennett switched on the lights, bathing the road ahead in a white glow, and moments later they began to accelerate. Clearly the men in the vehicles in front had had the same idea and were now some distance ahead.

Bennett grinned. 'That's more like it, sir. Permission to put my foot down.'

'Permission?'

The Bren carrier lurched forward into full speed, which, although only some 30 miles per hour, after the appalling slowness gave the impression to its occupants that they were on the racetrack at Broadlands. The trucks behind them followed suit. It took them just over another hour to manage the thirty miles to the outskirts of Athens, and as they left behind the final range of hills Lamb relaxed. The road flattened out quickly now and became straighter. He had kept the map before him and continued looking up to verify their position. But when he did so this time, he gasped. For the dawn was with them now and the sun's pink and orange rays began to pierce the night sky, falling upon the ancient capital and glinting off the whiteness of the Parthenon.

3

Athens was in chaos. The streets and boulevards, which only a week ago had seen the well-heeled drinking cocktails at the hotel bars and cafés filled with the locals, were now thronged with a quite different type of visitor. Refugees had of course been arriving in the city for more than a year, from Smyrna, Rumania, Russia, even Poland. But now the place seemed to Lamb to have become the hub of the world, brimming over with every nationality, and there was no mistaking the mood of the newcomers. The place stank of fear. The local people, though, seemed strangely sanguine.

Driving more slowly now into the ancient city, the company were greeted by several Greek civilians with a thumbs-up sign. It seemed bizarre to Lamb and singularly inappropriate.

Valentine, who, as he spoke Greek of a sort had transferred to the lead vehicle, whispered to him. 'Sir, they think it's the way we always greet each other.'

Lamb suspected, though, from their smiling faces that they might be some of the Greek fascists about whom they had been told. The streets were daubed with anti-Italian slogans but he wondered whether these men hadn't come out from hiding in the expectation that soon their friends the Germans would be among them.

Most of the Greeks, however, he knew to be a proud people, and President Metaxas himself had refused the ultimatum to submit to Italian occupation. Unanimously Greece had united against the Axis when it had seemed that only Britain stood against Hitler and Mussolini. And now, thought Lamb, this is what they get for all that faith and defiance. We were put in here as a political move, and now, when they need us most, we're leaving them, abandoning them to their fate.

The little convoy made slow progress, hampered by the press of civilians as they smiled and waved. A pretty, dark-haired girl with brown eyes stepped up to the carrier and planted a kiss on Bennett's cheek. He shied away as the others laughed. Mays joked, 'Oi. Careful, miss. He's a married man.'

Funny, thought Lamb, how it feels as if we're being welcomed as liberators, when they know all too well that we're about to abandon them. What sort of people could they be to have such strength of spirit?

While he and every one of his men knew that time was of the essence, they were glad at least that there was no apparent present danger on the rooftops and in the streets of the ancient capital. The danger from the skies, of course, was ever-present.

Lamb was not sure quite where he was aiming for, but it had occurred to him that, with so many Allied soldiers trying to find senior officers, the British Legation might be a good alternative starting point for discovering a means of escape. He clutched his tattered and spineless copy of Baedecker's *Greece* and thanked God he had brought it with him.

The Legation, he knew, was in the Hotel Grande

41

Bretagne, and according to the book that was in Constitution Square. Turning left, they found themselves beside the terrace of a large building, Italian in style and baked by two centuries of sun. On the terrace in front, among the carefully manicured gardens, some steamer chairs lay broken and surrounded by empty wine bottles. The army's been here, he thought. He sniffed, and Valentine saw him do it. 'It's gum, sir, that smell. Sap from the pines. Nice, isn't it.'

Lamb turned to him, bemused. 'Uh yes, very pleasant.'

'It always says "Greece" to me, sir, don't you agree?'

'You know Athens well?'

'Didn't I tell you, sir? A trip to study the antiquities, when I was up at university.'

Lamb shook his head. 'Where haven't you been, Valentine? In that case you can point us in the direction of the British Legation.'

A few blocks on they found what he had been looking for. The Hotel Grande Bretagne was a huge neo-classical building built a little like a wedding-cake, with a colonnade of Romanesque arches running the length of the front. Lamb told the men to wait and, jumping down, climbed the steps to the massive entrance doors. Inside the place was in uproar. The air was filled with the stench of burning papers. The few civil servants still remaining ran from room to room. He tried to stop one of them but was brushed aside. Looking around he saw a sign: the words 'Billiard Room' had been crossed out and 'Information Office' written in. Lamb walked towards it and found himself at the rear of the old hotel. There was a large mirror on one wall, and catching sight of himself he was momentarily horrified at his appearance. His brown, almost black hair, which in peacetime and on leave had been cut in a neat, military style by Truefit and Hill, had grown ragged in the month since the regimental barber had last had a go at it. The stubble to which he had grown accustomed, shaving just once every four days to save water, had grown almost beard-like, and the face that it hid was sallow and despite the tan somehow pale. But it was his eyes which most shocked Lamb. They seemed sunk into their sockets, as if all the misery he had seen in the past few weeks was hidden in their depths. He looked away and carried on. At the end of the corridor was a green-painted door.

He knocked and, not waiting for a reply, went in. A bespectacled man in his late forties, in a black suit, aided by another, much younger, was shoving pile after pile of papers on to the fire, which was burning gloriously. He turned and saw Lamb, his face ruddy from the fire glow, his grey hair tousled to the point of absurdity.

'Army? You're not needed here. Your chaps have cleared out. I should find your own place. Wherever that is now.'

'Sorry, sir. I was just trying to find out about transport and someone told me . . .'

'Yes, that's the trouble, you see, Captain. Everyone knows better than the other person. Everybody tells someone something but nobody has the right answer.' He paused for a moment, distracted from the burning. 'This is the British Legation, Captain, not the Quartermaster's stores. We do not deal in matters of military transport. I have quite enough to do packing the place up before the Germans get here. Now please leave us alone and find your own people.'

Lamb nodded and left, closing the door on the scene as the man threw more papers on to the cheerfully blazing pyre.

Outside Lamb found the men waiting, eager-faced. 'Sorry, no joy there I'm afraid. The top brass have cleared out and the place is full of pen-pushers from the consulate. And bloody rude ones at that. We'll just have to make our own way.'

He was about to get back into the truck when he turned, distracted by the noise of a commotion across the square. A group of civilians were arguing. There was nothing so remarkable about that. The thing was that this group of people was so obviously English.

There were three men and a woman. One of the men was tall and well-built, another short, thin and bespectaled, the last squat and slightly overweight. They wore a variety of clothing – tropical suits, blazers and even an Argyle-patterned jersey. The fat man was dressed in an astrakhan coat and sweating profusely. The woman was dark-haired and wore a fur coat and a silk scarf. They stood around a pile of small but expensive-looking suitcases, a single cabin trunk and, bizarrely, a portable gramophone. A little moustachioed Greek in a shabby black suit, white shirt and black tie – presumably someone's servant – hopped and muttered around them as if he intended to physically propel them out of the town and out of his responsibility.

Lamb stared at them. The British civilian population had reportedly been evacuated several days before and he was just puzzling as to what on earth they were still doing here when the woman saw him and fixed his gaze with her own. She had dark eyes and a shock of auburn hair, which fell in the style of a Hollywood star about her shoulders, spilling over her scarf and on to the collar of her coat. Lamb was transfixed by her eyes, like a rabbit in a spotlight, and before he knew it, as some predator might when focusing on its quarry, she was running across the square towards him.

'Sorry, I'm so sorry. Can you help? We're English. Well, most of us are. All apart from poor Mr Papandreou, who lost his wife in an air raid.' She put out her hand and for a second Lamb wasn't sure whether she expected him to kiss it or shake it. He chose the latter. 'Sorry. Miranda Hartley.'

She spoke with a clipped voice that betrayed an upbringing in the home counties and for a moment Lamb was transported back in time to another world, the world of his ex-wife and her friends. Lamb was frozen, lost for words, but only for a second. 'Yes. I can see that. I'm not sure . . .'

'Where have you come from? Have you any news?' She smiled. 'I suppose you're sworn to secrecy. Have you been . . . at the front?'

He looked at her and tried to work out what she might be doing here. Was she the wife of a diplomat? An aristocrat who had missed the boat? He muttered, 'No, no news I'm afraid. No good news, at least. We're just looking for a way out.'

She smiled. 'So are we. We must get away before the Germans get here. My husband is very important. He's a writer. A novelist. You've probably heard of him. Julian Hartley. Over there, with the glasses.' She waited for the acknowledgement, the recognition, the nod of the head, but none came.

Lamb saw her disappointment. 'Yes, of course. Julian Hartley. Yes, you must get away.'

'We were here on a lecture tour, you see. Julian's publisher's idea. Good for his public image, and Julian took Classics at Magdalene. In fact he knows Greece quite well. Actually he desperately wanted to come back to find material for his next book. It's set here, you see. Lovely story. We were guests with the university. That's how we met Mr Papandreous. Well, of course, I just had to come. And then all this happened. But you know you have to admit it. The Greeks are pretty indolent, aren't they. Don't you think that Rome is by far the

45

nobler civilisation? Il Duce wants to return them to that time.'

'You admire Mussolini?'

She looked shocked. 'Don't you? You know he's really done wonders for that country.'

'But not too much for its army.'

'I wouldn't know about that. I'm not a soldier. Not like you. So you will help us, Captain?'

'Well, I don't really see how I can. You see I have orders. You know how it is.'

A man detached himself from the group and approached them, not her husband, the apparently famous writer, but a heavy-set man in his early thirties, dressed in white flannels and a blazer. A man, thought Lamb, dressed more for a riverside regatta than a war zone. He beamed at Lamb and spoke in a deep, self-consciously masculine voice, oozing confidence.

'Comberwell. Freddie Comberwell. Have we met?'

Lamb did not make a habit of taking an instant dislike to people, but this man was an exception. Smiling, he shook his head. 'No. I really don't think so. Peter Lamb, North Kents.'

'The Jackals. Golly. We are in safe hands. Seem to have got ourselves into a bit of a pickle. I was here on business, of course. I'm in oil. Cod liver oil. The Greeks can't get enough of it. Worth a fortune. All those babies, you see. We actually had a factory here in Athens. Direct hit, wouldn't you know it. It's going to cost the company thousands. I've got to get home. Make my report. What a bloody shambles.'

This was becoming ridiculous, thought Lamb. The last thing he wanted was to find himself responsible for a bunch of civilians. Lamb went on, 'Now look, I'm sorry but I have to reach my regiment in Egypt. I really don't think . . .'

Comberwell was not to be dissuaded. 'The thing is, old man, we're really a bit stuck. Thought perhaps you might help.'

'I'd love to, but as I was saying to Mrs Hartley I have orders. There's nothing I can do. The British consul should be able to . . .'

Comberwell became agitated. 'The consul's gone. Didn't you hear? Took a sea-plane to Alex yesterday. That's why we're stuck, old man.'

'Isn't there anyone else at the Legation?'

'No, no one. We've been there. Just an odious little man called Dobson. Burning papers. Turned us away.'

Lamb nodded. 'Yes, I met him too.'

'Well, how do you suggest we are going to get out of here?'

Lamb shrugged. 'I should get down to Piraeus, if I were you. The harbour. Get aboard whatever you can. There's sure to be a boat.'

'But what I mean is, how on earth are we going to get there?'

Lamb bit his lip and counted to ten. As he did so a stick of bombs fell less than half a mile inland in a series of explosions. Mrs Hartley jumped and gave a little shriek.

Lamb looked at Comberwell in desperation. 'Oh, use your initiative, man, for God's sake.'

He turned away in momentary disgust and despair. Very soon, he thought, this is the sort of man who if he manages to ever get back home is going to be conscripted into the army. And then God help us all. For the moment, however, the man is a helpless fool. If we leave him he will die, and who knows what will happen to the rest of them, including the woman.

The harbour quay and the beach below were filled now with soldiers, RAF ground crew by the dozen and all

47

manner of civilians, all trying to find a ship or any other means of getting away from the Germans.

A New Zealand sergeant saw Lamb and spotted his pips. 'You in charge, sir?'

'No. Not really, Sarnt. Just trying to get my men away.'

'Well, you'd better look sharp about it, sir. They're only up the road. At Acharnes, someone said. The Jerries, that is. We've left the 4th Hussars as a rearguard and then they'll just have to fend for themselves. Poor bloody cavalry. It's another bloody balls-up.'

Lamb nodded. 'Yes, Sarn't. I think you may be right. Have you got a plan?'

'We found some taxis parked up in the main square. A whole bloody fleet of them. I'd help you if we could, but they're full already. I've got about 100 men to get away myself. You're welcome to try your luck with our column, though, sir, if you've got your own transport. The harbour at Piraeus is fucked, though. Blown to shit. We're off east to see if we can't find a ship at Rafina. You might do the same, mate.'

Lamb bristled. 'Thank you, Sarnt. I'll take your advice. Good luck.'

'Good luck, sir.'

On the corner of University Street a section of New Zealand infantrymen were setting up a machine-gun post, sandbagging it with sacks taken from the wall of a nearby café. Outside the same café several Greeks sat and watched the men at work, quietly drinking their coffee, saying nothing.

He turned to the men and then glimpsed the English beyond. They had stopped arguing now but were still talking. It was just too bad. He was an officer and, no matter what his personal feelings might be towards these misfits, his duty was to get his men to safety as soon as he could and back into action. As he was looking at the group a British major walked up to them, heading for the Hartleys. He was intercepted by Comberwell, who began to speak to him and pointed towards Lamb. The officer nodded and then spoke with Mrs Hartley. Then he looked across to Lamb and walked over.

'Captain Lamb? Guy Whittaker, RHA. Look, I've a bit of a favour to ask you. Those people over there.' He pointed to the British party.

'Sir?'

'You know who they are?'

'Sir.'

'Well, we really have to get them away. I know it may seem strange but Hartley's quite a senior chap, actually. Friend of the GOC. At least their wives are buddies. The other chap I'm not concerned about, but he seems to have attached himself to them. Can you manage it?'

'Is that an order, sir?'

The man looked at him, 'Yes, you'd better take it as one. Don't want to rattle the GOC, do we?'

'No, sir.'

'Fine, that's settled then. Good luck.'

He walked back to the civilians and as he spoke to Miranda Hartley Comberwell turned to give Lamb a smile. Lamb strolled across to him, biting his lip.

'Change of plan. I've been given orders to get you away. But I'm afraid you'll have to look sharpish if you're going to come with us.'

Comberwell smiled at him. 'I say, that's awfully decent of you. Righto. I'll just find my kit.'

Lamb bristled. He seemed almost a caricature of an Englishman.

Hartley, the famous writer whose work he had never read, turned to Lamb. 'It is frightfully decent of you. Let

49

me buy you a drink. There's a bar across the road. They're bound to have some champagne. The good stuff.'

'With respect, Mr Hartley, I don't think this is quite the time. But that is very kind. Let's postpone it till we're all safe in Alex, shall we?'

'Quite. Yes, of course, quite right. Should never have suggested it. Bad idea. Must get on and get your men away. Can't keep the Jackals waiting. You know when I join up, which won't be before long, I'm sure, I've half a mind to put in for a commission with your mob. Will you put in a word for me?'

Lamb looked at him. Could the man really be serious? Lamb wondered what the recruiting officer would say, and the adjutant for that matter. And then he realised that it was true, that before long men like Hartley, along with the bumptious idiot Comberwell, might be the only officers they had. 'Yes, of course I will. Good show. I'm sure there'll be no problem.'

Hartley turned to his wife. 'Miranda, the captain here says he can get me a commission in the Jackals. Isn't that splendid?'

Lamb muttered. 'I didn't actually say that I could do that. I will put a word in, of course.'

'That would be so kind, Captain. I really don't want Julian to fight, but if he must then . . . Well, he's always wanted to be a soldier. Like Dr Johnson.'

They smiled at each other and Lamb began to wonder whether he might not have been rash in suggesting he might help them to get away. There was a respectful cough behind him and Lamb turned to see a corporal. Lamb returned the salute and, looking for his buttons, saw that he belonged to the Grenadier Guards, which was strange, as, to the best of his knowledge, there were no Guards units in Greece.

'Captain Lamb, sir?'

'Corporal.'

'I've been sent to fetch you, sir. A matter of urgency. Would you come with me, sir?'

'Where to, Corporal? On whose orders?'

'My commanding officer, sir. It's not far.'

Lamb called across to Charles Eadie. 'Lieutenant, take command. I shan't be long.'

He followed the corporal across the street and down an alleyway. 'I hope this is not going to take long, Corporal. You do know that Jerry's about to pay us a visit.'

'Not long, sir, no.'

They kept walking at a brisk pace and eventually Lamb found himself in a back street that might have come from any eastern town. It reminded him of his one never-to-be-repeated visit to the Birkah in Cairo, with washing strung across the road and scantily clad women hanging out of the windows, touting for custom.

'Where the hell have you brought me, Corporal? If this is some sort of practical joke I'll have you . . .'

'No joke, sir. Sorry, sir.' The corporal pushed open a door. 'The colonel's just in here, sir.'

Glancing at the man, Lamb entered and followed the Guardsman into a house and down a narrow passageway. It was stiflingly hot, dimly lit by one bare light bulb and smelt of incense and spices, masking an underlying stench of disinfectant. They turned to the right and then left and at last the corporal pushed open another door. 'Here we are, sir.'

Lamb walked in, past the corporal's arm, and saw an officer sitting at a desk before him. Another soldier, a towering Grenadier warrant officer, was standing against one wall. The man looked up and Lamb recognised him instantly.

'Hello, Peter. Do sit down. WO Pullen, would you leave us for a moment?'

The Guardsman nodded, 'Sir,' and walked smartly out of the room, closing the door behind him. Lamb seated himself on a small upright chair in front of the desk and looked at the man who had summoned him to this unlikely office.

He was a colonel, and even though he was sitting down it was obvious that he was a tall man, lean and fit with it. He smiled at Lamb and Lamb wanted to return the smile, but instead he frowned. For this was the man who had seen to his quick promotion, and it had been the colonel too who had suggested to Lamb that he might join that new elite unit. Lamb knew as soon as he saw him that an encounter with Colonel 'R' could only mean trouble. Particularly when he smiled.

The colonel spoke. 'How wonderful to see you, Peter. I could hardly believe it when they told me you were in Athens. What a stroke of luck. About all we've had so far in this damned campaign.'

'Yes, sir. It has been rather rough.'

'Well, it's going to get rougher. For all of us. Now you're probably wondering why I called you here. And you're probably thinking that I've hatched another mad plan.'

'Yes, sir.'

The colonel smiled again. 'Well, I'm afraid you're absolutely right. Don't worry. It's nothing to do with Section D, and I don't want you to join the commandos. Those are purely voluntary. You won't need to leave your men. In fact they're integral to the whole scheme.'

'Sir, are you quite certain that you've got the right man?'

'Absolutely. As I said, I couldn't believe it when I heard you were here. Last-minute miracle. I was beginning to despair.'

'Can I ask how exactly you did hear, sir?'

'No. Not really. Let's just say that someone whom you know, knows who you are. That is to say they knew that you were here. And they told me, and as soon as I heard that I had you brought here. That any clearer?'

'Not really, sir. No.'

'Well, that's it. The walls have ears, you know, Peter. Can't be too careful.'

'Evidently not.'

It was instantly apparent to him that the colonel's spy, whoever he or she was, had to be one of the British party. Either that or one of his own men, or most unlikely of all a Kiwi or an Aussie. He called to mind the civilians and had begun to wonder which one it could be before he realised that the colonel was speaking.

'Now come on, Peter. There's no need to be like that. This is hardly the man I know. The hero of St Valéry.'

'Well, perhaps I've changed then, sir. Greece is a shambles.'

The colonel nodded. 'Yes. I couldn't agree more. And to stop it becoming an utter farce is the reason you're here. What do you know about the Greek monarchy?'

'Not much, sir. I know they've got a King at least and that he may be somehow related to Queen Victoria. And that he was deposed and then put back on the throne. That's about it.'

'That'll do. For starters. They do have a King. King George II. And yes, you're right, he was deposed and reinstated. And where do you suppose he is now?'

'Probably *en route* to somewhere a long way away from here. We saw Prince Peter driving for the coast.'

'Did you now? That's the King's cousin. Important chappie. In the Greek army. Liaison with us. Good sort. And yes, right again. The King is getting away. In fact . . .' He looked at his watch. 'By my reckoning he should be making landfall in Crete just about now.'

'Crete, sir?'

'Yes, island to the south of us.'

Lamb nodded. 'Yes, sir.'

'Delightful place. Stayed there myself once. Full of old buildings and ruins. Very important. Well, that's where the King has gone to get away from Jerry. And well he might.'

'Sir?'

'Herr Hitler has seen fit to declare King George an enemy of the Greek people. Damned impertinence. An enemy of his own people! That little man has no concept of manners. Well, now. What I want you to do is to go to Crete and keep an eye on him.'

'Keep an eye on him, sir?'

'Yes. Just that. Well, a little more. Forget about going to Alex. Get yourself and your men off to Crete. Find the King as soon as you can. Don't let him know what you're there for until you're needed. That'll be soon enough. We want to try to keep the thing as hush-hush as we can. In fact you may not even have to meet him. Just keep yourself aware of where he is, and if the Germans invade the island be prepared to help with his evacuation. Is that clear?'

Lamb shook his head. 'Quite clear, sir. You want me to babysit the King of Greece and if the Germans come for him help him escape to Egypt.'

'Precisely. Although I wouldn't say "babysit" was quite the right expression. "Unofficial bodyguard" is how I would put it.'

'Without his knowing?'

'Yes.'

'And if I refuse?'

'You can't.' The colonel had stopped smiling now. 'Try it and I'll see to it that you lose your captaincy.'

'Can you tell me why the King is so vitally important? Greece itself I think I can see. It's part of Mr Churchill's grand plan for a southern alliance against the Axis. But the King? Wouldn't I be better off fighting?'

'King George is a figurehead. Whatever Hitler might say, many of his people love their King. It's equally obvious that the Führer loathes him. He's 40, almost 41, and pretty fit. He trained with the Prussian army before the last war. His great grandmother was Queen Victoria and our own King calls him "cousin". George and his father the King were exiled in 1917 and replaced by his brother Alexander and a republican government. But Alexander died, and by 1920 George and his old man were back by common vote. His father was deposed after being defeated by Turkey, and George was given the throne. Four years later he was out, and in 1932 settled in London at Brown's Hotel. He divorced his wife in 1935 and the following year was back on the throne. There are no children. So. There you have it. There's your charge, Peter.'

Lamb stared at him. He realised that this was a defining moment. His instinct was to say no and to suffer the consequences. He had doubted the integrity of the Greek campaign since the outset, and now this. This was politics. Hitler against Churchill. A spite match, with the King as pawn. The colonel watched him carefully. Gauged his unease.

'Peter. Remember. When all this is over, when we've won the war, you'll need people who can help. You're a young man. Your whole future's ahead of you. You'll have done something good in the war, have already, but what will you do in the peace? I can help. I'm your guarantee of a future, Peter. You can still be someone when the lights go on again. Believe me, there will still be someone to fight, and I'll be leading that crusade too. If that's what you want then I'll be right behind you. But only if you play along now. You know what the alternative means.'

Lamb thought for a moment. 'All right. I'll be your babysitter, sir. I'll look after your King and I'll do my best to get him out if the Jerries attack. Do you suppose they will?'

'Yes, to be frank. But we don't know for certain and we don't know when. Good, I'm glad that's settled. Now you had better go back and find your men before the Jerries get here. Pullen.'

The WO came through the door. 'We're pulling out of this dive. Escort Captain Lamb back to the town and let's get ourselves off, shall we? Before Jerry walks in.'

Back in the square Lamb found the men milling around the tailgates of the trucks. Bennett stubbed out a cigarette. 'Blimey, sir. You all right? Look like you've seen a ghost.'

'Yes, you're not far wrong, Sarnt-Major. Come on, we need to get a move on. Get the civilians on first.'

The Hartleys, Comberwell and Papandreou and their retainers piled into the back of one of the trucks, and Lamb's men followed suit. Looking at them again he wondered which of them had told the colonel of his presence and how.

Lamb opened the passenger door of the lead truck and climbed in. They started up and the little convoy began to clatter and jolt down the road through the city and out eastwards towards Rafina. Despite the streams of fugitives, it didn't take them long.

Piraeus might well have been, as the Aussie sergeant had told him, 'fucked up', but as far as Lamb could see the little port of Rafina was certainly in a mess as well. The little harbour, normally more used to fishing boats, was now full of ships of all sorts, some of them half submerged, having been hit by the Luftwaffe. The water, usually clear blue, had turned a filthy black with the floating, charred wood from destroyed vessels, and everywhere, it seemed to Lamb, masts and funnels of ships poked through the oily scum of the surface. The cloying stench of oil and burnt wood was everywhere.

On shore most of the houses were in ruins, their rubble giving many of them the appearance of ancient monuments.

Valentine saw Lamb gazing at them. 'I think I can guess your thoughts, sir.'

'Really, Valentine, surprise me.'

'You're wondering whether this place will end up looking like the rest of ancient Greece. Whether it will sink back into antiquity where it lay for 2,000 years after the Peloponnesian wars, before we rediscovered it. That's what war does, sir, isn't it? Destroys civilisations.'

Lamb looked at him. 'You're right, actually. That was what I was thinking. But that's why we're here, isn't it, Valentine? To stop this bloody war. To stop a German madman from destroying our own civilisation.' He looked again at the shattered ships and houses. 'Come on, let's get going. Jerry can't be far behind.'

A number of caiques, fragile-looking Greek fishing vessels with a sail and a small motor, were lying at anchor in the harbour. Most appeared to have been requisitioned by the army, and men and stores were being loaded aboard. One, though, no less ramshackle than the rest but marginally more seaworthy, caught Lamb's eye. It bore the name *Andromeda*, which had been painted with some care by its owner on to a wooden sign on its bows along with a large all-seeing eye which gave it the appearance of a war galley. On its fore-deck he could see several khaki-clad figures tinkering with a deck-mounted Lewis gun – two British officers in shirt sleeves, a corporal and a handful of men. If that was the total on board then she would manage a few more bodies, he reckoned. Lamb walked over and stepped on to the deck. He walked over to the senior officer, a thin

57

young captain with slicked-back dark hair. Lamb introduced himself.

'Hello. Peter Lamb, North Kents. We're trying to find a passage to Crete.'

The captain looked up from his work. 'Toby Hallam, Queen's Own Hussars, and this is Lieutenant Corrance, my 2/IC. We've twenty of our own men on board and a few Greek civvies, mostly women.'

Lamb noticed the lack of any offer of transport.

Hallam continued. 'Most of this lot want to get to Alex. But it sounds like you've got the right idea. If we've got any chance at all with the bloody Luftwaffe up there on our tails, it'll be to try for Crete. Some of our chaps are there already. They've stopped embarking men at Navplion now, and you know that Piraeus has had it.'

'Yes. We didn't really see any rearguard to speak of. Who's holding the town? Is there a rearguard?'

'First Rangers. At least that's what I heard, and a squadron of the divisional cavalry, 4th Hussars, plus a few gunners and the Kiwis from the Hassani airfield. There's a few stragglers too, mind. All the odds and sods. That's all there is, though, between us and the Jerries.'

Lamb stared at him. 'You're probably right about Crete. We'd never make it to Alexandria alone. Not now, with the Luftwaffe in control of the skies.'

Hallam nodded. 'Bloody Stukas. Did for seventeen of our light tanks three days ago. Not much bloody use, are we? Cavalry without any tanks? Bloody joke. God knows where the rest of my lot are.' He paused, 'Do you know how many ships we've lost in the past few days?'

'No.'

'Well,' he hesitated '. . . nor do I, exactly, but I can tell you it's one hell of a lot, and I for one don't intend to join them. It's Crete for me.' He paused again and then added, by way of an afterthought, 'Though I dare say that once the Jerries have Greece that'll be next on their list. You can come along if you like. I should if I were you. I should think we'll cram you in. According to the admiral down there the convoy sails at 3 a.m. So the last boat has to leave the beach by 2.15.'

'That's very good of you. Crete it is then. I'll tell my men, shall I? You do have room for us?'

The captain looked at the lieutenant and shrugged, then turned back to Lamb. 'Don't see why not. How many have you got?'

'About forty, including a few British civilians.'

'That's fine. We could do with some help on the guns. Dare say we'll need it when the Jerries spot us in the middle of the Med.'

Lamb walked back to the trucks. 'Everybody out. We're going to Crete.'

Bennett smiled. 'Crete, sir? I thought we were headed to Alex.'

'Change of plan, Sarnt-Major. Only ship we can get is going to Crete. So that's where we're going.'

Comberwell was at his elbow. 'Crete? I say, Lamb, that's impossible. I mean, that's just not on.'

Lamb turned on him. 'Sorry? Not on? Mr Comberwell, do I have to remind you that you're damned lucky to be getting away at all? We are going to Crete. And if you want to come with us, then that's where you're going too.'

Comberwell smiled. 'Yes. Of course, Captain. I'm so sorry. Didn't mean to make a fuss. Just came out. I was so looking forward to going to Alex. Drinks at the Cecil and all that, you know?'

'Yes. I know. All that.'

Lamb turned away. The beachmaster, a commander in the Royal Navy equipped with a megaphone, was barking orders to a group of New Zealand infantry on the quay, trying to get them to move more quickly on to the tug which would take them out to a waiting destroyer.

'Come on, you men. Keep going there. Keep it going.'

Some of them called back. 'All right, Popeye. Keep your 'at on.'

'Where's yer bloody parrot?'

Lamb smiled and called to his own men, directing them on to the *Andromeda*. 'Get on the ship. Quick as you can, boys. Make it snappy. Sarnt-Major, make sure we don't take on anyone else. The civilians and our own men, and that's it. That's all we have room for. And for God's sake keep the noise down. If we make too much of a din you can be sure Jerry will get upset and send the Stukas back.'

It was only half a joke. They wanted to make sure they did not attract enemy attention sooner than was inevitable.

As the men filed aboard, Lamb saw that the ship anchored alongside the *Andromeda* was also filling up. On the beach below the harbour Lamb could see another party waiting its turn for the tug. Some of them were standing up to join the queue, which was moving with incredible slowness. Among them, a group of men, Australians by the look of them, seemed to be drunk. One man in particular was singing, some ribald ballad that was barely discernible but included a few recognisably filthy lyrics. The worst thing was that he was singing it at full volume. That and the fact that he was tone deaf.

As Lamb looked on he heard the harbourmaster again. 'Someone shut that man up there. The Jerries are at the city gates. Keep it quiet, can't you?'

A British officer wearing the single crown of a major walked down the gangplank that led to the tug. As Lamb watched, he went up to the group of Aussies and told them in measured tones to be quiet. The men laughed and the singer cranked up the volume and began again. The officer smiled and repeated his order. Most of the men shut up and looked resentful and Lamb wondered what else the officer had said, but the singer began his song again and now he was really belting it out, at the top of his voice. As Lamb looked on the officer took out his service revolver from the holster at his side and in a single, fluid motion, before anyone could stop him, put it against the singer's head and pulled the trigger. The far side of the man's head disintegrated in a spray of blood. There was a pause and then the body crumpled to the beach, the blood seeping into the sand. The officer muttered something, and before the others could do or say anything he was walking back up the gangplank on to the tug. The other drunks, recovering themselves, began to shout and scream at the man and rushed the gangplank, but the officer had turned to face them now and they could see that behind him stood a guard of half a dozen helmeted men, neat as new pins, their rifles levelled and ready to fire. The soldiers turned away and went to bury their dead friend.

Bennett shrugged. 'Bloody shame, sir. Mind you, he had it coming. Don't give much for that major's chances, though, once they get away, sir.'

Lamb banished his natural revulsion at what he had just witnessed. 'No, but it had to be done. The bloody noise was putting everyone at risk. Anyway, I don't think he plans to take them.'

As they watched, the harbourmaster held up his hand to stop the line of downcast, shuffling men and the gangplank was raised and flung aboard the tug, which began to pull away from the harbour. The men turned around and walked slowly away from the quay as the harbourmaster began to look for the next vessel.

Back on the *Andromeda*, what remained of Lamb's company was almost aboard now and Hallam was busy with his own men. The civilians too were moving on. He heard Comberwell call out to them. 'All aboard the skylark!'

Lamb watched as Eadie and Wentworth directed their platoons.

They had both come on since Egypt. Greece had made officers of them and he wondered what the future now held, what Crete would bring. From his vantage point on the harbour quayside, the beachmaster had spotted another ship and was motioning the desultory queue of men forward once again. As he did so, another, smaller ship caught Lamb's eye, a caique like their own, which was moored just beyond where the tug had been berthed.

It was slightly smaller than the *Andromeda* and the deck was crowded with people, sitting, standing and pressed against the sides. They seemed to be mostly civilian and among them were a number of British.

A naval officer on deck in white shirtsleeves and shorts was shouting orders to a crew who included several civilians in shirts and flannels, while an English woman in a smart, floral-printed frock and a slouch hat was attempting to herd four terrified children on to the tanker with the help of a Chinese amah. A greyhound was pacing the deck nervously, held by another servant.

On the fore-deck nearest to Lamb a young man in army uniform but without any clear insignia was trying to take charge of two others. 'Come on there, Charles, try to untie her. Peter, get that gun into action, can you. Get it loaded. We might be bombed at any time.'

He watched as the man referred to as Peter tried to secure a Lewis gun to a mounting, aided by a private. Three times they attempted to fix it to the base plate but it was only on the fourth that they succeeded.

Standing on the deck of the *Andromeda*, Lamb noticed for the first time the heavy swell that was rocking the boat. He had never been a particularly good seaman and hoped that the crossing would not prove too nauseous. He imagined, though, that seasickness would be the least of their problems.

He shouted to Bennett. 'Finish getting them on board, Sarnt-Major. Captain Hallam's in charge now. It's his ship. Report to him. Don't stow your gear. Every man must keep his own to hand in case we have to abandon ship.'

Miranda Hartley walked up to him, swaying with the motion of the boat.

'I say, it's a little choppy, isn't it? Still, we can't have everything. So clever of you to help us, Captain. Don't know what we'd have done. How long do you think it will take us to get to Crete?'

'I'm afraid I have no idea, Mrs Hartley.'

'Miranda, please.'

'Captain Hallam might know. He's in charge of the vessel. He's over there.' He pointed, hoping to deflect her attention.

'Well, we'll just have to sit it out and be jolly brave, shan't we.'

The sun had gone now and the harbour was lit by the moon, giving an eerie light to the figures who went to and fro about their duties on the deck. Lamb looked at his watch. It was nearing 11 o'clock, so there were another four hours until they sailed. He wondered if they would have that long before the Germans broke through the city and whatever scant defences there were left. Out on the sea he could see the looming shape of a transport ship and several destroyers, waiting to take on more men. Lamb paced the deck and looked at his watch. The minute hand had moved on four places since he last looked. This he knew to be a pointless exercise. He found Bennett. 'How are we, Sarnt-Major? All squared away?'

'Good as, sir. Men are dog tired, sir. There's some asleep already.'

'The more that sleep, the better. Especially in these seas. You should get some shut-eye too.'

'I will, sir. When the time comes.'

There was a huge explosion from behind them and they both turned and saw the silhouette of the port and the ancient city beyond lit up by a ghastly combination of moonlight and the flames from burning houses. The light fell too on the harbour and they caught sight of the staring, static figures of the men, hundreds of them, who had not as yet found sanctuary on a ship.

'Poor buggers,' said Bennett. 'Funny, innit. War, I mean, sir. How some get away and some don't. I mean there's got to be losers. Sometimes, though, it don't half make you feel guilty. I mean, why me and not them?'

Lamb laughed. 'Ask yourself that, Sarnt-Major, and you'll end up going mad. And what's more, you'll go and get yourself killed.'

As they watched, the beachmaster barked again, and the long line of the damned and the passed-over followed the orders from the area commander and began to move to the low ridge on the southern edge of the beach. And there, in the shelter of the laurels, the myrtles and the olive trees, they took cover and looked to the dark horizon for the return of the ships.

Three hours and a mile and half out to sea later, Bennett stood with Lamb at the rail, looking back at the shrinking coast of the mainland of Attica. 'Just like St Valéry, sir, ain't it? An' all in the nick of time again. You could hear them Jerry guns getting closer and closer. I can tell you, sir, more than once I thought we'd all be in the bag.'

Lamb nodded. 'Me too, Sarnt-Major. We've been lucky so far. And yes, I do have a sense of *déjà vu*. The only worry is, and make no mistake, it is a real worry, that this time we're not heading back to the safety of home. We're bound for an island in the middle of the Med, and it's my guess that very soon that place too is going to be very far from safe. And if you ask me, the sooner we get off that island and across to Alex, the better.'

4

He woke at dawn, as the sun's rays touched the deck of the caique and he sensed their warmth as they crept their way slowly up his sleeping face. Lamb shook himself awake and moved his aching shoulders. He had slept on deck from choice, given the heavy swell and his poor record of seafaring, but his attempts to create a passable bunk by laying his battledress tunic and a blanket on the slimy wooden boards had had little effect. His body felt as though he had slept on rocks.

He had woken with a start at some point during the night and had felt utterly alone and strangely frightened. He was not immune to the feeling, of course. Felt it always before any action. Would have questioned any man who said he didn't. But that was something you learnt to conquer. This fear was something else: a fear in the night, lonely and hopeless and cold on the darkened deck of their boat in the middle of the sea. To conquer it he had thought of home. Of Kent in summer and cricket, beer and racing through the lanes on his old motorbike. The fear had passed and he had slept then, praying for the dawn. And now he should have been glad of it, but he knew that while the night had

66

felt more vulnerable the real danger came with the light.

Lamb got to his feet and steadied himself on the rail. Looking around he saw nothing but empty sea. Ahead of them, lying on the surface, lay a bank of fog, or it might simply have been the mist of early morning. Instantly his fears of the night returned for, as he had imagined, their ship was apparently quite alone. The convoy with which they had sailed had gone, it seemed, and with it their greatest defence against air attack. Lamb turned to Hallam. 'We've lost them. The bloody convoy. It's gone.'

Hallam yelled back. 'No fault of mine, Lamb. I told you, I'm no sailor. I did my level best.'

Lamb swore. Of course the man was no sailor, he was a cavalryman. But then neither was he. Another two hours and the mist began to lift and Lamb realised that without it they were sitting ducks for the Luftwaffe.

There was still no sign of the convoy and he wondered how far they were from Crete. The sea was calmer now, but his head was reeling with the motion of the boat. So much so in fact that he was not sure, later, whether he had heard the noise first or seen the black speck in the sky. It was Eadie, though, who shouted first. 'Aircraft. Get down.'

Lamb stared at the approaching black dot. It was hopeless. In a few seconds the fighter would be upon them, and then it would just be a matter of time. For all their Lewis guns they were defenceless against an Me109, and God knew what other planes were close behind it. And then, in a split second, he had it.

He looked around. How many of them were up top? About half his men and a good dozen of the hussars, including Captain Hallam. The British civilians had chosen to take their chances in the hold. On the deck, though, was a party of Greek civilians on whom Hallam had taken pity at the last minute before they set sail.

He yelled. 'All you men, down below. Now. All of you.'

There was a frantic scramble. Still the plane was a black dot, but it was getting bigger with every second. The men threw themselves down the hatches and Lamb turned to the Greeks. Hallam saw him. 'Lamb?'

He shouted back. 'Down. Get in the hold.'

Not questioning him, the cavalryman slipped down the narrow ladder and was gone just as Lamb began to speak. 'All of you.' He had no Greek, he gestured. A waving gesture. Desperate. What to say? Where was Valentine? He looked into the sky. The plane was almost above them now. Lamb flung himself into the top of the hatch and collided with Valentine, who was climbing out on to the deck, his head and shoulders covered with a black scarf. He brushed past Lamb, then turned and spoke quickly in Greek to the women, as Lamb ducked into the hatch.

The Messerschmidt fighter came in over the mast and as it did so it dropped its height and swooped down over the little boat. Lamb, his head just below the opening, froze. He saw Valentine, sitting alongside the Greek women, his head still covered in the scarf.

Obeying Valentine to the letter, the women in the front looked up and waved. Valentine too. The plane passed and Lamb watched it go. But then, to his horror, he saw the plane bank and then turn. It was returning now, diving straight towards them at greater speed, and he thought, This is it. You are going into your attack dive. On it came, and any second he waited for the machine-guns to open fire. But instead the pilot rolled his wings and as he passed them came close enough so that they could see him wave back. Then, as Lamb watched the German fighter turn tail and run, he pushed up through the hatch, his feet slipping on the steps, and found Valentine. 'Valentine, you're a bloody marvel. You had the same idea. Did you see him?'

'Yes, sir. Only too pleased to help. It's easier if you speak the lingo.'

'Well, we'd better keep an eye out. He may have bought it but I'm not convinced that he won't be back with some of his mates.'

However, another two hours came and went and neither the fighter nor any of his mates returned.

The sun was high in a cloudless sky now and Lamb leant against the painted rail of the ship's forward deck and peered at the sight that was gradually unfolding before him. There were other men at the rail now, pointing and chattering, as yard by precious yard, across the azure sea, the coast of Crete drew closer. What had first been merely the line of a land mass soon became an island and Lamb was able to make out a town with whitewashed houses. He saw lush avenues of green, poplars and lemon trees, and imposing larger villas. On the slopes behind the town endless rows of olive groves stood in knotted groups amid the vineyards. He could see the quay now, already a mass of ships, men and material. In the distance, beyond the White Mountains, the rising sun pushed higher in the sky with a crimson light – a surreal, theatrical backdrop to this scene of ethereal beauty. Lamb was aware of a presence to his right. Charles Eadie, puffing on a heavily scented cigarette.

'Pretty sight, sir, isn't it?'

'Very pretty, Charles. Just like a picture postcard. You know I've always wanted to visit the Mediterranean islands. Ever since I was a boy. Must have been all that Homer at school.'

Eadie laughed. 'Oh yes, the Greek myths, sir. Odysseus and all that stuff. My favourite was the one about the

Cyclops. You know that giant of a chap who lives in the cave and only has one eye.'

'And ends up by eating half of Odysseus' crew before he's killed. Yes, I think that's one of mine too. I wonder how many of our lot have got away from Greece to here. There seem to be a hell of a lot of ships in the harbour.'

'I expect we'll be off to Alex soon, sir, anyway, won't we? You never know, you might be able to get a bit of sightseeing in. You know, ancient ruins and all that.'

'Yes. I believe the palace of Knossos is rather special. They've been digging it up for years. Some English professor.'

They were suddenly conscious at that same moment of a humming noise and both knew instantly what it was as it built above them in the sky. Lamb shouted, 'Aircraft, get down,' and instinctively every one of the men and women on board the *Andromeda* cowered and sheltered their heads with their hands, waiting for the scream of the siren as the Stukas fell upon them. But none came. Instead, the noise passed over them. Lamb raised his head and saw silhouetted against the brightening sky the shape of two Hurricanes, bearing the tricolour target roundels of the RAF, which as they passed over the ships off the coast tipped their wings from side to side in salute.

'Thank God, sir. They're British. I never thought I'd feel safe again.'

'Well, I shouldn't depend on feeling that way for too long, Charles. It's my honest opinion that what just flew over our heads might well be the entire air defence capability of this island.'

The ship drew closer to the island and as it did so Lamb was quickly aware that his vision of Eden was not quite as serene as it might at first have seemed. Gazing at the clear blue waters near the shore he could now make out that one of the ships which he had presumed

70

to be riding at anchor was actually tilted at an awkward angle. Her bridge had been blown away and there was a huge gaping hole in her forward deck. He looked to his right and saw another wreck, a tanker. Squinting, he was able to make out the lettering on her hull: *Eleanora Maersk*. There was smoke coming from her decks and now and then he saw a lick of flame. There were other ships too: half-submerged Royal Navy vessels, caiques and smaller boats, funnels and masts protruding from the water and debris. He stared down as they passed by one of the hulks and saw that what he had presumed to be driftwood was in fact a dead body, bloated and floating face down. He realised that the sea was full of them and that there was nothing that could be done to clear them. As they drew closer the smell which had begun to permeate the air of burnt metal and wood, cordite and oil grew stronger and he felt at first just nauseous, then suddenly cold and filled with a sense of foreboding. Prompted by Eadie, his schoolboy Greek mythology came back to him again and for an instant he thought of Charon, ferrying the dead in his boat across the river Styx to Hades.

He turned to Eadie. 'I say, Charles, you haven't got one of those fags to hand, have you?'

The lieutenant clicked open his silver cigarette case and offered it to Lamb, who drew out a thin white cigarette from behind the elastic strip.

'Turkish?'

'Egyptian, actually,' said Eadie. 'Got them from an old Jew in Cairo. Damned good smoke, sir. Hard to find.'

Lamb lit up and puffed away, his nerves calmed by the sweet smoke. Within minutes they were through the ghastly debris. Lamb let his gaze drift to the quay, which appeared to be littered with military equipment and stores of every kind, from lorries and miscellaneous crates to ammunition boxes, stacks of artillery shells and even a single light tank around which a crowd of local boys had gathered. Beyond the town he could see quite clearly now rolling farmland rising away to the south towards the snow-crested White Mountains.

Many ships clustered in the bay, some afloat, others resting on the shallow bottom – further evidence of enemy air activity. He couldn't help but allow himself a feeling of relief at having eluded the enemy on the mainland, and in the fresh morning sunshine he knew that his troops, though very weary, were in the same good spirits. They were almost at the quay now and he could see that it was thronged with locals and men in khaki of all descriptions going about their duties with ant-like precision and purpose.

Valentine had joined them close to the rail and stood staring at the closing coastline, and then without warning burst into verse.

'The isles of Greece, the isles of Greece!
Where burning Sappho loved and sung.
Where grew the arts of war and peace,
Where Delos rose, and Phoebus sprung!
Eternal summer gilds them yet,
But all, except their sun, is set.'

He finished and waited for a comment, but none came. 'That's Byron, sir.'

'Indeed.'

'I just thought it somehow appropriate for our situation, sir.'

'Which is?'

'Well, as I see it, sir, the sun is going down on this little part of civilisation. The cradle of civilisation if you like, sir.'

'You think too much, Valentine.'

'Yes, sir. Terribly sorry, sir.'

A tug drew alongside them and a naval officer yelled

at them through a megaphone. 'Ahoy. See that caique, tied up to the quay? Moor alongside her and disembark across her. Is that clear?'

Hallam called back. 'Quite clear, thank you.'

Their boat drew up alongside the caique and, once the crew had fastened the two together with ropes, they began to move across. Lamb turned to the men on deck. 'Sarnt Mays, take your section off first and form a guard. Civilians off next, and then the rest of you, by section.'

Mays led his men off and over the floating dock. Once ashore, they fanned out either side of the gangway. Lamb watched Miranda Hartley and the others step gingerly from their boat on to the caique and walk across its rocking deck before going down the gangway. They stepped ashore as if they were leaving a P&O cruise liner. He half expected to see her turn to Hallam and shake his hand to thank him as she might the liner's captain. Then, in as orderly a manner as possible, the rest of them followed.

There was a sudden wailing. Air-raid sirens. Lamb craned his neck and scanned the skies but saw nothing. Nevertheless the ack-ack guns on shore in their little sandbagged half-moons opened fire. Mays' section ducked instinctively and the civilians looked up to see the danger but to his surprise none of the crowd on shore seemed very concerned and the khaki figures carried on about their business. The sirens stopped as abruptly as they had begun and the guns ceased a few seconds later. More wasted ammunition, thought Lamb. And why? Because, he guessed, some jittery young artillery spotter in a slit-trench on a hill outside the town had thought he had seen a Jerry plane. It had probably been a seagull.

Lamb found Hallam by the mooring. 'Thank you. You got us all here safely.'

'No thanks to me. I lost the convoy, didn't I?'

'Probably sailed straight on to Alexandria. But it was your work that got us here.'

'Perhaps, but it was thanks to your sergeant that we weren't shot to pieces. He's an extraordinary man, isn't he?'

'Yes, he is. That's one word for it. But anyway, thank you. What will you do now?'

'Try to find a tank if I can. I reckon a few of our mob will be here already. I'm sure to find them. They're not very good at keeping out of mischief, especially in a place like this.'

Lamb walked down the gangway and no sooner had his feet touched the stone of the quayside than he heard a voice shouting. He looked around.

A neatly turned out British staff officer in a peaked cap liberally adorned with brass was addressing Mays' section. 'Pile any heavy weapons over there, you men. Everything but rifles and side arms. Over there. We're going to pool all the heavy weapons. Orders from the GOC.'

Bennett looked at Lamb and raised an eyebrow before taking him aside and speaking to him quietly.

'Things must be bad, sir. But I'll be damned if I'm giving up the Lewis guns. I thought this might happen, sir. Took the precaution of having them dismantled. We've got a piece each, all us NCOs. We took the ones from the boat too, sir. Course we'll have to leave the mortars. Can't do much with them.'

'Well done, Sarnt-Major. Quite right. Important to keep something with us. Hand them in now and we'll never see them again. Whose brilliant idea was this, I wonder? No one will notice. Stubbs will be furious about his precious mortars, though.'

The last men off were unloading what few pieces of everyday kit they had managed to bring away from the mainland, which consisted mainly of blankets and rations, and a box of company documents including maps and a copy of *King's Regulations*, along with the civilians' travelling cases.

The crowd of Cretans that had gathered on the quayside moved towards them now and Lamb saw they were holding objects in their hands. One of the women, an elderly matron in a black dress and shirt, caught his arm and, saying something in a guttural Greek dialect he had never before encountered, smiled at him toothlessly as she pressed something into his palm. Lamb looked down and saw it was an orange. He saw other girls and women giving his men and others newly arrived on the quayside ceramic bowls of milky-white ice cream and spoons with which to eat it. At first the men just stared at them in disbelief, but it did not take long for them to accept the gifts. Lamb said thank you to the old woman, who nodded before turning and walking back to her house, just as if this was something she did every day.

Miranda Hartley came up to him. 'Ice cream and fruit. They seem very pleased to see you, Captain.' She spotted the orange in his hand. 'I say, do you want your orange?'

'No, you have it, please.'

Bennett found him as he handed it to her. He gestured to the men who were greedily eating the ice cream. 'Sir, is this all right by you?'

Lamb smiled. 'Fine, Sergeant. Of course. For all we know the men might not see oranges or ice cream again for a very long time. Let them take it if they want.'

Mrs Hartley, he saw, was already tucking into his own orange and at least half of him wished he hadn't given it to her. Valentine saw him. 'It's all right, sir. I've got two. Have one of mine.'

Lamb took the orange and, peeling it quickly, began to bite into the juicy flesh and pith, savouring it as he had enjoyed no orange before.

The staff officer, a major, walked over to Lamb. He was holding a large pad and a pencil. 'And who are you, Captain? Where have you come from?'

Lamb swallowed hard on a piece of orange and tucked the rest behind his back. 'Lamb, sir. Captain Peter Lamb. A Company, North Kents. We've come from Athens, sir.'

'North Kents.' He jotted it down on his pad. 'From Athens. Yes, you will have done. Well done, Captain. Well, now you're in Creforce holding Area A. Take your men off up that road there. How many are you?'

'Forty men, sir. We've lost a few. We fought through Greece.'

The major ignored the last comment and pointed to the east. 'Take yourselves off up that road there and make camp in one of the olive groves. If you can find one, that is. We've got thousands of chaps like you. Odds and ends. Don't worry. We'll decide what to do with you and where to send you soon enough. We're building a transit camp up at Perivolia. But you know what the army's like, Captain. For the moment I should just make camp. And do keep your men in control, Captain, if you can. There are some men out there – Australians and New Zealanders mostly – wandering through the vineyards and taking the law into their own hands. It's a nightmare, I can tell you. And it makes my job no easier.'

'We have some civilians with us, sir. British. A woman and three men.' He indicated Miranda Hartley. 'Where are they to go?'

'They'll have to fend for themselves, I'm afraid, British or not. Too many civilians here too now, and no legation. Nothing. Can't help everyone, you know. Enough to sort out with you lot. Just find yourselves an olive grove and await further orders. I'm off to the GOC. More bloody paperwork, I expect.'

And with that he was gone. Lamb stared after the man

76

as he rounded on some other hapless new arrivals. He began again on the orange, and as he chewed Miranda Hartley came over. 'I say. What luck. A friend of Mr Papandreou's says we can stay with him. In his villa. Isn't that nice? Where are you staying?'

'To be honest, I was just wondering the same thing myself.'

'Oh, I'm sure you'll find some lovely house somewhere. You officers always land on your feet.'

There was a loud and insistent 'parp' from a car horn. 'That'll be for me, I expect. Better go. Mustn't keep them waiting. See you soon, I hope, Captain. And thank you for all your help.'

She shook his hand and then ran off towards where Hartley and the others were waiting in two long, elegant, highly polished convertibles. Watching her go, Lamb smiled and summed up their current situation to himself.

They were standing on a narrow harbour-front street of Italianate villas with neat, walled gardens of palm and lemon trees. Two cafés sat directly opposite each other on a corner, their gaudy awnings draped over rows of empty chairs. The larger of the two bore a sign: 'Plaza Bar Tourist Hotel'. Lamb pointed to it. 'Sarnt-Major. Ten minutes' rest. Sit the men down over there.'

'All right you lot. Ten minutes. Savvy?'

As the men fell out and rested on chairs which until only recently had been occupied by holidaymakers, Lamb turned. 'Valentine, you seem well versed in the area. Tell me exactly where we are.'

'Place called Canea, sir. It's an old Venetian trading port. Popular with the tourist trade. Very picturesque.'

'So I see. Where's Mr Wentworth?'

'Over there, sir. Eating an ice cream.'

Lamb walked across to the lieutenant. 'Wentworth, are we all present and accounted for?'

Wentworth, who was licking slowly at a spoonful of ice cream, straightened up. 'I think so, sir.'

Lamb smirked. 'Think so is not quite what I asked, Lieutenant. What are our numbers?'

'Thirty-eight, sir. But we have five walking wounded and six with dysentery.'

'Right. So effective strength of twenty-seven.'

'Sir.'

His company had become a platoon. They were low on rations, had ragged uniforms and few of them were properly armed.

'Weapons?'

'We're missing twelve rifles. But we do still have the Brens and the two Lewis guns from the boat.'

He looked at his men. Most, like him, had not shaved for more than a week and the tired, drawn faces and sunken eyes told their own tale of what they had witnessed. As if to emphasise their state, at that moment around the corner came a platoon of British soldiers. They were marching in time, in a column of twos, with a sergeant-major at their head and to the right. As they passed several of Lamb's men gave them a wolf-whistle but the soldiers did not even look towards them. Lamb searched their uniforms for insignia.

Fred Smart was standing beside him. 'Blimey, sir. Who the hell's that lot? The Coldstream Guards?'

'No, Smart. I would hazard a guess that that's the Welch Regiment. They're the official Crete garrison. Well, part of it at least. They weren't in Greece.'

'I should coco. Sorry, sir.'

They might look, he thought, as if they had just come off parade at Horse Guards, but Lamb was grateful for their presence and their appearance. It brought him back to order. And despite the wolf-whistles he knew it was just what was needed to restore his men's confidence in the army. And they desperately needed that now.

Having reached the quayside, the newcomers stopped and divided into three sections, one of which moved across to Lamb. Their sergeant approached him.

'Beggin' your pardon, sir, but you would be new arrivals, would you?' He spoke with a just discernible Welsh accent.

'Yes, Sarnt. Just got here.'

'Did you see the major, sir?'

'Yes, thank you, Sarnt. I saw the major.'

'Well, sir, he will have told you, I'm guessing, to go up that road there to the olive groves. Didn't he? It's a good mile, sir.'

Lamb smiled. He knew that 'a good mile' meant an 'army mile', and an army mile meant any distance you wanted it to mean.

The man continued. 'You'll find a lovely field kitchen, sir, up there. It's not that far. Each of your men will get a nice mug of tea, some bread and cheese, an orange, some chocolate and some fags. You too, if you want them, sir. The assembly points and your bivvy area will be about seven miles farther on, isn't it.'

Lamb wondered if the sergeant meant seven 'good miles'.

'Thank you, Sarnt. That's very clear. We'll set out in five minutes. I'm just letting the men have a rest. We've had a bit of a journey.'

'Yes, sir, I understand it was a bit sticky.'

Lamb laughed. 'You could say that, Sarnt.'

'Well, sir, if you take my advice I should get up there and find yourself a billet as soon as you can. See, there's more coming in from Greece right now, sir, and them olive groves are already heaving with Aussies and Kiwis.'

'Thank you, Sarnt. I'll bear that in mind.'

The Welshman went to rejoin his men and Lamb found Eadie. 'Charles, I'm just off to tell the civilians that we're moving out. They'll have to fend for themselves. Give the men five minutes, then get them into marching order, will you.'

Lamb walked along the waterfront to where he had last seen Miranda but she was not there.

Another ship was unloading its cargo of refugees. It was a bizarre sight – the four civilians, waited on by a waiter bearing wine and coffee, surrounded by groups of broken men. Lamb walked up to them.

Miranda Hartley saw him coming. 'Captain, will you join us?'

'No, thank you, Mrs Hartley. I'm afraid we have to leave you here. We have orders to proceed to our assembly positions outside the town. I'm sorry. You'll just have to do the best you can.'

'Oh, we'll be absolutely fine, Captain. Mr Papandreou here has a friend with a villa outside a place called Galatas.'

Lamb was speechless yet relieved. Of course, he hadn't doubted it for a moment. They would have a friend with a car and a villa. How could he possibly have thought otherwise?

'That's splendid news. Well, goodbye then. I imagine we might meet again. Perhaps in Egypt.'

'Yes. Perhaps. And thank you again for all your help.'

Comberwell stood and offered his hand. 'Yes, thanks awfully, old man. Couldn't have done it without you.'

There was a general murmur of thanks as the other men stood and shook Lamb's hand. He turned and walked back along the waterfront to his men, somehow sorry to leave them.

Arriving outside the Plaza Bar, Lamb found that Eadie had already formed the men up on the road and was about to give the order to move off. It was then, though, that he caught sight of another boat which had just dropped anchor. As their own boat had done with the berthed caique, it had heaved to alongside a tanker, over whose deck the passengers were now moving. The unloading ship was somehow familiar, and then he recognised it as the caique they had seen in the shattered harbour of Piraeus, with its motley crew of British aristocrats, navy and soldiers. Lamb felt glad they had made it across and was turning back to get the men moving when he became aware of a commotion in the air. From out of nowhere there appeared three Stukas. They had clearly sighted the yacht pulling into shore and as Lamb watched they hovered in the sky above, like three cabs waiting on a taxi-rank, he thought, queuing up for their fares. Where were the air-raid warning sirens now, he wondered, or the bloody ack-ack? He was aware of Bennett beside him. 'Bloody hell, sir. Where did they come from? Those poor buggers'll get it now.'

Suddenly the first of the dive-bombers peeled off to the side, flipped and tilted its nose before going into a screaming descent down at the ship. There was a burst of small-arms fire from the deck where Lamb could see the men scurrying in panic, and then the pop of a Lewis gun. The plane loosed its bomb, which hurtled down and missed the vessel, sending up a huge plume of water which flooded the deck. The bomb exploded down at the harbour floor and shook the wall, the shockwaves sending the ship rocking several feet in the air. People screamed and fell about on the slippery deck, smashing themselves against metal stanchions. As Lamb looked on the second plane went in to the attack.

Eadie's neat ranks had disintegrated as the men had dived for any cover, even under chairs and tables. Lamb turned and shouted. 'Lewis guns, quick.' But instantly he remembered that their weapons were still in bits, hidden from the gaze of the staff major. He tried again. 'Rifle fire. Quick. At the aircraft.' He knew it was useless but he had to try something. Any man who could grabbed a weapon and began to pop off shots at the plane, but within a split second the screeching Stuka had jettisoned its bomb, which hurtled down and hit the caique clean amidships. Lamb looked on in horror as the stricken ship exploded in a sheet of flame.

At that moment the twin Bofors on the high ground opened up along with the sandbagged guns on the waterfront and puffs of cotton-wool smoke began to appear in the sky around the aircraft. But the first two planes had done their work and the third did not bother to dive. Taking no risks, the three planes pulled up sharply and climbed away, to vanish into the clear blue morning, leaving behind them a vision of hell.

Lamb's men had stopped firing now, and as they all watched two small boats, motor launches manned by men in khaki, pulled away from the harbour and headed towards the burning fishing boat. For a few moments Lamb was frozen to the spot. Then he turned to the men. 'Right, let's get moving. You've seen worse.'

But in his heart he was not sure he had.

They formed up again and marched off towards the olive groves, but the road took them up a hill right above where the caique had berthed and there was no escaping the sight.

They watched in silence as the two launches returned with all who had survived from the burning ship. Burnt, bloody and blackened men stumbled ashore. And there was the woman he had seen in Piraeus, before so elegant, now near naked and in rags, her clothes torn from her by the blast. In her arms lay the body of a child. Two other children were being helped up on to the quay close to the

Plaza Bar, and with them what remained of the crew. Three VAD nurses had rushed across now and were ripping shirts to pieces to clean the wounds and dress the burns.

Lamb turned his head back to the road in front of them, certain that there was nothing he could do or could have done. Yet still he felt an absolute gnawing revulsion at what they had witnessed. They walked on in silence, none of them capable of speech. Each man was sunk in his own thoughts but united in grief. The relief and optimism which had raised their spirits and banished their fatigue had been shattered by the mindless violence of the act, and each step now seemed harder than the last.

Before long they found themselves leaving the outskirts of Canea and among the first of a seemingly endless landscape of vineyards and olive groves.

It seemed to Lamb that every inch of the olive groves was filled with khaki-clad troops. Each unit was marked out by a whitewashed wooden signpost on which had been painted their brigade, battalion and company designation. There were British, Australians and New Zealanders, with not a few Maoris among them. Most had been organised by battalion and company as they had arrived on the ships from Greece, and it did nothing for their morale to realise that they were on their own and at half strength.

He found a New Zealand captain. 'Any idea of where my men can wash?'

The man pointed. 'There's a stream just past that wall, with a deep pool. My lads have been using that. But make sure you're far enough upstream. Some of the boys have been using it as a latrine as well.'

Lamb thanked him and wandered away, bemused. It was basic fieldcraft, he thought. The first thing you learnt was not to take a piss in the same stream you used for washing or drinking.

They walked on a little further until they came to a break in the lines of men and an area that appeared to be as yet unoccupied. Lamb called his men to a halt.

'All right, lads. This looks like ours. Charles, your platoon can organise the perimeter. I want a wooden sign, you know the style. Good clear lettering. Use boot polish if nothing else. See who our neighbours are and use some sticks to stake out our claim. Tape between them if you can find any. Hugh, you can set up the HQ area. I'll need a table. See what you can scrounge. Ammo cases, anything. Anyone with ground sheets, join them together with a mate and make a shelter. Then we'll try to get some food going. All clear?'

Within a few hours they had made the place feel a little more homely.

Bennett told the men off in sections to freshen up in the stream, and then they pooled their rations. By evening Lamb was sitting on a packing case in front of his ammunition box desk sipping a mug of tea. Around him the men chattered about their improvised fires, eating tins of Machonochie stew and cold beef. They had queued up earlier on for the promised distribution of cocoa, and Lamb had made sure they knew to make it last.

As evening fell the birds began to sing in the branches of the trees around them and a sense of contentment settled on the hillside. How very bizarre, thought Lamb, after the horror of the harbour.

Off in one of the other camps someone was singing in a fine baritone. Lamb caught snatches of 'Danny Boy' and concluded that it must be some Irish Australian. They might have been at a holiday camp, particularly as most of the men had discarded their tin hats and their weapons were piled together.

Earlier, he had held a parade in the trees and inspected the company properly for the first time since Thermopylae.

Every man was armed with something – rifles, revolvers, captured weapons. One man – Partridge, from Corporal Simmonds' section – had only a hand-grenade and no other equipment or arms. Otherwise Lamb was pleased that their personal equipment was very nearly complete, apart from Private Lyne who, appearing with no bayonet, revealed that they were using it for opening the rations.

The good turn-out, he knew, was chiefly Bennett's doing. A good sergeant-major was indispensable. And although they had given up the mortars to the depot in town, and as predicted Corporal Stubbs had been desolate, Bennett's plan with the Lewis guns meant that they still had some heavy weapons at least.

Lamb opened his cigarette case, took one out, tapped it on the improvised desk and lit up. As he did so Valentine walked past him for what seemed to be the third time in less than five minutes.

'Anything wrong, Sarnt?'

Valentine looked at him and shrugged. 'No, sir, not really. What it is, is that I'm still trying to work out where might be the best place to sleep for the night. You see, with the sun setting over there that line of trees is going to get the last of it this evening. But when it rises, that line of trees will get it. Where do you suppose might be warmer, sir?'

'I have absolutely no idea, Sarnt. I should just find a pleasant spot and stay there.'

'Yes, sir. That would probably be the best thing to do. The army way, sir. Thank you.'

Lamb watched him go and shook his head.

Three times in the past year since their return from France he had recommended Valentine for an officer training course, and time and again Valentine had failed. It was clear that it was deliberate. The man was set against the idea. They had fought through France, and Valentine had twice saved his life. That aside, he had also shown all the attributes required of an officer. Yet still he refused to accept promotion.

Well, Lamb had given him some, despite the man. Had encouraged Colonel de Russet to promote him to sergeant. Valentine had grunted at his new stripe and then laughed it off. But Lamb knew he resented it and all the responsibility that went with it.

Lamb looked at the sign beside his command post. 'C Coy, 2nd North Kents. Capt P Lamb.' Walker, one of Wilkinson's men and a talented artist, had done the lettering in dark blanco on a piece of wood they had found and beneath it had drawn the regimental cap badge, the jackal. Lamb pulled on his cigarette and, exhaling, watched the smoke climb against the peerless evening sky. He closed his eyes for a moment, thinking he might enjoy the peace even more, but within a few moments he was more fully awake than ever. He closed his eyes and tried again. But it was no use. His mind was consumed now by a vision of the face of the woman on the burning boat as she cradled her child in her arms, her pleading eyes staring at him in an expression of disbelief and her gash of a mouth open in a noiseless scream.

5

It was on the fifth day after their arrival on Crete that Lamb realised how much he missed being in action. The past few weeks had been so frenetic and their flight from Greece so desperate that he had initially been as glad of a rest as the others. But on this day he woke and knew instantly that he had had enough. Enough of lying in olive groves and trying to invent activities for the men. Enough of inspecting weapons and polishing kit. Enough of morning physical training exercises. He had had time now to dwell on all that had happened to them in Greece and on the fury and ruthlessness of the enemy invasion. And always, etched on his mind, was the image from the harbour of the desolate mother. All he wanted now was a chance to fight back and to do what he had joined the army to do. Yet all that his orders directed him to do was to find the King of Greece.

He had not been idle over the past days. He had not had much chance to enquire about King George but he had learnt from some of the other officers that the defences of the island had been split into two basic sectors by the GOC, Major General Freyberg, a doughty New Zealander who everyone said was the protégé of no less than Churchill himself.

The bulk of the British forces, consisting of a battalion of the Black Watch and one of the York and Lancs, were holding the major town of Heraklion in the midpoint of the north coast. The western sector, where they had landed, was held by the New Zealanders, Australians and some Greeks, plus the Welch Regiment and a handful of Royal Marine gunners, plus the 'odds and sods' of which they were now a part.

Lamb could see – anyone could – that when the battle came, as it no doubt would, the island would be not one but several isolated battlefields. First there was the far north, with the town of Kastelli Kissamos and its vulnerable, unmade airstrip. Beyond that was a coastal plain running from the Rodopos peninsula to the strategic airfield at Maleme and on through Canea to Suda Bay. It was difficult terrain with olive groves and orchards of orange trees. Worst of all for any attacker to negotiate would be the bamboo plants which had been planted to protect the crops from the winds which scoured the coast.

The talk throughout the temporary camps was that the enemy would attack the island soon, but no one seemed to know when. It was clearly imperative, then, that Lamb find the King before it happened. An amphibious landing was forecast by some, probably at Suda Bay. Others, though, Lamb among them, thought a paratroop attack would come first and then, with that toehold established, a heavier landing from the sea. It had worked for the Germans at Corinth and before that last year when they had dropped from the skies and taken the Eben-Emael fort in Belgium. But however it came, Lamb knew that it must come. And when it did, he thought, he would be more than ready for a fight.

In the meantime all he could do was keep his ear to the ground and try to get in with the High Command. He had made a couple of good contacts on Freyberg's staff at Creforce HQ and that of General Weston, commander of Suda Force and CO of their own brigade sector under Brigadier Kippenberger. There were far too many generals on the island, he thought, all jostling for position. It was said that every time General Weston sent a telegram or a memo to General Freyberg he had to send a duplicate to General Wilson and even to Wavell. Some said he even had to send one to Churchill. With so much paper flying about it was hardly surprising that information, right or wrong, had begun to leak out. There might be a general rule of 'hush-hush' but every day seemed to bring fresh rumours. Some even said there were German spies on the island, who had come across from Greece dressed as New Zealanders. If there were, Lamb laughed to himself as he looked in the shaving mirror, he certainly hadn't seen them. None of the Kiwis he had encountered to date looked anything like German soldiers. For a start, they tended to be dressed almost in rags. Thank God his men had managed to keep most of their uniform intact, and their weapons for that matter. He thanked heaven for Bennett and his other NCOs. Even Valentine.

He had just finished shaving and was wondering where he had put his comb when an officer walked into the area of olive grove in which his men had made their home. The sentry snapped to attention, and the officer spotted Lamb wiping the soap from his face with the filthy towel which was the best Smart could find.

'You the North Kents? I'm looking for a Captain Lamb.'

Lamb pointed to the painted sign bearing his name and that of the unit, which the officer appeared to have missed. 'You've found him.'

'Ah, yes. Good morning. We're moving you, Lamb, you'll be glad to know. There's a transit camp down at Perivolia for the odds and ends. Sorry, didn't mean anything by that. It's just that you're not on your own. There are at least a couple of hundred who've lost their units. In fact, your command seems to be one of the more intact. Well done.'

'Thank you. When do we move?'

'Oh, whenever you want, really. It's very relaxed. But I should get there sooner rather than later or all the best places will have gone. Got any tents?'

'None to speak of.'

'Well, then, I'd say that was all the more reason to get a move on, wouldn't you? Cheerio.'

And with that he was gone. Lamb seethed for a couple of minutes, then, finding his comb, slicked back his hair with the contents of a half-empty bottle of Trumper's Eucris that Smart had managed to find in someone's haversack, and turned to Bennett.

'Sarnt-Major, they're moving us to a camp. Get the men moving. Tell them it's first come first served and if they want a bed or a tent they'd better snap to it.'

Even Lamb was surprised by the short time that it took to get the company on the road. They marched the three miles to the transit camp, which lay south west of Canea, in column of threes with Lamb and the two lieutenants at their head and reached it by late morning. It was a desolate place, a huge field of tents and a cluster of corrugated iron sheds, spanning an area 1,000 yards wide, between the tiny hamlets of Kharakia to the north and Galaria to the south. The tents, Lamb thought perhaps a hundred of them, were laid out in long lines like any military camp you might have seen for the last 200 years. At the end of every seventh line stood a camp stove, and

90

around these stood clusters of men with tin cups and mess tins, waiting for tea. Others sat on the parched grass and earth between the tents, reading or writing, while on the far north side a group of men were kicking a ball about.

Eadie spoke. 'Well, it's better than what we've come from, sir.'

'If we can get a tent. Look.'

Lamb walked up to a corporal who was leaning on his rifle at what he supposed was the camp perimeter. The man, seeing an officer approach, managed a semblance of smartness and saluted. Lamb returned the gesture.

'Corporal, who's in charge here? We're the new arrivals.'

'Captain Page, sir. You'll find him over there.' He indicated a tent, standing on its own. Lamb walked across. Outside the tent a wooden signpost had been hammered into the ground. It read:

'Capt. WS Page, RTR, O/C Transit Camp A.'

He pushed back one of the flaps and walked in and coughed. Inside a young officer was seated at a table covered with sheaves of paper. He was writing. As Lamb entered he looked up.

'Yes? Who are you?'

'Lamb, North Kents. We were told to report here.'

'Oh yes. You're the last ones, aren't you? Sorry. Not much left for you. We did keep a couple of lines of tents but the Hussars took them earlier this morning. Should have been quicker. I think there may be one line left. How many have you got?'

'Around forty of my men, and three officers.'

'Well, you'll need one tent for the officers of course, one for the NCOs and another seven for the men.' He flicked through the sheaf of papers and shook his head. 'Sorry, by the look of things we only have five. That'll have to do. Anyway, I've just had a signal from the GOC.

He's of the firm opinion that the entire division is to be sent back to Egypt, and that goes for us lot too, you included, I imagine. So you won't be here for long.' He looked back down at the paperwork and then had a thought. 'Oh, the officers' mess is over on the right. Dinner at eight. Not obligatory.' He looked back down and Lamb saw that their conversation was over. He turned and left the tent.

Bennett was waiting. 'Any luck, sir?'

'You might call it luck. We've been given five tents between us.'

'What, all of us, sir? That'll be cosy.'

'We've had worse, Sarnt-Major. At least we're under cover and we might have better mess tins to use than petrol cans.' He paused. 'The good news, according to the commandant here, is that we're due to be shipped back to Egypt. So I shouldn't get too comfortable.'

They found the tents and, much to their delight, a blanket waiting for them upon each of the beds. The disappointment, however, was that between the five tents in the remaining line there were only thirty beds. The men drew lots for who would be the first to sleep upon the ground, and Bennett drew up a rota. By the evening they had settled in.

The new billets were more comfortable, certainly, but Perivolia was no more than a tiny village. Whenever he could he would walk the mile or so from the camp and sit for half an hour in one of the local *kafeneios* in Galatas on what passed for the main square, watching the world go by. A couple of cups of strong Turkish coffee and somehow everything seemed, unaccountably, slightly better, even if he could still see the German bombers flying in on their daily run to bomb Heraklion or Suda, and even if his sips of the bitter black liquid were occasionally punctuated by the tremors of falling bombs. Sometimes he would take Eadie or Wentworth, and sometimes both, designating their coffee mornings as impromptu order groups about nothing in particular. The atmosphere was torpid and in this lotus-eating climate of quiet anticipation the island seemed to function as it must have done for hundreds of years.

While the women never seemed to stop working, the local men drank their coffee and their *raki*, read their newspapers in the cafés and talked of goats, women, the climate and the crops as they had for hundreds of years. They smiled and played with their moustaches and made thumbs-up signs at the British and New Zealand soldiers as they passed by. Lamb noticed how when they were not working the women tended to stay inside and how the older women were clad almost head to foot in black. The younger girls, of course, were quite different. For one thing, some of them were disarmingly pretty and not a few favoured a more European style of dress.

There was an air of unreality after the horrors of the mainland, and he wondered when it would come to an inevitable end.

The few lightly wounded they had brought away from Greece were being treated at the 7th General Field Hospital which had been set up three miles to the west of the old port and was staffed by seventy British nurses. It was filling up too with cases of dysentery and Lamb prayed that his men would not succumb. He had lost too many already. They all had lice, of course; the camp was rife with them and they were no respecters of rank.

Life at Transit Camp A was better than sitting in another olive grove, but only just. It held about 600 men, his own men and others like them who had missed their parent units during the retreat from Greece. Each group had some sort of cohesion, though he wondered how they would come together in the event of action.

The daily routine became a grind and still there was no word from any of his contacts of the whereabouts of the King. Waking from habit at 6 a.m., Lamb found himself at a loose end by 8. Luckily that was the precise time every day that the Germans chose to come over. And this morning was no different.

Overhead he heard engines but experience had taught him that this was no raid, just a recce plane, the local 'shufti' flight from Rhodes which the Germans sent out every day at the same time. No one bothered to fire at it.

'There he goes again, sir. Like clockwork.'

'Yes, that's the Jerries for you, Sarnt-Major. They certainly make things run on time. Very efficient.'

Bennett laughed. 'Let's hope not, sir.'

'Mr Wentworth tells me he's organised a swimming party for his platoon, down on the beach.'

'Yes, sir. Very nice idea too, sir. Just like Tottenham Lido. Lovely.'

'We need to make the most of this phoney war, you know. It does the men good, Sarnt-Major, even though we all know it can't last forever. Make sure they take their weapons with them, will you, just in case. We can't be too careful.'

'D'you think Jerry'll attack here, sir?'

'Yes. It stands to reason, if he wants the desert, and we know that for certain. It's my opinion that they'll hit us with whatever they can. But by that time you and I may have been sent to the desert again.'

'Back to Benghazi? Not again? Oh, my good lord. I think I prefer it here.'

Lamb laughed. 'But you might not when Jerry comes to call.'

They had made a new company HQ at the end of the first row of tents. It was slightly better than the effort back in the olive grove and consisted of a table set up beneath a tamarisk tree with beside it the original blancoed sign with Lamb's title on it. He was sitting at it later that morning when a man in black rode past on a donkey. Lamb waved at him and muttered a hello, to be rewarded with a nod and a smile. The local priest had become something of a celebrity every day riding his donkey straight through the middle of the camp, as he had done for years before it existed.

The church bells rang out the hour and Lamb stood up and brushed back his hair with his hand. The weather was becoming hotter by the day and he reminded himself to give another talk to the men that afternoon on the importance of staying in the shade and keeping fluid levels up – which did not imply drinking as much of the local wine as they could get their hands on.

He called for Smart, who appeared, as he always did, within a few moments. He was bearing a pair of gleaming, polished shoes.

'Your shoes, sir.'

'I swear I don't know how you do it, Smart. You're a marvel. I'd given up on those.'

'Never give up, sir. You know that.'

Lamb tied his laces. 'I shan't be here for lunch, Smart. Get yourself something, and remember to stay out of the sun. Last thing we want is you going down with sunstroke.'

For lunch it had become something of a habit for Lamb to mess with his fellow officers from the transit camp and occasional visitors from neighbouring New Zealand units. The food was hardly *haute cuisine*, no different in fact from the men's rations: bully beef and biscuit, supplemented with local olives, oranges, lemons and when they could get it ice cream. Eaten in convivial company it became more passable, and Lamb had struck up a rapport

95

with a few of the officers, in particular a large, broad-shouldered Kiwi major named Macdonagh and a pleasant young lieutenant in the tanks named Roy Farran, who knew Hallam.

Today, though, he had decided to pay a visit to the Hartleys and the other civilians in Canea. He had no interest in Miranda Hartley, of course; it was merely that he still felt responsible for their welfare. While Papandreou was pleasant enough, he hoped the buffoon Comberwell might not be there with his odious 'gung-ho' chatter.

There was precious little transport to be had on the island and Lamb walked the two miles from the camp to Canea. He was rewarded by a thick deposit of dust on Smart's beautifully polished shoes.

The house owned by Mr Papandreou's cousin, a professor of archaeology in Athens, was set back from the road about half a mile outside Canea on the Galatas road. Lamb had sent a runner to find it the previous day, saying he would drop by, and he found Miranda Hartley in the walled garden, waiting for him.

'Captain Lamb, Peter. What a lovely surprise to get your note yesterday.'

She tidied her hair and gave him what he presumed she thought was her most disarming smile. 'Now tell me, is there any news? What's to happen to us all? Are the Germans going to attack us here? When will we get away to Egypt? It's been days, you know. We've heard nothing.'

'Hasn't anyone been to see you from the legation?'

'No, not a soul. I know that there are some of their people on the island but we haven't seen hide nor hair of them. We keep asking but no one tells us anything. And now everyone's saying that the Germans are coming.' Miranda looked at him. 'What are we going to do? Do you think they'll attack?'

Lamb thought it best to be honest with her. 'Yes, I'm afraid I do. They must. Hitler needs Crete if he's to take Egypt, and that most certainly is his plan. They'll come, I'm sure of it. The real question is, will we still be here when they do? Will you be here?'

She looked away. 'You'll be staying. If they come?'

'It's my job. My duty. But we should get all of you away before that happens.'

She looked at him and he said nothing. He had guessed that she had been attracted to him but, while she was attractive, it was not mutual and he had hoped there might be nothing in it. This was the last thing he wanted.

'Mrs Hartley . . .'

'Miranda, please . . . Peter.'

'Of course. Miranda. I'm sorry.'

A servant appeared from the house bearing a silver tray and on it two large glasses filled with ice and a clear liquid, each topped with slices of lime. She said, 'I thought you might want something. Gin and tonic?'

He took one of the glasses. 'Thank you. That's perfect. Where's your husband?'

He cursed. That had not been said at all as it had been intended. One look and he knew at once that she had misinterpreted his purpose.

'I don't know. I think he went off with Mr Papandreou to look at some archaeological site. He's a desperate Classicist at heart. Quite far away. He won't be back for hours. Neither of them will. And heaven knows where Mr Comberwell is. He disappears for hours at a time and never tells anyone where he's going.'

She looked at him, pleadingly. He ignored it. 'You should keep track of him and your husband, and I strongly advise you both to get your things together. You can be sure there will be a ship for you soon, and you should be ready to leave at a moment's notice. I mean it.'

Puzzled at Lamb's apparent sudden departure from the idea of an illicit afternoon liaison among the lime trees, she changed the subject. 'The King's here, you know. The King of Greece. On the island. Isn't it exciting?'

Lamb tried to disguise his very real excitement. 'Yes, I had heard that, and his new prime minister.'

'Julian says he's heard that General Freyberg wanted the King to go to Egypt, out of harm's way. But that General Wavell and the Government in Britain think it better that he should stay. So he's staying.'

Lamb said nothing for the moment, but he wondered whether Freyberg, the GOC Crete and one of the few men on the island in direct contact with Britain and privy to all the Government's intelligence, knew something about the timing of a German invasion that he did not.

Lunch was cold cuts, but to Lamb it might as well have been a five-course banquet at Simpson's, such had been the monotony of his recent diet. He ate voraciously, worried that he might look greedy, and throughout it all Miranda Hartley smiled at him indulgently, looking at times, he thought, like someone who was fattening up a pig. Her conversation now turned to things back in England, to the social season and the sort of subjects he thought he had left far behind when he had divorced his wife – society subjects, racing, the latest débutantes and some court scandal about which he had not a clue. He nodded politely and bluffed his way through. For pudding they had ice cream and peaches, not tinned as he had become used to, when he could get them, but fresh from the tree. As they sipped at the dessert wine, a Tokay from the house's excellent cellar, Miranda expounded the theories of Mussolini and explained to Lamb why Il Duce was so very different from Herr Hitler, who was a nasty, priggish little man.

'At least that's what a friend of Julian's says. Quite common. Not a statesman at all. Not like Il Duce.'

'Yes, it's a shame we have to fight him, really.'

'Yes. My thoughts entirely. We are alike, don't you think?'

Lamb smiled, amused and annoyed that she hadn't detected the obvious sarcasm in his tone. She was an extraordinarily simple woman, he thought, capable of giving her allegiance to one person. War was so very simple in her mind.

After lunch she suggested a walk and Lamb was only too pleased to accept. It made the perfect excuse to finally get away from the house and avoid any further hints of a more complex relationship. He hoped she might have got the message.

They walked towards Galatas, enjoying the afternoon breeze, which blew in from the sea, across the hills. As they entered the village, Lamb was surprised to see Valentine walking towards them up the road. He was with a New Zealand corporal whom he had befriended. As he passed Lamb and Mrs Hartley he smiled knowingly.

Miranda Hartley did not notice the two men. She was still talking. '. . . and there's a frightfully nice young English officer here whom Julian used to know in London. Michael Hathaway. You should really meet him. Perhaps we can organise dinner, or lunch.'

Lamb looked at her. 'What, oh yes, that would be good.' He was still thinking about her throwaway comment about Freyberg and the King of Greece.

Aware that she was being ignored, Miranda smiled at him. 'I should go. Lots to do. People to see. You know.'

'Sorry, yes, of course. Let's meet for a drink some time. I should like to meet your husband again. And Hathaway.

99

Fascinating about the King. But where's he staying? Surely there are no royal palaces on the island. Apart from Knossos, of course.'

She laughed. 'Oh, apparently he's in a big house quite near here. At Perivolia or somewhere. Lovely to see you, Peter. Goodbye then.'

She bent up towards him and planted the smallest of kisses on his cheek. It was not much, but just enough to leave him uncertain as to whether she thought of them as more than friends. Lamb could hardly believe his luck. A villa in Perivolia! Without knowing it he had already been carrying out the colonel's instructions, shadowing his charge from a safe distance, from the transit camp outside Perivolia.

As he watched Miranda Hartley walking away, Lamb could see Valentine returning, minus the Kiwi corporal. He walked over to Lamb, still smiling. 'Ah, sweet Isle that hath such voices in it.'

Lamb did not look at him. 'Sorry?'

'I only said, "Ah, sweet Isle that . . ."'

'Shut up, Valentine. I know what you said. And why. And you're wrong.'

'Yes, sir. Sorry, sir.'

'And don't be so bloody facetious.'

'But don't you think it's funny, Captain, how our companion, the lovely Mrs Hartley, is named after the very character from Shakespeare who turns up on a desert island?'

Lamb sighed. 'I know what play you were quoting from, Valentine.'

'Sorry, sir. I forgot that you had a Classical education. I can only suppose that I might be her Caliban. But who can we cast you as, sir? Ferdinand, perhaps?'

Lamb said nothing.

Valentine continued. 'Prospero, then.'

100

'Even more absurd. I'm no magician.'

'No, sir. I think I'll settle on Ferdinand for you. You could do with a happy ending. A little romance.'

'I'm warning you, Valentine.'

'Yes, sir.'

'Now get back to the camp. I'm sure there's something useful you can do.'

He walked further into the village, where he had earlier arranged to meet Charles Eadie, and found the young lieutenant in the centre of the village looking at the church with its twin whitewashed towers.

'Lost in thought, Charles?'

'I was just thinking, sir, how strange it is to be here, as if one were a tourist. I mean, here we are enjoying life in this extraordinary place, and any moment it might all come to an end.'

'Yes, I know what you mean. It's as if life goes on regardless. Perhaps we should make the most of it. We might be back in Egypt before you know it.'

'Do you think so, sir? But just say that we don't get away and the Jerries do invade. How many men has General Freyberg got?'

'According to my sources there are something over 30,000 Allied troops on this island, along with the odds and sods. That's with a population of 400,000 Cretans. And some of them might be pretty handy with a gun or whatever else comes to hand. If he does come, he's going to have a fight on his hands.'

'How do you think they'll do it, sir? Paratroops, like Corinth? Or from the sea?'

Lamb nodded. 'Both. If I were invading this place I'd want to make sure I had a bridgehead first, and the best way to do that, if you control the air, is by dropping men out of the sky. Then you take the airfields, and then you land more men by plane and invade from the sea.'

There was a sudden commotion in a street behind them, just off the square. Raised voices. Both men turned and instinctively walked towards them. Getting closer, it appeared that something was happening in the little *kafeneio* that lay down the narrow side street close to the corner. The voices from inside were louder now. Lamb could hear English voices, and above them a woman was screaming.

6

A crowd had gathered around the door of the *kafeneio* as, running now, Lamb and Eadie made their way past the low wall outside the bar, ducked under the awning and went inside. The smoke-filled room was packed with soldiers. Lamb pushed his way through the press of bodies, with Eadie close behind him.

Someone he pushed into half turned. 'Oi, watch it mate.' Then, 'Oh, sorry, sir.'

Seeing an officer, several of the men closest to the door melted away outside. The others, though, seemed oblivious, and Lamb knew why. The place reeked of cheap booze.

The room was cool and sparsely decorated with a religious icon, a poster advertising *raki* and a large mirror, while hanging from a beam were baskets of bright pink plants. There were four tables and a long wooden bar with a highly polished top. Against this, with their backs to the bar, stood two British soldiers in shirtsleeves, one wearing a forage cap. At the table nearest to the bar an officer in staff uniform was standing, and beside him stood two more British privates. One of them had to be the biggest man Lamb had ever seen. He was an ordinary soldier and in his right hand he was holding a fighting knife. Next to him stood his mate, a fraction smaller but clutching a broken bottle. As Lamb and Eadie entered, the men looked round and smiled. One of them spoke in a slurred Liverpudlian drawl.

''Ere we go, Mick. Two more jokers, by the look of them.'

They turned back to the officer. Lamb half recognised his features: a long, aquiline nose, slicked back dark hair and a moustache. The one who had spoken continued. 'Look 'ere, chum. We told you, hop it. No one gonna stop us having a drink. Least of all some ponced-up wop.'

The officer spoke. 'I'm not a wop, as you put it so politely. I am Greek and I'm an officer. If you talk to me again in that manner I will have you all on a charge. Leave now and I will say nothing more.'

The big man pressed himself up against the officer. 'You'll what? Have us on a charge? I'll tell you what you'll do. You'll fuck off out of it while you still can.'

He turned to the bar, behind which Lamb now saw two people were standing. One was a man in his fifties, tall and with typically Cretan looks: the angular, hawk-like features above a bushy moustache now turning grey. His face was red with fury, and Lamb could see why. One of the soldiers at the bar had a pistol trained on him. Beside him stood a girl. She looked terrified.

The big man spoke. 'Two more *rakis*, Niko, or whatever your name is. No, make it a bottle. Let's have a party. Get the girl to bring them over.'

He leered at his friends and made an upward motion with his fist. 'All right, sweetie. You bring us drink, yes? Jaldi jaldi.'

That got a laugh from the room. But not from Lamb or Eadie. It took a matter of a second for Lamb to draw his pistol. Eadie had done the same, and both were pointing at the two soldiers by the officer. Lamb spoke across the room, silencing it. 'What the hell's going on?'

He hardly needed to ask, but the Greek officer gave him the answer he needed. 'Captain, thank God. These men are drunk. I have forbidden the owner to give them any more, but they disobey. They have also insulted a superior officer.'

Lamb looked at the ringleader. 'Is this true?'

'Piss off. This is our beef. This bastard won't let us drink. Greek bastard! What are we doing here, saving his bloody skin?'

Lamb continued. 'Unless you drop your weapons, I will shoot you.'

'I said piss off.'

'Can't you see, man? I'm an officer.'

'Piss off, sir, then.'

'Put down the knife, you fool. You'll do time for this, war or no war. Make it better on yourself. Put down the knife.'

'Think you can make me, sir?'

'Put it down, man. Don't be stupid.'

The man lurched slightly and Lamb could see that his drunkenness had the better of him.

'Bastard barman won't let us have any more wine. We've come here to save the bugger from the bloody Jerries and he won't let us have any wine. What does he want? Bloody wop.'

That was enough for Lamb. 'He's not a bloody wop, soldier, he's a bloody Cretan. And he owes you nothing.'

The man turned and, it seemed in slow motion, made a stab at the Greek officer, who backed away, but Lamb was faster. In an instant he had moved across the room and, his pistol still clutched tightly in it, brought his right fist hard up and straight into the soldier's face. The man fell back screaming and, dropping the knife, clutched at his bloody face where the gun had connected with his nose, pulping it to one side.

Then, recovering, he turned on Lamb. The girl screamed as the man threw himself across the room, roaring with rage. His bloody fist caught Lamb in the stomach, winding him and knocking him back. Lamb tried to blot out the pain and focused, sidestepping another swing from the man's left fist. In swinging the soldier had overbalanced and tried to straighten up. But it was too late. In a swift motion Lamb brought the butt of the revolver hard down upon the man's bare head with a sickening crunch, and the soldier slumped to the floor unconscious, blood pouring from his head. The other soldier dropped the broken bottle and stood staring at his friend for a moment before quickly putting his hands up, his face ash-white.

'Don't shoot, don't shoot me. Jesus. Please.'

Lamb kept the gun trained on him, and for a ghastly moment thought of himself as the major on the beach at Rafina, shooting dead the drunken Aussie. Snapping out of it, he motioned to Eadie to grab the two men at the bar who were sidling towards the door. It was over in an instant, and not surprisingly, when Lamb turned back to the room, he found that along with the other two officers and the three remaining drunks, apart from the owner and the girl, the bar had cleared.

The Greek officer approached Lamb, stepping over the bloody body of his unconscious assailant. He had fine features and a tanned complexion, and from his hands it was clear that he was obviously no working man, nor ever had been.

'Thank you, Captain. That was quick thinking. I'm in your debt. Shall we get out of here? Away from all this.'

Lamb turned to Eadie. 'Charles, get this lot under guard, will you. I passed a guardhouse on the way in.

See if you can find any redcaps. Oh, and he might need a medic.'

Once outside, the captain brightened up. 'That's better. Now tell me whom I should thank for saving me.'

'Peter Lamb. North Kents.'

The officer snapped to attention. 'Thank you, Captain Lamb.' He paused. 'I take it you don't know who I am?'

'I'm afraid not. Do I take it perhaps that I should?'

The man laughed. 'Funnily enough my name is Peter too. But the army list says simply Captain, the Prince Peter. Does that help?'

Lamb stared. 'Good heavens. I'm terribly sorry, Your Highness. Of course.'

Prince Peter of Greece smiled at him. 'Yes, I'm sorry. You realise that it makes it rather more important that it didn't get any nastier in there. What's most annoying, though, about what's just happened is that I'm with liaison.' He laughed. 'I'm chiefly responsible for making things work between our two armies. But you might say it's also my job to ease relations between all the Allied troops on Crete and the local population. I wonder what your general would think of what just went on in there. I'll have to file a report.'

'It wasn't your fault, Your Highness. Those men got drunk and threatened you.'

'Yes, but as far as records are concerned I was in a dispute with some British soldiers and one of them was badly injured.'

'Sir, with respect. That was not the case, and I will swear to it.'

'Will you? Thank you, Captain. It's just that my family have never been that popular in parts of Greece, Crete included, and there are certain people who will look for every excuse to discredit us.' He replaced his hat, which he had been carrying. 'I'll say goodbye. My driver was with me before those animals arrived. Better find him. Thank you again, Lamb. I shan't forget it.'

Lamb saluted and went back into the *kafeneio*. So now at least he had met a member of the King's party. He had been careful not to mention his mission, nor to enquire any further as to the King's whereabouts. It had been a productive day.

Inside, he was pleased to see that Eadie had found some men to remove the unconscious man and that the girl from the bar had mopped the floor. He went over to her as she cleared up behind the bar. She had wiped her tears now and Lamb noticed her striking features – strong, yet with a powerful, sculptural beauty, dark, almost raven-black hair and bright blue eyes.

She smiled at him. 'Thank you. My father is very grateful too. We didn't know what they would do.'

'It was nothing.'

She nodded. 'Yes, I agree. It was not much. Perhaps I would have managed.'

He smiled, taken aback. 'Would you?'

'I don't know, really. Since my mother died I manage most things. But that? I don't know. Would you like a drink?'

Lamb was going to refuse but saw the look in her eyes.

'Please, Captain. I'd like to say thank you.'

He laughed. 'In that case it would be rude to refuse.'

She poured a shot glass of *raki* and he took it and downed it in one, feeling the fiery spirit burning his throat. 'You know who that was? The Greek officer?' he asked.

'Yes, I know.' She shrugged. 'We don't care for them much, the royal family. But that would not have been a good way to die.'

'No. Not for anyone. Even a prince.'

'They're not all bad, you know,' she said, smiling again. 'Your soldiers, I mean. Just a few of them. They get drunk.

108

We don't really understand it. Of course we drink too, but only at parties. Not like that.'

'They want to forget. And they're not my soldiers. But they should know better.'

'What are your soldiers? New Zealanders? Kiwis?'

'English.'

'Oh. You live at the camp?'

'Yes. It's pretty dire.'

'Dire?'

'Sorry. It's not very comfortable. Or pretty.'

He looked at her again, then, conscious that he might be seen to be staring, looked away at the poster on the wall, which showed a smiling old man in Greek costume raising a glass of *raki*.

She spoke quietly. 'I wish we could forget. Perhaps we should drink, like them. One of my brothers is missing. In Albania. I think he's dead. My father is half mad with worry, but he will never show it. But I know.' She wiped her hands on her apron and extended one to Lamb. 'Sorry, my name is Anna. Anna Levandakis. My father owns this bar.'

'Lamb. Peter Lamb. I'm sorry about your brother. I hope you're wrong.'

'I'm usually right. But sometimes I think it would be better for him. What hope have we got here? Oh, I don't mean you. I'm sure you will fight bravely. But I know that you will have to leave. The Germans will have too many men, and then you will go and we will be left to fight them alone.'

'Will you fight?'

She smiled and nodded. 'Of course I will fight. We all will. We're Cretans. We will never let an enemy take our homeland. We fought the Greeks five years ago and before them the Turks, for centuries. Why should the Germans be any different? After you have gone we will take to the hills and they will go. We may lose many people, but in the end they will go and we will survive.'

Lamb looked at her in admiration. She reminded him of a girl he had taken out from France last year and left behind in London. She had been a fighter too, a true Frenchwoman who had vowed to help liberate her country. But this girl was something more. He had never heard anyone, particularly a woman, speak with such vehemence and such certainty of winning.

She held out the bottle to him. 'More?'

'No, no, thank you. That was good. But I have work to do. My men . . .'

She smiled. 'Will you come back? I mean, will you come and drink here again?'

Lamb nodded and smiled. 'Yes, of course. I will. Thank you, Anna.'

It was enough to say, for now. He wandered away from the village back towards the camp and thought of the drunken soldier and wondered what damage he had done. He had had no alternative, he supposed. It was clear that the man would have made a mess of Prince Peter. Surely, it was what anyone else would have done, and for anyone? He wondered whether there might have been an alternative and then thought again of the major at Rafina. Of course Lamb had not killed the man, and he was thankful for that. That had been a stupid way to die, a waste of a man's life in a war where all life had become cheap, where men were expendable and were sacrificed daily for the greater good. Entering the camp perimeter he returned the sentry's salute and walked to his tent. Smart was waiting for him, and as Lamb entered he looked down at the officer's dust-encrusted shoes and smiled.

The following day Lamb found himself summoned by runner to the HQ of the newly appointed commander of 10th Brigade, Colonel Howard Kippenberger, a famously forceful New Zealander. The HQ for the Canea and Suda battlegroup was based in one of the few grander houses in Galatas, not far in fact from the Levandakis' *kafeneio*, and Lamb wondered whether his audience with the colonel might have something to do with yesterday's incident. Summary justice and martial law were the norm now. Surely, he thought, he was not going to be asked for a full report and a justification of his actions?

He walked past the sentry, returned the salute and entered a marble hall with a sweeping staircase. Two officers were talking at the foot of it and Lamb, recognising one of them, approached him.

'Geordie Crawford.'

'Peter, good God, what on earth are you doing here?'

'Adrift again, would you believe? Lost the rest of the battalion in Greece and then came over here. And you? I suppose you're with the Black Watch at Heraklion.'

'Yes, in a manner of speaking. It's actually not my battalion, but I asked the colonel if I could come along for the ride, and then all this happened. So now I'm acting liaison officer with Brigadier Chappel. We're just on our way back there now. You know Paddy Leigh-Fermor, our IO?'

Lamb nodded at the suave, thin young man, who smiled back.

'This is Peter Lamb, Paddy. I told you about him. We came through Normandy together. Keeps losing his battalion.'

Leigh-Fermor smiled. 'Ah, so you're the chap who got those men away at St Valéry. Well done. You should be with our lot at the Military Mission. I could put in a word.'

'Quite happy where I am, thanks. I still have a company,

whatever Crawford might tell you. I'm here to see Colonel Kippenberger.'

'He's through in the office. In quite a good mood today, actually. Better see WO2 Morris over there first, though. Good luck, Peter. I'd say we'd see you soon, but I doubt it. It's bloody murder trying to get here from Heraklion. The coast road's shot to hell and there's no transport to be had for love nor money. Try to get across to us. I'll stand you dinner. You'll find us at Brigade HQ.'

As they left, Lamb walked through the bustle of other officers and NCOs and reported to WO2 Morris, who directed him into what had been the salon.

Colonel Kippenberger was seated behind an ornate mahogany and ormolu desk with gigantic cabriole legs which, while it complemented perfectly the style of the Venetian villa, looked absurd as the office furniture of an army officer in service dress. When Lamb came in he rose to greet him. He was a tall man in his mid forties, with heavy eyebrows and a broad smile.

'Captain Lamb, heard a lot about you. All of it good, I'm afraid.' He laughed. 'What do you think of this place? Biggest house in Galatas, I'm told. Fascinating island, don't you think? Shame we don't really have time to explore it properly. I'm told that the palace at Knossos is extraordinary.'

He looked down at his paperwork. 'So, Lamb, you've quite a reputation, it seems. Didn't you hold a bridge against a Jerry division in France and then get some men away in Normandy?'

'Yes, sir.'

Kippenberger flicked through some papers.

'You also got some British civilians away from Athens, and now it seems you've saved a member of the Greek Royal Family. The point is, Lamb, I've just been given some Greeks. Two battalions of them, in fact, and a spare company. General Freyberg has taken it into his head to mix in a few locals and make them into some sort of militia. The Crete Home Guard, you might call it.'

Lamb smiled.

'But there's a problem. The King's not very keen on the idea. You see he's fine with the Greeks, but he doesn't want the Cretans to get their weapons back. Thinks they'll rise up against him again, like they did in 1935, under Venizelos. But they're all damned useful men and I think they'll fight damn well, given the chance. So that's where you come in. Particularly since you seem to be in with the Royal Family.'

Lamb winced and hoped that Kippenberger had not somehow got wind of his mission. 'I'm not exactly in with them, sir.'

'You saved the Prince's life, Lamb. If that's not "in", tell me what is? Fact is, some of the Greeks need training, and bloody quick, and keeping out of mischief, and someone with a title has suggested that you might be the man to do it.'

'So we are digging in then, sir? All of us, defending the island?'

'That's about the long and short of it. The German army is about to descend on this place and we need every man we can get, including your mob.' He looked up. 'You're quite a man. Reckon you can knock a few Greeks into shape?'

'I'll do my best, sir.'

'Good. That's settled then.'

'Do we know when they'll attack, sir? I mean, how much time have I got?'

Kippenberger hesitated. 'No, naturally we can't say for sure when they'll come. But it's my guess they'll attack soon enough. And when they do, well, as I said, we'll need every man we can get. D'you speak Greek?'

'No, sir. Just a few words. But one of my men does.'

'That's lucky. Only their officers have any English. I'm giving you the odd company, Lamb. You'll need to rearm them. They're using ancient Austrian rifles at the moment but we're expecting new stuff to arrive from Egypt at any time. Oh, and they're down to ten rounds a man, if that. See what you can do with them, Lamb. I'm not expecting any bloody miracles. Just an effective fighting force to hold a defensive position. That's all.'

He pushed the papers away to the sides of his table to reveal a map of the area, and beckoned Lamb. 'Look here. At the moment they're encamped near here. 6th Greek regiment are between Pink Hill south east across Cemetery Hill down to the Alikianou–Canea road. The 8th Greeks are stuck out on a limb. They're on this stretch of hills further down Prison Valley, just to the north of Alikianou. I've signalled General Weston that I intend to pull them back, but as yet I've had no response. So at present there's a socking great gap between the two Greek regiments, and that's where you fit in, Lamb, with your Greek odds and sods. Your men are going to fill that gap. Just here.'

He pointed to an area on the map, stretching from the lake just north of Alikianou, up the main Canea road to Pink Hill.

'When Jerry does attack I'm willing to bet that it'll be at Maleme first. He'll want that airfield to bring in the second wave. But I've no doubt that Galatas will be the second line. Oh, and look out for another bunch of Greeks up by the cemetery. Funny lot. Some regulars, some civilians. They're under another one of our chaps. Man named Hathaway. Part of the military mission. Not your "run of the mill" officer, if you get my drift.'

Lamb smiled. 'Yes, sir, of course. I've heard of him.'

He got the colonel's 'drift' all right, and he was cheered

114

by it. Kippenberger might have supposed that he was agreeing with him in a shared abhorrence of the unorthodox. But inside, Lamb found himself suddenly more optimistic. There was nothing that bored him more than 'run of the mill' officers.

7

Lamb's Greeks, when he found them, proved a sorry-looking bunch.

The first thing he noticed was the state of their clothing. He could hardly make a fuss given the fact that his own men were dressed in a mixture of serge battledress, denims and khaki drill, but he had thought that, with the Greeks being in what passed as part of their own country, they might have at least had more recourse to a change of uniform. He looked them over, drawn up in an area among the vineyards on the upper slopes of Pink Hill, and they stared back at him, some of them grinning, some simply perplexed.

Lamb turned to Bennett. 'Think you can lick this lot into shape, Sarnt-Major?'

'Well, sir, I reckon we can do something with them. If we can't, who can? Could do with some new togs, mind you.'

'Yes. I'll have to see someone about that. What really matters right now, though, is the man inside the togs. Just remember, we don't want this lot to go on parade at Horse Guards. We're here to make sure they can fight well and kill well, when the time comes.'

116

He turned back to the bemused Greeks. 'Right. First things first. What have we got for them to fight with? Sarnt Mays, where are their weapons?'

Piled on a cart on the dirt track which curved up the hill beside the position lay the ancient Austrian Steyers with which they had originally been equipped, together with all of the precious Lee Enfields that Hathaway had been able to scrounge from the depot. There were bayonets, too, and ammunition, but Lamb noticed that there was not much of that and he did not intend to waste any more rounds than he needed to in exercises.

Lamb did a quick head count and noted 120 other ranks, thirteen NCOs and two lieutenants. That would do. 'Sarnt-Major, tell them off into three platoons of forty men, each of them to have a platoon commander and four NCOs. I'll take one of the platoons, and you can give one each to Lieutenant Eadie and Mr Wentworth.'

As the Greeks and Cretans were sub-divided, he turned to Valentine. 'Sarnt Valentine, I need an interpreter, and it looks like it's you. Let's kick off with some basic field-craft, shall we?'

Lamb thought for a moment who among his own men might be the best to demonstrate, then called out, 'Corporal Hughes, Corporal Hale. Would you assist us?'

Under Lamb's instructions, the two corporals showed the Greeks first of all how to walk forward with your head up and your rifle at the ready. Then there was the leopard crawl, in which you slithered along the ground, with the rifle held in front, the monkey run, the roll into cover, and of course the ghost crawl for use in long grass. The Greeks seemed to enjoy it. There was certainly a deal of laughter, though whether they had actually learnt anything Lamb wasn't entirely sure.

He shouted at his new platoon, his command was echoed by Valentine, and it occurred to him that without an interpreter the other two officers might not be making as much progress, if any at all. It was lucky that he had taken on poor Harry Sugden's platoon as his own, made up as it was mostly of the newer intake. Eadie had Wilkinson and Perkins to demonstrate, and Wentworth, Mays and Butterworth. They'd manage. After all, hadn't he taught them everything they knew?

As the corporals dusted themselves down, Lamb looked at the grinning Greeks and adopted a sober tone which he hoped Valentine could interpret. 'Soon the Germans will attack,' he told them. 'Whatever you might think and say, they are good soldiers, the Germans. Some of you have fought them before. If you listen to me you will have a better chance not to be killed and a better chance to kill more Germans.'

As Valentine translated in his half ancient-Greek patois they stopped chattering and became serious. The officers nodded. Lamb went on.

'The Germans know how to fight. They know how to use cover and terrain and how to creep up to you without being seen. And by then it's too late. Because by then you'll be dead.'

Valentine translated. There was now utter silence among the Greeks.

He walked across to the nearest Greek and motioned to him to hand over his rifle, one of Hathaway's. Lamb looked at it. The Lee Enfield. Standard issue, 44 inches long, bolt action .303 calibre. The classic infantry rifle was almost nine pounds in weight, with a maximum range apparently of 3,000 yards but, as Lamb and most of his men knew well, an effective range of just over 500 yards. It held a magazine of ten rounds and it could be horribly effective. He remembered one of the first

118

things his musketry instructor had taught him in training. The Enfield had been used since before the First War, but in the right hands it really was a remarkable killing weapon. The instructor had told them with glee how in the First War the Germans had reported that they had come up against British machine-guns which had cut them down in great sweeping fields of fire, a never-ending rain of lead. In fact their enemy had only been a platoon of infantry equipped with Lee Enfields.

In theory the gun was capable of firing 15 rounds per minute. But any well-trained rifleman Lamb knew, could fire off 20 or even 30 rounds in the same time. Of course, he mused, that rate of fire would hardly be a problem here on the island, given the shortage of ammunition. But he thought it might just help to give them the ability for rapid fire should they ever have the chance. And, more importantly perhaps, it would raise their morale.

'Sarnt-Major, set up a target against that tree.'

Bennett found a piece of sacking on the cart and tied it to the olive tree so that it splayed out in a square shape.

Lamb continued, 'I want you to imagine that that sack is a man. Watch me. Don't look at the target. Look at what I'm doing. Watch how I shoot the gun.' Valentine translated, and Lamb flipped up the bolt and fired. Again and again and again he did it, in an easy, fluid motion. He jettisoned the first magazine and slammed in another, reloading 'in the shoulder', with the rifle still aimed at the target. The Greeks watched closely as he worked the bolt with just his thumb and forefinger and used his second finger to squeeze the trigger.

Again and again the bullets slammed into the target on the tree. And then he was done. The Greeks burst into spontaneous applause. Gun smoking, Lamb walked across to the tree, followed by the first few ranks of the Greeks.

'There you are. Not bad for starters. Now who wants a go?' Seven of the shots were grouped around where the heart might have been, with ten in the torso area of vital organs. Three had gone through the top of the sack – through the head.

Bennett looked at the target and smiled. 'Not bad, sir.'

The Greeks laughed and clapped him on the back, and those without weapons began to queue up to get their rifles from the cart.

He allowed them only a few rounds each, just enough to get their eye in. Besides, he was more concerned that they should learn bayonet and knife fighting.

Had they been the Cretan division left in Albania, of course, there would have been no problem, for the inhabitants of the island were brought up in a culture of self-defence and street brawls to protect their family honour. These Greeks, though, seemed to Lamb to be as mixed a bag as he had ever seen in his own or any British battalion.

Lamb walked towards a man in the front rank and, reaching into his own belt, pulled out the fighting knife that, unusually for an officer, he kept attached to it in a sheath. It was seven inches long, and Lamb had won it in Cairo from a furious British officer of marine commandos who had just come out from England. It was sleek, foil-gripped and double edged and looking a little like a stiletto, but like nothing he had ever seen or handled before. Apparently it had been designed in Shanghai and was only currently in experimental development. But the moment Lamb had seen it he had wanted it, and a game of backgammon after dinner in Alex had brought him his chance. He had had no opportunity to use it as yet, but knew that the time must come soon. He turned it in his hand now and its blade caught the sunlight. Lamb slipped into an attacking pose and began to move towards one of the Greeks. The man froze, panicked and then, when he saw that Lamb was in earnest, tried to mimic him. Lamb circled and, before the man could think, had his head locked in his left arm, with the knife dangerously close to his throat. The other Greeks said nothing; they just looked on in horror. Some were smiling.

Lamb let the man go. 'Sorry about that. But that's how they will fight you. There is no more deadly weapon than the knife. You may not have a knife like this, but you can easily find yourselves a knife. Now, do you want us to teach you how to fight like that? Because that's what you're going to have to learn if you want to survive.'

They surged forward.

'All right, stay back. I'll show you all, slowly. Watch me.'

For another ten minutes Lamb himself, and then Bennett and the two corporals, showed them fighting techniques with knives. Then they went on to bayonets.

He turned to Bennett. 'Right. Now we'll see what they can do. Get the bayonets out.' Bennett barked the command and Valentine tried to translate. The men fumbled and attached their bayonets. A few of them dropped them to the ground in trying to clip them on.

'I think we've got our work cut out here, sir.'

'We'll see. Don't worry. I'm not going to give them all that bloody "hate and blood training" stuff, Sarnt-Major.'

'Thank God for that, sir. That's a bloody farce, that is.'

'We're going to do it the old way. Valentine, ask them if anyone knows how to use a bayonet.'

Valentine spoke and one of the men who had dropped his bayonet stepped forward. Lamb took his rifle and fixed the weapon's eighteen-inch, standard sword-type bayonet on to the boss below the end of the barrel, before returning it to the man. The bayonet was almost half as long as the rifle itself. 'Right, let's see if he's as good as his word.'

He pointed to a spot on a wall where Mays and Bennett had rigged up four sandbags to resemble the head, torso and legs of a man.

'Go on. Attack that. There, my friend, is your German. Kill him.'

Valentine gave the order and the man assumed something like the ready position before launching himself at the sandbags. Reaching them, he raised his rifle and plunged the bayonet deep into what would have been the unfortunate man's guts before withdrawing it and stepping back. He turned to Lamb and gave a huge smile.

'Very good. That was good. Now, Sarnt-Major, would you care to show them how we do it in the British army.'

Bennett took his own rifle, its bayonet already fixed, and, snapping smartly into the ready position, charged at the sandbags, at the same time screaming at the top of his voice so loudly that some of the Greeks flinched. Reaching the dummy, Bennett thrust the bayonet in, close to the heart, and gave it a firm twist to the left before withdrawing it and going back to the 'ready'.

The Greeks applauded. Lamb spoke. 'You see, gentlemen, what you have to do is give it a twist.' He demonstrated with his hands. 'You need to mess the bugger up.' Valentine struggled to translate, but then the Greeks understood and began to nod. 'Right, who wants to try that?'

They began to put up their hands.

Over the next hour they learnt to parry, block and the other basic thrusts, and then went on to horizontal strokes with the rifle butt. There was the smash and the slash, aimed at the neck. Then, for good measure, Lamb taught them how to use the butt, combined with some very unsportsmanlike kicks to sensitive areas. That had them grinning. He caught Bennett yelling at one of them, 'Stab the bugger. Kill him, go on. He's a bloody Jerry and he wants to rape your bloody sister.'

Lamb turned to Charles Eadie. 'I wonder what the Greek is for that.'

By the end of the morning, Mays, Perkins, Hughes, Butterworth and Wilkinson between them had the Greeks running around and screaming like a platoon of the best that Aldershot could offer.

Bennett stood with him, watching in admiration. 'By hell, sir. That's something, that is. They're not half bad. Some of them even scare me. D'you reckon it'll work on the day? When Jerry does get here?'

'I'm blowed if I know, Sarnt-Major. But if we work hard enough on them we might have a chance. Besides, whatever happens it'll make them feel as if they can do it. And you and I know that's half the battle.'

In fact it took ten days to knock the Greeks and the handful of Cretans into some sort of soldierly shape, and by the end of that time Lamb knew that he could do no more. He and the others had improved their skills as soldiers. There were other things, though, with which he was unable to help. For a start, like his own men they were riddled with lice. He tried to get the camp CO to allow them to use the canvas showers, but was met with a steadfast refusal. Worse than that, many of the Greeks had contracted malaria. He lost thirty out of his company in the time it took to train them, evacuated to the field hospital. Those that remained, however, were good, and it was with renewed confidence that Lamb was able to send a report to Colonel Kippenberger with the assurance that his Greeks would stand and fight when the time came.

But still it did not come.

Dawn broke on Monday 19 May and Lamb's depleted company, strengthened by their Greek comrades, stirred themselves for another day in paradise. Like clockwork the enemy bombers came in for their daily run at 8 a.m. but the camp and the forward position on Pink Hill remained untouched. Lamb watched the planes move away above Heraklion, circling and diving like so many angry wasps.

After morning parade, as had become his custom, Lamb wandered up to the little *kafeneio* in Galatas and sat drinking his coffee, reading through Part One orders. There was nothing to report. He had come here every day for the past week, driven not only by the chance for a moment's peace and the time to think, but also by the knowledge that Anna would be here, working for her father who owned the place.

The men had a mutual respect for each other, not least on account of Lamb's ridding his establishment of the drunks. Fortunately, however, Anna's father seemed in the dark as to the identity of the Greek captain he had rescued. For one thing he had learnt well was that the Cretans had no great love of the Greek royal family.

Each time Lamb came, he would walk up to the bar before sitting down and he and Anna would exchange a few words. She had taught him several words of Greek. Now her face, her smile and her world had become part of his daily routine. He had said nothing to anyone about her. She and her café were his refuge, an utterly private place in which he could lose himself, drinking in the heady aroma of fresh coffee, baking pastry, honey and tobacco.

Always of course, while at the *kafeneio*, he would make

sure that he kept himself busy. Despite his command's ramshackle situation there always seemed to be paperwork to attend to. Captain Page made sure of that, treating Lamb almost as a camp adjutant. This morning he had signed a couple of forms for the camp MO, hoping that what seemed to be two cases of food poisoning were not dysentery. He looked again through the daily orders and took another sip of coffee, and then looked up to see Anna standing in front of him, smiling down. How had he not noticed her?

'Good morning, Peter. Busy?'

'No, just the usual paperwork.'

'Oh yes. Your officer's work.'

'Officer's work.'

'Will we see you at the party tonight? My little brother Andreas' birthday. Remember? I told you.'

'I was hoping to come, but I can't be sure. I might be needed.'

'Try to come. Please. I would like to see you. I mean, I think you would enjoy it. And who knows when we will have the chance again?'

Then, for the first time since they had met, she pressed her hand down on to his, and as she did so a man walked out of the shadows beside the bar and crossed the room towards them. He was tall, with huge hands and the moustache so typical of Cretan men of a certain age. Anna's father, Nikos Levandakis, smiled at Lamb.

'So, you are coming to the party tonight, Kapitan?'

Hearing him, Anna drew her hand away.

Lamb stood up and shook his head. 'I was just explaining to Anna, sir, that I might be rather busy. We don't know when or where the Germans might attack.'

Nikos shrugged. 'Pah. What of it? Whenever those bloody cuckolds attack we will be ready for them.' He patted a knife tucked into his belt. Lamb had seen him use it for cutting bread but was sure he would use it just as readily on a man. He continued, 'Be honest, you will have finished your work by then, Kapitan, and your men are good enough to take care of themselves. Bring some of them too, if you like. I like the man Valentine very much. He tells good jokes.'

Lamb laughed. 'Does he really? What are they about? The Germans, I suppose.'

Levandakis laughed and shook his head. 'No, Kapitan Lamb. He tells jokes about you.'

Still smiling to himself, Lamb emerged from the quiet, cool darkness of the *kafeneio* and found himself confronted with a street filled with soldiers. They were Greeks, all in uniform of various conditions, a few with tin hats, but on closer inspection Lamb was fairly certain that they were not his Greeks. They lolled against the walls in front of the church's twin towers, smoking and chatting as their officers did the same, and Lamb wondered why they had congregated here. He did not have a long wait before he found out. A tall man wearing a regulation-issue British army yellow jersey, which came almost to the turn-ups of his baggy khaki shorts, emerged from a side street to the right. On his feet he wore brown boots topped by long yellow socks and beneath the jersey a khaki drill shirt and tie. But the most striking thing about him was his hair, which was yellow, almost golden, Lamb thought, and slicked back against his head.

He walked up to one of the Greek officers, who dropped his cigarette and snapped to attention to greet him. Then, seeing Lamb standing by the *kafeneio*, he walked across. Lamb noticed that he wore a captain's three pips on his epaulettes, and strikingly, contrary to all advice when in the field, they had been Brasso-ed to an impressive sheen.

'Hello. Michael Hathaway, the Buffs. Do I know you?'

126

Lamb shook hands. 'No, we haven't met, but your name has been mentioned. Peter Lamb, North Kents.'

Hathaway nodded. 'Ah, a Jackal. You're Lamb. Of course. I've heard a lot about you from the colonel and Prince Peter. You saved his life.' He gestured to the Greeks. 'You've met my new command, I take it? Likely-looking bunch, aren't they?'

'Almost as prepossessing as mine. But I'm sure they'll fight well enough, once you've given them a bit of extra coaching.'

Hathaway laughed. 'Yes. But, you know, I've nothing but respect for them. Saw them fighting the Eyeties in Albania, and by God they can fight. They prove the lie for the British style of things. And I've got some help. We've had some chaps out here for quite some time, you know. Undercover. Sort of secret agents. All a bit too John Buchan for me. Eccentric.'

Lamb looked again at the man before him and said nothing.

Hathaway continued. 'But they've got the natives fairly fired up, and now the whole thing seems about to kick off I'm jolly glad of them. In fact, if you stick around you'll meet them. Cigarette?' He offered an open case, and Lamb accepted. Hathaway lit it for him.

'Thanks. Yes, I knew that we'd been working with the locals. They seem to be spoiling for a fight.'

'Everyone is, if you ask me. You can't blame them. Cooped up in this place for weeks with nothing but lice and the runs. I blame the oranges. Eaten far too many myself. Dreadful bad. You were in Greece?'

'Fought our way down from Thermopylae and got away by the skin of our teeth as the Jerries were at the gates of Athens. You?'

Hathaway nodded. 'I was with the Military Mission out here, working with the Prince. We had a high time of it. Managed to get across the bridge at Corinth before it went. We got away in a boat full of civilians on the 24th. The captain was blind drunk so I took over, but we ended up back on the mainland. Next day we pitched up on Kithera. We didn't get here till the 30th. I'm staying in the Prince's cottage now. Pleasant place. We've got his cook, too. Marcos. Damn good. Where are you?'

Here was another link to the royal party, thought Lamb, hardly believing his luck. 'In the transit camp at Perivolia, I'm afraid.'

'Oh, bad luck. Place is rife with lice, I hear. Still, the word is that the attack will come soon, so I shouldn't get too comfortable.' He laughed and looked at his soldiers as they stood around the square, then spoke again. 'You know, I can't help feeling we've let them down. The Greeks, that is. Perhaps we can make up for it here.'

There was a noise on the other side of the square across from the *kafeneio* and a group of men entered. Instantly they were mobbed by the soldiers. Cheers rang through the village.

'Ah,' said Hathaway. 'Our guests have arrived.'

He beckoned Lamb to come with him and together they walked across the square towards the church. The soldiers, seeing Hathaway, moved aside to reveal a party of armed men, in local civilian dress, the largest of whom was standing at the front, with his arms folded.

Hathaway led the way. 'Captain Lamb, allow me to introduce Kapitan Bandouvas.'

The newcomer was dressed unlike anyone Peter had ever seen. He sported a pair of short riding boots, the sort of thing a Napoleonic hussar might wear, and above them baggy trousers in a richly coloured purple cloth. His shirt was full and white and topped with a black embroidered waistcoat, and on his head he wore a round black cap, hung with tassels. It looked to Lamb like a cross between the sort of thing his aunt might have hung around a teapot and something that might be sported by a tart in one of the cheaper Cairo brothels. His heavy-set face was defined by a huge handlebar moustache. Taken as a whole he looked like a cross between one of the chorus in a production of *The White Horse Inn* and an extra from *Desert Song*. What really marked him out, though, was the assortment and number of weapons that he carried. His rifle, a Lee Enfield that had been heavily decorated, principally with silver, was slung over his right shoulder. Over his left he carried a British Thompson gun, and around his waist in a belt were at least sixty rounds of ammunition for both. Lamb was certain he would also have had a knife tucked into his boot and wondered where he had put the grenades he undoubtedly carried.

Manoli Bandouvas looked Lamb up and down and nodded. 'You are Kapitan Lamb? Lamb? We say *"Arni"*.' He laughed, and it was echoed by his men. 'I am a farmer, Kapitan Lamb. I keep sheep. Many hundreds of sheep. And lambs. *Arni*. It does not sound much like the name of a warrior. Baa, baa.' More laughter.

Lamb rose to the slight, but steeled himself, determined not to let it go any further. He was well aware that this was a culture driven by honour feuds and that the slightest slur would mean time wasted in a useless vendetta. Bandouvas had had his say and had impressed his men by besting a British officer. That was enough for Lamb.

He spoke calmly and with a smile. 'You will know, Kapitan Bandouvas, being a great and experienced leader of men, that often things are not as they might seem, or as they might sound.'

Bandouvas said nothing for a while. Then he smiled and nodded. 'Yes, that is right. And if they say you are a fighter, then who am I to doubt them. Good. I hear that you saved the Prince. We need men like you to kill the German cuckolds when they come.'

Good God, thought Lamb. It was as if he was being recruited by Bandouvas. This man in fancy dress was no more than a glorified bandit. But he knew that he had to play along. 'As long as we can be of some help in your struggle, Kapitan.'

Hathaway turned to Lamb and raised his eyebrows out of sight of Bandouvas. 'Kapitan Bandouvas has kindly offered to help me train my men here in the ways of mountain fighting. I'm sure that if you were to ask him he might do the same for your Greeks.'

Lamb smiled at him. 'Actually I've just spent ten days with my NCOs training them in warfare as waged by the British army. But I grant you that some local knowledge would be useful. I might do that.'

At that moment a car drove up behind Bandouvas' men, the driver sounding the horn. It stopped abruptly and two men emerged into the crowd, both of them heavily armed. One, the passenger, a fair-haired man in his mid-thirties, walked towards Hathaway and spoke in a loud voice that sounded as if it would have been more suited to shouting encouragement across the playing fields of an English public school.

'Good morning, Michael. Kapitan Bandouvas, good morning. I've come to see what the hell's going on over on this side of the island. Are you aware that there is absolutely no wireless communication between west and east? It's absurd. We are fighting a war in the manner of nineteenth-century warfare. No, I'm mistaken. Ancient warfare. We are Priam's men. Well, I'll tell you one thing, all of you. You're a damn sight better off here than where I am at Heraklion. Brigadier Chappel's HQ is a cave. Nothing more. I've just come from there, via your Colonel Kippenberger and his lavish mansion. I ask you, a cave,

130

between the town and the aerodrome. It is neither secure nor suitable.'

The man, who was a fraction under six foot tall and of slim, athletic build, was dressed in an officer's service uniform, complete with Sam Browne, but he had added a few stylistic twists of his own. His peaked service cap was worn at a rakish angle and he wore a rifle slung like a Cretan mountaineer's, around his shoulders, and a cartridge belt round his middle. Most noticeably, though, he carried at his side, thrust into an improvised holster on the Sam Browne, a leather-covered scabbard containing what Lamb recognised to be unmistakably a swordstick. Clearly he was a British officer, but, thought Lamb, a temporary officer rather than a regular. And there was something more to his appearance – a strange squint.

'Came to see your GOC, Brigadier Weston. Couldn't be found. Saw Colonel Kippenberger instead. Nice chap. Just offering my services, Michael. If needed.'

He turned to Bandouvas. '*Yasou*, Manoli. What brings you here?' He clapped the big Greek on the back and they began to talk rapidly in Greek, and soon both of them were laughing. Lamb caught the word '*arni*' again and thought he could see them both looking in his direction.

Hathaway saw the danger. 'Sorry, John. Let me introduce you. Captain Peter Lamb, John Pendlebury. Peter, John here is the authority on everything on Crete, ancient and modern.'

Pendlebury shook his head and smiled. 'Nonsense. I'm an archaeologist.'

Hathaway continued. 'John was Vice Consul until recently, and now he's Liaison. Which means he helps the Greeks. Like me. But he's in a different sector.'

Pendlebury extended his hand. Lamb took it, and as their eyes met Lamb realised what it was that gave

Pendlebury that curious squint. His left eye was made out of glass, and long habit had encouraged his right eyebrow to become permanently raised, as if he were perpetually questioning something. It was with this expression on his face that he now looked Lamb square in the eye, with disarming candour.

'John Pendlebury. A pleasure.'

'Peter Lamb, North Kents.'

'Ah, the famous Jackals. What on earth are you doing here? This garrison's all Kiwis and Aussies. There are few Jocks too, up at Heraklion, and the Welsh of course, but not your lot. Thought you'd got away to Alex.'

'Most of us did, but some of us missed the boat. Jerries took the canal before we could catch up. We came via Athens.'

'Did you, by Jove? Must have been a little hairy. Haven't been to the old place for a while.' He looked wistful. 'I'm actually in Liaison with Brigadier Chappel, at Heraklion. You're the chap who saved Prince Peter, aren't you? KOed a drunk squaddie. They can be an ugly lot, our soldiers, can't they, when their blood's up.'

'Or their drink.'

Pendlebury laughed. 'And it's all this cheap wine. *Krassi*. The men can't take it. Getting "krassied up", they call it. Drink it as if it were beer. You should try it, though. They pass down the method to family and friends. You never know how strong it actually is.'

'What about raki? I thought that was the local drink.'

'It is. The local name is *tsikoudia* and it's not at all like the stuff you find in Greece or Turkey. It's brewed in very old breweries and back yards from the leftovers from wine production. Basically it's the seeds and skins from grapes. The sweeter the raki, the stronger it is. The Greeks down it in one. But listen, here's a real tip. If you're going to drink a lot of it or drink it over a long night, you're best to drink a little water with it. Or even the same amount. Then you can keep going for as long as you like. But for heaven's sake don't switch to drinking other alcohol like beers or wines in the same evening. I tell you, Lamb, if you do that you'll wake up with the worst hangover of your life. An absolute corker.'

He turned to Hathaway.

'You know that Freyberg has forbidden me to move the arms and explosives from Suda island without his specific, written permission?'

Before Hathaway could reply he turned back to Lamb. 'Now will you kindly tell me how the hell I'm expected to arm the civilian resistance, home guard, call them what you will? They were his idea in the first place, and now all my efforts are being blocked. And why? I'll tell you why. Because the government is frightened that if we arm the Cretans they'll keep the guns and then revolt again like they did in '35.'

He paused for breath. 'If London would only send me 10,000 rifles we could hold this bloody island. A few guns and that division of top-notch Cretan soldiers that they had the brilliance of forethought to abandon in Albania.'

Lamb thought he should say something. 'Yes, I heard that their general was assassinated here a few weeks ago, in the street, after leaving them there.'

Pendlebury nodded. 'He knew it would happen. It was the only honourable thing to do. Well, what would you do?'

He stared at Lamb and his face changed from the jovial man who had walked into their midst to that of someone quite different. A fighter.

'The Germans are coming, Lamb, and we're going to be ready for them. And if the High Command decide that we have to evacuate, do you know what we're going to

133

do on this island? We're going to hold out. Whatever happens.'

He was almost oratorical now, playing to his audience.

'I know this land. We will take to the high ground. To the Nidha plateau, high on the slopes of Mount Ida. Thousands of sheep, inaccessible by road and riddled with caves. Do you know the locals believe that Zeus was born in one of them? Place can only be reached through the village of Krousonas. And that place, my friend, is held by Kapitan Satanas.'

There was a murmur among the troops as they heard the nickname of Antonis Grigorakis. 'You have to go through Krousonas and through Anoyia too. Anoyia is the stronghold of my two friends Stephanoyianni Dramoudanis and Mihali Xylouris. And with their men, armed with new weapons from me, I tell you, Lamb, we will hold out for as long as it takes. Until this scourge is wiped from the face of the earth.' The Greeks applauded, although Lamb was not sure that they had understood.

His speech finished, Pendlebury turned back to Bandouvas and began to talk very quickly.

Hathaway shook Lamb's hand. 'It's been good to meet you, Lamb. Always good to know who you'll be fighting alongside when the balloon goes up. I say, would you join us for dinner this evening? It won't be much. At the Prince's villa. He's dying to meet you again, to say thank you properly. You helped him out of a hole. He's hugely grateful, you know.'

'It was nothing, really. Anyone would have done the same.'

'Nevertheless, come and dine with us this evening.' Lamb remembered Anna's party for her brother.

'Of course. But I'm afraid I might have to leave early.'

Hathaway laughed. 'Oh, we shan't keep you late. We eat early. Shall we say 7 p.m.? It's just south of Perivolia.

134

I'll send a man to show you the way. Do please come. You won't regret it. Oh, and I should be on your best behaviour; there's every chance that the King might drop in. He's moved from that house near your camp that he was in, but I think he prefers Marcos' cooking. Dare say you'll know a few others there too. The Hartleys and their hangers-on. Should be a jolly party.'

8

It was with a sense of some unreality and no little annoyance that Lamb wandered down to the company lines on Pink Hill. A jolly party? It hardly seemed likely, with Miranda Hartley making eyes at him all night and Comberwell cracking lewd jokes. It struck him, though, that it was a very British thing to do, to gather for a dinner party when the enemy were damn nearly at the gates. His thoughts turned to Hathaway, Bandouvas and Pendlebury. There were some very curious people on this island. Perhaps Valentine was right after all: it was a little like *The Tempest*, filled with strange noises. At least, he thought, there was the prospect of making contact with the King and it appeared that, with all the talk of a forthcoming attack, that was hardly soon enough.

Lamb reached the camp and walked up to his HQ tent to find Valentine sitting on an ammunition box close by, cleaning his Thompson gun. He sat down at his desk, a table liberated from the village, which had been laid with maps and a pair of binoculars.

'Busy morning, sir?'

'Yes. I met some very interesting people, Valentine. Have you heard of Captain Pendlebury?'

'Oh yes, sir. The one-man army, they call him. Old man Levandakis has told me all about him and his glass eye. Takes it out all the time. Sort of a bit like a Cyclops. One-eyed and making weapons. You remember, sir. They made thunderbolts for Zeus' and Apollo's bows and arrows. You could say Captain Pendlebury's doing the same for the Cretans, couldn't you, sir? I mean, trying to arm them. He's apparently about as stubborn as the Cyclops were meant to be, too.'

He clicked back the bolt of the gun and slid it back into position with perfect precision.

'You know too much, Valentine – far too much for a soldier.'

'I thought soldiers were meant to know everything, sir.'

'Officers, Valentine. Only officers know everything. You're still an NCO. At the moment.'

Valentine swiftly diverted the subject away from the bugbear of his commission. 'Did you hear about those poor Kiwis from 19 Battalion, sir? Went for a swim at Kalamaki and got strafed by some 109s. All dead.' He carried on cleaning the gun.

It was happening almost every day now. The holiday atmosphere of the island had induced a false sense of security. General orders were supposed to have put an end to the practice of taking yourself off for a swim, as the Luftwaffe's presence in the skies had escalated, but still men stole away to take a dip in the Med, as they had become accustomed to doing for the last month. It was an ignominious way to go, he thought, and a bloody waste of precious resources.

Lamb ignored the comment. It invited no reply. 'Have you seen the Sarnt-Major?'

'He's down in the forward positions, sir.'

'Will you kindly tell him that Mr Wentworth will be officer of the watch tonight, and his platoon on first stag. I've got myself embroiled in an official dinner at Platanas.'

'Sounds intriguing, sir.'

'Oh, I shouldn't think so. All brass hats and brouhaha. The Hartleys will be there.'

'Fascinating man, Mr Hartley, don't you think, sir?'

'Really?'

'Very good on the sites here. He got a first in Classics at Oxford.'

'I'm sure the two of you get along very well, Valentine.'

'As a matter of fact we do, sir.'

Lamb shook his head, 'I'll leave the address of where I'm going. Just in case the Jerries decide to pay us a visit.'

There were no raids that night, and no unwanted visitors. At 7 o'clock precisely Lamb found himself at the bougainvillaea-shaded entrance to the villa where the Prince was staying.

As Hathaway had promised, the dinner party was prompt and mercifully short, although the food itself, of fresh fish, concussed that morning by the German raiders, proved as delicious as anticipated. Of course there was no mess kit or dinner jackets, but the ladies had made an effort and for an instant the war seemed very far away.

Pendlebury's very presence, with his extraordinary blend of erudition and ribald humour, had spread a feeling of optimism and raised drooping morale. It also helped that someone, he never did find out who, had discovered a wind-up gramophone and a stack of dance band records ranging from Al Bowlly and Ambrose to Ray Noble, so they had dined to the strains of 'Goodnight Sweetheart', 'Dancing in the Dark' and 'The Very Thought of You'. And as the music played Miranda Hartley had been as irritatingly flirtatious as ever, flashing him knowing looks that played on the lyrics. Her conversation was different now, though – similar observations but tainted with a sense of *ennui*.

'Do you suppose the Germans will attack? Julia says your man Valentine told him they would.'

'I have no idea, I'm afraid, and I suppose Sergeant Valentine has even less.'

'Oh no. Julian says he's most knowledgeable. He's been very grateful, actually, to find such a kindred spirit here on the island. Of course, Captain Pendlebury is encyclopaedic, but he's so very busy. Valentine seems to have all the time in the world to talk about the Minoans. Just the sort of stuff Julian loves. I must say, how I long for someone to offer the same sort of companionship. Someone I can really talk to.'

She went on.

'I do so hope that they get us all away to Cairo soon. Or Alexandria. Anywhere but here. Do you ever feel that we're trapped in paradise? I wake every day to the same blue sky and wonder what on earth I'm going to do. I can't think what Il Duce thought he was doing when he invaded Greece if it was going to end up stranding us here.'

And so she continued. Lamb was thankful when after dinner she and the two ladies who accompanied the Prince – the wife of the prime minister and a former lady in waiting – had reluctantly retired, leaving him with the men. The port, a Croft 1912, was surprisingly good and it had been annoying to have to hold back, but he had done so, partly because he needed to be alert and partly because he did not want to miss Anna's party.

The Prince had spoken volubly about the state of the island's defences and the general state of the garrison. There had apparently been a few courts martial since the curfew had been introduced two weeks ago – less, though, than in the first week.

'I would say it's been a bit of a success,' said the Prince. 'They finally seem to be under control. Better, certainly, than when Captain Lamb had to rescue me.'

Hathaway shook his head. 'We may be better able to control them, Your Highness, but I don't know how long Creforce as a whole can remain in good spirits. It's all this damn waiting.'

Pendlebury smiled. 'It may not be an issue very much longer.'

'What, you mean you have an idea of when they'll come?'

'Well, think about it, dear chap. How long have we been here now?'

'Well, clearly, John, you've been here since time immemorial.'

They all laughed. 'Thank you for that. Sometimes it does feel as if I have. No, I meant how long has the garrison been here?'

'Since last September.'

'So effectively we've been expecting an attack for the past eight months. Hitler's had his hands on Greece since the end of last month, and we know he's not a man for hanging about. Take my word for it. It will be any day now.'

'Do you know something that we don't, John?'

'Perhaps. Let's just say I have connections. That's the principal advantage of being attached to the GOC at Heraklion. In fact I should really be there now. But the coast road is a bloody shambles, so why not enjoy this splendid wine while we can?'

Eschewing the port, he poured Lamb a glass of one of the better wines they had liberated from the cellar of the new prime minister, whose house, Bella Campagna, this happened to be.

As the wine flowed the Prince became more talkative.

He turned to Lamb. 'My cousin the King is on the island, you know. In fact I'm surprised he isn't here tonight. I've told him about you, Captain Lamb. He's very grateful. It's very difficult for him here. The Cretans do not like us very much, so he has appointed a Cretan as prime minister, a banker. Mr Tsouderos. This house belongs to him. He's with my cousin now. Of course we sent Maniadakis off to Egypt with all his damned secret police. He would have been killed here if he had stayed.'

Lamb nodded. 'Like General Papastergiou. Shot dead in the street.'

'Well, it was bound to happen. For a Cretan general to abandon his division in Albania and save his own skin, then to return to his homeland – he must have known what would happen.'

'Perhaps he wanted it.'

'Perhaps. It was an honourable way out.'

Pendlebury chimed in. 'It was an excellent sign, actually, Your Highness. Don't you think? I think something would have been very wrong indeed with the morale of the Cretan people if Papastergiou had not been promptly shot.'

They stared at him, but Lamb for one realised he was absolutely right.

The Prince nodded. 'Yes. But it was a pity. It's bad for any man to be shot by his own people.'

Comberwell poured himself another glass of port. 'Where did you say your cousin was, Your Highness? Is he quite safe?'

'Oh, yes, Mr Comberwell. He's in a little villa quite near here. Closer to Perivolia. He was at a bank in Suda for the first day or so, and then at the Villa Ariadne for a few days. You know, Pendlebury, Arthur Evans' house.'

Pendlebury nodded.

'Then he was with the general for a while at Heraklion,

but the continual bombing unsettled his nerves. So then they came here, he and the government. He has a guard too, a platoon of Kiwis with a highly entertaining young chap in charge of them. Lieutenant Ryan. You know, Michael, we must ask him to come for dinner some evening, and a swim.'

'I'll see to it, Your Highness.'

Lamb had listened with interest. 'Just one platoon? Do you really think that's enough?'

Hathaway nodded. 'Yes. I don't think we'll need to reinforce. Mr Tsouderos is going to get together an escort of armed locals. Everything's been arranged with Colonel Blount, the military attaché to the Embassy. He's got some secret up his sleeve, apparently. Probably one of these new "elite force" chaps. If the Jerries attack we'll have the King and his chums off to Egypt faster than you can blink. That rather brings me to an important point. Comberwell, Mr Hartley. It has been suggested that you and the other British civilians might accompany the King, in the event of an attack.'

Julian Hartley said nothing as Hathaway began to explain, but nodded and turned to Lamb. 'It's frightfully good material, you know, all this. Couldn't have wanted anything better. To tell you the truth I was having a bit of a block. Sometimes gets you that way. I thought this trip might provide the kick to get me started again. Can't really believe my luck.'

'What sort of books do you write? I mean, I'm terribly sorry, I've never read any of your novels.'

Hartley laughed. 'Well, no, I don't expect you have. Let me see, how can I define the indefinable? They're sort of social satires, really. You know the kind of thing: a group of people, our sort of people, in a house or in a situation which accentuates their relationships. Archetypes. Lots of tension. It's nothing new, of course. Aristophanes was doing the same thing here 2,000 years ago. I'm sort of the same without the wasps and frogs.'

Lamb smiled and nodded. 'Yes, I see.'

Hartley went on, 'Read any Huxley?'

'No, can't say I have.'

'Thought not. Some of the critics have drawn comparisons. Of course others say I have more in common with Waugh, but I think they're missing the point. I'm not that lightweight.' He inhaled from his cigarette and blew a large smoke ring. 'I feel like an observer on the periphery of a society which has accepted me as one of its own, but to which I've never really belonged. Do you understand?'

Lamb nodded. Of course he understood. Perfectly. It was exactly the way he had felt at university and among his ex-wife's friends. Always on the edge, looking in. He felt a strange affinity for Hartley suddenly, for all his pretensions and bohemian attitudes. And Lamb knew that was why he felt so at home in the army. He said, 'Yes. I know how you feel. I think I was like that. Once.'

Hartley nodded. 'Thought so. I pride myself on being able to read people. All part of the novelist's art, you see. I knew you and I had something in common. Outsiders. That's what we are. Looking in on the world.'

Lamb smiled. 'I'm not sure I still feel that way.'

'Really? I wouldn't be so sure. Sometimes these things are bred in the bone. We're all a cast of characters. Look at us, for instance. Here, like this. It's perfect. Just perfect for a plot.' He laughed. 'You never know, Captain, you might find yourself one of my characters.'

'I shall have to be very careful what I say then.'

'Oh no, please don't do that. What you say is exactly what I need.'

Lamb nodded, but he had one ear on Hathaway who was still talking about their impending evacuation.

Comberwell, flushed with the port, shook his head. 'I'm damned if I'm running away. Can't we make ourselves useful here? I'm not a bad shot, you know. Well, I've accounted for a good few pheasants in my time. Guest of the Devonshires, mostly.' He turned to Lamb. 'Ever shot there? Chatsworth?'

'No. I'm afraid I'm not that well connected.'

It silenced Comberwell, temporarily, as if he knew he had spoken out of turn. Hathaway spoke again. 'I'm sorry, that's just not going to be possible. Besides, this island is a real fortress now. The Jerries still believe we're only about 10,000 strong. At least that's what the intercepts are saying. Do you know how many men we really have, combat ready? 28,000. They'll get a bit of a shock when they do come. And we've tanks, albeit just a few of the light ones, but at least we have them. And those AA batteries at Heraklion and Canea – they haven't spotted all of them. They're in for a surprise. We'll give them a bloody nose.' Knowing perhaps he had said too much, he reverted to form. 'As civilians, you do realise you'd be shot if you were captured with weapons. We have it on good authority that the Germans have been ordered to give no quarter to *francs-tireurs*. You must get away. It won't be easy, but those are our orders from Whitehall.'

Prince Peter spoke again. 'It's a real problem for His Majesty. If he stays until we are attacked and then goes, he will be accused of cowardice, but if he goes before the Germans come he will perhaps seem an even greater coward. The King is of the opinion that to leave before would seem less cowardly, but your General Wavell in Cairo has told him to stay, for the sake of morale.'

Pendlebury was the first to leave, suddenly impatient to get back to Heraklion, and when he rose from the table Comberwell somewhat predictably said, 'Do show us your swordstick!' Pendlebury drew it from its leather scabbard with comic drama and flashed it round with a twist of the wrist before slipping it deftly back.

They applauded and Lamb had a fleeting vision of Pendlebury using the thin blade in battle against the Germans, whirling it round his head like some officer from the time of Marlborough leading a headlong charge of his Greeks. Pendlebury bade them all farewell, bowing to the Prince, and as the door closed behind him Lamb heard him start to whistle a tune. Unmistakably it was 'Lillibulero'.

Hathaway explained. 'He sings it everywhere, or whistles it. No idea why. You can always hear him coming. How are your Greeks?'

'Fine. They've really come on. They're good fighters, you know. Gave my men a real run for their money.'

'What did I tell you?' He paused and took a drink of wine. 'What d'you make of John Pendlebury?'

'He's quite a comic turn, isn't he?'

'Yes. But he's actually rather good news. And I'm damned glad he's on our side. You saw his left eye?'

Lamb nodded.

'Lost it in an accident at the age of two. Stuck a pen into it, I heard. He's worn a glass one ever since. When he leaves his office to go on a mission he leaves the glass eye on his table to show that he'll be back soon.'

'What was all that about being here all his life?'

'He's an archaeologist. Been in Greece since God knows when. Did some of the excavations at Knossos. Then our government got hold of him and made him Vice Consul, although really he was doing undercover stuff with the Cretans.'

'They obviously respect him. Especially Bandouvas.'

'You could do worse than getting some help from Manoli Bandouvas, you know. And you'd earn his respect.'

'Is that important?'

'It'll be vital when the Jerries get here.'

'I thought we'd hit it off quite well this morning.'

Hathaway laughed. 'Don't be too sure. These chaps are grudging in their praise. And they're tougher than they look. I'm quite serious, Peter. Manoli Bandouvas is one of the most powerful chiefs on Crete, perhaps second only to the one they called Satanas. According to Pendlebury Bandouvas is as unreliable as he is brave. He's also arrogant, self-important and hugely influential. Oh, and Pendlebury's convinced he's a Communist. Probably curses you for saving the Prince.'

'And I thought we were all on the same side.'

Hathaway shook his head. 'First thing to learn on Crete: they're not Greeks, they're Cretans, and when they've defeated the Germans they'll still be fighting, whoever wins.'

The words came back to Lamb as he walked from Tsouderos' villa to the Levandakis' *kafeneio* through the warm, fragrant night. Cicadas chirruped in the trees and from the encampments dotted around the olive groves came voices and the occasional burst of song. He climbed the street as it snaked up the hill and had almost reached the centre of Galatas when another thought struck him, another troubling snatch of their conversation. It was when Pendlebury had made his comment about the imminent attack. It was almost, thought Lamb, as if he knew. As if he had a date in his mind. It seemed to him now that his sudden departure might have been because he had realised he might have said too much and that he must get back to Heraklion as soon as he could.

Lamb recalled the look on his face: the expression of supreme smugness. But if Pendlebury did know the exact timing of when the attack would come then why had

General Freyberg not taken others into his confidence? Surely if Creforce, or at least its officers, knew when the Germans would attack they would be defeated with ease? And then it struck him.

The only answer was surely that the British had some means of gathering intelligence that would reveal Hitler's plans. And of course, if that were known to be the case, if our forces were seen by the enemy to have been too well prepared, the game would be up. The Jerries would change their signals, their codes and all the rest, and the Allies would lose whatever advantage they enjoyed.

Once again, as had been the case in France, he was aware of wheels spinning within wheels, of the dilemmas that faced not just field officers but the High Command itself. For a horrible moment it occurred to him that Whitehall must consider preserving the integrity of its intelligence advantage more important than the lives of several thousand men. This thought sent a shiver through him. He realised he was one of those men.

By 10.30 Lamb was sitting at a table in the little *kafeneio*, drinking a glass of the good raki and trying to make it last. He had taken John Pendlebury's advice and poured himself a generous glass of bottled water to match it. Valentine was not with him, of course, but Charles Eadie had asked if he might come along and Lamb had not seen why he shouldn't, for an hour or so, and was keeping an eye on how much he drank, like some watchful father over a teenage son.

The men were happy enough in their trenches in the groves on Pink Hill just to the south of the village. Lamb knew he could be with them in a matter of a few minutes. Besides, he knew too that Anna would be there, and there was something about her that bewitched him. She was utterly feminine but at the same time exuded a fieriness of spirit that was close to his own. He half thought she was his female counterpart, and he was certain that when the invasion came she would be out in the fields with a rifle killing Germans with the best of them. He was watching her dance now as he sipped at the raki, admiring the way she moved her body, sinuous, even to the masculine rhythm of the bouzouki. The raki and the music had dispelled Lamb's morbid thoughts. But a better antidote than either of those things had been the sight of Anna's face.

Even though the door was open and the party had spilled out into the village square, the music filled the room, catching him up in its infectious beat. Suddenly she caught his eye and smiled, and he knew that what he had thought might be the spark of something between them was certainly something more.

He was glad he had come. It was good to see the local people enjoying themselves, despite the ever-present threat of invasion and the daily air-raids. For all his lack of Greek he felt he had somehow been assimilated into their company. There were not many British officers present. A couple of New Zealand NCOs he vaguely recognised had obviously been given leave to attend but kept themselves to themselves and away from the officers. Captain Page was there, but for the most part he seemed to prefer to sit alone. A few of Lamb's Greek officers had turned up and were dancing in the square. But Anna was the real reason he was there, and as he sipped at his raki and watched her as she whirled across the floor, dancing with her younger brother, he felt somehow complete.

She stopped in front of him. 'Peter. This is my brother. My little brother, Andreas.'

The boy, who was about fifteen and slightly shorter than Lamb, smiled and said hello before turning to find

148

another dance partner. Anna looked at Lamb. 'Thank you for coming. I did not know if you would.'

'I left a very important dinner to come here. With the King's cousin.'

She shrugged. 'Should I be impressed?'

'No. I was joking. But I would have come anyway. To see you.'

She laughed and tossed her hair, then grabbed at his hand and dragged him to his feet. 'And now I will make you sorry you came. I will teach you how to dance.'

He protested, but it was too late. Anna pulled him into the middle of the floor, pushing the other dancers aside. They carried on, but looked at the couple as they danced, asking each other why Anna Levandakis was dancing with the handsome British captain.

Lamb had never been a great dancer. His wife had told him on their first walk-out to the Café de Paris that he had two left feet. But if he had thought a waltz or a foxtrot difficult, this was something altogether different.

And so the bouzoukis played and Anna swayed and turned in front of him, pushing him around the floor and inviting him to mimic her movements. Lamb tried his best but could not help but feel he was out of time. He was sweating now, hot and confused as he felt the raki and her perfume filling his senses. At last the music stopped and, panting, she pulled him close to her and kissed him on the cheek. Then she walked to his table and in one swift movement drained the half glass of raki he had left in his place. She placed the empty glass down before him and offered him the glass of water, which he drank. She spoke softly.

'You dance well. For an Englishman.'

'Nonsense. I can't dance. Not like you.'

'Perhaps not. But I know you can fight, like us. I saw you in the *kafeneio*. I can fight for myself. This place is used to war. Everyone wants this place: Turks, Italians, Greeks. Now the Germans. We have only been part of Greece for thirty years. I am a Cretan. I'm not a Greek.'

'I'm sorry. Of course.'

She hadn't finished. 'And we don't like the King. Or his cousin. The one you saved.'

'I didn't know you knew that.'

'Of course I knew. But you saved me too, and my father.'

'I would have done the same for anyone.'

'I know. That's why I like you. So, please, none of this nonsense about the King. My father and his friends fought here after the last war. In 1935 they fought for Venizelos, against the King. Then in the summer of 1938 we fought again, against Metaxas. They beat us and took our guns away. But my father hid his gun. He will get it when the Germans come. And then we shall see what happens.'

'Why do you hate the Greeks so much?'

'This is my family. You met my little brother, but my big brother is not here. Metaxas took our men for his army. Your army came and he took my brother to fight the Germans.'

She was becoming angry now.

'Tell me why we should welcome you. Why? You British. If you hadn't come here to defend us, then our boys wouldn't have been taken to Albania. My brother would still be here. I should hate you, Peter Lamb, and all your comrades.' She paused and looked down. 'But how can I hate you?'

She looked up at him and he could see tears forming in her eyes. She shook her head and stared into his eyes, and for a moment for both of them the war ceased to exist. Then, without another word, she took his hand and silently, together, they walked away from the music and the dancing.

*   *   *

At that moment, in a villa just a few miles away, a pair of careful hands uncovered the wireless set kept hidden in the back of a wardrobe and, sitting down at the dressing table, began to tap out a message. And soon the Germans were in no doubt as to the real strength of the enemy they would face when they invaded. They had final confirmation, too, that the King of Greece was at Perivolia. They knew about the tanks and about the hidden anti-aircraft guns at Canea and Heraklion and about the massive underestimation they had made about the readiness of Crete's defenders. The hands tapped away in the code that the Germans still believed the Allies could not break, and the message concluded with the suggestion that they might perhaps choose to postpone the attack. But even as the hands typed out their advice their owner knew that it was now too late to stop it and that when it came the fight would be bigger and bloodier than they had been told to expect or could begin to imagine. Now all they could do was hope and pray.

9

Lamb stirred and pulled the blanket closer around him in the chill morning air. He opened one eye and then remembered. The girl lay close beside him on the tiny wooden sleeping platform in the back room of the house, and he drank in her scent along with the morning. He wondered what had awoken him, and then, before his eyes were open, he knew. The earth shook and glasses fell from the shelves, where they had been left the night before, to smash on the earth floor. Lamb sat upright. 'Christ, we're being bombed.' He shook the girl to life and then with a few movements pulled on pants, shirt, trousers and battledress top.

'Anna, come on, quick, they're bombing us.'

He had grown used to the daily early-morning raids, the 'daily hate' as the men called it. But that was no reason to think you were immortal. Bombs were not picky about whom they sent to kingdom come. Anna stirred languorously, and stretched. For a moment he stared at her. 'Come on, Anna.' He repeated it, shook her again. 'We're being bombed. Get dressed.' She opened her eyes and was suddenly awake and aware. She swung her naked body on to the edge of the bed and grabbed at her clothes while Lamb pulled on his boots and strapped on his webbing and watch.

'I've got to find the men. I'll see you after this is over.' He bent to kiss her, and as their lips met he caught her smell again, musky, infused with alcohol and honey and warm with sleep.

'Yes, Peter. Later. Be careful.'

Lamb smiled at her, pushed open the door and walked into the morning. The air was clear and fresh, the sky a peerless blue. Another perfect summer day. Apart from the fact that due east and west of where he stood some poor bastard was copping it.

He flipped open the leather cover of his wristwatch. It was 6 a.m. Jerry was a little early with his wake-up call this morning. The village was coming to life. Apparently oblivious to the bombs falling over to the west on Maleme and close to Canea in the east, a peasant was pulling a reluctant mule up the main street, goading it with a stick. The single bell was tolling on the church roof and the bombs seemed to have set all the village dogs barking at once. Looking west he saw the powder-puff balls of smoke from the Bofors guns as they strained to hit the bombers. Lamb rubbed at his eyes. Bombers. It seemed the whole sky was filled with them, sticks of bombs raining down on Maleme. Even here, some seven miles distant, he felt the earth shake as they hit home. Christ, he thought, what must it be like to be under that lot?

Smart appeared. 'Morning, sir. Cup of char?' He handed Lamb a mug of tea. 'Daily hate's a bit noisy this morning, sir.'

'A bit noisy, Smart, yes. Bit early too. Thank you.' He had no idea how Smart had found him in Galatas and did not like to ask. He presumed there was simply nothing Corporal Valentine did not make it his business to know, including the details of his commanding officer's private life.

153

Lamb took a long drink and thought about it. A bit early. That was unlike the Germans. This was more than the 'daily hate', he thought. This was something new. Perhaps this was it. Perhaps this was the prelude to the attack that he felt certain must come.

He looked at the planes as they came in. Stukas with fighter cover, wave after wave of them, circling round to drop their bombs and depart. Then another wave came in, and they kept coming.

Smart spoke. 'I think they're headed for us, sir.'

The man was right. They were making directly for Galatas.

'I think you may be right.' As he spoke a squadron of Stukas appeared almost over their heads. 'Christ, take cover.' Lamb threw down the tea and ran past the house towards where he knew there was a drainage ditch. Smart dived towards the opposite side of the road, into a culvert. Lamb was about to throw himself into the ditch when he remembered Anna. He rushed back into the house. He could hear the engines above them now; almost feel them. He opened the door. The house was shaking with the vibration of the planes. He shouted, 'Come on.' He found her still sitting on the bed, dressed now but clearly dazed by the noise. Quickly, Lamb dragged her out of the house by the arm and together they ran towards the ditch. She screamed, 'My father. Andreas.' Paying her no heed, he threw her in and followed, just as the first of the bombs came down.

It did not hit the village itself but an area just to the north of Galatas, near the beach at Kato Stalos. Nevertheless the earth heaved beneath them as the shock waves ran through it. She gripped him tightly.

He was aware of earth and grit pattering on top of them, clogging their noses and ears and making them cough. The noise was almost unbearable, from the deep

154

sucking drone of the bombers to the whine of the falling bombs and the massive boom of the explosions. Then it stopped, just stopped. His ears ringing, all that Lamb could hear was the receding drone of the engines and then, to his amazement, birdsong.

Pulling himself up, he brushed the earth from Anna's face and clothes and together they climbed from the ditch into a scene of destruction. At least four of the village houses were blazing, and another was now no more than a shell. The church was still standing, but lying in the middle of the road a little further on was all that remained of the old man and his mule.

He saw Smart climb from his culvert and cross the road.

'That was a bit close for comfort, sir.'

'Just a bit.'

'All done now, though, sir. Shame about your tea. I'll get you another, shall I?'

Lamb shook his head. 'Don't bother about that. We'd better get to the men.'

He could not help but think of the fact that the raid had come so early. He turned to Anna and, conscious that his batman was watching, waved at her. 'Until later.'

She smiled and turned. Lamb did likewise and watched as four villagers carried the body of the peasant into a house. He had walked a few paces along the road and was about to say something to Smart when he stopped, aware of another noise: a throbbing hum. Still with ringing in his head from the raid, he rubbed at his left ear but only came away with some grit. The noise could be in his head, he thought. Or it could be . . . more engines. Not the whine of the Stukas now, but a heavy, rhythmic throb.

Smart looked at him. 'You all right, sir?'

Lamb gazed up at the sky, and what he saw filled him

155

with both wonder and horror. More planes were drifting over them. Great banks of them. Dornier 17s and Ju 88s, twin-engine heavy bombers. He pointed. 'Look.'

He turned quickly and saw Anna, still walking away. He turned to Smart. 'Go on to the company. Tell them I'm on my way. Lieutenant Eadie's in charge.'

Running as fast as he could, Lamb chased after the girl, calling out her name as he did. She turned just as he reached her. He grabbed at her arm and pointed to the sky. 'Quick, back in the ditch.'

Together they ran back and threw themselves flat on the ground. It was not a second too soon. They heard the staccato patter of machine-guns as the Messerschmitt escort planes dived down on the town, strafing the streets with the guns in their wings, sending lethal shards of white-washed masonry spinning through the air. Directly beside the ditch he could hear the rounds tearing into the dusty road surface. He pushed her head further into the earth floor.

And then the bombs began to fall, not in single explosions like the Stukas but in sticks of thousand-pounders.

As the first of them came down the floor of the ditch seemed to roll and heave like the deck of a boat in a heavy swell. Anna retched. Then another bomb exploded, closer this time, and the air around them seemed momentarily to have been sucked away. He heard her gasp.

He could hardly breathe. It felt as though the very life was being drawn out of him. His teeth seemed to rattle in his head. There was another explosion and then another, the shock waves from each hitting both of them like a blow to the guts. Lamb's head was swimming with the pain from the relentless percussion of the bombs.

They were covered in earth from the walls, buried in a layer of it. He spat and motioned to Anna to do the same and then to close her eyes again but to keep her mouth open to avoid the deafening effect of the shock waves that he knew could have you bleeding from your mouth and nose.

More bombs came down, and more as they repeated the drill, spitting and inhaling as he told her with his hands, their eyes tight shut. He prayed that it would stop, certain that before long one of the bombs must find them as its target. And then, after perhaps ten minutes, he was aware that there were fewer explosions. And then nothing. That's it, he thought.

Then, with ears barely capable of sensing anything, he heard a low drone unlike any he had heard before. Surely not another wave, he thought. Haven't they done enough for one day? Or might it be something else?

No bombs had fallen for two or three minutes and Lamb peered over the parapet of their ditch at the devastated street. While one side of the main street was untouched the other row of houses and the yards that lay behind them had been all but obliterated. Amazingly, the church and the little *kafeneio* were still largely untouched, save for a few chunks of masonry which had been scooped from the church façade.

As they looked up more planes appeared in the sky above. Not bombers this time, but curious square-nosed and ribbed green Junkers 52 transport planes. Behind some of them he saw tow-ropes attached to gliders. They were flying like birds, he thought, in triangular groups of three.

This was it. He looked again at his watch. It was 8 a.m. There was no time to lose. He pressed Anna to him. 'Open your eyes. Quick. The Germans are here.' She looked at him and then at the sky, and gasped. 'I've got to find the company. Can you go back to your house? Find your father and brother. Are you all right?'

She nodded. 'Yes, of course. Take care.' She squeezed

his hand and kissed his cheek then turned and began to run down the rubble-strewn road.

Lamb turned west and made for the olive grove where the company was encamped.

As he half walked, half ran towards his men, he watched as the planes continued to come in overhead. There seemed to be hundreds of them in the air, filling the blue with their black crosses. The Dorniers were coming in low and strafing the houses with lead. Stukas banked and swooped, nose-diving gun emplacements, while transport planes plodded above them and tiny Me 109 fighters spiralled up into the high blue. How many of them could there be? he wondered. Were they sending an entire division to Crete? A corps of paratroopers? Reaching the grove, he found the men staring upwards.

'What are you doing? Where's the sarnt-major? Where are the lieutenants?'

He saw Bennett pointing skywards, his face a mask of schoolboy wonder. 'Look, sir, parachutes. They're parachutes. Now I've seen everything.'

In the cloudless azure sky above them dozens of white parachutes were blossoming. With them were other chutes of different colours: red, green and yellow. It was beautiful, hypnotic, like so much confetti raining down on them. The strange shapes tapered upwards to a mushroom balloon: umbrellas, twisting and swinging in the sky as they fell earthwards.

Mays spoke. 'Bloody hell, sir. They're not real, are they? They're only dummies, aren't they, sir?'

'No, Sarnt. They're real all right.'

Lamb stared at the falling objects, marvelling at their grace. They seemed so very serene. How, he thought for an instant, could anything quite so beautiful be dangerous? The men attached to them were small too. Like dolls. Harmless little toys.

Bennett broke the spell. 'They're Jerry paratroops. Stand to.'

Lamb joined him. 'They're paratroopers, all right. Get the men fallen in, Sarnt-Major. Lieutenant Eadie, Mr Wentworth, find your platoons. Get moving. There's more on their way.'

And there were. The skies above them were suddenly filled with parachutes. Lamb counted. Five, ten, thirteen, thirty. He gave up. He saw that the different colours denoted the nature of their load. White for the paratroopers, red, yellow and green for large canisters, presumably weapons, and equipment of different types.

Seven chutes, mainly white, came down to their immediate left.

'Over there. Get them.'

One man was down trying to untangle his chute. A man from Mays' section shot at almost point-blank range, blowing him off his feet. Two more chutes had landed in the taller trees. Bennett fired his Thompson gun at one of them and, riddled with holes, the man shook and then hung there limp, like the body of some pirate, suspended from a gibbet, thought Lamb. The other man, caught in a tamarisk tree, was trying to extricate himself from his chute while at the same time sending sporadic bursts of fire into the men on the ground. A round from one of them caught one of Corporal Beaumont's men in the shoulder. Eadie ran across. 'Don't worry. I'll get him.' As the panic-stricken German looked down he raised his revolver and fired hitting not the paratrooper but his load of grenades. The paratrooper blew to pieces, showering all in his immediate vicinity on the ground below with his blood and guts. One of the men threw up.

They were coming down faster now, more of them firing their submachine-guns wildly at the ground as they came.

There was no need for Lamb to give commands. His men knew what had to be done. As the shots hit their mark the falling Germans would shake, go limp and then suddenly straighten with a jerk before drooping again just as they hit the ground.

One of the new intake, Shaw, smiled at Lamb. 'I got that one, sir.'

'Just keep shooting them, son. They're still coming.'

And they were. But as fast as they came they were spotted, and as soon as they were spotted they were shot. The men did not have to aim, they just fired. It took only a few minutes to absorb the finer points of this new game. It was better to shoot at the feet, then you would be certain of hitting the target and disabling it at least. Or you could load an incendiary bullet and go for the parachute itself which, bursting into flames, would collapse and send its owner plummeting to the ground. This was absurd, thought Lamb, like shooting high pheasant. No, it was ten times easier than that. He wondered for a moment if they should stop, give them a chance. But logic dictated that they must be killed in the air, and another random burst from above him brought him to his senses.

'They're firing at us now,' he shouted. 'Keep firing. Shoot them before they land.'

He knew in his heart that it was beyond the principles of war to shoot a helpless man, but anyone could see that this was the only way the defenders were going to have anything like a chance. Quite apart from the machine-guns from above and the small arms, Tommy guns and Lewises from below, the noise was deafening now. Above them the sky was filled with planes. Stukas had returned with a fighter escort, and even as more transports came in, circling in a pattern above them, they were dive-bombing the British and Commonwealth positions. The stream of transports seemed endless. Observing them more closely, Lamb calculated that the paratroopers would jump out at a height of 300 feet. That was not without its dangers. Whoever had devised the V formation seemed not to have accounted for the airspeed. As Lamb watched he saw several of the figures who left the lead aircraft hit by the wings of the other two, killed in mid-air before their chutes had even opened. One man was decapitated. Another jumped, and his chute, opening too soon, was snagged on the tailplane of his own aircraft, pulling him along in its slipstream. It was a horrific scene. But even so, with all the mistakes, the Germans' tactic seemed to be working. For the most part the paratroopers were making it out of the transports and into the skies and descending on them.

The Bofors guns in the anti-aircraft pits around the airfield at Maleme and those near Galatas had opened up in earnest now, and as Lamb watched he saw the familiar puffs of smoke which marked their shots. One of them scored a direct hit on one of the gliders and it disintegrated before his eyes in a sheet of flame. Another shot hit one of the Ju 52s and the aircraft broke up, the men inside falling out of it like so many sacks of potatoes. He hoped for their sakes that they were dead already. The gliders came in over their position in a sinister silence, just a sudden swish. Looking at one of them, Lamb and his men were able to see their enemies' faces peering out of the windows.

Beaumont was beside him, and paused to reload. 'Did you see that, sir? Jerries. They looked bloody terrified.'

'Well, wouldn't you be, Corporal? Coming down on us.'

All around them it seemed that the units encamped in the trees had begun to fire now, and from the olive groves off to his left occupied by the New Zealanders came the staccato chatter of machine-guns, along with screams.

Behind him he could hear the woof of Bofors guns and then more German fighters, 109s, appeared in the sky and swooped down to machine-gun the positions to the rear of where the paratroops were landing.

Some of the Germans at least had made it to the ground, and Lamb knew that those vital few minutes when they had been at their most vulnerable were almost over. To their right he glimpsed a grey form running through the undergrowth. 'Over there. There's one of them.'

Simultaneously a dozen rifles opened up on the area where Lamb was pointing. There was a short shout and then nothing, but almost at once he saw other grey shadows – to their front this time. They must be searching for their weapons containers, which had been dropped separately. He had seen them come down, the ones with the coloured chutes. He wondered if there would be any chance of his own men getting their hands on them. Perhaps he might even get hold of the Schmeisser machine-pistol he longed for.

Lamb wondered where the gliders had landed and whether their passengers had made it. He turned to Bennett. 'Did you see where those gliders came down, Sarnt-Major?'

Bennett pointed towards the airfield. 'Somewhere over there, sir. To the west, I reckon. They're after that airfield.'

He was right, thought Lamb. Maleme would certainly be their target. That and the anti-aircraft batteries. Get the batteries, and you could bring in the transports to land on the airfield, and when you managed to do that there would be no limit to the number of troops you could bring to the party.

Sitting hunched up in a glider towed behind a Ju 52 transport plane, heading away from Athens towards Crete, Generalleutnant Wilhelm Sussmann, commander of the

7th Fallschirmjäger Division, looked down at the sparkling sea below them and smiled. They were clear of the Greek mainland now and the islands, and everywhere the sky seemed to be filled with other planes of his division. Nine battalions, each of 700 men, plus the support troops – a total of some 7,000 men heading towards their island objective. Heading towards glory. This was the biggest thing yet for his beloved Fallschirmjäger, the Führer's favourites. Sussmann's men had been all set to take Lemnos and then diverted to the Corinth Canal. That had been a glorious day. But this would be bigger by far.

After an initial glider assault on key anti-aircraft batteries there were 3,000 of them jumping in the first wave with another 3,000 in the second and then more glider-borne troops. Once the paratroops had secured the airfields, then would come the men of the 5th Gebirgsjäger Mountain Division, Ringel's men, skilled since their childhood in climbing alps not unlike the mountains which filled inland Crete, men who proudly wore the edelweiss as their badge and were now trained to fight in those mountains. How could the Allies resist them? Besides, intelligence reports had told them that the island was poorly defended, no more than a few thousand men. It had even been suggested that the Cretans, disaffected as they were with the Greek monarchy and Metaxas' regime, would welcome them with open arms.

Sussmann smiled and nudged his aide-de-camp, Captain Scheiber. 'All right, Scheiber? We're going to do it this time, eh? Something that's never been attempted before. We're jumping into history, my friend. We'll give those Tommies another bloody nose. They don't know when they're beaten.'

'No, General.'

A huge Ju 88, its twin engines throbbing, came perilously close to their glider, and then another.

Christ. They're getting too close. What the hell are they doing? Those bombers should be nowhere near us.

He turned to Scheiber. 'What the hell do they think they're doing? Can't they see they're in the wrong lane? They'll . . .'

At that moment there was a terrific lurch, enough to break harnesses. One of the men was thrown to the other side of the glider, another to the floor.

Sussmann knocked his helmeted head against the pierced metal of a fuselage strut. He swore and as he did so he was aware that they were suddenly not moving as fast as they had been. There was a yell from the pilot.

'Our tow-rope's snapped. Everyone brace yourselves. We're going down.'

Sussmann looked below at the sea and saw nothing but blue. They had already passed the island of Aegina and he knew there was nothing now between them and Crete. He had no way, though, of gauging how far they had gone.

He turned to the others and saw their ashen faces.

'All right, boys, we'll make it. Who's got a chute on, apart from me?'

He did not hear the replies, if there were any. As he spoke, there was a terrific crack and he looked on in horror through the tiny window as the left wing broke off the fuselage. One of the men yelled, 'Shit. The wing.'

Scheiber stared at him. 'General, what do we do?'

There was a split second that seemed to last an eternity and then he heard another voice mutter in the darkness ahead of him, 'Oh God, no. No.'

Sussmann said nothing. He looked at Scheiber's pleading eyes and knew what would happen next. But he was surprised, for instead of going straight into a spiral dive the aircraft stalled and then, with another crash, the right wing was gone. For a moment they seemed to be hanging, suspended in the air. No one spoke. There was no sound, save the rushing of the wind.

But only for a moment. Suddenly the glider gave a lurch. There was a yell from the pilot and they were all hurled forward as the useless capsule that had been the glider turned on its nose and began a headlong descent to the earth. Arms, heads and legs collided with weapons, metal and splintered wood. A huge shard of fuselage drove straight into Scheiber and skewered him to the roof. Dark blood gouted from his mouth. Sussmann turned away and, being at the rear, managed to pull himself up, out of the mass of bodies, kicking down on the soft flesh of someone's face with his jackboot. He reached for the jump door and wrenched on the handle, opening it to the rushing air, then with an effort that took every ounce of his strength he hauled himself to the opening. The pressure against his face was incredible and for a moment he thought he would not manage it. But then he kicked again against something, not knowing or caring what it was, and he was through the hole in the fuselage and out, free of the hurtling wooden coffin, in empty space.

He was falling, hurtling through the sky, a helpless Icarus without his wings. Sussman threw his hands wide in the crucifix jumping position and then turned his head to the right and watched as the wreck of the glider, still with the others on board, fell away below him. He could see their bodies falling from it as it neared the sea, black specks dropping into infinity, and for a moment he prayed that they might be still alive, trying to save themselves. But then he wished them dead, for he did not think they had any hope. But he was free.

Sussmann said another prayer to the God of soldiers and felt the jerk upwards as the chute opened. Thank heaven for that. Then he looked down, expecting to see nothing but the Aegean below him. But there, just beyond the tip of his boot, was land. Through a gap in the clouds the landscape of Crete opened out before him. He saw the tips of the White Mountains first and then, through the hurrying cloud, lying at an angle, the outline of the island, looking like a long fish. The area on which he might hope to land, if he were not to ditch in the sea, was on the bottom right of the island. He tried to visualise the map and saw that he was on the north-west coast, surprisingly close to their objective. Ahead of him and below he could see the other transports on their journey into battle. The wild idea came to him that, far from being doomed, he might actually find his men and go ahead as planned. It gave him new strength as above him he watched the stream of bombers on their way to destroy the waiting enemy. This was hardly as he had envisaged his arrival, but anything, thought Sussmann, was better than the fate of his poor comrades.

On the slopes of Pink Hill there was firing from all sides now, and although they could hear the firecracker rattle of small arms and shouting there was for a moment a strange lull in the airborne invasion, fewer planes in the sky, and it seemed, bizarrely, that no more paratroops were dropping on them.

Mays scanned the skies. 'Is that it then, sir? Do you think that's it?'

Lamb shook his head. 'I doubt it, Sarnt. They mean business.'

There was a noise behind him and Lamb turned, ready to shoot, but saw instead a khaki uniform. A runner. 'Captain Lamb, sir?'

'That's me, yes.'

'From Colonel Kippenberger, sir, 10th Brigade. Looks like a whole German paratroop battalion has dropped on top of us. Colonel says that some of them have dropped near here, sir, some way short of their objective. They're after the prison, sir. They'll be trying to regroup. The colonel says you need to counter-attack, sir. To link up with 6th Greek Regiment, up at Cemetery Hill.'

Lamb looked at him. 'Those are my orders? To counter-attack a battalion of paratroops with half a company and a few Greeks?'

'Yes, sir.'

'Very well, Corporal. Thank you.'

The man ran off back to Brigade.

Lamb turned to Eadie. 'You heard him, Charles. Move out with your platoon and clean them up.' Eadie raised an eyebrow. 'Yes, sir. Of course. Right away. The whole, er, battalion of them?'

'No, man. Just whatever you can see. The brigadier's right. We have to stop them regrouping. It's our only chance. You take the left flank down into the valley. I'll send Hugh to the right. I'll hold the centre with the Greeks.'

Eadie yelled across to Valentine. 'We're moving off, Sarnt. Twenty-yard gaps. We've got to stop them from regrouping. Got it?'

Valentine drawled, 'I think so, sir. Come on, you lot.' And then they were off, through the vines in the direction that Lamb had indicated, down towards the round hill which housed the village cemetery and beyond it to the valley and the low, white buildings of Ayia jail which lay at its base, and which had given it its new name: Prison Valley.

He called across to Wentworth. 'Hugh. You're on my right, all right? We must stop them from re-forming.'

'Sir.'

'Right, Sarnt-Major, we're moving up with the others. Sarnt Hook, Beaumont, Simmonds, you're with me. We're in the centre. Where are the bloody Greeks, Sarnt-Major?'

'Been off looking for Jerries to kill, sir. Their blood's up right enough.'

'That's good. They'll need it. Valentine, you speak the lingo. Go and round them up, get them back with their platoons. Right, let's go.'

They moved forward steadily and soon found themselves descending terraces of vines, past the slit-trenches of the forward troops, New Zealanders who offered their own verbal encouragement. 'Go on, mate. We're right behind you. We've got twenty-three of the buggers already. Beat that if you can.'

The slopes of the hillsides made a curious buffer to the noise of the battle, and the further down they went into the little valley the less frenetic it became. Lamb felt suddenly alive, as he always did when heading into battle. He still had the knot of fear that went with it, but his head was filled with certainties and perhaps just a little of the euphoria of the previous night, the dinner with the Prince and Hathaway and then the party, and then Anna. And then he remembered. Christ, how could he have forgotten? The King. He looked around and realised it was now too late. His men were committed to the attack. As soon as they had retaken the hill he would consolidate and they could make their way to Perivolia. He prayed he would not be too late, that the paratroops would not have found the King before he did.

They were almost at the bottom of the little valley now and Lamb could see the slopes of Cemetery Hill and, closer, the chutes hanging from trees across its floor, some of them with their owners still dangling in grotesque attitudes of death.

His eye was caught by a black shape in the sky as another glider floated in from the right and grazed the base of the valley before crashing into two pine trees. Lamb watched as the pilot and co-pilot, ripped from their harnesses, were catapulted through the windscreen and the fuselage broke in two midway along its length, the wings snapping off like a balsa-wood model. Two of its occupants staggered out, bleeding, but the others who followed were alert and had weapons in their hands. They looked around nervously and found cover in the gorse bushes.

Lamb yelled, 'Jerries, 2 o'clock.'

The men opened up with rifle fire and he thought he saw one of the men go down, but he could not be sure. 'Follow up, you men. And watch out.'

Beaumont called to him, 'Blimey, sir. Look at this.'

He hurried over and found the corporal staring at the body of a dead paratrooper. Beaumont was holding a canteen in his hands. He offered it to Lamb. 'It's coffee, sir. Bloody strong too.'

Lamb took a swig. It was. 'And look, sir, he's got rations. A bloody great sausage, bread, fruit and chocolate. Two bars, sir. Lucky bugger.'

'He's a dead lucky bugger now, isn't he, Corporal? Gather it up, we'll need it. Now all of you, keep your heads down. We don't know where they might be.'

He had hardly spoken when there was a crack and Corporal Beaumont fell, shot clean through the forehead, the chocolate and fruit tumbling from his hands. They dropped as one.

'Where the hell did that come from?'

'Front and left, sir, 10 degrees.' Bennett pointed and Lamb followed his finger towards a group of olive trees about fifty yards away beyond a field of vines. He could see white chutes among the vines and another couple on the trees.

Lamb brought his Thompson gun up slowly and aimed it at the target. He turned and nodded to the others. Then he breathed out, and gently squeezed on the trigger. There was a burst of staccato fire and then eight of the men opened up in the same direction. There were yells and screams and then the crack of rifles as the Germans returned fire.

'Sarnt-Major, where's the Lewis gun?'

'With Corporal Simmonds right behind us, sir.'

'Get it up here and give them some.'

Seconds later Simmonds had come up to them. He dropped to the ground, put the Lewis on its rest and opened up. There were more screams, but this time no return of fire. Only silence.

Simmonds spoke, his cheek still against the gun. 'Could be bluffing, sir.'

'Yes, perhaps they are. But we've no choice. Come on.'

Lamb moved forward at a crouch and slipped a grenade from his pocket. Then at twenty yards he pulled the pin and, holding the trigger, counted before throwing it. They all hit the ground. The explosion that followed ripped into the trees. Lamb shouted. 'Come on,' and together they charged towards where the Germans had been, through the smoke and stench of cordite.

There was no one left alive. Of the three paratroops who had fired on them, one had been killed by gunfire. It was hard to tell how the others had died but the grenade had certainly done its work. Lamb looked at the first man, as fine an example of blond-haired Aryan youth as you could encounter.

'Sarnt-Major, get their weapons and their rations and . . .' Lamb stopped. Ahead of them there was a commotion in the trees, and raised voices. 'Quiet, all of you. Get down.'

They dropped to one knee and waited, all of them raising their weapons, expecting at any moment to see a German helmet. Instead they saw khaki and moustaches. Greeks. Not his men but the battalion that had been beside them in the line. But what were they doing walking to meet him? He called out, 'Hold your fire. They're Greek.'

Lamb stood up and the men followed. 'Hey there. Captain. Yasou.'

The Greeks stopped and then, recognising a British officer, walked on. One of their officers approached Lamb.

'Yasou, Kapitan. Good to see you and not more of those German cuckolds.' He spat on the body of the blond Fallschirmjäger. Lamb breathed sigh of relief. They were not his Greeks but part of the 8th Greek Regiment whom General Freyberg in his wisdom had left down in Prison Valley at the foot of the hill.

'Can I ask what you're doing, Captain? Are you withdrawing?'

The man nodded and shrugged. 'We have to. We have no alternative. We have only three rounds each at the start. Now perhaps we have only one. And no bayonets. What can we do? How can we fight?'

'But I was led to believe that ammunition had been sent to your CO.'

'If it has then it hasn't been given out to us. Look.'

He held out his revolver, a Smith & Wesson, to Lamb and dropped open the chamber to reveal a single round.

'No, I agree. You can't fight without ammunition. You'd best get back to Galatas and see if you can scrounge any there.'

'Yes, Kapitan, I think so too. Good luck.'

The Greeks passed through them with thumbs-up signs, yasou-ing and hello-ing as if they were old friends. And then they were gone. Christ, thought Lamb, who was holding Cemetery Hill now?

He turned to Bennett. 'Sarnt-Major, better send a runner back to Colonel Kippenburger. Tell him the 6th Greeks have pulled off Cemetery Hill for lack of ammo. Tell him

171

we're going to try and get to it before the Jerries do. And you'd better send out someone to find Valentine and his bloody Greeks, wherever they are. We're going to need them now.'

Bandouvas had been sitting on a chair outside the door of his house in the little mountain village of Fournes when the second air-raid came and he knew that something was up. This was what Kapitan Pendlebury had told him would happen. Two air-raids would signal the attack. Almost as soon as he had come out of the cellar he had seen them, the white mushrooms, falling gracefully from the sky. He knew what they were. Pendlebury had shown him illustrations. Paratroops. The sky was full of them now, canopies of silk with their heavy cargo hanging beneath, a grey-black lump. He rushed into the house, where his wife was sitting in a chair in the kitchen recovering from the bombing and shaking her head.

'Quick, woman. Get the guns.'

Bandouvas' wife just stared at him.

'The guns. The guns. The ones in the barn. Quick, woman. The Germans are here.'

She got up with a start and ran to the kitchen drawer. Reaching in, she searched for a moment and took out a knife which might have passed for a kitchen knife but which looked in truth more like the cut-down Turkish scimitar that it was, a weapon used 100 years ago to attack another invader and oppressor. Bandouvas smiled at her. 'Good. Now get the guns while I find the bullets.'

She rushed out of the door and a few minutes later, as Bandouvas slung on a bandolier of bullets, came hurrying back in bearing in her arms three ancient rifles. Bandouvas looked at them.

'They'll still work. They're good enough. Now go and get Melina. Get bandages ready too. We'll need plenty of them. I'm off to find Giorgio and Andreas. We've no time to waste.'

He found his sons up on the hill. They came running towards him, the older, Andreas, followed by fourteen-year-old Giorgio.

Bandouvas pointed. 'Look, do you see them?'

'Yes, father, of course we see them.'

'Here, take a gun, and you, Giorgio.'

The younger one spoke. 'I have a knife.'

Then Andreas. 'And I have the axe, father. Grandfather's axe. I dug it up.'

He held it out. Bandouvas took it from him and looked at the axe that had belonged to his father. It was not a chopping axe for wood, but a Cretan fighting axe, a tomahawk of the type used by red Indians seen in the cowboy films they showed in the picture house in Heraklion. He turned the weapon over in his hands for a moment, feeling its perfect balance, noticing how sharp it still was.

'Good. Let's find the bastards. The British need our help. It's a good day for killing.'

High in the skies above Crete, Sussmann continued to fall, floating safely now on the air current. Christ, he thought, I am a lucky sod. If I can just pull on this thing, somehow will it to carry me over there, I might be able to make land. He was falling faster now, it seemed, and was carried on the wind. A favourable wind, a Greek wind of fate that was blowing him ever closer to the island. It rose to meet him and he knew now that he could do it.

He had seen his subordinates before they left the airfield in the other gliders and transports and knew they would be down there now. Brigadier Meindl in his own glider, and Major Count von Uxkull, his monocled Chief of

Staff, who had insisted on dropping by parachute. Somewhere. And the division was out there too now. He could imagine them, his boys: some of them caught in the trees, poor bastards, some of them would not have made it, but those who had, he knew, would be quickly stripping off their harnesses hunting for their weapons containers and supplies, getting ready to face the enemy and to take the island in the name of the Führer. Oh, Sussmann was no fanatical Nazi. He was a career soldier from a family of soldiers. But he was loyal to Germany, and at present that meant loyal to Hitler. And there was something else, something that even some of his commanders did not yet know – certainly not that strutting Austrian Julius Ringel and his mountain men. Sussmann had been given another mission. It was to be his personal honour to capture the King of Greece. He looked down and got ready. He felt like a trussed turkey. His lifejacket was cumbersome and he half wished he hadn't worn it, but Scheiber had insisted. His MP40 machine-pistol was slung around his shoulder to hang loosely at his left leg, and he hoped he would not encounter it on landing. Better that, though, than to land with just a Sauer pistol, good as it was, as was standard practice. At least with his Schmeisser to hand he had a better chance of survival against an instant enemy. And of course he had his knife, strapped to his leg. He tried to flex the muscles in his legs to prepare for the impact of landing.

Even at the age of forty-five, Sussmann knew in his heart that he was as able as the fittest young lieutenant, and now he would prove it to them. The poor buggers who had gone down in the glider would not have died in vain. He was here to take command.

He had passed out of the paratroop school with flying colours and had made a number of jumps, but that fear never left you. He was sure that your mental state counted just as much as your fitness and your technique.

The ground rushed up to meet him and he braced himself to take the impact, bending his knees to take the shock. Christ, he thought. Perhaps that was a mistake after all. Then, hitting the button which secured his harness, he slipped it off and grabbed his pack. He looked around and realised that he was now quite alone and in enemy territory. Where he was he had no idea, but he was close to the sea and in north-west Crete. He removed the Luger from his shoulder strap and checked it before placing it in the holster at his side. He felt around his uniform for the extra magazines for the Schmeisser and found they were all in place. Lastly he drew out the map of Crete from his breast pocket. Then, aware that every step might be his last, Generalleutnant Wilhelm Sussmann set out to find his men.

10

Sitting in his new command post, behind a low dry-stone wall, on the edge of an olive grove in the valley on the forward slopes of Pink Hill, Peter Lamb considered the situation. The entire floor of the valley was covered with parachutes. They filled it, like so many huge mushrooms, mostly white but with other colours too. He could see the enemy paratroops running between them, zig-zagging to avoid incoming fire, collecting weapons from the containers that had split open like pea pods. Occasionally one of the men would fall, crumbling like a paper doll as he was hit by gunfire. But as far as Lamb was concerned there was absolutely nothing he could do. The enemy were out of range. Behind him, dug in, was the Petrol Company, the New Zealand hotch-potch of Service Corps men, drivers, mechanics and the like under Captain Macdonagh. Lamb had his men around him, Eadie on the left, Wentworth on the right, with a total of about thirty. Valentine was somewhere to his rear with the Greeks, and he hoped that his training of them had been enough. He knew too that Michael Hathaway and his band of partisans were in Galatas. It was clear to him now, though, that the Jerries had taken Cemetery Hill. A few minutes ago his position had been raked by machine-gun fire from the heights. They had taken no casualties, but it had put the wind up the men and been enough to tell him of their presence. Since then there had been nothing. The enemy were clearly weighing up their chances.

Lamb reasoned that, if the Jerries were up on Cemetery Hill, in all probability they must have taken the prison and made that their base. Any fool would have done that – any fool but whichever Allied commander had taken the decision not to defend it. Time and again Lamb had thought over the past week that the prison would have made an ideal strongpoint, with its large, windowless buildings and high walls. A company of infantry could have held out there indefinitely. But whoever had had the option had not installed even a token garrison, and now it must be in German hands. The paratroops would have gained their first foothold on the island. However, now was not the time to apportion blame. That would surely come later, as it always did.

Anyone could see that Pink Hill was the gateway to the Galatas heights and that whoever controlled the heights controlled the entire area. Pink Hill also denied the village of Galatas itself to the enemy, and from it fire could be brought down on the surrounding area, in particular the vital artery of the road from the south. He had no idea whether the northern flanks down to the sea were still intact. Closest to the coast were the Royal Marines and on their left flank the 4th Field Regiment, artillerymen fighting as infantry or 'infantillery' as one wag had put it. It was anyone's guess how they would do when attacked by German paratroops. On Ruin Hill were the divisional supply troops, and next to them on Wheat Hill the 5th Field Regiment, more gunners with rifles. Then came Pink Hill and his men, and then the perimeter stretched back round up to the sea. It was a good position and Lamb knew that his men were as vital to it as any of the components that made it up. And that worried him. For if he were to pull back now, to try to reach Perivolia and find the King, the line might collapse. Perhaps, he thought, if I leave half the men with Eadie . . .

He turned to Bennett.

'You know, Sarnt-Major, we've made a pretty good fist of it so far if you think about it. I mean, what have we got here? Apart from us, that is? Under-equipped, non-infantry soldiers. Gunners without artillery and drivers without trucks who left their kit on the beaches of southern Greece. Down in Galatas there are 400 Greeks with precious little ammo or bayonets, and we've got our own company of Greeks who two weeks ago couldn't hit a barn door. But I can tell you I'm willing to bet that where we are, right here, is going to decide this whole bloody battle. It's going to be up to us. Any suggestions?'

'If you put it like that, sir, it looks a bit thick, doesn't it? D'you think those Greeks will fight, sir? The ones with no ammo?'

'The Greeks want the Jerries out more than we do, Sarnt-Major. If they can find some bullets they'll be back. Someone's just got to work out what to do with them.'

Valentine appeared, breathless.

'Sir. I've got our Greeks, sir. Found them back in the village, looking a bit lost. But they're fine now. What shall I do with them?'

'Split them up as they were before. One platoon to go with Lieutenant Eadie, another with Mr Wentworth, the third with me. That will give us each an extra twenty or so men, almost up to strength. If someone can get back the Greeks from the 6th, if we can get them re-armed, then we'll have almost 500.'

178

There was a sudden whoosh in the air above them, followed by a crump about ten yards away to the left.

'Mortars,' Lamb shouted and they all went to ground.

He looked up as another round came in. 'Where the devil are they coming from?'

Bennett looked up and tried to fix them. 'Looks like Prison Valley, sir. Up by the cemetery. They've almost got us zeroed in.'

'I knew that bloody prison should have been garrisoned.' Another mortar bomb landed five yards to their right. There was a scream. 'Christ, that was close. These are the heavy jobs. Right. Just tell everyone to keep down. There's nothing we can do.'

Another crump and then another. They were falling marginally short, he thought. But he wondered how long it might take for the Germans to find their range. There was a shout from the front. 'They're coming, sir. They're coming up the hill.'

There was a burst of automatic fire from their front. Too wild, it hit nothing but a few plane trees. Lamb yelled across to Mays. 'Get the Lewis working. Cut them down.'

Within seconds the Lewis gun was pumping out fire in the direction of the oncoming paratroops. More machine-guns opened up as the Petrol Company joined in the defence. There were shouts and screams from the forward slopes as the Lewis gun chopped its way through the advancing enemy. More mortar rounds came in. They could hear German voices shouting words of command.

A New Zealand officer appeared in a tin hat, wearing a broad smile: Macdonagh. 'Hi there, Lamb. Good shooting now, eh? Duck season's a bit late. Just doing the rounds of my boys. Great shooting.' Then he was gone as quickly as he had appeared.

Mays arrived at a trot. 'Sir, we've beaten them back but Lieutenant Eadie says there's a gap on the right by

179

the Petrol Company where the Greeks were and some Jerries look like they're pushing through.'

Lamb stood up. 'Right, my platoon, come with me. Sarnt-Major, bring the Greeks.'

They wound their way down the hill across the terraces and over the dead bodies of what seemed to be scores of Germans. Others, badly wounded, held their hands up for help.

Mays whistled. 'Blimey, it *is* like a bloody duck shoot.'

There was the occasional random round, but the mortars were silent now. Lamb stopped. 'Look, down there, Sarnt-Major.'

'Jerries, sir. A good dozen of them. More now.'

He was right. The paratroops had spotted the gap between the units and were moving as fast as they could through the vines to penetrate it. Lamb crouched. 'Come on, with me.'

Together they moved forward, their guns at the ready. Lamb was about to raise his hand to stop them when there was a cry from their left. As he watched a crowd of khaki-clad men erupted screaming from the undergrowth, their rifles with fixed bayonets, and hurled themselves shouting down the hill towards the advancing paratroops. At their head ran Michael Hathaway, his blond hair, without its customary oil, blowing behind him now. Wearing no form of headgear, not even a service cap, he presented a strange figure. His long yellow army jersey almost reached the bottom of his shorts, worn above long socks and ammunition boots. The brass on his canvas belt and his shoulder pips had been polished by his batman to such a sheen that it reflected the sun. He looked to Lamb like a character from P.G. Wodehouse heading purposefully towards a tennis court. To cap it all he held to his mouth a bright tin whistle – service issue – and it was on this that he now gave the command

180

signals. He was carried down the hillside by his own impetus, revolver in his hand, whistle in his mouth, blowing commands. Sporadic small-arms fire crashed out from the trees, and four of the men with Hathaway fell. Lamb watched as Hathaway reached the Germans ahead of his men and saw him, without taking aim, raise his gun and fire, hitting the first German in the forehead. His men were up with him now, and they could see that they were a body of Greek soldiers armed with rifles, bayonets and swords. They crashed into the astonished Germans, and their work was quick and deadly. A few seconds later ten of the paratroops lay dead on the ground, most of them bayoneted, while Lamb and Bennett watched the others streaming back down the hill. As they went, one of the Greeks dropped to one knee and, bringing up his rifle to his shoulder, shot at the man. The German fell forward.

Hathaway saw Lamb. 'Peter. What ho! Saw those Jerries had spotted the gap and knew we had to be quick. Imagine you did the same.'

'Yes, I was planning to surprise them. Well done.' He scrutinised Hathaway's men.

'They're the 6th Greeks. Managed to rally them in the village. Knew they'd do well. Did you see that last man fall?' Hathaway was catching his breath. 'I'd like to think they could stand and plug the gap, but truth to tell I think they're really only an effective force in that sort of attack. They've got nothing to defend themselves with. No bullets yet. We'll do it somehow, though. Pendlebury might find some ammo, and I've heard we've got a few tanks coming up. You know, the Divisional Cavalry.'

Lamb nodded and pointed to the dense olive groves. 'Useful in the towns and on the roads, but not much bloody good in this lot. What are you going to do now?'

'I'll take the Greeks back up to the top and hold them

181

there as a sort of mobile reserve. That's about all we can do until we get any ammo. If you need us, send a runner.'

Lamb watched them go and turned back to the front. 'We'd better go to ground, Sarnt-Major. They're sure to attack again.' The men slipped back into their trenches and waited. The shelling had stopped, and although they could hear the battle raging to their forward left and right, directly to their front nothing seemed to be happening.

It was close to midday when an officer appeared at Lamb's trench.

'You Lamb?'

'Sir.'

'Major Bassett. We met at Colonel Kippenberger's. The colonel's set up brigade HQ on the little ridge directly to your rear. It's a bloody mess out there. Petrol Company's been shot to blazes. Macdonagh's dead and all their other officers are out of action. You seem to be holding on.'

'Yes, we had a bit of trouble but they seem to have dug in. Expect we'll get it soon enough.'

'Well, actually we've other plans for you. We're expecting the Divisional Cavalry to turn up here any moment. Light tanks. We want you to counter-attack down the hill with the tanks and carriers on your left flank along the road. We must clear the prison area of the enemy.'

Lamb looked at him for a moment.

The order had been clear enough. With classic military brevity, he was being ordered to mount a counter-attack against unknown enemy forces, which would doubtless include mortars and other heavy weapons.

'Sorry, sir. You want us to attack a heavily defended position? A fortified position, with small arms and a few light tanks?'

'That's about it. And once you've cleared the area you

182

need to hold a position over on the left. Roughly where the 6th Greek Regiment was until Captain Hathaway took them to the rear. Covering the Canea–Alykianou road.'

Lamb nodded. 'I see. Fine. Of course, sir.'

It seemed to sum up the desperation of their situation, for in any other circumstances such an order would have been interpreted as suicide.

'Be sure to wait for the tanks, Lamb. No point going in without support. Good luck. Wish I was going with you. Better get back to the Old Man.'

Lamb rubbed his head with his hands and tried to ease the pounding in his temples.

Smart was standing beside him. 'I'd offer to make you a cup of char, sir, if I thought we was staying 'ere for a bit.'

'Well, we're not. But thank you. We're going to attack. See if you can find the Sarnt-Major for me.'

Bennett came at a trot, sweating in temperatures that were fast rising to the thirties. 'Sir.'

'We've been ordered to advance, Sarnt-Major. To take the prison.'

'What, sir? But we've no artillery. And no mortars neither.'

'Nevertheless, those are the orders.'

'That's madness, sir. We'll be cut to bits.'

'Yes. You're right.'

He heard a crashing over on his left. Someone was running through the vines. Lamb turned and raised his weapon. Called out, 'Look to your left.'

He heard a voice, breathless and indistinct, but English, and a second later a man appeared, a British corporal. Lamb recognised him as Hathaway's batman.

'Don't shoot. Don't shoot. I've got a message for Captain Lamb.'

'That's me.'

The exhausted man tried to stand to attention. 'Captain Lamb, sir. Captain Hathaway says to tell you that the Jerries have broken through a gap in the lines to the south east, between his men and the 2nd Greeks. At Perivolia. There's nothing between them and Platanas and the road to Canea. He says he's taken a company across to try to hold them but he's got no ammo and the Jerries are heading for the house where you were last night, Bella something, Campany. And the captain says he's not sure who's in there now.' He paused for breath. 'He asks for your help, sir.'

'He said that, Corporal? You're quite sure that's what he said? The house where we were last night? Bella Campagna?'

'Yes, sir. That's it. Those were his words.'

'Thank you, Corporal. Take a message back to Captain Hathaway and tell him we're coming.'

He saw Bennett. 'Sarnt-Major, we're going back to the camp.'

'Back to the camp, sir? That's in the rear. We're not retreating, are we?'

'No. There's no rear any more, Sarnt-Major. These bloody paratroops have dropped all over the shop. Seems the Jerries have broken through at Platanas. They're almost at Canea. Captain Hathaway's trying to hold them. We'll leave Mr Wentworth and his men here.'

He found Wentworth. 'Hugh, we're needed up at Perivolia. Captain Hathaway's in trouble. I'm taking Charles and the spare and leaving your platoon here to plug the gap. You might get a bit of flak from the GOC. We're under orders from Brigade to mount a counter-attack, waiting for the light tanks to show up. Now listen to me. On no account are you to mount that attack until we return. On no account. Whatever order Major Bassett or the colonel might send.'

'Yes, sir, I understand. Good luck.'

'And good luck to you, Hugh.' He turned to Bennett. 'Come on.'

Moving off, down through the terraces, Lamb thought for a moment. If the Germans were attacking Bella Campagna they might know the King and Prince Peter had been there. Lamb hoped the Prince had got out before the paratroops had landed and that the King had not returned there from the house where the Prince had told them his cousin had moved the previous day. He wondered whether Hathaway knew about his role as royal body-guard but decided that he could not and that this must be no more than coincidence occasioned by the events of the previous evening.

The villa lay two miles south west of Canea and about the same distance away from Lamb's present position. While he knew it might have been safer to get there via Galatas and Karatsos, under cover of the buildings, Lamb decided that, speed being vital, they would go directly along the road which ran up from the prison to Platanas and was likely to form the axis of any German attack from Prison Valley. Assembling his and Eadie's men and the Greeks attached to their platoons on the south-east slopes of Pink Hill, he led the way down towards the road. He looked down to the right in the direction of the prison and saw activity down by the huge white mass of the building. Clearly the Germans were consolidating their position there. He called to the others and turned left up the road, in the direction of the sea. With the heights above Galatas to their left, the Mediterranean lay before them, beyond Canea, shimmering in the sun, while in the bright blue skies above the swarm of black and green planes still circled. He watched the fighters going in, strafing the positions in Canea and Suda.

As they reached the outskirts of the little village of

Karatsos just to the east of Galatas, Lamb noticed the trees up ahead. Most of them had dead paratroops hanging from them, still strung up in their harnesses. As they passed, the Greeks spat up at them and shouted obscenities. Lamb's men said nothing, not wanting to invite the presence of death in their mockery. German, British, Commonwealth or Greek, there was still something universal about a dead soldier. Someone who must be honoured and respected, whoever he was. They averted their eyes. Before long they passed a troop of British artillery set out before their motorised quad transports on the right-hand side of the road. Lamb stopped and consulted his map.

'Right, we'll cut across country here. It's only about another mile and a half.' Walking through the fields and vineyards they crossed a small, meandering river and emerged on a road in the centre of Perivolia. Lamb turned to Bennett. 'As I remember, it's not far from here. If we keep going straight up this road we should hit it. We'll leave the Greeks here with Corporal Freeman and Corporal Stubbs.'

Lamb's instinct was right, and after another 1,000 yards they found themselves at a junction. It was damned lucky, he thought, that he had been here the previous night. He tried to recall the layout of the house and its grounds as best he could. The villa was arranged in the classic Italian fashion, in a curve around a courtyard. He called Eadie, Bennett and Hook towards him.

'The villa's up there, but it faces on to a narrow lane. There are two entrances. The main one, with an arch, goes into a yard. The entrance to the garden is through two wrought-iron gates. Careful how you go. They lead to a gravel path down the side of the house.'

He knew, from memory, that anyone in the house would be able to observe the courtyard and the formal gardens

186

to the rear, so they edged around the south side of the villa, shielded from view by the high stone walls which enclosed the formal gardens. He peered around the corner of the villa towards the arch. If the Germans had already taken the place they had not yet posted sentries, and there were none of the enemy in evidence. He stopped suddenly and listened. The noise of gunfire was coming from the garden. Lamb turned and waved the men on past him, Simmonds' section first and then his own HQ group, with Bennett, Stubbs and Turner, followed by the others, with Eadie's platoon following on behind. They made it along the road unopposed and reached the gate, outside which a large marble slab set into the wall bore the inscription 'Bella Campagna'.

Two of Simmonds' men were first through. There was no gunfire and Lamb moved them all on quickly into the gardens. They fanned out at speed, looking from side to side, as they advanced towards the rear of the house. Lamb looked up and glimpsed a face at one of the windows, topped with a German paratroop helmet. In a second his gun was up and firing into the window, shattering the pane. The man disappeared.

Hook spoke. 'Christ, that's torn it. Look out, sir.' From up ahead in the dark heart of the garden a stick grenade hurtled towards them. The men flung themselves away from it, into flower beds and across the neat lawn. There was a massive explosion followed by submachine-gun fire which raked across the grass and chopped into the trees. Lamb heard two men scream. He recognised Simmonds' voice. 'Shit, sir. I'm hit.' He dropped and began to moan.

Bennett spoke from his position behind a tall cypress tree. 'They've got Marks too, sir. He's dead.'

Lamb kept his head down as another burst of fire ripped across their path. 'Right, grenades.' He took a Mills bomb from his pocket, pulled the pin and held down the lever.

A count of four and he hurled it towards the gunfire, seeing it joined in the air by three others. Seconds later the garden exploded in a hail of shrapnel. As the blast lit up the foliage he caught sight of men and parts of men blown to pieces. There were screams from the bushes.

Lamb stood up and ran directly towards them. 'Come on.' Together the two platoons raced across the lawn towards the french windows at the back of the villa, Lamb and the two sergeants spraying the burning bushes and maimed men with fire from their Tommy guns. Lamb yelled behind him, 'Charles, clear the garden. Sarnt-Major, Sarnt Hook, with me. Inside.' Lamb kicked hard against the wood of the french windows and they splintered, shattering the glass panes. The doors fell open, and with Lamb leading the way the sixteen men entered the house. They found themselves, as he had thought they would, in the ground-floor morning room and were moving fast across it when the door on the other side flew open and three German paratroops burst in. In a split second one burst from one of the Germans' Schmeissers had ripped across Saunders' chest, with one of the bullets passing through his right arm to hit Griffin in the hand. At the same time Garner fired his Enfield from the hip and shot one of the Germans, a sergeant, in the groin, while Lamb and Bennett, squeezing the triggers of their Thompsons, hit the other two square on – not before one of them, though, had squeezed off a burst which flew across the room. One of the bullets smacked into the now dead body of Private Saunders, while another nicked Lamb on the forehead. He swore and put his hand up, feeling the warm blood. Lamb's bullets, angled high, got one man in the neck and face and flung him back out of the room while Bennett's rounds peppered the other man's chest and the door frame behind him. Instants later the room was a chaos of smoke, cordite, dead bodies and screaming wounded. With no time to deal with his own casualty, Lamb pushed over the dead Germans and moved into the hall, followed by the others. He looked right, Hook left, but there was no one to be seen. Ahead of him was a banister, the same one he had used last night to climb the staircase to the salon for drinks before dinner. It seemed surreal now, as he ran up the stairs.

He called behind, 'Sarnt-Major, stay down here with Corporal Simmonds' section. Rothman, Bunce, Grist, you lot, up here with me.' They took the stairs two at a time and hit the landing at a run. Upstairs the sound of gunfire came from the salon. Lamb turned and ran along the corridor and, without bothering to take cover and unaware of which of his men might be behind him, charged through the doorway into the room. It was all he could do to stop himself squeezing the trigger as he almost ran onto the outstretched bayonets of Michael Hathaway's batman and three of the Greeks. He pulled up. 'Don't shoot. Hathaway.' Across the room a man turned from where he had been firing from the window into the garden below.

Hathaway smiled. 'Just potting a few Jerries, Peter. Your lieutenant's doing a good job out there. It's been a bit hairy, mind you. Thank God you came. We'd never have got out. A truck arrived from Pendlebury but with only thirty rifles and barely enough ammo for them. I left most of my Greeks in Karatsos. Did you take many casualties? Oh, I say, you're hit.'

'Just a graze.' Lamb put his hand up and dabbed with a large, spotted handkerchief at the spot just above his right eyebrow where the bullet had gouged a furrow. He was bleeding profusely, but he had been lucky. 'Two dead, I think, and a few wounded. Plus anyone that Lieutenant Eadie's lost.'

'Well, at least we've got what we came for.'

'What you came for? Where? I thought we were saving the King.'

'No. He's still at the other house in Perivolia, unless they've moved him again. Didn't my man tell you? Jerry paratroopers were seen landing here, around the villa. I had a signal from Prince Peter to say that the King's state baubles and some vital paperwork of Tsouderos' had been left in the house when they moved to the new place. It was imperative that they be got out. That's why I sent for you. I knew you could do it.'

Hathaway opened a haversack at his feet and pulled out a large gold sceptre. Lamb looked at it, but he could not tell what it was and frankly he did not care. He just stared at Hathaway. 'Are you telling me that I've just lost at least two good men and had several others wounded, not to mention risked other lives, just to save a few pieces of tin?'

'Come off it, Peter. They're not exactly tin, are they? These are the King of Greece's bloody objects of state. They're irreplaceable. Part of the monarchy. You might say that without them in a way he ceases to be King of Greece. Don't you get it? What a coup that would have been for the Jerries. For Hitler. They've already declared a Greek republic and deposed the monarchy. This would have finished the job almost as well as killing the old man and his cousin. We had to get them back.'

Lamb shouted, 'Nonsense. He's the bloody King. This is just a load of old brass. It's you that doesn't get it. Christ, look at us. Two dead. Where's Eadie?' He yelled from the window above the staccato pop of random bursts of gunfire. 'Sarnt-Major.'

Hathaway was looking at the medals. 'Problem now is how to get them to him.'

Lamb turned. 'You are bloody joking, aren't you?'

''Fraid not, old boy. He can't govern without them.

190

Not that he's going to have much hope of doing that in the near future.'

'You're going to take the King's medals to him while men are fighting and dying here to save Crete from the Jerries?'

'No, you are. I've 400 Greeks to look after. You've only got a company. It's vital for Greek morale.'

Lamb was confused. Of course he already had an obligation to save the King, of which Hathaway was unaware, but the last few minutes had made up his mind that his duty to his men and the defence of the island must come first.

Now he boiled over. 'No, Hathaway. You're not going to do this to me. I left a platoon of my men on Pink Hill waiting to go into a counter-attack, as ordered by Colonel Kippenberger. Now, as if that wasn't against all the rules of war, you are asking me to take some crown jewels to a King who has just lost his throne. I won't do it, and you can't make me. You're not my superior.'

Hathaway looked down and stuffed the medals back into the haversack. 'Funny, I thought you were the man for the job. That's what the Prince reckoned. I'll do it, of course, but it'll leave my entire battalion leaderless, 600 men, at a time when we can use every man we can get.'

Lamb could see when he was being blackmailed. 'But you said yourself that the Greeks didn't have enough weapons. Only bayonets, you said.'

'Yes, I know, but they will soon. Once they've picked them up from the dead Jerries. Ammo too. They've dropped half of the weapons containers and supplies in our trenches. It won't be a problem. But if I'm not with them they'll just drift away again. And right now the Petrol Company needs them back at Pink Hill.'

Lamb knew when he was beaten. What was his meagre

company when set against Hathaway's battalion? If anyone was going to find the King, it would have to be him.

'All right, I'll take the bloody things. But before we find the King I'm going back to my men to execute that order. And then – if we survive this mad bloody counter-attack – I'll find the King and give him his sceptre and the rest.'

He turned to the door. 'Sarnt Hook, take this bag and keep it safe. The rest of you, come with me. Let's go and find the lieutenant.'

They made their way back down the staircase and out through the garden room. Lamb paused, bent down over the two dead Germans and the one wounded by Garner who had lost a huge amount of blood. His face was as white as a sheet. He whispered to Lamb, 'Wasser. Wasser, bitte.'

Lamb turned to Rothman. 'Find him a drink, will you. From the tap. Use anything.' Then he reached out to the man and prised his submachine-gun from his hands. It was slick with blood and Lamb took it and wiped it on one of the curtains. Then he returned to the two corpses and took their guns and did the same. As Rothman returned with the water for the dying German, Lamb laid out the three Schmeissers on the wicker table which stood at one end of the room. He picked up each in turn and inspected its mechanism, clicking off their safety catches, checking the barrels and clipping and unclipping the magazines. Then he slung one of the guns over his shoulder and gave the other two to Bunce.

'There you are, Bunce. Guard those with your life. See what ammo you can find on those two and the other stiffs upstairs. I'll check the garden.'

The garden smelt of death: cordite, charred wood and burnt flesh. The terrace on which Lamb had strolled with

Miranda Hartley the night before was now the resting place of two dead paratroopers, lying in a spreading pool of their own blood, while a third, fourth and fifth, caught in the blast from the grenades, lay mutilated below the charred branches of an almond tree. Two more of them, badly wounded, had crawled off and died beneath a tamarind. Eadie had done well, and Lamb congratulated him. Not only had he cleared the place of Germans in a matter of minutes, he had not lost a single man. Carter had been wounded in the arm and sent off to No. 7 Field Hospital, along with Corporal Simmonds and Griffin, and Eadie himself had been dealt a glancing blow from a bullet on the shin, but the bleeding had stopped and he could walk. Hathaway, sensing that Lamb had nothing more to say to him, made off for Karatsos with his Greeks, while Lamb, having picked up his own irregulars on the main road, detailed Corporal Hale and a dozen Greeks to bury the dead and follow on and led his men away down the Canea–Alykianou road, back towards Pink Hill.

He walked in silence, still fuming at Hathaway's behaviour. They travelled as quickly as they could, keeping an eye out all the time for any rogue paratroops, but all that they met were dead. They lay at the roadside in crumpled heaps, often missing their boots, looted by Allied troops, or entangled in their parachutes where they had fallen, dead before impact. Lamb felt in poor spirits and walked on next to Bennett, saying nothing, but the Greeks were full of the victory at the villa and insisted on singing.

As they neared Pink Hill, though, Lamb sensed that something had changed. Climbing back up the slopes, he struggled to find their original trenches and realised they were empty. The hill was almost entirely silent, save for a first-aid post in the New Zealand lines off to the right. He scrambled up the hill to a vantage point and looked out towards the prison, and there in the valley he saw what he had feared. The valley was filled with columns of smoke and where before there had been trees were now stumps, and among them dozens of bodies.

'Jesus, no.'

Through the half-light Lamb saw a party of men coming towards him slowly, up the hill. Sergeant Mays was walking at the head of a mass of walking wounded, his men and Greeks, while behind them came the others. Mays was holding his right arm, which was bleeding, and he had a deep gash across his forehead.

'Mays, what in heaven's name's happened? Where's Mr Wentworth?'

'Thank God you're here, sir. Major Basset came to find you. From the colonel. Told Mr Wentworth the enemy were making a landing ground by the prison, to bring in reinforcements by plane. Said we needed more men to press home a counter-attack, and wondered where you had gone. Then the tanks arrived and began to move down the valley with some of the New Zealand lads. Mr Wentworth just got up and said, "Come on, let's go." It was bloody murder, sir. For them and us. Never seen nothing like it. We moved down the hill just as it was getting dark. We kept finding paratroops in holes. They just opened fire on us. We'd go on for a bit and another would fire and then we'd get him. It was bloody hard going, but we mopped them up. I think we killed about twenty of the buggers. But we lost some men too, sir. I suppose we were about 800 yards north of the prison when this Kiwi officer came up and told us to dig in. Mr Wentworth asked him why, and the officer said we would carry on in the morning. Didn't make sense, sir. We knew we'd be pinned down. Then one of the tanks got hit, square on, just blew up. And that was when Mr Wentworth copped it too.' He dropped his eyes.

'He's dead?'

194

'Yes, sir. Hit by a mortar.'

'Who else?'

'Same blast got Corporal Vincent. Smithy lost his leg. Then there was Davies, Maggs and Corrie, and about a dozen of the Greeks. We've got a few wounded, sir, and Corporal Hughes is hurt pretty bad.'

Lamb cursed. 'Well done, Mays. Get yourself to the MO.'

He had known he shouldn't leave them, but he'd thought Wentworth would wait for his return. He should have known the lad would want to go. The attack had been ludicrous and badly mismanaged. But what could he say to Bassett or the colonel? He was the one in the wrong. He had effectively disobeyed an order and had not been there when required. Wentworth's death, and those of his men, had been no one's fault but his.

11

Wednesday 21 May dawned as it always did, under a cloudless sky. In the trenches the men stretched and scratched and spat and tried to find water with which to wash their faces and swill out parched mouths. They scraped together what food they could and took a swig from half-empty canteens. Then they turned, as refreshed as they could be, to face another day.

Lamb, however, was far from refreshed. It had been a sleepless night. He had posted sentries around the trenches but had been unable to find any rest himself. His mind had been filled with the image of endless parachutes coming down and the imagined vision of poor Hugh Wentworth and his men, sacrificed for nothing, as far as he could see. He saw Hathaway's haversack close by in the trench and wondered what new horrors and follies the coming day would bring. He had no idea, either, what had become of Anna, whether she might even still be alive. Perhaps, he thought, he might contrive to get to Galatas somehow and find out, although he also wondered how, in the light of yesterday's débâcle, he would ever extricate himself from the trenches. He knew, though, that he would have to do so. There was the urgent need to find the King. Perhaps he too was dead. Half of him still considered it a pointless mission, even though he had been ordered to do so by Colonel 'R' in Athens. Things had changed since then, hadn't they?

It was plain to Lamb that they would be better to remain with the Petrol Company and defend the hill against the inevitable German attack, but he knew Hathaway had passed him a poisoned chalice and that, given his original orders, there was nothing he could do to avoid at least attempting to find King George. The medals and the papers must be returned to their owners, otherwise Lamb was well aware he might find himself in deeper trouble than he evidently was in already.

Reports had come in throughout the night, and as the men began to stir and think of breakfast Eadie approached him. 'Situation stable, sir. Has been all night.'

'Good.'

'Shame about Hugh, sir.'

'Yes, it is a bloody shame. Just too bad. What's the sitrep with the Kiwis?'

'The Petrol Company's back in its own lines, sir. The enemy's gone from the bottom of the hill. Just pulled out. Back in the cemetery, according to the patrols.'

'That's something. You're looking tired, Charles. Bearing up?'

'I'll manage, sir. At least I'm still here.'

It was not intended to be a pointed remark. Charles Eadie had the greatest respect for his commanding officer. But Lamb felt the words prick his conscience. It had been his fault, he was sure, that Wentworth had died. He looked at Eadie and saw no hint of malice, but still the comment had done its work.

'I should keep the men on the alert. Something's sure to boil up.'

As Eadie returned to his trench, Smart poured a kettle of hot water into a tin bowl and Lamb tried shaving, using a blade that had seen better days and a piece of cracked mirror glass as a guide. Smart was an adept scrounger and Lamb wondered from which bar he had liberated the mirror. He splashed water on his newly smooth face and instantly felt better for it.

Smart presented him with a cup of tea.

'Thank you.' Lamb took a sip and dried his face, dabbing at the two inevitable cuts made by the razor. 'Sarnt-Major.'

Bennett doubled over to him. 'Sir.'

'I need a proper situation report. Everything. Status, numbers, dispositions and ammo. As soon as you like, Sarnt-Major.'

'Sir.'

'Smart, I don't suppose for a minute you've anything on that bloody WT?'

'No, sir, not for days. Reckon it's all them mountains, sir. Never had this in the desert, sir, but this island's different. Blooming great mountains all over the shop.'

Lamb wished he knew the situation in other parts of the island, and also wondered what the plans were for a possible evacuation, should the Germans succeed in taking the island. He was considering sending out a runner to General Freyberg's HQ at Canea, or at least seeing if he could discover what Kippenberger thought, when a Greek boy in his early teens came bounding through the olive grove from the north. Lamb recognised him as being from Galatas. 'Kapitan Lamb, Kapitan Lamb.'

Lamb called hello to him. 'Yasou. Over here.'

The boy smiled at him and Lamb knew him at once. 'Yasou, Kapitan Lamb. I come from my sister, Anna Levandakis. She says to tell you she is safe. Do not worry.' The boy smiled again as he saw that Lamb understood.

'Thank you. Tell her I am safe also.' The boy saw the bandage on Lamb's head and pointed at it with a frown.

Lamb shook his head. 'It's nothing, Andreas. It's just a scratch. Don't tell your sister.' The boy smiled again, nodded and ran back into the olive trees towards the village.

That at least, thought Lamb, was a relief. But while Anna might think she was safe, there was surely no guarantee of it. The dead paratroopers by the roadside on their way to Perivolia, not to mention the battle in the villa, had been proof that the enemy could be anywhere. He buttoned his shirt, walked over to the command trench and found a map. Carefully peeling back its almost ripped folds, he tried to work out where the enemy might have planned to drop. Clearly the prison at Agya was a key objective, but so, it seemed, was Canea and the heights where they now were above Galatas. He presumed the drop would not have been localised. There would have been other, similar assaults across the island, many dozens of them, probably, judging from the number of planes in the sky yesterday. There must now, he surmised, be similar fights to this one at Pink Hill going on at Heraklion and Maleme, for control of the airfields. Pendlebury would be in his element now. Bandouvas too, he thought, must have mobilised his men, and Lamb wondered where they would be. He would have been glad of their presence alongside his own. His principal concern, though, was the whereabouts of the King. Hathaway had not given him a clue as to where he might be, and Lamb cursed his own pride for not having asked him what if anything he knew.

He saw Bassett hurrying through the trees towards him. The major looked weary and flustered. 'Captain Lamb, a word if you will.'

Lamb walked across to the major, who had stopped in the shade of an olive tree. He looked at Lamb and rubbed at his red-rimmed eyes. Then he began. 'Captain Lamb, will you kindly explain to me what the bloody hell you thought you were doing leaving your post? Particularly after you had received an order telling you to expect to counter-attack at any moment?'

'I'm sorry, sir. I had another request to reinforce a position to the rear, at Perivolia. It was under attack, sir.'

'That's no reason to desert your own position. What position at Perivolia? Who gave you the order?'

'Captain Hathaway, sir.'

'Hathaway? Dammit, Lamb, Hathaway's only a captain like you, man. Why did you take an order from him? Are you trying to be funny, Lamb?'

'No, sir. Not at all. It was the King's house, sir. The King of Greece. Captain Hathaway led me to believe that the King of Greece was in danger. I took two platoons of my men to save him.'

'And was he? Was the King in danger? Did you save him?'

Lamb paused. 'No, sir. He wasn't. We didn't.'

Bassett shook his head. 'No. And I'll bet he wasn't even there.'

'Sir.'

'Christ, Lamb. I took you for a bloody good officer. God knows you're brave enough. But this time you've been a bloody fool. It'll have to go down in the Brigade order book, you know. You might be in the British army and not the New Zealand, but here you're attached to us, and under our orders. If we get away from this lot I dare say you'll still be in trouble, Lamb. Do you understand what I'm saying?'

'Yes, sir. Perfectly.'

Lamb was about to mention the fact that he was on a mission from Colonel 'R', but experience had taught him that in such a situation, with an officer in the field, he was unlikely to be believed. He let the major go on.

'Good. Right. Well, now I'm giving you some advice, and you'd do well to take it. Stick where you are, Captain. God knows what they're going to throw at us today. But when they do, you and your men are surely going to be on the receiving end. And you're going to stop them.'

However, the Germans did not attack again, not for the entire day. For a couple of hours Lamb sat in the command trench and at the table behind the wall and walked through the olives checking on his positions and thought about everything that had happened since he had arrived on Crete. The sun beat down on them and he had sent a man to try to get through to the transit camp and find some fresh water. But that had been four hours ago and the runner hadn't returned. The men had spent the morning on watch, playing cards and snatching some sleep when they could.

Valentine had cracked a few jokes. 'I suppose you could called it a "sitzkrieg", sir. Couldn't you? They don't seem to want to do anything.' He seemed in a particularly sombre mood and Lamb knew he was dwelling on something. Finally it came out, almost as a casual remark.

'Doesn't seem right, sir, does it? Mr Wentworth dying like that 'cos we weren't here. Not as if we were doing anything useful either. Just off to save the King.'

Lamb said nothing.

'I mean, what use is a king without a kingdom? Better off forgetting him, I say. What earthly good have kings ever done for their people?'

Still Lamb refused to be drawn. He turned to Smart. 'I'm sure they'll attack soon enough. Eh, Smart? That's it. Always good to face the enemy with shiny shoes.'

The men who were within earshot laughed. 'We'd better make the most of this. It won't last forever.'

Sure enough, within the hour the Germans had begun

to mortar the slopes of Pink Hill from their positions on Cemetery Hill.

The shells whooshed in and landed with a sickening crump, and wherever they landed, almost without fail, someone screamed. Mays was beside Lamb at the forward OP. 'Blooming heck, sir. How much ammo did they bring with them?'

'Enough. And it's my guess they've a great deal more.'

A mortar round came over their heads and landed to the left in a trench. There was an explosion followed by screams. Lamb yelled, 'Stretcher-bearers,' but he knew there were precious few of them around. 'Medic. Get a medic.'

He scuttled over, head down in the hail of missiles, reached the scene and almost vomited. Two of his men, Webb and Lyne from Wilkinson's section, were lying in the bottom of the trench in a pool of their own blood. One of them had had his head practically severed by a piece of shrapnel. The other, Lyne, had lost his forearm and been blinded. He was screaming, high and long. Corporal Wilkinson himself was sitting on the edge of the trench into which he had been climbing when the round had hit. He was looking at a hole in his stomach from which his entrails were protruding and trying to stuff them back in.

Lamb yelled again, 'Medic.' Two Kiwis came dodging through the falling tree branches which were being severed by more incoming rounds. Between them they carried a makeshift stretcher of a door of a house. It was covered with dried blood.

Lamb turned back and hurried into the command trench. Gradually the shelling ceased, to be replaced by the moans of the wounded.

Bennett had given him the casualty figures. They had been down to twenty-two men before this, including himself.

Plus the Greeks, but they'd lost twelve of them, perhaps more. Well, you could add a few more to the tally now. Wentworth was dead and with him Hale, who had come with them through France. And now Wilkinson, another French veteran, and the two privates. Lamb knew there would be more. He waited for the reports.

'All secure, Sarnt-Major?'

'Yes, sir. Perimeter's tight now, sir. We took five more casualties, sir. Lyne and Webb . . .'

'Yes, I saw them. And Corporal Wilkinson.'

Bennett looked at him and shook his head. 'Yes, sir. And two of the new lads from Cross' section, Waterman and Butcher. And some of the Greeks, sir, but I couldn't tell you how many.'

'So we must be down to seventeen of us now, Sarnt-Major. That's too bad. Some bloody Company.'

Bennett shook his head and lit a smoke. He had seen his officer getting a dressing down from the Kiwi major, and he resented it. And now this.

That had been no way for the major to treat Captain Lamb. In Bennett's eyes he was an exemplary officer. One of the best. The men would have followed him anywhere. For that jumped-up New Zealander to have ripped him off a strip was just wrong, however you looked at it. Yes, they had gone off on a wild goose chase, but how, he asked himself, had the captain been able to know that? Captain Hathaway had seemed sound enough to him too, and Bennett prided himself on being a good judge of officers. At least they had killed a few Jerries, and hadn't they got what Hathaway had been looking for? Lamb was being too hard on himself. And it hadn't been his fault about poor Mr Wentworth. Bennett had thought that boy was marked from the start, had just been waiting for the moment to come. Old soldiers could see that sometimes. You just knew.

Bennett himself was getting restless. Being shelled and mortared was worse than being in the thick of it, and the lull between made you think too much. He kept on wondering about those things that never crossed your mind when you were in combat: his wife, Vera, expecting their first, at home in London; the poor bloody German kids strung up in their parachutes; and, worst of all, whether he would make it out of this lot and ever see Blighty and Vera again. He wondered if he would ever see his own child.

He turned to Lamb. 'I really thought they'd try again, sir. I don't like it. What's Jerry playing at?'

'That's just it, Sarnt-Major. He's not really playing at anything. Apart from the fact that you might say they're playing with us.'

'But they're not giving up, sir, are they? They're just getting ready to come again. Do you think we'll hold them? With this lot?'

'Yes, Sarnt-Major, I do, and I'm sure you do too. But I'm not sure I know what we would gain. We might have won the day. We took back the hill and knocked out some guns and mortars, but think about the bigger battle. The Jerries have got time on their side. Stands to reason. They've landed more men today, and I dare say more supplies and heavy weapons, and if they carry on doing that then eventually they'll outnumber us and outgun us.'

'All we can do is pray for a miracle. That, or more reinforcements to allow us to mount a proper counter-attack.'

Bennett changed the subject. 'Did you see Colonel Kippenberger today, sir? Walking around the top of the hill, sir, bold as brass, carrying that captured Schmeisser of his. Just like yours, sir. He was just talking, sir. Talking to the men. Now that's an officer for you. That's the way to do it.'

'Yes, he's a real leader. Makes a difference to the men. With a man like that to lead them they think they are indestructible.'

'Let's hope the Jerries think so too, sir.'

Lamb looked at the ground for a moment. 'Tell me, what would you do, Sarnt-Major?'

'Sir?'

'You know the score. In that canvas bag over there are some bits of tin and pieces of paper that somehow I've got to make sure get to His Majesty the King of Greece. But how can I do that when I've been ordered to stay here and fight?'

'That's a hard one on you, sir, and no mistake. As I see it, both ways you lose.'

Lamb shook his head. 'There's sure to be an answer somewhere. I've just got to find it, and soon. One thing I will tell you, Sarnt-Major. I'm damned if I'm going to sit here on my arse for days and then find that the battle's been lost and we're all in the bag.'

The night was warm and Lamb lay propped up against his kit bag and the King's haversack. The cicadas seemed noisier than ever, and a barn owl was obviously high in one of the nearby trees, calling for its mate which answered at intervals throughout the night. He could also hear the men in the trenches around him as they snored and mumbled through the small hours. Of course he had not been able to take Bennett into his full confidence, but just to have told him about the fact that he was torn between delivering the King's medals and fighting on here had helped. He drifted in and out of sleep, troubled by dreams in which Wentworth's face kept appearing. He was aware of the change of sentries and then of the dawn coming up on the hills over to the right, and beyond them the towering mass of the mountains. Finally he fell into a good, deep sleep, but it seemed only minutes before Smart's hand was on his shoulder.

'Sir. Captain Lamb, sir. Nice cup of tea for you?'

Lamb muttered his thanks and took the mug in both hands. His neck and back both ached, and he peered at the landscape down the hill. There was nothing to be seen but the interminable vineyards. Far down in the valley, though, there was ant-like movement going on as men moved around, and he guessed it was the Germans standing to. He looked at his watch. It was 6.30. Around him the men were beginning to stir. The last sentries of the night had come in and reported no movement. But Lamb knew they could not afford to sit it out for another day. If the Germans did not mount another assault on the hill it was inevitable that he and his men, along with the other defenders, must sally out of their trenches and counter-attack. He had still not resolved his dilemma and he half hoped that the attack in which they must be involved might come sooner rather than later and remove the problem.

Smart bought him some shaving water. 'Here you are, sir. Mr Eadie says could he have it after you and to tell you he'll be using it to wash in too. Just so you know. Have you heard, sir? The Kiwis have cancelled the attack from the forward position. 19th Battalion.'

'What?'

'The attack they postponed from last night, sir, where Mr Wentworth was killed. They've stopped the attack. They're pulling everyone back.'

'Where did you get this?'

'Batman of one of their officers, sir. He keeps me up to date.'

So he was right. And poor Wentworth, too. It had been madness to entrench down there, so close to the enemy lines.

*   *   *

206

Behind him, from around Canea, he heard the sound of explosions now as the Luftwaffe launched another raid. How very different it would have been, he thought, had the RAF managed to maintain a presence on the island. But they were long gone. The planes that had not been shot out of the skies or destroyed on the ground were shipped off to Malta and Cyprus by night to keep them intact for whatever came next.

He had just finished a meagre breakfast of corned beef and biscuit when Charles Eadie came up. 'Message from the colonel, sir. We're going to attack.'

'When? What on earth with?'

'Says we've got to kick them off Cemetery Hill before they do worse to us with the mortars than they did yesterday. I suppose he has a point, sir. That was merry hell.'

Lamb rubbed at his tired face, then looked up at Eadie. 'Well, thank God for that, Charles. At least we'll have a chance to make a difference. I suppose we must outnumber them still. They can't have flown any reinforcements in yet, can they? I just hope they haven't got all their heavy weapons, though on yesterday's showing they must have a good deal.'

He reached out and grabbed hold of the Schmeisser he had taken from the dead German. It was a lovely weapon, in good condition. Lamb had managed to get a handful of magazine clips from Bunce and had stuffed them into his battledress pockets. He was sure that when the time came it would do the job. And it pleased his sense of irony that the Germans would be killed by their own beautifully made weapon. He looked back at Eadie, whom he noticed had also appropriated a similar submachine-gun, which he wore slung around his neck.

'Of course, Charles, we do have right on our side.'

'But you know as well as I do, sir, that no amount of

'right" will do us any good against an 81 mill mortar and a nest of MG34s.'

'Talking of which, how are we doing with salvaged weapons? I see you've got yourself one of these.' He patted his gun.

'Yes, sir. Managed to pick it up in the garden back at the King's villa. Very nice, aren't they? Actually, we're not doing too badly at all, sir. We managed to get two whole canisters of Jerry weapons. That's six heavy machine-guns and a couple of the smaller mortars. There's a reasonable amount of ammo with them too. Very considerate of the Jerries, to drop it in our laps.'

'Yes, very. Charles, I'm going to give command of Hugh's platoon to Mays. He deserves it, and he's one of the best I've got, but that will have to wait until he gets back from the Field Hospital. Who d'you think I should give it to in the meantime?'

'Well, I'd say the sarnt-major, sir, but we can't really spare him. What about Valentine?'

'What, and cause a bloody riot? He'd refuse.'

'It would be a battlefield order. He wouldn't dare.'

'Are you so sure?'

'Hook, then. It would mean moving him from No. 3 platoon, of course.'

'And replace him with Simmonds? Yes, it might work. Thank you, Charles. Most helpful.'

There was a shout from the sentry to their right. 'Runner coming in, sir.'

The man, a New Zealand lance-corporal, came leaping into their position and blurted out a breathless message.

'From Major Bassett, sir. He says would you support Captain Hathaway and provide the left wing of the attack. The captain has the 6th Greek on his right, all fully armed, and he's leading his own Greeks in the centre. The major needs you on the left, sir.'

208

Lamb paused for a moment, counted to ten, then spoke. 'Yes, Lance-Corporal. You can tell the major that I'll be there. We'll support the left flank. When does he intend to go?'

'He'll give the command by whistle, sir. But H Hour is at 1 p.m.'

'Fine. We'll be waiting.'

Whistle signals, thought Lamb. He reached into his top pocket and pulled out his own silver tin whistle. Right. They would see what the Greeks had learnt over the past couple of weeks. He would do the same in the attack.

The runner turned and ran back the way he had come.

Lamb turned to Eadie. 'Well, 1300 hours it is, then. Had some breakfast?'

'Just got in from the forward post, sir.'

'Of course. See what Smart can find you. Better be quick. We don't want to miss the party, do we? Oh, and by the way, pass the word. I'll be using whistle signals.'

Valentine came with a message for Eadie, something about a jammed gun, and after the lieutenant had gone to deal with it and scrounge whatever food he could, he turned to Lamb.

'Are we attacking then, sir?'

'Yes. We go in at 1300. We're on the left. Captain Hathaway's Greeks will be on our right.'

Valentine smiled. 'That man's got a way with him, wouldn't you say, sir?'

'Yes, Valentine, you could say that.'

Lamb knew that Valentine had immediately sensed his annoyance that Hathaway and his rabble were taking centre stage in the attack. How he had managed to pull that off, God only knew, but there it was. Hathaway would lead the attack, and good luck to him. It irked Lamb that they should have fallen out. Lamb had liked the man at first, had thought he had seen in him a soldier like himself, a man willing to bend the rule book when necessary and to use real initiative, but the business at the villa had soured their relationship. Now, however, he most definitely saw him as a creature of two parts. On the one hand he was undoubtedly brave; on the other he was ruthlessly ambitious and eager to cover himself in glory at another man's expense, even if his actions were to threaten that other man's credibility as an officer and mean his ruination as a soldier. Now, though, was no time for spite, or for awkward questions.

12

Lamb looked at his watch. Three minutes to H hour.

Bennett snapped to beside him. 'Men are standing to, sir.'

They were on the start line, if you could have called it that. A line had been taken along the lead trenches, and Lamb's men with their Greeks were standing loosely where it ran. They held their rifles at the ready and looked, he thought, as had any line of infantry about to go into battle for the past 300 years. He was damn sure they felt that way, because he certainly did.

He did not think the Germans were yet aware of what was about to hit them. Their mortars had not yet started up, though he knew they would feel their bite when at last they began to advance.

The line seemed to go perfectly silent for an instant, and then from just to their right and rear a whistle blew three times, then a fourth, and then again very fast, and at the same time from their right the ground seemed to erupt. Dozens of Greek troops seemed to rise from nowhere, and with them, to Lamb's initial surprise, came civilians, scores of them.

At their head walked Hathaway, dressed as before in

his yellow jersey and with his tin whistle in his mouth. He blew it, and from among Lamb's men someone spoke as they moved off to the attack.

'Blimey, it's the bleedin' Pied Piper.'

'Shut it, Dawlish.'

'Sorry, Sarge.'

Perhaps even more bizarre a sight than Hathaway himself were the band that followed on behind him. Their core was provided by half of the 6th Greeks, but this was supplemented in number by civilians. A Greek farmer in a shirt, waistcoat and boots advanced down the hill brandishing a shotgun on to which he had tied a serrated-edged bread knife. Behind him came a woman wrapped in a black shawl, waving above her head a huge garden spade. Another man held a pitchfork, and behind him Lamb saw an Orthodox monk in a flowing robe, armed with a rifle and an axe tucked into his broad belt. Others had whatever knives, rocks and clubs they had been able to find in the rush to get to the Germans. There were young boys with game guns and a man in a business suit, tieless and carrying a scythe.

Hathaway suddenly broke into a run and gave another long blast on the whistle before dropping it from his mouth and letting it hang from his neck on a ribbon. The Greeks were hot on his heels, waving and shouting. Lamb yelled at his men. 'Forward the Jackals. Up and at 'em.' He put the whistle in his mouth and gave a blow. Four short blasts, four more, then again and again and then two short and a long.

As one, what was left of the three platoons of C Company, plus their Greek additions, ran to the left and slightly behind Hathaway's battalion towards the German positions. Over on the far right he could see the long lines of the advancing New Zealand infantry of 19 Battalion.

212

Lamb let the whistle drop around his neck on its lanyard and began to yell – a long war cry, the sort he had been taught in training. It just seemed to come. And now he could hear it being taken up by the others. The Greeks were shouting too, as Hathaway had encouraged them to do, a short war cry he had taught them. They could see the Germans ahead now, some behind a low white stone wall which they were using as a defensive parapet. There was a burst of machine-gun fire from the wall and Lamb saw men go down to his left and on his right, among them several of the civilians. Women were falling as well, and for an instant he half thought that Anna might be among them. But Hathaway was still there, godlike at their head. He was walking forward now, firing his pistol as he went, deliberately, choosing his targets with care, oblivious it seemed to the bullets flying past his head.

Lamb scudded down the slope, sending clods of parched yellow earth flying, and when he was about fifty yards from the enemy he pointed the Schmeisser and gently squeezed the trigger. The gun fired, a stream of bullets shot out from the muzzle and cut into two of Germans behind the wall who had their rifles raised towards Lamb. He saw them fall, the shots ripping into them, and then he turned the gun slightly to the left and sprayed another burst with similar effect at an officer and a sergeant, ripping into them with staccato dots of lead and throwing them back like hideous marionettes. His men were hurling grenades now and he was aware of Hathaway's group in the centre closing on the wall, ready for a mêlée. Christ, thought Lamb, this is going to get very messy. The men behind the wall seemed on closer inspection to be no more than boys, but they were still tall and fit and well trained. He did not give much for the Greeks' chances.

And then the miracle happened.

In the centre of the enemy line, as he watched, awestruck, a green-grey form jumped up, turned and ran. After ten yards the man threw down his pack and, faster now, ran for his life. He was followed by another, and then another. The Germans were running away from them! The first of the New Zealanders had hit the parapet now, and other Germans were raising their hands in surrender. Now all along the line he could see men in grey running or surrendering. He called to his own men, who had now reached the wall.

'Don't shoot them, but be careful they don't try anything. Sarnt-Major, leave the Greeks to guard them. And Hobdell and Corporal Stubbs, come on. Follow up, they're running. Don't let them get away.'

The men were whooping now, with the Greeks firing random bursts. Bennett yelled at the charging mass, 'Hold your bloody fire. Save the ammo. Jesus Christ.'

It was of little use. Lamb knew that when the blood was up and your enemy in retreat, saving ammunition was the last thought on your mind.

He pulled up. Found Smart and Turner. 'Corporal, take a message to Colonel Kippenberger. Cemetery Hill retaken. Enemy in retreat. That should do it.'

But Lamb knew as well as the next man that they could not remain in possession of the hill, exposed as it was in front of their lines. They might have helped push the enemy from its summit and brought about a respite from the shelling, but now they would have to retire back to Pink Hill. Perhaps further.

And then they would have to secure their position.

He was just wondering how on earth you did such a thing when your enemy was on all sides when Major Bassett appeared, with the repetitive predictability of the angel of death and looking just about as happy.

'Captain Lamb.'

214

'Sir?'

'Well done back there, Lamb. Damn good show. I knew you had it in you. This is the battle, man. Well done.'

Lamb resented being addressed like some green second lieutenant, but said nothing. 'Thank you, sir.'

Bassett's face looked grave. 'Right. Here's the gen. 10th Brigade has effectively ceased to exist. We're now 4th Brigade. Colonel Kippenberger still commands, but you are now under Major Russell, along with the Greeks and the Petrol Company. Take your orders directly from Major Russell.'

'May I ask, sir, where Captain Hathaway might be?'

'Hathaway's in Galatas with his Greeks – on the eastern side at Colonel Kippenberger's new HQ. He's still brigaded with us, though. Good luck, Lamb.'

'Yes, sir. I expect we might need it.'

Bennett had been standing just behind Lamb and had heard everything. 'What now, sir?'

'Now, Sarnt-Major, we sit here and await new orders from our new commander.'

So again they waited, and their patience was rewarded. It was a quiet morning. Well, as quiet as it could be with the bombers over Canea. As far as Lamb's men were concerned there were no air-raids and the enemy only shelled them once. At 2 p.m. there was a signal from Major Russell, delivered by runner. Lamb read it to Eadie.

'The Jerries have taken Ruin Hill. Seems they just walked up there and now it looks as though they can lay down fire on any of us. We're to fall back on Galatas and hold a line across the west of the village. And we're to expect an attack.'

Lamb had been here before. He had disobeyed an order from a superior and come damn near to being court-martialled. Then he had had a mission with the objective

215

of saving thousands of men trapped in France. Now, though, he only needed to save one man. He knew it was vital, but something in him could not abandon his position. He had seen the faces of the men and knew what would happen if he withdrew his company, even though it might only be some thirty strong. The new order was the final decision-maker. He would stay and fight, and then and only then would he lead his men to find the King.

'Sarnt-Major.'

'Sir?'

'You recall what I was saying to you earlier on about the King of Greece and his pieces of tin.'

'Sir.'

'Forget it. We stay. We're going to hold this line and deny the village to the enemy. No Jerry's going to sit down and put his feet up in my bloody café.'

Wilhelm Sussmann stopped in his tracks beneath the olive trees, threw himself to the ground and lay as still as he could manage. He could hear his heart pounding in his head and thought they must hear it too – the soldiers out there, in the vines. He heard them calling in their strange accent. Made out words: 'Jerry', 'Para' and others. He would lie here until they passed. They were yards away now, a group of them, spread out in line.

He had been able to recognise the terrain for the past half hour – the big hill to the right and, beyond it, the town of Canea. The road before him was as clear as day. He had finally made it to his objective.

Sussmann steadied himself and shuffled down the slope. He could see the house below and had heard the sound of gunfire. Ahead of him in the undergrowth he could make out moving shapes, helmeted figures, but the shapes of their helmets stopped his heart from racing. Slowly, not wishing to alarm them, Sussmann climbed down the hill until he was no more than a few paces away from their backs. He thought of the best word with which to announce his presence.

'Sieg Heil.'

The two men turned, both with levelled machine-pistols. Then the bigger one spoke and pushed the barrel of his comrade's weapon down towards the ground. 'Christ, sir. I mean, General.'

'Who are you?'

'7th Company, 2nd Battalion, 3rd Fallschirmjäger, sir.'

'You're more than two kilometres off your drop zone. Has it taken you two days to get here? Where are the rest of you?'

'It was dreadful, sir. They shot us as we were coming down. Half the men were killed. They're still hanging on the trees, sir. Some came down in flames. It was terrible, sir.'

Sussmann said nothing. Then, 'Where are the enemy? How many of them are there?'

The other man spoke. 'They're everywhere, sir. More than we thought too. Much more.'

There was another noise from the left. Voices in German, and two more paratroops came through the vines. They stopped dead.

Sussmann smiled and spoke. 'Major Derpa.'

'Good God, General. Sir, we thought you were dead.'

Sussmann shrugged. 'Yes, so did I – for a while.'

'But your glider crashed, sir. The pilots saw it go down with everyone on board.'

'Not quite everyone, Major. I am here now, am I not? Tell me, what's your situation? I want everything. What's the sitrep on the landings? How many men have you managed to collect? Do we have heavy weapons? What about the other containers?'

Derpa shook his head. 'Not good, sir. Not good at all. It all hangs on that little pink hill and the heights above Galatas and the village.'

'I know that. That was in the plans. What else?'

'Lieutenant Neuhoff led an attack on the first day, but his company was wiped out. We didn't take Maleme or Canea. That was the first day. We had no contact with Colonel Sturm at Rethymno, then yesterday they counter-attacked. Tanks too. We tried to take back the hill with the cemetery on it but every time we took it they just wiped us off it. We took a lot of casualties, sir. But then they just stopped, sir.'

'What?'

'They didn't follow up. I don't know why, but it saved our bacon.'

'So how many do you have?'

'I . . . I'm not quite certain, sir.'

'Jesus, Derpa. You must have an idea.'

Derpa fidgeted and looked exasperated. The last thing he wanted at this moment was his commander-in-chief – whom he had thought dead – tearing him off a strip.

'It's very difficult to keep track of where anyone is here, sir. And at night the civilians sneak in and kill the sentries. We've lost two men every night. Throats cut. One of the men was beheaded.'

'Beheaded?'

'Yes, sir. They're savages here. We really didn't expect this.'

Sussmann bit his lip. No. Even he had not expected such stuff. Until they had received the last message from the agent on the island, last night. Then he had felt a fear in the pit of his stomach and had realised this would be a battle like no other the German war machine had fought to date. France had fallen, its people surrendering with war-weary readiness. The Greeks had put up a fight. He had known they would; Sussmann had studied the

218

Classics and respected the ancient Greeks, the victors of Marathon and Salamis, and he saw no reason to suppose their descendants would be any less warlike. His brother officers, of course, had not agreed, but then they were Nazis for the most part and unlike him believed in the absolute superiority of the Aryan race. Sussmann was not so sure. Of course the German army was superb, probably the best in the world, but there was no room for complacency. And now it seemed his worst fears had been realised.

This was something new. Even the spy's message had not warned them of such savagery.

'Where's Colonel Heidrich?'

'His HQ is in the prison down there, sir. It's a good defensive position, and the idiot Tommies didn't even garrison it.'

'And what now?'

'We're going to attack, sir. That's the colonel's plan at least. He's formed a new battlegroup from 3 Battalion and the Engineers under Major Heilmann.'

Heidrich had responded well to his new responsibility.

'Good. That's no less than I'd have expected from him. Right. You two, find me a cup of coffee, for God's sake. The real stuff. Good and strong.'

He waited until the others were busy and then turned back to the major.

'Derpa, one thing. From what I can see it's a fiasco. But what about the other thing? Where's the King? And don't tell me he's got away. This is the Führer's personal mission. Remember? Who's down there in the villa?'

'We don't know, sir. We think the King has got away but we can't be sure. He may still be there. There was a big fight there two days ago. We lost some men.'

Sussmann thought for a moment. 'Right. First things first, Derpa. First we attack the hill and take the village, and then we get the King. It's the Führer's orders, but I'm a soldier first. We're here to take this bloody island. We're Fallschirmjäger. We have a reputation to defend. I don't want Ringel and his damn mountain men to claim all the glory. That's not to say my mission is compromised, but you know I really feel like killing some of those Tommies and those bastard Greeks who butchered my boys. We'll make them pay, eh, Derpa? Now, where's that coffee?'

On Pink Hill dusk came down fast, and Lamb's men dug in for the night. For once Lamb managed to sleep, but towards dawn he was awoken by voices. He looked up, grabbing his gun in alarm, but saw that the noise was coming from groups of New Zealand infantry who were walking into the position from the west. Lamb climbed out of the trench which had been his bed and found one of their officers, a thin lieutenant who looked utterly done in.

'What's happening? Who are you? Where are you from?'

The man stared at him, hollow-eyed. '20th Battalion. We were up at Maleme. It was like bloody hell up there, sir. There's thousands of Jerries up there, coming in by glider and transport. Guns too. Big stuff. Anti-tank. We've been pulled back. Whole of 5th Brigade has. Jerry's taken the bloody airfield. Left the wounded and the chaplain. We're heading for Canea, sir. Can you point me the right way?'

'You're going the right way, Lieutenant. Just keep walking along that road and you'll find it.'

So that was it, thought Lamb. They'd taken Maleme.

Charles Eadie wandered up. 'Who the devil are they, sir? They look all in, poor sods.'

Lamb spoke without turning. He just kept looking at

the lines of dispirited soldiers shuffling along the road to Canea.

'The Kiwis have pulled out from Maleme, Charles.'

'That can't be right, sir. They must have got it wrong. They wouldn't. That would mean that the Jerries . . .'

'. . . had taken the airfield. That's precisely what it does mean.'

It confirmed what Lamb had been thinking over the past few weeks. What mattered to him, what was really important, were the men. It was all about the men you led in battle, the company and the regiment. Pendlebury could keep his special operations. He would never become involved in that. He'd already turned down the potential appointment to the much-lauded, top-secret 'Section D'. Cloak-and-dagger stuff. If only they all knew. That was not for him. He was a soldier. There would be no covert missions for him. Lamb was a man who fought at the front. But now he had been coerced into helping to save the King of Greece.

Eadie brought him back to the present crisis. 'Can't we counter-attack, sir? Send reinforcements.'

'From where? Freyberg doesn't have them. Don't you see? We can't win now. They have an airfield, a bridge-head on to the island. Give them a few hours and they'll have thousands of men in there. And what's more, artillery. They've already got anti-tank guns. We've lost the bloody battle. All we can do now is work out a means of getting off this damned island with as many men as we can save. First, though, we've got another job to do. We're going to stop them taking Galatas.'

13

It was 8 a.m. They had been awake for some hours now and still the steady stream of Kiwis had not stopped coming. Lamb and his men had struck camp and moved their position as directed a few hundred yards back in the direction of the village.

There was a familiar noise in the sky above them. Lamb didn't need to look up. 'Aircraft. Take cover.'

Across the road and into the trees and vineyards men dived to the ground, not bothering to look where they might land. There were fewer trenches here but most of the men managed to find some sort of cover from the planes, which came in low from the west. That's it, thought Lamb. The Luftwaffe are using Maleme already. The Stukas fell on them from out of the blue, whining down in their siren call and loosing their bombs almost directly into the slit-trenches. The skies were filled with aircraft and the sticks fell in staccato bursts now. Lamb kept his head down but sensed that above him the air was alive with whirring metal. Another sound now: rather than the whine of bombs, the whoosh of artillery shells. They were being fired on from the heights as well as from the air. He pressed himself still further into the trench and began to pray, the familiar soldiers' prayer that simply asked for deliverance from present danger.

After half an hour it stopped. Lamb sat up and surveyed the carnage. The road to his left and the vineyards before him were littered with dead and wounded men and body parts. Blast craters pitted the ground. Men had been flung in weird, unnatural poses and hung over walls or shattered against the walls of houses. There was masonry and wood everywhere, and the smell of burning and death.

He called out, 'Sarnt-Major, Sarnt-Major Bennett, over here.'

For a horrible moment he heard nothing, save the ringing in his ears. Then there was a familiar voice. 'Sir. Yes, sir. I'm here.'

Bennett had been wounded, but not badly by the look of things. He was holding his left hand and it looked as if he had been hit by shrapnel on one of his fingers.

'You're hit.'

'Not bad, sir. Hurt my bloody finger. That was horrible. Not many of our lads hit, though.'

'Not many left to hit, Sarnt-Major. Seen Lieutenant Eadie?'

'He's fine, sir, though he got hit on the head by a piece of wood from the house he was in.'

'Taking cover from shellfire inside a house – he should know better. Eadie.'

'Sir.' Charles Eadie was winding a bandage round his head.

'What the devil have you done?'

'Bit of a headache, sir. Silly, really.'

'Yes, it was. Bloody silly. Right. That was the softening up. They'll be on us soon. Let's make them welcome, shall we? How many of those Jerry mortar rounds have we left?'

'Ten, sir. But we've a good deal of ammo for the machine-guns.'

'Right. Set them up to enfilade the road, and put the mortars well to the rear. Has anyone got any more Schmeisser mags?'

'Here, sir, have some of mine.' Eadie opened up a canvas bag on his shoulder and Lamb saw that it was full of magazines.

'Good God. Where the devil d'you get all those? Thank you.'

He pulled out six and stuffed them into his pockets and belt. 'Sarnt-Major, better get the men in position. We've no time to clean up this mess, ghastly though it is.'

But for once Lamb was wrong. As they looked into the olive groves his men were unable to spot any advancing enemy. The same seemed to be true along the entire line. The hours ticked past. They did manage to bury the dead and get the worst cases back to the field hospital. Ten. Midday. Then at 12.30 precisely the air filled again with black silhouettes and they dived for cover. This raid lasted fifteen minutes, but hardly had they had time to climb from the trenches than another attack came in. Lying flat on the trench floor, Lamb looked at his watch. 1.15. This would be it. A short last burst, and then they would come. As soon as the planes climbed and banked away into the blue he jumped up and peered through his field glasses up at the hills. Slowly, green-grey figures began to move across the landscape.

'This is it, boys. Here they come. Get ready.'

He could hear the wounded from the last attack, but there was no time to be lost now. They and the rest of the dead would have to wait. As the enemy came on, the covering fire began. What had seemed intense fire before was now as nothing in comparison as the Spandaus opened up at long range among the mortars and artillery. The Germans seemed to have captured at least two British Bofors guns and the familiar pop could be heard above the din. Lamb timed the bursts. Ten in thirty seconds, twenty every minute. And now the infantry were closing upon them. From their rear he heard the air-sucking whoosh of a shell and one of the British batteries behind Galatas opened up. There was a ragged cheer but it was short lived as more enemy rounds came crashing in. Lamb looked up to his right, and on Wheat Hill, to the west of the village, he could see huge explosions among the defending trenches of the 18th New Zealanders.

Valentine summed it up. 'They're copping it, sir. Glad I'm not up there.'

As they watched, khaki-clad figures began to emerge from the top of the hill and, still firing, walk slowly back down the hill towards the village.

'Christ, they've broken.'

'No, no, they haven't. Look, they're falling back in order. They're withdrawing. Look.'

But then Mays pointed to the figures following up the New Zealanders, for the top of Wheat Hill had turned into a mass of field grey.

Lamb called out. 'The right flank's falling back. Wheel to the right. Refuse the right.'

The men who heard him, some of his own, a few Greeks and part of the composite battalion that was on their right wing, began to turn and make ready to form a line with the now retreating 18th. Lamb could see the attackers now. These were not paratroopers. That was easy enough to tell from the shape of their helmets. These troops wore the more usual Wehrmacht infantry pattern, though there were other things about them that suggested they were another elite unit – not least the speed at which they advanced.

Bennett pointed to their front where the Divisional Petrol Company had been standing alone in defence of Pink Hill. 'Look, sir, they're pulling back.'

It was true; the stalwart mechanics who had done so much over the past few days to hold up the German advance were finally falling back. They seemed to be pivoting as they did so on an axis of the hill itself, in order to join up with the remnants of the 18th.

Bennett whistled. 'That's as good a manoeuvre as I've seen on parade at Tonbridge. That's something for a bunch of grease monkeys.'

Lamb turned on him. 'Oy, just you mind who you're calling a grease monkey. You know what I do when I'm not playing at soldiers.'

Bennett smiled. 'Sorry, sir. Forgot you was one yourself. But look at them.'

Lamb watched, impressed, as they carried out their manoeuvre, denying every inch of ground to the advancing enemy. He saw one man stand and fire a Bren gun from the hip, spraying the hill and the road that ran across it, and watched as the Germans dived for cover. Several failed to get up. The man pulled out an empty magazine, jammed in another and fired off another long burst, and then another. Then finally, with no magazines left, the man ran back to his comrades, leaving the hillside covered in crumpled grey-green mounds, most of them dead.

The enemy had gained some ground and with it closer positions on which to site his mortars. Lamb yelled to the men, 'Fall back into the village. Try to find cover.'

As he said this, several mortar shells landed close by. One man was hit by a small fragment and fell but managed to get up again. More shells came in, smashing into buildings and sending stones flying into the street to become deadly projectiles in themselves. The southern outskirts of Galatas were burning now, and Lamb's thoughts turned again to Anna. He hoped with all his heart that she had got away, not just for her safety but because he did not want her to witness the destruction of her home. Slowly the remains of his company fell back into Galatas. They were nearing the square now, close to Anna's *kafeneio*, and glancing to his rear momentarily Lamb glimpsed the white façade of the church. It seemed surreal that, despite everything that was happening around it, the church's bells were pealing out to summon the devout.

'Some bloody hope,' said Valentine. 'His congregation's scarpered.'

Lamb shook his head. 'Not entirely. It's Sunday, remember?'

'Really? God. That seems a long time ago.'

'What's that, Valentine?'

'Church on Sunday. A sense of normality. Be nice to get it back.'

'Were you ever that normal, Valentine?'

'No, not really, sir.'

There was a whoosh as an artillery shell scudded across the sky above them and hit home in the rear of the village. At the same time, as they watched in awe and surprise, a line of villagers, mostly old men, women and small children, all of them dressed in black and preceded by a priest bearing a cross and four other men in black robes, came from a building near the back of the church and walked through its tall doors.

Valentine was incredulous. 'They can't be serious, can they?'

'I'm afraid they are. Perhaps it's their way of fighting back. The power of prayer.'

'Mumbo-jumbo. No offence, sir. But really, it's all a lie, isn't it?'

'Is it? How can you be sure?'

'If your number's up, your number's up. That's my belief.'

'Careful, Valentine. You're beginning to talk like a soldier. Can't have that.'

Eadie interrupted them. 'They're getting a bit close now, don't you think?'

He was right. From the edge of the town they could hear the rattle of small-arms fire.

Lamb waved to them. 'Right, we'll fall back on the square. On the church.'

They turned to walk across the square and found their way blocked by a motley collection of soldiery, headed by a New Zealand officer. The men were dressed in every manner of uniform; some of them even seemed to be wearing civilian clothes. One with a forage cap on his head wore a striped jersey, another was clad in a battle-dress top above brightly coloured slacks and wore sandals on his feet. A less warlike group of infantry Lamb had never seen, even though all were properly armed.

Valentine spoke. 'Blimey, sir. Now we're really scraping the barrel. That's the Kiwi concert party. I saw them at the picture house in Canea. They weren't bad either, mind you. Don't know if they can fight, though.'

'They seem keen enough to have a go. We need every man we can get.'

Their officer called to Lamb. 'Sir, can we join you? I mean, could you take command?'

Lamb looked at him. He was a second lieutenant, a mere boy of only about nineteen and obviously out of his depth in this situation. Lamb reckoned that he had been lucky to survive thus far. 'Of course, Lieutenant. I'm Captain Lamb. North Kents.'

'Lieutenant Riley, sir. We're the . . .'

'I know. You're the ENSA concert party. My sergeant here's a fan of yours. Well done in getting yourselves properly armed. Stick with us and you'll have a sporting chance.'

He turned to Eadie. 'Charles, you take care of this lot, will you? Right. Let's try to form a defensive position across the square. We might have to use the church.'

They were directly outside the *kafeneio* now and Lamb could see that it had been shuttered up and padlocked. So far, though, it seemed to have remained intact and there was no sign of any inhabitants. He wondered whether Anna was in the church. He did not have her down as being over-religious, but then war did strange things to people. They moved across the square towards the church, collecting the concert party on their way, and were forming a line behind whatever cover they could find when the first elements of the Petrol Company began to enter the square, firing behind them as they came. Seeing Lamb's men they made for the position, and within moments Lamb saw why. Behind them came a mass of the enemy, oblivious to the target they presented, running and firing in pursuit.

He shouted, 'Covering fire. Give covering fire.'

The Jackals began to snipe at the oncoming Germans, and Lamb saw some of the shots strike home. They were not yet in effective Schmeisser range so only the riflemen were firing. They were joined by the concert party, and Lamb was impressed by the number they brought down. The German bullets zipped and cracked off the low white-washed stone wall before the church. The remaining Greeks with them were firing too now, and the combined effort forced the German assault party to take cover inside the houses at the far end of the square.

On the left side of the square more New Zealanders began to appear, some of them badly wounded and being carried. Seeing Lamb's men and the Greeks, they turned and formed a line from the houses on the northern side across to the centre. Behind them a man was shouting. 'Stand for New Zealand. For New Zealand, boys.'

Lamb saw that it was no less than Colonel Kippenberger himself, his Schmeisser slung over his shoulder.

Bennett yelled out, 'Come on then. If they can do it for New Zealand, we can do it for Dartford, boys, and Dagenham. Up the Jackals.' They fired into the Germans with new vigour, making every shot count. They had smashed their way into the *kafeneio* now and were firing down from the upper windows, from Anna's bedroom. Lamb thought how strange it was that buildings and streets which had grown so familiar over the past few weeks had now become battlefields. Houses of friends were no longer dwellings but strongpoints or hazards to be taken or defended. This place was transformed, a battleground ripped from the heart of one of the most peaceful, civilised villages he had ever known.

Kippenberger was running down the line now, shouting encouragement everywhere he went. He saw Lamb. 'Captain Lamb, glad you're here with us. We've got to hold them, Lamb. If they get through this line and debouch out of the village then the whole front's gone. Stick with it.'

Lamb's men continued to pour fire into the houses, and he prayed that their ammo would not run out before the Jerries halted for the evening. The sun was dying now and, looking at his watch, he saw that, incredibly, four hours had passed since the first attack had come in. Around him the firing line was filled with wounded men. Looking across the square he saw one of the concert party, the man with the bright red trousers, lying in a spreading pool of blood. Lamb wiped the sweat from his forehead and fired off the Schmeisser at a group of five Germans who had run from cover and across the square in an attempt to move forward. Three went down, one jerking and twitching on the ground, and the other two were taken out by single shots of rifle fire.

Suddenly to his left a man jerked back, hit by fire from one of the snipers. It was Valentine. Slowly, he raised himself from the ground and grabbed at his left arm and his shirt, which had been ripped open by a bullet just below the bicep and was stained with blood. 'It's all right, sir. Think I'll live.'

'Get it seen to, Sarnt. Get back and find an MO. Ask the colonel if you can't.'

There was a shout and a sudden surge of grey-green uniforms through the gap between the houses. Lamb yelled out, 'All of you. My men and the Kiwis. With me. We're pulling back.'

Still firing, they backed away as far as they could from the advancing enemy. At the church they found the doors open and the congregation streaming out, their faith now interrupted by the need for earthly salvation. They ran headlong to the rear of Lamb's small force, which continued to pull back. More men fell: three of the Greeks and two more Kiwis, along with another of Lamb's men, Dennis, a bright lad of eighteen, shot through the head.

Another quarter mile and they were clear of the village. Turning, Lamb saw two of their light tanks advancing down the road.

'Get behind the tanks. Take cover behind our tanks.' He could see two groups of men in khaki on either side of the road, picking out what cover they could. This then was the front line.

At the edge of the village the Germans stopped and Lamb and his men took the chance to run as fast as they could for the tanks. They half fell into the new positions. The tanks had stopped now and were spraying the German-held houses from their Vickers machine-guns.

They began to move again, and Lamb watched from behind a wall as they entered the village. He could hear the sound of their machine-guns. Looking to the rear he saw Kippenberger in conversation with a New Zealand captain and imagined what he was saying as he pointed into the village. The only course of action now was to try to retake Galatas.

He turned to Bennett. 'We've got them pinned them down, Sarnt-Major. A couple of mortars would have them out of the houses. And then what have they got? Two companies just come up, by the looks of it. And we'd give it a go, wouldn't we?'

'Yes, Kapitan. I think we would.' But it wasn't Bennett's voice that came from behind him.

Lamb turned and saw, crouching to his rear, the huge figure of Manoli Bandouvas, complete with tea-cosy hat and moustaches. 'Kapitan Bandouvas. Yasou. You've no idea how glad I am to see you.'

Bandouvas grinned and Lamb noticed that he now had a long scar running down the left side of his face. Bandouvas noticed his interest. 'I had an encounter with a paratrooper. Don't worry, he came off the worst.'

'Are your men here?'

Bandouvas nodded. 'Yes. All of them. Look. Grigorakis, Petrakogioros, Bardakis. They're all here, Kapitan, here to fight with you against the Germanos. We are up in the church tower and on the roof.'

'It was you. You just about saved our bacon.'

'And we have new recruits too.'

He moved aside and Lamb saw that there were perhaps twenty other armed men behind him, and a few women. Among them stood Anna, a rifle and bandolier slung over her shoulder. Her white shirt was covered in blood. She walked towards him. 'Hello, Peter.' She smiled.

'Are you all right? You haven't been wounded?'

232

'No. Not my blood. But you have.' She pointed at his head. 'I heard from Andreas.'

He felt the bandage at his forehead. He had quite forgotten it. Lamb turned back to Bandouvas. 'But I thought you would be with Pendlebury. Where is he?'

Bandouvas shook his head. 'You didn't hear? I thought you would.'

'He's not?'

'Yes, it happened near Heraklion. There was a big battle. Did you know?'

'No, we've had no contact. WT's out, and they've cut the wires.'

'There was a very big battle. The Germans attacked the city and it looked as if they would take it but then Pendlebury led a charge. We were there, on the old walls. It's where I got this.'

He felt the scar. 'We all charged. He used his sword-stick. It was wonderful. But then he left the city with just his driver and Kapitan Satanas. After that he left Satanas and ran into some Germans at Kaminia. He got out of the car and climbed a spur to look down on the German position. They were closer than he thought and opened fire. Pendlebury and the driver fired back. Some of the Greeks came up – regulars who had been with us in Heraklion. They all fired on the Germans. They were still firing when the Stukas came over, and he was wounded in the chest. They captured him and shot him in cold blood. A British officer.'

'I'm so sorry. He was a good man. He did much.'

'It was how he would have wanted it. He was a great man. Truly great. And soon we shall avenge him.'

There was the noise of tracks on the road and Lamb turned to see that the tanks were returning. He had a better look at them now: two old Mark VIs, built between the wars and pretty much useless as tanks. Totally

233

outdated. An armour-piercing bullet fired from an ordinary rifle would go straight through them. They were really only effective against ordinary bullets. But Lamb knew that their value lay in boosting morale. The tanks reached their position, and one of the hatches opened and a fair-haired officer jumped down, quite close to Lamb.

Kippenberger went up to him. 'We have to retake the village, Farran. It's our only hope.'

The tank commander spoke in a British accent. 'We can try, sir, but the place is stiff with Jerries. They're everywhere, in the orchard behind the church, behind chimney stacks, on all the roofs and in the school. They've run up the bloody swastika by the church. I took two casualties. When we were coming back, an anti-tank rifle put a shot through the turret of my corporal's tank. Got him and the gunner. They're not dead but the tank's U S without a commander and a gunner.'

'We'll just have to replace them then.' Kippenberger turned to the men behind him. 'Right, I need two volunteers to replace Lieutenant Farran's wounded men and go again. Any takers?'

There was a clamour of voices and at least a score of men began to walk forward. Lamb got to his feet and walked up to Farran. 'You know, I'm pretty good with motor vehicles, Lieutenant. Not a bad shot, either.'

Kippenberger turned. 'Lamb? Sorry, can't spare you. You're one of the most senior officers we have left here.'

'But sir, please.'

'I've given you an order, Lamb. Obey it.'

In the end they found two privates, and as soon as the wounded had been taken out the volunteers jumped into the blood-stained, sweat-drenched turret.

Kippenberger was busy briefing the men he had selected to follow the tanks, C and D Company of what was left of 23 Battalion. Lamb approached him. 'Can I at least go in with the infantry, sir? Look, you can see my boys are spoiling for a fight.'

Kippenberger nodded. 'Very well, but remember this is a counter-attack, not a suicide mission.'

He turned to Farran. 'Do not go any further than the village square. I want your tanks back intact and my lads and yours alive. Is that clear?'

'Yes, sir, I'll do what I can. But you seldom come out of these things alive.' Farran climbed into his turret and closed the lid.

Lamb checked the magazine on his Schmeisser and that he had three others tucked into his belt. Hand-grenades too. He watched as, well trained by Bennett and the other NCOs, his men and the Greeks did the same. He was conscious of someone standing behind him and turned to see Anna. He whispered, 'I wanted to talk to you, but I don't think now is quite the time.'

She smiled and reached to hold his hand, as if she were shaking it, but then held on for longer. He looked into her eyes and mouthed a few words which she seemed to understand. Then she let go and she swung the rifle from her back and checked the magazine.

'You're not coming with us.'

'Yes we are.'

'That wasn't a question. It was an order. You're not coming with us, Anna.'

'Try to stop me, Peter. Just try.'

The tanks started off down the road on the 200 yards back into the village, from which they could see plumes of smoke rising. It was not quite dark now, at around 8 o'clock. The infantry followed them through the clouds of dust from the dry road, marching at first, well spread out, and then over the last fifty yards at a run. C Company went up the road with D Company moving to the left flank. Lamb took his men and all the Greeks over to the right and saw that they had been joined there by another force led by a familiar fair-haired officer in a yellow jersey.

Hathaway blew frantically on his whistle, and at the same time, above the din of the small-arms fire from both sides and the clank of the tanks, there came another sound. From the whole of the advancing battle line came an assortment of war cries. Lamb had never heard anything quite like it. He found a New Zealand corporal on his left. 'What the devil's that racket?'

'It's the haka, sir. Maori battle cry. They started it, at least, Maoris did. Those lads, over there on the other side of the road. But the thing is, sir, back home every school and college has its own haka. Try to stop us.' And he joined in the yell in a deep, rumbling, primeval voice.

En masse the noise was appalling and at the same time blood-chilling. Lamb thought he should yell himself and smiled at Bennett as he did so. 'Come on the Jackals.' He followed it with the sort of thing he had been taught at bayonet drill and it blended well into the mix, which was now just a primitive roar and enough to put the wind up anyone on the receiving end.

Charging down the right edge of the village Lamb could see that most of the enemy fire was concentrated against the tanks and the infantry on the main road and was damn glad that he hadn't gone that way. After 300 yards he signalled to the men to turn in and they found themselves in the main square by the church. About a dozen houses were on fire, including Kippenberger's former HQ. The tanks were in the centre of the square and it was clear that one of them was in trouble. Lamb could see that it had been taken out by a grenade hit and that Farran and his crew, all of them wounded, were lying and sitting beside it. He ran across and bent down. 'Don't move. You're all right.'

As Lamb watched, crouching over Farran, the second tank lurched into a gutter. He pressed a dressing on Farran's wound and, thinking that the tank might have slipped a track, ran across to see if he could help, only to find the commander emerging from the turret. The man was jabbering. 'It's useless. I can't speak to the driver. The bloody speaking tube's gone.'

Lamb climbed up and grabbed him by the shoulder. 'Nonsense, man. Get back in there. We need you. Come on.' The man dropped back down and Lamb leaped off the tank, which turned and began once again to lead the way for the advancing infantry.

Valentine was beside him now with what was left of his section. 'Sir, look.' The far side of the square was full of Germans and New Zealanders, fighting hand to hand. As Lamb watched them a huge German picked up one of the smaller Kiwis by the neck and used him as a human shield to ward off another's jab with a bayonet. The lunge just missed the man who was yelling and kicking against the massive German. Lamb ran over and, taking out the commando knife he had won at gambling, stuck it deep into the German's side and pulled it out, wiping it on the grey-green uniform which he saw was embroidered with a small white and yellow flower. The dying man dropped the Kiwi and sank to the ground. More of the enemy were forming up across the square.

Lamb turned to Valentine and his men. Saw Eadie. 'Charles. We must charge them. Can you do it?'

'Yes, sir.'

Lamb found Bennett. 'Sarnt-Major, we're going to charge. Bayonets, anything. Come on. With me.'

The company, together with the Greeks and Bandouvas' men, turned behind Lamb and Eadie and raced across the square, smashing into the Germans before they had a chance. The sheer weight of them bowled the Germans over and Lamb saw eighteen-inch bayonets thrust deep into throats and chests. He saw Anna, in the thick of it, fire from the hip and shoot a man at point-blank range, leaving a scorch mark on the crumpling body. Above the din he heard Farran's distinctive English voice. 'Come on New Zealand. Let them have it.' Then it was subsumed by the high-pitched scream of a man who had been stabbed through the stomach. There were dead and wounded all around him now, it seemed, but still their charge went on, out across the little square and into the alleyways, chasing the Germans back the way they had come towards Pink Hill.

Lamb and his men went with them, clearing the houses with grenades and bayonets in a blur of combat. Parry, lunge, twist, withdraw, again and again and again. Lamb knew that in this sort of fighting every split second would count. Panicked, the Germans turned and fled.

Lamb was leading from the front, but as they cleared more houses he became aware that men from other units were losing their way, doubling back on themselves, so that he would see the same faces over again. He knew the reason. Their officers were all down, dead or wounded.

He found Eadie. 'We've got to restore order. Find any Kiwi officers you can. They must reorganise. The Jerries could counter-attack at any moment.' Aware that it was all too easy in a pursuit such as this to get ahead of yourself and end up out on a limb, Lamb ran back into the square.

There, as if to answer his request, he was met by a New Zealand major. 'Thomason. I/C of the 23rd. Well done. You seem to have cleared them out.'

Lamb shook his head. 'Yes, sir, but your lads don't seem to want to give up. They're after them down the

238

hill.' The major turned to a colour sergeant. 'Colour Sarnt Macleod, get down the hill and pull them back before we lose the lot of them.'

It was approaching midnight when Lamb at last sat down on one of the pock-marked walls in the church square. The clear night sky was lit by the leaping flames from a score of burning buildings, but amazingly Anna's *kafeneio* was not among them. He had seen her a few moments ago and knew she had made it through the fight. He wondered how, though, for it had been perhaps the fiercest engagement in which he had ever taken part. He supposed it had been worthwhile.

They had retaken Galatas. The front line had been stabilised, and the New Zealanders had gained a vital breathing space. But what, he wondered, had been the cost? Hallam, whom he had encountered on one of the side streets, covered in blood, his own and that of others, had told him that of all the New Zealand officers only four subalterns were left standing by the end of the action.

Kippenberger had wanted to go again, but Thomason and a few others had refused, telling him the men were on the verge of exhaustion. In any case, thought Lamb, the Jerries seemed to have dug in for the night. They had taken the village, but as far as any military purpose went they had effectively lost 10th Brigade. And he still hadn't got to the King.

Charles Eadie interrupted his thoughts. 'Sir, I think you should see these.' He presented Lamb with a bloodstained bundle of papers. 'Mays found them on a dead German major.'

Lamb took the bundle and began to read. His German was worse than rudimentary, almost non-existent, but even he could make out references to 'der Koenig'. And there was a map of a house.

'What d'you make of it, Charles?'

'I've only a little German, sir, but I know that it's about the King. The King of Greece, sir. I'll find Valentine, shall I?'

Valentine had to be extricated from celebrations among the Greeks, who had opened a bottle of raki. He returned bearing a Schmeisser.

'Look, sir. Isn't she a beauty? May I be permitted to keep her?'

'You may. But only if you can translate this for me, Sergeant.'

Valentine scanned the papers. 'Hmm. Yes, this is all about the King of Greece, sir. Says he's on Crete and the Jerries want him, dead or alive. Seems he's a threat to Greece and the Reich. It's signed . . . oh, what do you know? It's signed Adolf Hitler.'

He held out the last sheet to Lamb, who took it and ran his hand over the signature.

Valentine continued. 'There are details, sir. Exact details of where the King was, erm, yes, four days ago. Look, there's a plan of the house. Their intelligence really is astonishing, isn't it?'

Lamb gazed at the plan of the villa Bella Campagna, with its German annotations, and thought for a moment. As far as he could recall Hathaway had told him they had moved the King only recently, which meant that somehow the Germans had got this knowledge from the island in the past week. He knew that there were spies around them and that some of the Greeks at least were sympathetic to the German cause. But the detail here was extraordinary.

'Thank you, Charles. Of course you know what this means.'

Eadie looked sheepish. 'That the Germans want the King?'

'It means he is now in real danger, more than we had thought. It also means that what Hathaway was saying wasn't complete tosh. For some reason the King and his tinplate medals really are important to the Germans. To Hitler himself, it seems. It means we've got to get to him before the Jerries do.'

Eadie tapped the side of his head. 'Oh, sir, one more thing. Captain Hathaway gave me a message for you. Said to tell you that he had good word that the King was safe in an old Turkish fort outside Pirgos, to the south. And that Mr Tsouderos never did get the Greeks together. The King's only got Lieutenant Ryan's men, and it seems a few of them haven't made it.'

Lamb swore. 'That bloody man. Christ, he's got a nerve to pass that message on. Where the hell is he?'

'Last seen taking his Greeks back to Canea, sir.'

'So he's ducked out again.'

'Steady on, sir. He hardly ducked out yesterday.'

Lamb nodded. 'Yes, that was unfair of me. Still . . .' He turned to Bennett. 'Do you suppose we've done enough here, Sarnt-Major?'

'We've helped them all we can, sir, and more, if that's what you mean.'

Lamb looked across the square and saw the triumphant Kiwis returning from their pursuit. 'Well, that's it then. We've gained Galatas but we've lost most of the brigade, and anyway it looks like we've lost the bloody island.'

It was true. One thing he knew, though, was that he and his men had done their best. 'Well, one thing's for certain. We're not going to lose the bloody King. Come on.'

241

14

They had been walking for some hours. Lamb had led
them from the lines shortly before dawn. Amid the chaos
and exhaustion they had not been missed. They were a
small party: his own men, Bandouvas' brigands and some
villagers, including Anna. Lamb had been surprised that
Bandouvas had come with them. Of course he had asked
the man if he could spare a guide and had told him in
confidence the nature of their mission. But with all the
talk, not least from Anna, about how much the Cretans
hated the royal family he was astonished at Bandouvas
having volunteered to lead them down to the little harbour
of Sfakia on the south coast. He reasoned that there was
now little option for the Greeks, other than fighting on
in a hopeless position with the British. Crete was a lost
cause.

Valentine as usual had got the gist of Kippenberger's
plan from his batman after the colonel had gone to give
his report to Brigade command in Canea. He was going
to be forced to pull out of Galatas. There was nothing
for it. Despite their victory, the village could not be held.
The idea now was to form a line from just outside Canea
down to the area of the hills around Pirgos, to the west

of Perivolia and their old camp. This was the precise location, in fact, of the fort in which Hathaway had told him the King was now in hiding. It was clear to Lamb that they did not have a moment to lose.

They marched across country towards the south east, moving as directly as they could towards the fort. As far as Lamb was aware the 2nd Greek Battalion still held the ground around there, if they existed as a unit after the German onslaught. But God alone knew where the Germans were.

Bandouvas led the way, keen to show off his local knowledge and to prove the most useful member of the party. He was acutely conscious that he was a better warrior than any of the British officers, even if they were off to save a man whom he vehemently detested. Anna went with him and his partisans, and Lamb and his men followed on behind. They had left the Greeks at Galatas. Lamb knew they would find their way to Hathaway soon enough.

Crossing the bridge to the east of the village, they made for Karatsos, but then at a little hilltop church Bandouvas turned south. The sun was rising in the sky as they came down the slopes towards the main Canea road, and Lamb realised there were two ways they could choose to go. One would take them further east through their own lines and straight down through Platanos and Perivolia. The other took them cross-country across the road and the river, through the lower reaches of Prison Valley and then directly up the mountain to the fort. That of course was the shorter. It was also by far the more dangerous. There was no doubt in his mind that the Germans who had been in Prison Valley must by now have advanced further along the road. For all he knew they might even hold Perivolia. He looked up ahead at Bandouvas and ran along the road to catch him up.

'Kapitan, which way are you taking us?'

'Why, the quickest way, of course.'

'Across the river.'

'Yes, naturally.'

'You do know that it will be swarming with Jerries?'

Bandouvas nodded. 'My gun is hungry for more of them.'

Lamb chose not to argue. For one thing he knew it would be bad form to appear to Bandouvas like someone who wanted to avoid the enemy. For another, he knew they had to get to the King first, and if that meant cutting through the enemy lines before the Germans found him themselves, then so be it. 'Good. I was just checking.'

He paused for a moment to exchange glances with Anna and then, returning to the men, found Valentine and Bennett marching together at their head. Valentine spoke. 'I was just telling the Sarnt-Major, sir. You know what they've christened us. Some clever dicks in the Kiwis?'

'No, surprise me, Valentine.'

'The Royal Perivolians, sir. On account of the fact that we went off to save the King at the villa and . . .'

'. . . that we came from the transit camp at Perivolia. It's quite catchy.'

'I prefer the Jackals, sir. That's always been good enough for us, hasn't it? Anyway, who wants to be a royal regiment?'

'Yes, perhaps it is a bit long-winded.'

Bandouvas led them sharply off the road and across a long, low stretch of vineyards. He waved them down into a running crouch. Looking to their right Lamb could see down the valley towards the white blocks of the prison. There seemed to be a frenzy of activity going on in front of it and he hoped they would make the cover of the hills before they were spotted. They had reached the base of the slope when there was the sound of motors from the valley and to his horror six trucks, captured from the Allies by the look of them, began to drive directly towards them up the road to Canea. Lamb broke into a proper run and dashed for some long grass. He was followed by the rest of the men and could see that up ahead Bandouvas and his party were already in cover behind a rocky outcrop. Moving slowly to their left they began to edge around the north side of the hill. The trucks were closer now, and Lamb and the others ducked down in the grass. Then one of the trucks began to slow down and came to a stop parallel to where they were lying. As Lamb watched in trepidation four men got out, all armed with Schmeissers, and moved to their side of the truck. Surely, he thought, they couldn't have seen anything. We must be out of sight. The four Germans began to walk into the vineyard and then, reaching a wall, they stopped. Turning away from one another they began to fumble with the front of their tunics and Lamb realised the reason for their having stopped. As they peed against the wall, the men laughed with each other. He shook his head and then saw that the men were walking back towards the truck. The bizarre interlude had him worried. If the enemy felt confident enough to stop in the open to pee, they must have been under the impression they were some distance from their opponents. And if that were the case, then somehow he and Bandouvas must have got deep inside their lines.

He saw Bandouvas move off, and within a few hundred yards he and the partisans were hidden from the road in a gully on the north face of the hill. The big Cretan was loping up the hillside now, like a huge gazelle. There was nothing to do but follow.

'He's up there. There's an old Turkish fort at Pirgos. That's where he must be.'

They climbed from the main road up a steep slope,

and looking back down Lamb could see the fight still raging on the slopes around Galatas in the north of the valley.

Pirgos was just a tiny hamlet, nothing more than a few dilapidated houses. The old fort stood slightly away from them on a rise in the ground. They approached it with caution. It was impossible to know if any paratroops had fallen up here. As they reached the foot of the high walls, Lamb heard a noise. A stone tumbled from the top of the battlements, and moments later was followed by a shout.

Waving the men on behind him, he ran, his gun held at the ready, into the ruins – and collided with another man. Their two bodies tumbled to the ground, and instinctively Lamb grabbed the man's neck and twisted his head to get him in a grip. The man struggled, trying to speak, and Lamb heard an English word, a familiar accent. He relaxed his grip and at that second another figure appeared: a lieutenant in British uniform.

The newcomer yelled, 'Stop, or I'll shoot.' Then he froze, seeing several submachine-guns and rifles levelled at him.

Lamb looked up and gently laid the gasping sentry down on the ground. He scrambled to his feet. 'You're British.'

The officer lowered his gun. 'New Zealand, sir. Lieutenant Ryan.'

'Lamb. North Kents.'

'Thank God. I tried to get a message back to someone. Captain Hathaway.'

'Well, he did a good job. Here we are. You have the King? How many are you?'

Ryan nodded, 'There's me, sir, and what's left of my platoon. Twelve men. Then there's the King, of course, Prince Peter, the Prime Minister and the two ladies.'

'The Prince is here. Good.'

'And then there are two other gentlemen from the Greek government, and the English party.'

'English party?'

'Yes, sir. They were at the villa when we got the King out. There's Mr Hartley, the novelist, and his wife. And Mr Comberwell. Oh, and there's a servant.'

Lamb rubbed at his chin thoughtfully and swore under his breath. 'That's quite a full house we have, Lieutenant.'

'Yes, sir.'

'Still, we'll just have to get them all away, won't we?'

'Yes, sir.'

'Can you take me to the King?'

'He's in the back of the fort, sir. There are a few rooms which still have their original doors. We thought it safer.'

'Very good. Seen anything of the Jerries?'

'There was a patrol that passed by the base of the hill a day ago, but they've shown no interest in the fort so far.'

'Can't be long, though. They're moving damn fast.'

They walked through the courtyard of the old fort past the lieutenant's platoon and reached a door under the ramparts on the far side.

'His Majesty's in here, sir.'

Ryan opened the door to reveal a dimly lit cell of a room which indeed might at one point have been just that. Inside, seated at a simple table, was a man in the uniform of a Greek general. He looked up as the door opened and stood to greet Lamb but did not extend his hand. King George was similar in looks to his cousin, tall and lean, with the same broad, high forehead, receding hairline and beak-like nose. He smiled. Lamb felt he should produce some sort of a bow and nodded.

'Captain Lamb?'

'Your Majesty.'

'I had thought we might never see you. I was informed of your presence on the island some weeks ago.'

'You were, Your Majesty?'

'Please, Captain, it is Your Majesty only the first time. Sir will do quite well from now on.'

'Yes, sir. I'm sorry.'

'Yes. I had a wire from London telling me that your Section D were sending out one of their best men to protect me. Of course I didn't have your name until my cousin informed me.'

'The Prince knew it was me?'

'Oh yes. Quite a chance encounter, though, between the two of you. And very fortunate for Peter.'

Lamb was angry and confused. Had Colonel 'R' told the King he was in Section D? And if so, why? Why too had he been told so specifically not to alert the King to his presence? It occurred to him that perhaps there might be someone else on the island from whom the connection between him and the King had been kept. He also realised with a ghastly shock that here he was back again among the English party, one of whom he knew for certain must have been the agent who had disclosed his presence in Athens to the colonel and started all this business. Someone who had passed on information about the King's whereabouts to the enemy. The thoughts jostled inside his head, creating a web of befuddlement.

The King spoke. 'Well, you're here now, Captain, which is the main thing, with your men. And I must say, although I mean no offence at all to Lieutenant Ryan, I do feel that I must be in safe hands. You have quite a reputation, Captain. I know all about you.'

He spotted Bandouvas and his men. They were standing in a huddle, dressed in similar attire to their leader, unshaven and armed to the teeth, with weapons ranging from an MG34 to a scimitar.

248

'Are these the gendarmes I was told about? Tsouderos, is this your doing? Surely not?'

A soberly dressed man looking as much like a banker as you could without a tie approached from behind the King. 'No, sir. I have never seen these men before. These are not the gendarmes.'

Lamb continued, 'No, sir, they are not. Far from it. May I present Kapitan Manoli Bandouvas. He is from Krousonas. A great warrior. He has been fighting against the Germans with me. These are his men. And women.'

The King eyed them warily at first. Then nodded and smiled. 'Wonderful. Wonderful. Welcome, Kapitan, and thank you. You have earned the gratitude of your King.'

Bandouvas shrugged.

Valentine muttered, 'Thank God for that.' Bennett hissed at him.

Bandouvas spoke. 'The pleasure is mine, Your Majesty,' and gave a short bow. Lamb hoped that the sarcasm, so evident to him in Bandouvas' tone, was not so obvious to the King. Mr Tsouderos scowled, however.

Lamb went on, 'Kapitan Bandouvas will be our guide through the mountains, sir. We're going to head for Sfakia. We should be able to find a boat there, or hopefully the Royal Navy will be waiting to take you off, sir.'

The King nodded. 'And how do you intend to take us there, Kapitan?'

Bandouvas scratched his stubble. 'Well, Your Majesty, as I see it the simplest way, avoiding the Germanos, is to go from here to Canea, then to Suda and Vrises, taking the hill roads if we need to.'

Lamb interjected, 'One of my sergeants got the gen from Kippenberger's man. We have no reason to believe the enemy has taken the main road through Askifou yet.'

Bandouvas continued, 'So that's the way we'll go. If we find them or they find us, we will have to leave the road and climb into the mountains. Then we drop down into the gorge of Imbros and we reach the coast. Will that suit you, sir?'

The King laughed. 'I may not be as fit as I was, but I think I will manage it. When do we start?'

Lamb spoke. 'As soon as we can, I would suggest, sir. The Germans are closing in up the Alikianos road and I've no doubt that they'll try to take Canea soon.'

The King nodded. 'Good. Tsouderos, is everyone ready?'

'Yes, sir. All our party.'

'And the English?'

'I believe so. Lieutenant?'

Ryan nodded. 'Yes, sir. They're as ready as they'll ever be.'

Lamb took charge. 'Right then, let's move out.'

As Lamb walked over to Eadie to explain the situation he felt a hand touch his shoulder. He turned and found himself looking at Miranda Hartley.

She looked very different from when he had last seen her at dinner on the day before the invasion. Her make-up was hardly visible and her skin seemed dirty and in places quite raw from exposure to a combination of sun and wind. The hair, so neatly kept, now hung loose and her dress had a few tears where it must have snagged against bushes. She looked utterly exhausted and her eyes bore the classic red-rimmed signs of fatigue. She spoke in a breathless rush of words and fidgeted throughout with her filthy hair. 'Peter. Thank God. I knew you'd come to save us. I kept telling Julian. Captain Lamb will come, I said. I was so sure of it. Thank God. He was certain we'd be killed or captured by the Germans and I had horrid thoughts of what they might do to me. One hears such dreadful things. And I think between you and me Julian would kill himself if he was forced to spend any time in captivity.'

250

Lamb stopped her. 'You're not safe yet, I'm afraid.'

'No. But we will be. I'm sure that we will be now. Now you're here. Dear Captain Lamb.' She leant up and pulled him down to her quickly, kissing him, not on the cheek this time but hard on the lips.

Lamb recoiled and managed to detach her arm from where it was around his neck. 'Please.'

But it was too late. Valentine caught his eye.

Lamb shook his head. 'Where's your husband? And Comberwell?'

She tried to look natural, straightened her dress. 'Julian's over there, with Freddie. We're all a bit shaken up, I'm afraid. They've done their best, though. To look after me. But now you're here, Peter. Thank God.'

Lamb ignored her and walked over to the two men. Hartley was struggling with a large pack, trying to hoist it on to Comberwell's back. Lamb took it from him. 'Here, let me do that. There, is that better?'

Comberwell let the pack settle on his broad shoulders and beamed at Lamb. 'Fine. Never better. I say, what a spot of luck your turning up here. We'd almost given up hope.'

Hartley spoke in a rush as he hoisted a smaller rucksack over his own shoulder. 'We were with the King and Prince Peter at their villa – well, of course you know the place – when the Germans came. We saw them land on the road between Alikianou and Canea. It was very exciting and actually rather terrifying, there being so many of them. But the New Zealanders just shot them out of the sky. Most of them, that is. But then Blount from the legation turned up and took the King and the rest of us off to Alikianou. Well, that was no use because pretty soon the place was swarming with Germans. So we left and pitched up here. Of course Mr Papandreou had already gone off with his friends, ages ago. I heard they

251

were trying to get to Alex. There's just Julia and me and Comberwell here with the King and Prince Peter. And the others, of course.'

Lamb did a quick head count. There were his own men, twenty of them now, plus himself, Ryan's platoon of Kiwis, numbering eleven, the King, Prince Peter, Tsouderos and his wife, the Hartleys, Comberwell and the two servants. That made a total of forty all told, including two women and one, perhaps two, men who might not make it across any mountains they had to climb. It was not the ideal party for an escape on foot through hazardous country pursued by the enemy. But it would have to do.

They moved out of the fort and down the hillside towards the east, Lamb and Bandouvas leading the way with their men, the King and Prince Peter directly behind them, followed by Tsouderos, then the English and finally Lieutenant Ryan's men bringing up the rear.

The sound of battle was all around them. To their rear he could hear the thump of artillery, but there was no small-arms fire close by, which was a relief at least. It implied that they were within their own lines, although with this new airborne enemy you could not know for sure.

It worried him that they had not encountered any sign of the 2nd Greeks, and as they emerged into the countryside north of Perivolia Bandouvas suddenly stopped. 'Listen.' Then, 'Look.' He pointed north, in the direction of Canea. They all stood on the hillside, transfixed. It looked as if a huge black cloud was over the town. Lamb counted the planes as they grew closer. Ten, fifteen, twenty, thirty, forty. At fifty he gave up.

The Stukas came screaming in first, as they always did. They hovered over the ancient port like a swarm of angry wasps and then one by one descended, hurtling towards the domes and spires, sirens wailing, bombs dropping, before they pulled steeply up. Explosions rocked the coastline. Then, as they watched, a great cloud of heavy bombers came into view from the west: Dorniers, Ju 88s and above them the smaller shapes of fighters, Me 109s. They throbbed across the blue afternoon sky, calmly and deliberately jettisoning their sticks of high explosive directly on to the town. More explosions followed, bigger now, so heavy that they shook the ground of the grassy slope on which they stood. Lamb heard Miranda Hartley whimper behind him and mutter something, and Bandouvas' men began to curse. Then to his astonishment and horror another wave of heavy bombers came in. The fighters had peeled off now and dived down on the town, strafing its streets with machine-gun fire from their wings. He saw some of them head towards the nearby woods on the east side of the town, intent on machine-gunning whoever might have been trying to seek refuge in them. Birds rose from the shattered tree-line, flying off in confusion in every direction. The bombers were coming in at five-minute intervals, and still their party did not move. The bombs fell on Canea and by the time of the third wave their blasts had created a huge dust cloud, which rose from the town and filled the sky above. The centre of the town was blazing now, and they could see from their vantage point above the vineyards the black specks that were people streaming from the burning houses into the countryside beyond, heading anywhere to escape the bombs. Again and again the black planes came in. The party stood and watched, oblivious for the moment to danger, bewitched by the awful sight unfolding before them. Lamb felt physically sick. He found Anna standing beside him. For the first time since they had been reunited she placed her hand on his arm, and grasped it tight. She turned to him. 'Why, Peter? Why are they doing this?

What have the people done? Why . . .' She shook her head and bent it away from him to hide the tears.

Lamb knew why. Back in Athens, or even in Berlin, he supposed, someone had given the order that Canea should be destroyed. And with good reason. It would terrify the civilians. It would lower the morale of the remaining Allied soldiers, and it would destroy the communications systems and curtail any further use of the town as a centre of operations. That was why. That and the fact that the Nazis planned to show the Cretans that resistance was useless, that it would not be tolerated. But how could he explain that to Anna? Even Anna, the fighter, would not understand the bland military logic which meant that hundreds of innocent men, women and children would die, were dying as they watched, and that others would be driven from the homes they had loved, the only homes they had ever known. It was the end of the world. He looked around and saw the King shake his head in despair. Several of Bandouvas' men were in tears.

As yet another flight came in Lamb came to his senses and turned to Bandouvas. 'Let's move. There's nothing we can do to help them. We can make good use of the noise and the distraction.'

The Greek nodded. 'Yes, you're right. We had best not go much nearer to Canea. We'll take the road through Mournies.' Motioning them on, he led the way down the hillside.

From the vineyard-covered slopes they emerged on to a road and took the way that led east, skirting the southern outskirts of Canea. The ground beneath their feet shook with every explosion and Lamb could sense the fear among the group.

A lone fighter screamed in over their heads. Bennett shouted, 'Take cover. Get down.' They threw themselves away from the road and huddled at the side as the plane opened up. One of Bandouvas' men was not quite fast enough and tripped, and falling in the road lay for a moment unable to avoid the bullets which ripped through him in a bloody line, from groin to head. The fighter carried on over their heads and swept round to the left into another diving attack across the town. Lamb got to his feet and the others followed suit, leaving the dead man in the road. Quickly they set off again towards Mournies. To their left Canea was blazing more fiercely now, red and yellow flames twisting upwards from every quarter. They could hear the crackle of the fires and the explosions of the dying town, and feel the searing heat.

Still on the dust road, they rounded a bend and found themselves confronted by an Allied defensive position with soldiers entrenched on either side of the track, which had been barricaded with wire and two lorries. The officer on sentry hailed them and after a brief exchange they passed through the barricade and very soon found themselves on the outskirts of the town of Mournies, directly to the south of the port. The place was a mess of vehicles, serviceable and abandoned, and everywhere there were Allied troops. They stood about in units and sections, in various states of order. They leant listlessly against walls, singly and in groups. Many were wounded, some badly. All, thought Lamb, made Miranda Hartley's fatigue look trivial in comparison. And through them all wandered the officers attempting to retain some semblance of order.

Lamb found one of them, an Australian gunner captain, and asked, 'What's going on?'

The gunner shook his head. 'Where have you been, mate? The Jerries have taken Galatas. They're advancing here double-quick. We've been pulled back. No one's sure where we're going to stand and fight. There's not many officers left. This lot yours?' He pointed to the party.

'Yes. We've got to get to Suda. What's the quickest way through?'

'Well, I wouldn't go anywhere near Canea. It's bloody chaos. Poor buggers. We've had loads of them through here. Bloody butcher's shop. Field ambulance has gone in. It's just carnage. I'd carry on along here if I were you. Good as any.'

From out of nowhere, it seemed, a company of British infantry appeared, marching smartly along the road in the opposite direction. Lamb stood and watched as they passed by.

The Aussie spoke. 'Bloody hell. That's it then. They must have put in Force Reserve. That's the bloody Welch. On parade as usual. But I'll tell you something: they fight bloody well too. Better get back to the men. God knows how we're going to get off this bloody island now, though. Good luck, mate.'

They walked on, through the streets of Mournies, as quickly as they could, dodging to the side of the occasional truck and carrier, moving swiftly round the black-clad Cretan civilians who dawdled in front. Coming to a junction, they stopped as, crossing their path from left to right, came a convoy. It was led by a Jeep in which sat an officer of the RAMC and his driver and behind them two wounded men, both with their heads completely swathed in bandages. Behind the Jeep came a field ambulance, and behind that an open 3-ton truck filled with people. They were civilians, and as they passed Lamb could not help but look in. What he saw made him shiver. A mother was cradling her daughter whose bright golden hair was matted and thick with blood. Half of the girl's face had been torn away and a field dressing applied to the mess. Beside her sat a man holding another dressing to what appeared to be the stump of an arm. He stared past Lamb into the far distance with agonised eyes. But it was the eyes of another person that Lamb saw now. A girl of perhaps sixteen was sitting beside them, and while he could not see any visible wound her eyes said it all. He caught sight of them, and for that instant his very soul turned black. They were the eyes of despair and the eyes of hatred. For as long as he lived they would forever be for him the eyes of Crete. The pitiful convoy had passed now and he was glad that none of the women in their party had witnessed it.

It was not far to Suda. As they entered the port area Valentine whistled, for what met their eyes was a very different place from the sunlit harbour at which they had arrived a month before. The docks had gone, for all practical purposes, swept away by incessant daily bombing. In their place lay ruins, while in the bay the masts and funnels of more ships proclaimed the triumph of the Luftwaffe.

Lamb turned to speak to Bandouvas and saw that Miranda Hartley and Tsouderos' wife were lagging far behind. The King was helping them along the road. He called out to Bandouvas. 'I think we might rest for ten minutes.'

The Cretan nodded, and they sat on and around what remained of the harbour wall as the planes still screeched over Canea and the earth shook. Lamb took out a cigarette and lit it, and noticed for the first time that his hand was shaking. Bandouvas did the same.

Lamb spoke. 'We should head south, along the coast, yes?'

Bandouvas nodded. 'Yes. Down to Sfakia, through Babali Hani. How much further can they walk today?'

Lamb shrugged. 'I don't know. My men could manage another ten or fifteen miles.'

'Mine too, or more. Twenty miles. But the others? Perhaps we can make it to Vrises?'

'How far is that?'

'Twenty kilometres.'

'Call it thirteen miles then.' He shook his head. 'They'll never do it.'

'We'll stop at Kalives then, before we turn off to the south. That's only another fourteen kilometres. And it should be safe.'

Lamb nodded and walked across to where Bennett was sitting with some of his platoon. 'Sarnt-Major, we're going to try to get on a bit, another ten miles if the ladies can manage it.'

'The Greek lady's not bad on her feet, sir, and the partisans are as fit as fleas. But that Mrs Hartley's failing a bit, and if you ask me, sir, the King's a bit weak himself. He makes out he's hanging back to help her, but I reckon it's him what's feeling the strain. Look at him.'

Lamb looked over at the King and saw that Bennett was not wrong. King George was sitting on the wall, breathing heavily as he smoked. He was smiling, but it was clear he was not feeling at his best.

'Right. We'll press on, nevertheless. Get them up.'

They left Suda with its ruined, blackened villas and scorched gardens and emerged on the coast road. To their right lay a domed church among a grove of olive trees. Looking at it as they passed Lamb saw that the ground was full of slit-trenches and that in the trenches were men in khaki. Someone yelled at him, 'Get off the bloody road, you fool. The Jerry planes'll see you.' But he paid no attention.

Then, four hours after they had begun the destruction of Canea, the bombers stopped and turned for home. At the same time Lamb and his weary party reached a bend in the road, high above the coast. At the roadside sat two men with an anti-tank rifle, and in the vineyard which straddled the hill behind them he could see more trenches.

Seeing the motley column of British, Kiwis, civilians and Greeks, two officers, a major and a captain, both in British uniform, came forward from a sandbagged position.

The major spoke first. 'Who the devil are you lot?'

'Peter Lamb, sir. North Kents.'

The major stepped towards him and shook Lamb firmly by the hand. 'Are you, by God? Good. Very good. Graham, Freddie Graham. Layforce.' He half-turned towards the man behind him. 'This is Evelyn Waugh, our Intelligence Officer.'

Lamb shook the captain's hand. He might not have heard of Hartley, but he at least recalled Waugh's name as a novelist.

The major went on, 'So, bit of a shambles, isn't it, eh? Of course, Lord Randolph told us the battle was as good as won before we came out by you lot, don't you know? Somewhat different in reality, eh?'

'Yes, sir. Somewhat different.'

'Our CO's away at General Weston's HQ at 42nd Street. If you ask me, Weston's finished. Exhaustion, d'you see. Can't get a coherent word out of him. Colonel Bob reckons this is a bloody awful place to defend, and I agree with him. But those are our orders from on high. From Freyberg.'

Waugh, who had been lost in thought thus far, spoke at last. 'I say . . . Peter Lamb. Weren't you married to Julia Maitland?'

'Yes, as a matter of fact I was.'

'Not any more though, eh?' He smiled, as if aware of something that Lamb was not privy to.

'No, not any more.'

Waugh paused for a moment before speaking again. 'How is she, Julia?'

'I've no idea.'

He laughed and shook his head. 'No, of course you wouldn't, would you? Haven't I seen you in White's?'

'Possibly. I'm not a member but I did occasionally dine there with friends, before all this. Not really my world any more anyway, not since the divorce.'

'No. Suppose not. Not really your set any more, eh? What regiment did you say you were?'

'North Kents.'

'Oh yes. The Jackals. Very good.' He smiled, and Lamb felt the sneer.

They had been joined by another officer now, and Bandouvas was talking with Ryan to the major. Waugh turned to the newcomer. 'I say, Algie, this chap was married to Julia Maitland. Peter Lamb.'

The other officer's face brightened. 'Were you? I say. Good man. Lovely girl. Shame she's not yours any more. What did you say your name was?'

'Lamb. Peter Lamb. North Kents.'

'The Jackals, eh? Didn't know you were here. Your chaps got a bit beaten up at Corinth, didn't they? Where are you making for? I say, what are all these civilians doing with you? Isn't that . . .? No, it can't be. It's Prince Peter, isn't it? And the King. Good God. I must say hello.'

And before Lamb could stop him the officer had pushed through the men and was talking to the King. Lamb and Ryan hurried to join him.

'You do remember, Your Majesty, don't you? We had dinner together in London at St James's. Two years ago. I was on guard at the palace and you were visiting the King. His Majesty had an awful problem persuading you that you couldn't stay at Brown's.'

The King nodded and laughed. 'Of course, I remember. How are you?'

'Worledge. Algie Worledge. Grenadiers.'

'Of course. How nice to see you again. You know my cousin?'

He turned to the Prince. 'Yes, sir. Hello again. We met in Egypt. At the embassy.'

He turned to Lamb. 'I say, Lamb, this is extraordinary. What are you doing with the King?'

'Taking him out of danger, if I can. We're trying to get down to Sfakia and find the Navy. Get His Majesty away to Alex. Those are my orders, at least.'

Worledge shook his head. 'No go, old chap. Sorry. I'd forget Sfakia if I were you. Out of the question. That road's fine for the men, but not with the King in tow. Far too dangerous. It's *sauve qui peut* down there. And Jerry will be hot on all our tails. No, I'd definitely find another route south if I were you.' He turned back to the King. 'I say, sir, what about that dinner at Mount Stewart? The Londonderrys.'

Lamb gave up and, leaving the King to reminisce about a previous and probably irretrievable life, went back to where Bandouvas was talking to the 2I/C.

Another officer was with them now and Lamb recognised him as their CO, Robert Laycock, 'Colonel Bob' to his men.

Laycock squinted at Lamb. 'Don't I know you?'

'Yes, sir. Peter Lamb, North Kents.'

'Oh yes, the chap from St Valéry. I offered you a place in my commandos and you turned us down. Pity. Looks like we're in for a bit of sport here. What exactly are you doing?'

'I've orders to escort the King of Greece to an evacuation vessel, sir.'

Laycock raised his eyebrows. 'Have you, by Jove. Someone else got to you then. Top secret and all that.'

'No, not really, sir. I'm just obeying orders.'

Laycock laughed. 'Witty too. Shame we don't have you aboard, Lamb. Where is His Highness?'

Not for the first time, Lamb was glad he had refused Laycock's offer of a place in his force of commandos. Even when Laycock had offered to take on Bennett too, and Smart, Lamb had said no. He was a regular soldier, bound by unbreakable bonds to his regiment, his battalion and his company. Besides, if Waugh's form of wit was anything to go by, that form of soldiering was certainly not for him.

Ryan had taken Laycock to the King and Lamb heard the colonel's distinctive voice. 'No, Your Majesty. I really wouldn't advise it. The major's quite right.'

Lamb walked across to them.

'I was just telling His Majesty, Lamb, that the road to Sfakia is quite unsuitable for your party, and the major here agrees with me. I do have an idea, though. Where's your map?'

Eadie produced the map and they gathered round in an impromptu 'O' group. Laycock pointed. 'Look here. The Jerries have taken our left flank as far as Galatas and reduced Canea to a ruin. They'll be there soon in force. They're also advancing here, up the Alikianos road, and there are more reinforcements being landed all the time at Maleme. Mountain troops as far as we know, and damned good. Problem is there are pockets of their paratroops too here, at Rethymno, and at Heraklion. They'll be trying to break out, and it won't be long before they try to come round and cut us off by meeting up with the main body. If you want my opinion your best bet is to go back up to Canea before they get there and then head off down here.' He pointed to a small road south, some miles west of their intended route.

Laycock looked at Bandouvas. 'Is that possible, Kapitan?'

Bandouvas nodded and scratched at the stubble on his chin. 'It is possible. It may not be desirable, but it may be possible. Yes.'

Laycock turned and began to talk again to the King. Lamb looked back to the map and studied the route proposed by the colonel, who for all his faults seemed to him to be the one officer fully apprised of all the facts, or as many as could be known. First, he thought, they would have to get back from where they were, through Suda, back to Canea, with whatever dangers that might hold for them. Not least they would be moving towards the main German forces that must by now be closing in on the town. Then, branching off to the south, they would take to a path off the road across the foothills of the White Mountains and then up higher on to a plateau, before dropping down into the area known as Samariá, with its notoriously steep gorge, which would eventually take them down to the sea at Agia Roumeli.

He spoke quietly to Bandouvas. 'Can we manage it? Truly?'

Bandouvas said nothing, but traced a line with his dirty fingernail down the map from north to south. Then he nodded. 'God willing, we can do it. In truth, Kapitan, I don't think we have any other choice.'

15

The walk back into Suda along the same dusty road was mostly spent in silence. There was no point in trying to persuade the men to sing. They all knew the situation and no one was in anything approaching good spirits. Lamb led the way, with what was left of his HQ, Bennett and Eadie's platoon. Passing through the roadblock unopposed this time, they found themselves walking against a tide of men. There were more now than before, it seemed, and all of them were walking in the opposite direction. Lamb looked at them more closely and saw clearly the lack of equipment and the torn uniforms. The larger men were carrying the rifles and ammunition of the weak. Such officers as remained among the listless throng shouted orders in an attempt at discipline. 'Change those Brens.' 'No one to carry heavy weapons for more than half an hour.' 'Keep closed up.'

An officer, a captain, stopped in front of them and, eyes wide, shook his head at Lamb. He had lost his hat and his uniform was ripped. Lamb noticed an old, dark stain on his shorts that looked like blood. He shouted into Lamb's face, 'Where the hell are you going? The Jerries are right behind us. You're mad, all of you.'

'We have to get to Mournies.'

The captain shook his head again. 'It's pointless. Stupid. No point in going that way, old man. The road's been blown to pieces. You'll never get round it. Have to go into the town and out again. That's what I should do. But it's still madness. You're mad. Come with us. Save yourselves. You'll all be killed, all of you.'

Lamb ignored him and walked on, letting him go. He was not sure whether or not to believe him, but he saw no reason not to do so. With a wave of his hand he signalled that they should turn right, and instantly wondered whether he had been right to do so.

The streets of southern Suda were deserted, and everywhere they looked lay piles of rubble and possessions. And among them, strewn like dolls, lay the bodies. A rat ran across Lamb's path and vanished into the basement of a bombed-out building. On all sides the fires licked and crackled in the shells of houses and shops, and every few minutes an explosion somewhere would signal that they had reached a gas main or a cache of ammunition.

As the noise of one explosion died away, Lamb heard someone whistling. Lillibulero. For a moment he could hardly believe it. Pendlebury. His tune. He looked around but saw no one, only the column of his party. But how could that be? Bandouvas had sworn he was dead. He turned, still hearing the tune, and saw Valentine, lips pursed. Then it stopped. Lamb went over to the sergeant. 'That tune you were whistling.'

'Sir?'

'Lillibulero.'

'Yes, sir. Lovely tune, isn't it? Do you know it was sung on campaign in the Duke of Marlborough's times?'

'Why were you whistling it?'

'I don't know, really. I suppose because I like it.'

'Well, don't.'

265

'Sorry, sir?'

'Just don't whistle it. Or sing it. It was Pendlebury's tune.'

'Was it, sir? Didn't know that it was anyone's tune. Just a tune.'

'Well, now you know, don't you. All right?'

'Yes, sir.'

Lamb rejoined the head of the column and wondered whether he might have over-reacted. He had hardly known Pendlebury. It was just that that tune seemed to conjure up something: a vision of hope, a spirit of joyfulness, an England he hoped he might see once again, some day. It seemed totally inappropriate.

They walked on through the bombed ruin that had been Suda. The sound of falling masonry was all around. But it was the smell of the place that hit them the worst. It was extraordinary: olive oil mixed with burning brick and stone, strong wine and the distinctive sweetness of burnt flesh.

Although Canea must have suffered worse, he thought, Suda was dead. The heart of the little town had been ripped out.

They headed west, trying to stick to the roads south of the town, passing what had until recently been elegant Venetian-style seaside villas and tall houses, too many of them now no more than façades. Several were still smoking, and in dozens the fires raged. On Lamb's right stood a ruined monastery and on his left the shell of a church, but it was hard to tell immediately whether either or both were the result of the ravages of time or the new vandalism of the German air force. A party of civilians, the women clad in black, the one old man in his shirt-sleeves, ran across their path out of the town, pushing their possessions on two handcarts. They gave the party a look without stopping and hurried past. Ahead of them they could hear the boom of the guns. Startled by a noise and looking right, Lamb saw a group of three soldiers. It was obvious they were looting, but he did nothing to stop them. One of them was holding a case of something and arguing with one of the others when the third drew a revolver and shot the one with the case through the head. Falling, he dropped it and it smashed on the stones: a dozen bottles of red wine. Then, leaving their dead comrade, the two survivors clambered off in search of more plunder.

As he was contemplating the sheer waste, Smart came up to Lamb. He was carrying an ammunition box. 'Found this in one of the houses by the road, sir. Sort of a ware-house sort of place. Door smashed in. There's loads of stuff. Rifles, good 'uns. Enfields. Boxes of ammo.'

'Well done, Smart. Leave the guns but get the lads to take as much ammo as we can all carry.'

As the men broke ranks to fill their pockets, Lamb saw that Bandouvas and his men had already taken some of the rifles and were busy re-arming themselves. The Greek smiled at him. 'Kapitan Pendlebury's guns. Thank God for him.'

Just outside the port they found themselves suddenly in an Allied position, dug in and sandbagged. Bennett, who had been silent throughout, chimed up now. 'Blimey, sir. It looks like we're going to make a stand.'

'Yes, Sarnt-Major, there does seem to be an element of organisation.'

He looked about for an officer and found a Royal Marines sergeant. 'Is this the front line?'

'Yes, sir. You could say that. It's where we've been told to hold, anyway.'

'Can we get through? I have to get down to Mournies.'

The sergeant shook his head. 'Shouldn't do that, sir,

not if I was you. Jerry's right over there. See? He's come through Canea and all. We're just waiting for the attack. Whenever it comes.'

'Have you any officers left?'

'Not in our mob. All dead. But there's a bunch of Kiwis down the road on the left flank who are in command. You could try them, sir.'

Lamb looked back at the group behind him. He saw his men, as exhausted as any he had seen that day, and beyond them the Greeks and the civilians. Miranda Hartley looked as if she was about to drop. He found Bandouvas.

'There's no way through. The Jerries have taken Canea. Mournies too, I'll bet. What's to the south of here?'

Bandouvas thought for a moment. 'A village. Tsikalaria. Then no roads. Just a hill up to Kondopoula. But I don't know if they'll manage that.'

'They'll have to. I'll talk to them.'

Lamb turned and called them together.

'I'm not going to beat about the bush. We're in a mess. The front's collapsed. This line here, these men in these trenches, that's all we have of our rearguard. The problem is we've got to get beyond these lines to get down to the road south. They're going to stand and fight here to try to let the men on the Sfakia road get away. We've got one chance. When the Jerries do attack, this place is going to be chaos. The only thing we can do is slip through the lines away to the left. There are no roads, and it's rough country, so I won't pretend it'll be easy. But if we don't try we have less than any hope.'

He paused, allowing them to take it in. 'I have to try to get the King away. Those are my orders. I'm afraid that the weak and the wounded, anyone who doesn't feel they can manage it, you'll just have to stay here. That's how it is, I'm afraid. I'm sorry.' He turned to Bennett.

'Sarnt-Major, see to the men. The light cases can come with us. Any other wounded, even the walking wounded, will have to stay here and take their chances.'

'Sir.'

Miranda Hartley was at his side now, as he had known she would be. 'Captain . . . Peter, please. Is there any way? I'm really quite good on my pins. Quite steady. It's just that these shoes aren't the best.'

He smiled. 'To be frank, I don't think you'd manage it. Better for everyone if you head back down to Sfakia and try to find transport south that way. I can give you an escort.'

She looked at him. 'Peter, please. Just let me find other clothes. Other shoes. Boots. I can do it. I know I can.'

He shook his head. 'How on earth do you think you can find boots your size here? Even if you strip the dead. I'm sorry. No.'

As he turned and walked away Comberwell approached him. 'I say, Lamb. When d'you suppose they'll come? The Jerries, I mean?'

Lamb sighed. 'I've no idea, really.'

'I told you, I'm really quite handy with a gun. You know, the pheasants. And look.'

He was brandishing one of the Lee Enfields that Smart had found in Suda. 'Cartridges too. Look. Sorry, I mean bullets.'

'Mr Comberwell, I don't think there's any need.'

'Oh, but there is. There is a need. You need every one of us. And I'm armed and ready.'

'Thank you so much. I'll keep you in mind.'

Christ, he thought. That's all I need: a bloody armed civilian with a death wish.

Lamb was about to tell Bennett of Comberwell's offer when a New Zealand captain hurried over to him. 'Crikey. What the hell are you doing here? Who the heck are all

269

these civvies and Greeks? We're about to get it. You'd better get them out of it, sharpish. We could use your men, though. Better look sharp. They're moving forward.'

Lamb had started to reply when there was a terrific whoosh over their heads and an artillery shell flew in and crashed behind them, exploding in the rear of the position.

The captain frowned. 'Christ, that's it. Come on, if you're coming.'

Lamb ran over to Bennett. 'Sarnt-Major, where's Lieutenant Eadie?'

'Haven't seen him, sir. Must be with his men.'

'Get any man who can fight and come with me, and get the women into cover, and the King, the Prince and the others. I'll give you a signal when it's time to move out.'

He found what remained of the company, including Eadie, close to the front-line trenches. 'Charles, how are you for ammo?'

'Fine, sir. That cache of Smart's was a bloody godsend.'

'Good. Looks like we're going to need it. Just remember, we're not here for the big fight. We're using it to get away. All right?'

'Sir.'

'When I judge it's time to go, I'll wave at you like this.' He cut the air three times with his right hand. 'Or if I can, I'll whistle. Three short blasts. Got it?'

'Sir.'

'Right. On either of those signals you disengage and fall back on the others. Then we get away. Follow Bandouvas if you're in any doubt.'

Another shell flew in over their heads, and then another, and then the whole place seemed to explode in a frenzy of small-arms fire. The ground to their front was lit up with criss-crossing streams of tracer.

Lamb found Bennett. 'Establish a line, Sarnt-Major, wherever you can. Let's take a few with us before we go, shall we?'

The Kiwi captain ran over. 'OK. We've got a plan. We're going to charge.'

Lamb was incredulous. 'What? You're bloody joking.'

'It's the only way. We're going to charge them. It's all we can do.'

He moved away at a running crouch, and Lamb turned to Bennett. 'Did you hear that? Charge them? And he's serious. We can't do that. We have to get away from here.'

'But we can give them covering fire, sir.'

'That's it. You're right. Covering fire. Tell the men. I'll find Eadie and Valentine. Better fix bayonets all the same.'

The word was passed around, and within minutes the Enfields had sprouted their eighteen-inch-long slivers of razor-sharp steel and the men had taken position behind the sandbags to the front of the Kiwis' slit-trenches. Bandouvas' Cretans were with them, the new rifles keen in their hands, and among them Anna. Lamb had sought her out.

'Remember, we must get away from here. You may want to kill Germans, but we have to get away. We have to use the battle.'

'Yes, Peter. I know. Don't worry. But first I will kill some of those bastards.' Then, after a moment's thought, 'What will you do about the English woman and Madame Tsouderos?'

'They can't come with us. You can see that. Not dressed like that. Besides, Madame Tsouderos is too old to go into the mountains. And I'm not even sure if Mrs Hartley would make the pace anyway.'

'No? So you think women are weaker than you?'

Lamb smiled. 'Well, yes, I suppose I do. Not you, of course. But look at her. She'd never manage it.'

271

There was a burst of fire over to their right and a rush of grey-green uniforms up the hill. At the same instant the entire position seemed to erupt as a mass of men poured out from the trenches that had been named by the men 42nd Street and ran headlong down the hill. Lamb watched them go and was conscious of the glinting, reflected light on hundreds of bayonets as they went. But what held him gripped was nothing that he saw, but what he heard. The sound seemed to come from the very earth itself. A terrible, primeval roar – the haka, which for centuries had preceded generations of Maori warriors into battle – came down upon the Germans. Lamb glimpsed the New Zealand captain waving his company forward. The German guns opened up, and that same moment Lamb saw the officer fall, torn by bullets from three directions. But his men moved forward. Forty yards, fifty now, sixty. Lamb and Eadie shouted at the same moment, 'Covering fire now,' and their rifles opened up along with the last remaining working Bren.

More men were walking forward now, taking over where the others had gone to ground. More Maoris. Still chanting, they moved on, another twenty, thirty, forty yards, and then after 100 yards they were on the enemy. In the half-light Lamb could see the silhouettes of individual battles, men locked in deadly combat with bayonet, rifle butt, knife and fist. Part of him longed to be in that fight with them, but equally he was aware that he had another duty. He could see the Maoris clearly now, lit up by the firefight. They were pushing in on the German positions, and then he was aware of something else, figures running headlong down the slope. The haka had done its work and achieved the impossible. Where guns had failed the fighting spirit of the New Zealanders had prevailed, and as Lamb looked on the entire German attacking force before the Maoris broke and fled. The

Kiwis kept on after them, but Lamb knew he had to act fast. He turned to Eadie. 'Charles, find the sarnt major. I'm going to get the King. You stay until the last, then follow us.'

Lamb raced to the rear and found the civilians with the King, Prince Peter and a guard from Ryan's platoon.

'Right, Your Majesty. Now's our chance. Everyone, come with me.'

He led the way back until they were almost level with the original front line. In the distance he could see that isolated groups were still fighting, but the bulk of the attack was far down the hillside now. He found Bandouvas standing by a path which led off to the south and into the village of Tsikalaria. Silently the kapitan showed them where to go, and one by one, led by Ryan and his men, the royal party moved up the trail. Lamb watched them go and was conscious that someone was missing. Two people: Comberwell and Miranda Hartley. He found Hartley. 'Where the devil's your wife?'

The writer stammered, 'I don't know. I really don't know. I only just missed her.'

Lamb looked around them but saw no sign of her. Then further down the slope he caught sight of a familiar figure. Comberwell was standing a little distance down the slope with the rifle at his shoulder, pumping shots into the night. Lamb ran down to him and grabbed him by the shoulder.

'You bloody fool. I told you to stick together. You'll get killed.'

Comberwell turned to him, and Lamb saw that his smile was of a man brought alive by the heat of battle. 'Did you see that? Did you? I got one of the buggers. Hit square on. Big bugger too.'

Lamb pushed him up the slope. 'Get back to the others. You may not be a soldier but you will obey orders.'

Comberwell muttered something inaudible and moved up the hill, and perhaps ten yards away from the rear of the party he stopped. 'Wait. In that bush, there. You come out. *Hande hoch. Hinaus. Schnell.*'

As Lamb watched, a German paratrooper emerged from the bush, his hands on his head, and walked towards them, mumbling as he came. '*Nicht schiessen, nicht schiessen. Freund.*'

There was a crack and the man fell to the ground, a bullet hole in his forehead. Lamb looked at the smoking muzzle of the rifle in Comberwell's hands.

'He was surrendering, you idiot. That was bloody murder.'

Comberwell cocked the rifle and shook his head. 'Was he, old man? Didn't look like it to me. Anyway, one less of the buggers.'

Lamb snatched the rifle from Comberwell and shoved him towards the group.

Comberwell hesitated. 'Steady on, old man.'

Lamb pushed him towards them with the butt of the gun. 'Get on with them. Get away from me.'

He turned towards the rearguard, saw Eadie and Bennett and the others. 'God help me. Come on. Has anyone seen Mrs Hartley?'

Eadie shook his head. Bennett said, 'I did, sir. A few minutes ago, with the Greeks.'

Just then two figures appeared from the rear. Anna was running towards him, followed by Miranda Hartley, who to his amazement was clad in a khaki service-issue shirt, shorts and a pair of boots. She was smiling. 'Told you I could do it. Look. She helped me.'

He looked at Anna. 'Where did you find this lot, then?'

'We stripped the dead. The boots came from an Australian boy. The shorts too. He was very small. His body had no wounds at all.'

Lamb found the others. 'Right, come on, before it's too late.'

They caught up with the rest of the party who were hurrying away from the battle, down the southern slopes.

As they did so Lamb thought about Comberwell's actions. He had clearly seen that the German was surrendering. So why had he shot him? To prove something to himself. To Lamb perhaps? And was the shot in the head just luck, or was he really that good? He had thought for some time about the identity of the agent who had revealed him to the colonel back in Athens. Now, absurdly, it seemed as if Comberwell might be the real contender.

Bandouvas was beside him now, urging on his men. 'He likes killing Germans, your friend.'

'My friend?'

'Comberwell. He enjoyed it.'

'He's no friend of mine. You think so?'

'Didn't you see his face? I tell you, he's a good man to have on our side.'

'If you like murderers.'

'Kapitan Lamb, I like any man who likes to kill Germans. Don't you?'

They reached the tiny hamlet of Tsikalaria and did not pause but carried on climbing. Then, at 400 metres, Bandouvas called a halt, not for rest but because the road curved round here and was open above the slope down to the sea. Anyone standing on it would be visible from the north east, and he wasn't taking any chances. Placing his men lying down on the slope facing the enemy, Bandouvas ushered everyone across the road in groups of three until at last he followed on. At Kondopoula they passed the little church and then continued to climb, but on a road now. Lamb found himself walking with the King, who spoke, quietly and more than a little breathless.

'Captain Lamb, this is a great thing you are doing. Thank you. Not just for me. You see, Hitler has declared me an enemy of my own people and Germany's number one enemy in Greece. He has deposed me. There is talk that he would like to place my brother Paul on the throne as a puppet. He's married to a German. It would suit him well. But he has to get rid of me first.'

'Yes, sir. I know. We were told. That's why I'm here.'

'Is it? You don't strike me as like the other Section D men I've met. You're more of a soldier's soldier. Aren't you?'

'Yes, I suppose I am, sir.'

'I dare say you'd far rather be fighting the Germans down there than up here with me.'

'To be honest, sir, I have to say I would. But, as you've just said, ensuring your safety is vital.'

'Thank you, Captain, but I really don't believe you mean that.'

The King walked on and Lamb fell back to where Valentine was treading nimbly over the boulders that lined their way. 'Valentine, tell me why I'm here.'

'Because you're an officer and a gentleman and a born leader of men, sir?'

'Very funny. Now tell me again.'

'Because someone in the high command has decided that you're the man to save the King of Greece, and you've agreed, and because someone has to take responsibility.'

'Thank you. That was what I wanted to hear.'

Lamb pondered. Responsibility. Bloody word. Who was really responsible? he wondered. The one who gave the orders, or the one with the blood on his hands who did the dirty work?

Bennett came running over. 'Sir, there's something you should see. Before anyone else does.'

*   *   *

276

They had come down the road now to Panagia, directly south of Canea, and he followed Bennett ahead of the main party on the outskirts of the village. It seemed to be deserted, but then he saw that the shapes he had taken to be rocks were actually bodies. Bennett called him over. 'Look, sir, Bunce found them.'

There were dead bodies strewn through the streets of the village. And, to a man, they were German. Evidently the fighting here had been heavy, but who exactly had accounted for so many of the enemy, Greeks or Allies, there was no way of knowing. He walked across to one corpse, looked down at it and almost retched, for he found himself staring into two empty eye sockets. The man's nose, too, seemed to have been ripped apart, through the septum.

'Christ almighty. What a bloody mess. Who the hell did this?'

Eadie's platoon were moving through the village now. There was a call from across the road. 'Same here, sir. No eyes, and the face is a mess.'

'And here, sir.'

They moved around the dead young men, counting them. Of the thirty-two who had lain out in the sun for at least a day, their bloated bodies stretching their uniforms to bursting, all but two had lost their eyes.

Lamb found Bandouvas staring at them too. He looked for the royal party and the women.

Bandouvas spoke. 'It's all right, Kapitan, they are not here. They are behind us. My men will move these cuckolds before they get here.'

'Is this the doing of your partisans? If it is, then you are even more savage than I thought.'

Bandouvas shrugged. 'No, this is not our work, although given the chance some of my men might do the same. This, I think, is the work of the crows and the ravens. We have many here on Crete. They like the eyeballs, just as we like to eat the eyes of the sheep. The nose too is a delicacy for them. That I think is how these men lost their sight. And after death.'

Lamb looked around. The stench from the corpses was stomach turning, made all the worse as Bandouvas' men moved them into the empty houses. The unforgiving heat, he supposed, had helped the decomposition as much as the crows.

Valentine was standing with them. 'It's the Cyclops again, sir, isn't it? D'you see? Losing their eyes. Like Odysseus . . .'

Lamb turned on him. 'If I hear you spouting one more bloody Greek myth, I'll have you on a charge. Or worse, God help me.'

'Sorry, sir. I was just making an observation.'

'Well, don't. I've enough to worry about without your bloody observations.'

But as the sergeant walked away, he couldn't quite help feeling that Valentine had touched a nerve of truth. What at first had seemed to be a straightforward if questionable mission was now turning into something far more complex and potentially disastrous.

Back at 42nd Street the Maoris had been recalled to their positions and stood triumphant, looking down at a field strewn with hundreds of enemy dead. Every one of them, however, knew that this was just a temporary victory, that any time now the order would come for a general withdrawal. For the Kiwis it had been a last hurrah.

A few hundred yards away the Germans licked their wounds and waited for the morning, which they knew would bring fresh troops and ultimately victory. But one man among them did not intend to wait.

278

General Wilhelm Sussmann had seen something in the midst of all the fighting that had changed his plans.

As the Maoris had charged home, pushing his men down the hill, he had caught a glimpse of the face of a man in the light of battle. The face of a King. The last few days had been hell: so many men killed, even after the initial horror; Derpa was gone, other old friends too. Well, now he was going to do something that would avenge them all, that would make the name of the Fallschirmjäger live through history. He turned to his new 2I/C, Captain Baron Friedrich von der Heydte, commander of 1st Battalion, who was squatting in the cover of a stone wall at his side.

'Von der Heydte. Get word to Colonel Heidrich. Tell him that he's in charge.'

'Sir?'

'I'm taking a platoon of our own men and whatever mountain troops I can get to come with me, and I'm going south. That matter of which we spoke earlier has just become a reality.'

'The King?'

Sussmann nodded. 'And I intend to get him myself. Think of the Führer's face, von der Heydte. Dead or alive. Well, we'll see. Either way the glory will be mine. Wish me luck, Friedrich. I dare say I'll need it.'

16

Sussmann climbed up the rocky path and cursed his uniform. It had not been designed for a hot Cretan summer, and even at this time of day it was still unpleasant. He wished that instead he might have been wearing a pair of the shorts worn by the British and their Allies. He had contemplated stripping them from one of the dead, but had thought better of it. It did not suit the dignity of a general of the Wehrmacht. Even the mountain troops who came behind him were dressed in a more fitting way than he. At least they had managed to bring their shorts with them, nor were they encumbered by the sweltering and heavy paratroop helmets. Well, Sussmann had stuck to his *feldmütze* at least. But if only he could lose these damned trousers! He turned to the young lieutenant whom he had brought with him and the platoon from 1st Battalion.

'Well, Becker. This is better than being stuck in a damn trench.'

'Yes, Herr General. It's good to be on the move and away from the guns.'

The young man had been bemused when his general had come to him ordering him to accompany him on a chase through the hills.

He had managed to find a platoon of Gebirgsjäger, the mountain troops that were being landed by the hour at Maleme, and had ordered them as a general of the Reich to come with him. Their lieutenant, Müller, had at first been reluctant, but he had eventually ceded to Sussmann's superior authority. This was after all, the general had said, a mission from the Führer. Perhaps, thought Müller, it might even be a shortcut to glory and promotion. One heard about such things. The Führer's favour. Whatever, a stroll in the hills was certainly better than dying at the hands of those yelling savages, as so many of his comrades had done.

It had taken Sussmann the best part of two hours to assemble his little force and they had followed the route taken by the Tommies and their royal charge. It had not been hard, particularly for the mountain troops, men from the alps of Austria and Bavaria who had grown up tracking animals and reading the signs. Besides, according to Sussmann's map, if they were going south from Suda there were only two paths open to them. That on the east, through Kambi, was one. But that would take you high into the heart of the White Mountains, up to 2,300 metres and the highest mountain on Crete. No, the second way was sure to be their path – the track that led down through Theriso to Samariá and then off to the sea at Agia Roumeli.

So it was, as the moon rose, that Sussmann and his men reached Panagia. As they entered the village he knew that something was wrong. It was not just that the place was deserted. There was something else: a smell, a sense of evil. One of the mountain troops called to him. 'Herr General, over here, sir.'

He looked at where the man was pointing, at a stain on the ground under the moonlight. 'It's blood, sir. And look, there's more.'

They began to walk up the street and every few yards he could see, even in the half-light, were marked by more of the stains.

He turned to Becker. 'What is it, d'you think? Where are the bodies?'

There was another shout. 'Sir, in here.'

Sussmann entered the house, which was lit inside by a shaft of moonlight. It fell through the open window, across the stone floor and the wooden table, and fell across the faces of the dead. The general looked down and found the eyeless corpses. He stared, wide-eyed, and then turned and walked from the building. The stench of dead flesh had reached into his nostrils now. 'Becker, did you see? Did you see what they had done to those boys? Christ. Holy Christ. How could they? Those poor boys.'

He reached into his pocket and pulled out a small flask. Schnapps. Sussmann took a swig, then another, and passed it to Becker, who followed suit.

Lieutenant Müller was with them now. 'Did you see them? Those poor boys.'

'Yes, sir.'

'They're savages, these people. No better than barbarians. The cradle of civilisation? Don't give me that.'

He took another swig from the flask and, walking back into the house, took another look at the corpses and felt the tears coursing down his face.

Sussmann had come to do one thing on this cursed island. He had come for a King. But as well as that, now he knew he had another mission: a mission from a higher authority even than the Führer. He would teach these savages a lesson. He would somehow atone for the blinding of those poor young boys, for the hideous torture. And then, when he caught up with the royal party and found the animals who had done this thing, he would take his revenge. After that he would deal with the King.

As Sussmann had guessed, Lamb's party had spent the night at the village of Theriso, five miles into the mountains from Panagia, sheltered by its tiny population of old men, women and children. Casting propriety aside, after posting sentries and ensuring that the King and his party were comfortable and the civilians secure, Lamb had decided to spend the night with Anna. He had kept his distance from the Hartleys and Comberwell, staying with his men during the climb. He wanted no more to do with any of the civilians. He no longer felt it his duty to get them away.

His men, the King and Anna were what concerned him now, although in what order he was still not entirely certain. His orders, love and loyalty vied for position in his addled mind. What he knew above all, though, was that he needed rest.

The woman whose house he had made his billet for the night welcomed them in almost as newlyweds. Anna had explained, but it had not mattered. The woman's husband had been killed in Albania. She cared for nothing now. And to see two people happy was enough. The little room had a single bed made up on a wooden shelf. It had been cramped, but better than the ground. Yet all night long Lamb's sleep had been disturbed, haunted by visions of the eyeless corpses. Once he had cried out, waking at the end of a shout, and had found Anna's hand stroking his head. It was another three hours before the light woke him again. The dawn smelt of thyme and of the sweet scent of the hillside flowers. Lying there, cradled in her arms, he shivered with the cold, pulled the goatskin that had been provided tighter round them and cursed the fact that, in their haste to leave, more of the party had not brought blankets, and what covering they could find had been given to the King and the women. Anna was awake too now. He heard a cock crow. She said, 'You cried out in the night.'

'I know.'

'Why? What was it?'

'A dream. A nightmare. Nothing.'

'The men in the village, back there?'

'How do you know about them?'

'I saw them too.'

'Is it true about the ravens?'

'Perhaps. Maybe not. We hate the Germanos and we will hate them more soon.'

'You know what they will do when they find those men. And others like them?'

'Yes. Soon this island will be filled with hate. But by then you will be gone.'

'And you? Aren't you coming with us?'

She said nothing.

A soldier appeared in the doorway. Turner.

'Captain Lamb, sir. The Greek captain. He wants you.'

He found Bandouvas crouching down over a fire he had set on the floor of one of the outbuildings, kept low to avoid detection. The kapitan offered Lamb a mug of tea.

'Your servant made it for us. He's good. I like your British tea. Very sweet.'

Lamb took a swig as Bandouvas walked to the door and gazed at the rising dawn before he spoke.

'Today we will go higher. Up there.' He pointed towards where the mountains touched the sky. 'Twelve hundred, eighteen hundred metres perhaps. We will take it slowly, for all our sakes. At Samariá there is a little monastery. Not many monks now. I know the abbot. He's a friend.'

Lamb drew the faded map sheet from his pocket and

traced their path. He saw the climb go from 2,000 feet at their present location up through the mountains to Lakki. Then it branched off the road on to a track, which followed the line of a stream. Bandouvas was right. At its height it touched over 5,000 feet. There was no point in worrying. It was their only hope. They might lose some of their group. Saving the King was his mission now, although he could not help but feel that his real duty still lay in saving his men. He knew too now through a runner from Layforce that they had German mountain troops behind them, men who were used to this sort of terrain. He imagined they must be twice as nimble over the rocks as his own men, let alone the civilians.

Leaving Bandouvas at the house, Lamb walked through the village, which was coming to life. A few old men stood staring at the soldiers, and he passed a group of inquisitive children and two dogs before he came to the positions on the perimeter where Ryan's men had spent the night, with a picket of his own. He could only wonder what they thought of what he was doing. He hoped they would have followed him anywhere, knew in his heart that some at least would. But he knew too that they must be questioning, as any soldier would, why they were being taken into the hills when the rest of Creforce was making its escape along the road down to Sfakia. His reasoning, of course, was that they should at all costs avoid being mixed up in the potential rout that was taking place on the Sfakia road. It troubled him. He called across to Smart, 'Morning, Smart. Got your hands full this morning, eh?'

'Yes, sir. They can't get enough char, sir.'

'Hello, Dawlish. Bearing up?'

'Thank you, sir. It's just me feet. Bit raw. Don't suppose you've a spot of vinegar about you, sir?'

'Sorry, I'm all out. But I'll see if it can be managed

when we get back to Alex.' He turned to Bennett. 'Taken the roll, Sarnt-Major?'

'Yes, sir. All present.'

'Very good. Ask the lieutenant to find me, will you. "O" group in ten. You as well, Sarnt-Major. Oh, and you'd better get Mr Eadie to ask the King to come along.'

The King, along with his cousin and the Prime Minister, had spent the night in the best house in the village, that of a farmer, and they emerged from it looking better than most, shaven, fed and rested. There was more for Bandouvas to resent, thought Lamb, and for his own men to question. He knew that. Valentine was watching the King, and had been for some time.

He knew too that they were being followed by the enemy. Somewhere, not too far away, the Germans were on their trail. And with every slow step they took into the hills, as his pack became heavier and his feet grew more weary, he realised more and more that on their own they might have been able to double their pace, be back on the Sfakia road and with a real chance of escape. That, or they could have stayed with the rest of the army. Now he sat, sipping at his tea, waiting for the order and questioning, with the mind of a born general, quite what military logic lay in saving one weak and ailing man at the potential expense of twenty trained soldiers. And the question began to gnaw at his mind.

The road from Theriso to the hilltop village of Xiloskalo is a road in name only. In fact it is barely a track. But it was by this route that the royal party made its way to the monastery of St Nikolaos.

They had come via Meskla and as they passed the tiny white church in the village Lamb had seen an old woman at the door. She had called him in and, stepping out of line for a moment, he had peered into the darkness to be rewarded by a candle-kit glimpse of wall paintings of exquisite beauty. Christ the Saviour, surrounded by angels. It was only for an instant, and he had quickly backed out, thanked her and rejoined the column, saying nothing, but the image stayed with him, and now in his mind as he trudged on along the path the face of the painted Christ seemed, at least for the present, to blank out those of the eyeless German dead.

They pushed on across country up one of the rubble-strewn corries that led directly south from the village, rising 300 feet in five miles before they hit the track. They rested then, lying on the hillside in the morning sunshine, among the olive groves and chestnut trees, the sweat seeping through their shirts. Twice Miranda Hartley glanced at Lamb, hoping for some acknowledgement. He gave none, no sign of any interest. And he hoped that might be an end to it. Scouring the landscape down the mountainside behind them, Lamb could see no trace of their pursuers.

But Bandouvas nodded sagely. 'They're out there all right. I can feel it.'

Within minutes they were back on their feet, but at least the track here had been cleared of boulders and stones. Walking on the smaller paths was hell, a bit like trying to climb an old staircase where every third or fourth step has a habit of giving way. And although it was clearer, at times their new route did not seem much of an improvement.

They stopped at the foot of another mountain. Bandouvas pointed up. 'Mount Psari.'

Lamb shook his head. 'We're surely not going up there?'

Bandouvas smiled. 'No, don't worry, Kapitan. That would be too much. We go here.'

The road wound westwards, twisting and turning its way around the mountain, until at last they came to a wooden hut perched on a precipice.

Lamb looked down, and wished he had not. 'How high are we?'

Bandouvas laughed. 'About 1,300 metres above that.' He pointed down beyond the rock face. 'Down there is where we are going. Samariá. But don't worry, we won't go straight down.'

They rested in the refuge hut for ten minutes and then carried on, leaving the gorge behind for the moment, as the road turned north again. This was a very different landscape, he thought, with no trace of the hand of man. All that he could see around him among the acres of cedar trees was evidence of the force of nature, and before them the White Mountains soared amid the clouds. Within minutes they emerged on to the last mile of the metalled road from Lakki, and then, walking at the head of the column, Lamb stopped in his tracks. Ahead of him lay another precipice, and beyond it one of the most breathtaking sights he had ever seen.

He was looking directly down a gorge, with mountains falling into it from left and right. Mountain after mountain succeeded one another, rising directly before him, perhaps four miles distant, and behind that another, higher, and another higher still.

Bennett was beside him, gazing in awe. 'Blimey, sir. I never thought I'd see the like.'

'No, Sarnt-Major, nor me.'

Bandouvas spoke behind them. 'Beautiful, isn't it? This is what my people fight for. This is our land. Our mountains. Look, in the distance. You see that? That is Mount Pachnes. The Mountain of the Gods. Two and a half thousand metres high. It is the birthplace of Zeus, the king of the gods. That is why we fight.'

And that, thought Lamb, was why the Germans had brought their mountain troops here. That was why Creforce and even the commandos had lost this battle, and that was why the Cretans, men like Bandouvas and his partisans, the *andartes*, would ultimately win it.

'Now we go down.'

Bandouvas ushered Lamb and the others down on to a flight of steep stone stairs cut into the side of the cliff face. They had been finished carefully with a waist-high wooden handrail. 'Be sure to hold on and walk slowly.'

Carefully, they made their way down the steps, conscious that at any moment the slightest slip could mean death. Bennett was right behind Lamb. 'Bloody high, sir, isn't it? Can't say I care for it much myself.'

There was a commotion from their rear. Someone was shouting. It sounded like Hartley's voice. Somebody shrieked, 'No, no, I can't.'

Christ, thought Lamb. Hartley. He must have vertigo. Lamb pushed past Bennett and, climbing back up, yelled back after him, 'You go on. All of you, keep going.' He reached the top of the staircase and found Hartley and one of his own men, a young lad named Hollis, locked in a struggle. Thankfully the writer had the better of it.

Hollis was shrieking, 'No. Can't you see I'll die? I hate heights. I can't do it.'

Lamb was about to interfere when Valentine stopped him. 'No, sir. Wait. Just wait.'

Hartley shook the young soldier. 'Stop it, man. You'll be fine. Here. Take this.' From his trouser pocket Hartley produced a green spotted handkerchief and tied it around Hollis's head as a blindfold. 'There. Now all you have to do is to hold on to me and we'll soon be down. Don't worry about anything. I've got you now.'

As Lamb watched, saying nothing, Hartley led Hollis on to the top step and very slowly began to descend. The boy let out a whimper and an 'Oh my God,' but that was it and soon the pair were on their way. Lamb smiled at Valentine, and behind him noticed Miranda Hartley. She too was smiling, and he knew why.

The steps curved down the cliff face some 2,000 feet before reaching the bottom of the gorge. The surface was worn, and from the outset Lamb realised the danger. Sure enough, hardly had ten minutes passed before there was a cry from in front of him and he saw someone, one of Ryan's men he thought, slip and fall. The man tumbled down several steps and for a moment Lamb thought he was sure to fall off into the abyss. But he managed to roll into the cliff face and lie there, yelling in pain. They stopped, and after a few moments Mays, who was some way in front of him, yelled up, 'Broken ankle, sir. They're going to have to carry him down.'

Their progress now was even slower, and Lamb was half tempted to leave the man behind. For what seemed like an eternity they edged down the steps, occasionally knocking a stray rock over the edge. Finally, a good hour after they had started, the first of them touched the ground of the valley below. One by one they staggered off the steps and sat down under the plane trees which grew at their base, until Bandouvas urged them to their feet. Lamb came last, after ensuring that they were all safely down.

Bandouvas welcomed him. 'That was the hard part. From here on it is less steep.'

They moved in silence down the valley, and gradually the sides of the ravine through which they were walking became closer together. As they went they crossed a little stream which flowed along the base of the gorge. Then, after it seemed that they had hardly gone any distance at all, perhaps three miles, they found themselves approaching a group of whitewashed buildings enclosed by a six-foot-high wall.

Bandouvas shouted back, 'We will stop here. This is Agios Nikolaos.'

He led the way towards two huge iron-studded wooden entrance gates which were set in the wall, pulled hard on an old and rusted chain, and from within they heard a pealing bell. The noise echoed down the gorge. Lamb cursed. The bloody fool, he thought. If their pursuers had not heard them on the steps they would now be in no doubt as to their location.

One of the doors swung open and they saw a small man, heavily bearded, dressed in black and wearing a cylindrical black hat. Behind him was one of Bandouvas' *andartes.*

The monk clasped Bandouvas' hand in his and looked at them. 'Kapitan. Welcome back. God's blessing be with you, my friends. Please come in.'

They walked in through the gates and found themselves in a wide enclosed courtyard. All around them figures in black robes moved in silence in and out of arched door-ways, evidently preoccupied with their tasks and disinterested in the strange newcomers. The gatekeeper led them across the courtyard to the grandest of the buildings which was crowned with a dome, topped with a stone cross. He said something to Bandouvas, who turned to Lamb.

'The abbot wants only me, you, the King and his cousin.'

Together the four of them followed the monk inside. Lamb gasped. The walls of the room were hung with tapestries twenty feet high and some fifty long, and underfoot was a thick, dark red carpet. Around the room sat gilt-wood chairs upholstered in crimson.

Father Sofronios was seated at the end of the room, behind a huge polished desk on which lay a bible, a gold cross and various documents. He was, Lamb guessed, in

291

his sixties and his long, once black beard was now quite grey. He looked at them with kindly eyes as they entered, but said nothing.

Bandouvas walked towards him, speaking fast, then turned. 'This is Father Sofronios, abbot of the monastery. Father, this is Captain Lamb of the British Army, of whom I told you. And this man, this is His Hellenic Majesty, the King of Greece.'

Lamb was caught off guard by Bandouvas' lack of respect for the King, but moved aside and gave a slight bow. 'Father Abbot, may I present His Majesty King George and His Highness Prince Peter.'

The abbot stood and nodded his head in deference, and the King and the Prince, Lamb noticed, did the same. Bandouvas did nothing.

The King muttered some words of Greek and the abbot smiled and nodded.

He approached Lamb. 'A pleasure to meet a fellow warrior in Christ. God is gracious to grant me such company.'

'Warrior?'

Bandouvas explained.

'Yes, the abbot was mobilised by me ten days ago. He took an oath with all the other *andartes* and kapitani in a cave at Agios Sillas. It is his role now to act as hospital for the fighters, and also a place where we can meet in secret.'

'A field headquarters.'

'Exactly. Here in the monastery. Actually it's only an annex to the main monastery, which is a few kilometres away at Frangokastello, on the coast.'

'I'm sure this will do. I'm just surprised that monks should fight.'

The abbot spoke. 'I hate the Germanos as much as you do, Captain. Perhaps more. I have hated them for years.

Long before you left your country to fight them here I had people from all religions here who had been hunted from their homes by these Nazis. Their stories were so filled with tragedy that they would make even you weep, Captain Lamb. They are a scourge and must be wiped out. You are safe here, for the moment. I don't think the Germanos know of us. We can help you get to the coast. You must get His Majesty away.'

Bandouvas scowled.

Lamb ignored him. 'Thank you. We need to rest, and some of our men are wounded.'

'My monks will look after them. Come, you must rest and eat.'

In the refectory off the courtyard Lamb and the officers ate with the civilians and the royal party.

Meanwhile, across the yard, the monks had set up a great table for the men, who could hardly believe their good fortune. Dinner consisted of chicken and oysters with as much bread as they could eat, washed down with wine from the monks' own vineyards. Bennett and the other NCOs kept them in check, but when they had finished eating, as the wine did its work, Valentine turned to the sergeant-major.

'Tell me one thing, Sergeant-Major. Can you tell me why we're resting here? I mean, it's all very nice, all this, but if it wasn't for the King we could have been long gone from here by now, down at the coast finding a boat to take us off. Either that, or we could be back there up in the north, doing what we're meant to do: kill the bloody Jerries.'

Bennett rounded on him. 'That might sound like mutiny to anyone else, Valentine. I'd keep your lip buttoned up if I were you.'

'It's not mutiny and well you know it, Sergeant-Major. It's just common sense.'

'I'm telling you, Valentine. The captain was given an order, and that's what we do. We follow his orders.'

Valentine said nothing more, but now what had been the germ of an idea had begun to grow in his mind and it would not be denied.

17

They slept that night in cells vacated by the monks, the other ranks two or three to a room, the royal party and the officers on their own. The abbot had allowed the Hartleys to be together. Neither Lamb nor Anna of course had made any mention of their relationship, and so it was that the following morning he awoke alone with the sun streaming in through the tiny window. He rose and washed his face from the ewer on the table before dressing and walking out into the courtyard. The monks were already about their business and, shaking off the cobwebs of the night, he walked across the dusty yard to the refectory where they had been told they might find breakfast. He had not got half-way across when the bell rang for the gate. The keeper peered through his grille and opened the door, admitting three *andartes*. They looked exhausted and, seeing Lamb in the uniform of a British officer, their leader made immediately for him.

In an instant the man's way had been barred by Valentine, who stepped out in front of the unarmed Lamb, his Schmeisser held at the ready.

The man stepped back and grasped for his own weapon.

Lamb held up a hand. 'All right, Sarnt, I'm sure he means no harm.'

The man was in his forties and wore a turbaned hat and a black waistcoat above his crap-catcher trousers and hessian boots. Behind him came two boys, one wearing a bandanna. Like Valentine, they were armed with captured German weapons, two Mauser pistols and a Schmeisser, and had bandoliers of bullets slung round their necks.

Valentine stood down and Lamb turned to him. 'Thank you, Sarnt. See if you can find Captain Bandouvas.'

'I could try translating myself, sir.'

'Very well.' Lamb addressed the leader. 'Where are you from? Who are you with? Whose band? Who is your kapitan?'

The old man smiled. 'Kapitan. Yes, kapitan.'

'What do you know about the King?'

'King.' The old man spat on the ground and wiped his moustache with the back of his hand.

Lamb tried another tack. 'Do you know where the Germans are?'

The old man smiled again. 'Germanos. Yes. Here, Germanos.'

He reached deep into his right pocket and, drawing out his hand, opened it to reveal three severed human ears.

'Germanos, yes, Germanos.'

Lamb stared in horror at the grisly trophies.

Valentine gasped. 'Bloody hell.'

Bandouvas appeared beside him and spoke to the man, who nodded. 'These are my men. They know where the Germans are.'

'Evidently,' said Valentine.

'They know, Kapitan. They have told me.'

'And?'

'They say they are eight cigarettes away.'

'What?'

'It's how they calculate distance. One cigarette takes eight minutes to smoke so they think how many could I smoke in that time. Eight cigarettes. They're at Theriso. They are following us. Two platoons at least, maybe more.'

Valentine said, 'Seems a pity we can't fight them, sir, doesn't it?'

'What?'

'Well, don't you feel we should be fighting back instead of getting the King away? I mean, sir, what real worth is that?'

'Valentine, I've warned you before not to question orders.'

'I'm not, sir. I wouldn't ever do that. I'm just saying that in my opinion we should either be fighting them or we should get away as fast as we can. As it stands, sir, we're doing neither. And if we keep doing what we are then we're going to get caught and we'll all end up in the bag, or worse. It's just a case of ethics, sir. A soldier's ethics, isn't it? I mean, what are we fighting for? Justice, freedom, call it what you like. And we end up saving a King who if he survives this war will get back on that throne and do his best to make life hell for his people. He's done it before. Just ask them. They'll tell you. That's why they threw him out. Twice.'

Lamb sighed and shook his head. 'Thank you, Sarnt. I'll bear that in mind. Now go away and do something useful.'

Bandouvas, who had been talking to the three *andartes*, now dismissed them and turned to Lamb. 'I was listening to your sergeant. He's right, you know.'

'About what?'

'Why are we saving the King when we should be killing

297

Germans? We could turn back and face them. Kill them as they come up the mountain. It would be like a bird shoot. And why save the King anyway? What is he to you, Kapitan Lamb? Whatever it is, he's less than that to us. Do you know Hitler wants to put his brother on the throne? His brother, who is married to a German cow. Did you know that his whole family is Germanos? They have more in common with the Germans than with any of us, Greeks or Cretans. I say we turn back and face the Germans. Leave the women here.'

'And the King?'

Bandouvas smiled. 'Well, he could just meet with an accident, couldn't he? He's not a well man. You've seen that. A foot placed wrong on one of these mountains. A casual slip and . . . no more King. And no more trouble for you, Kapitan. I know you worry about your men. You are a good soldier, a true warrior. But you have not been given a soldier's job to do. Get rid of him, Kapitan. Then we can go back and kill more Germans, and then I will take you and your men to a better place to get away to Egypt. And we will all be happy.'

Lamb looked at him. 'Have you finished?'

'Yes. For now.'

'Good. I'll forget I heard that. It's treason.'

'No, Kapitan, it's reason. It's just common sense.'

Lamb was impatient to get moving. He drummed his fingers on the table and sat and stared at the map and then out at the morning sky. Valentine's words had made him think, but it had been Bandouvas who had really rattled him. For an instant, no more than that, he had actually been tempted by the idea of faking the accident – of 'losing' the King. But then of course you also had Tsouderos and the Prince to deal with. And what about the civilians? He wondered, too, what his men would

298

think of him if he were seen to be party to such an act. He was sure that other, similar treatment was being meted out to officers and other ranks across the island at that moment. It was always the case in times of war. When things descended into chaos old scores were quickly settled with a bullet in the back of the head when no one was looking.

Bandouvas' proposition aside, for once Lamb could see Valentine's logic, and it annoyed him. For a moment it crossed his mind that perhaps the man was actually more like him than he cared to admit.

He had seen one or two of the monks sitting in a quiet spot beneath the trees at a place between the cloister and the cell block which was largely hidden from view, and he went there now and sat in the shade. He allowed himself a few minutes to think.

At length it struck him that perhaps there might be a compromise. If he were to turn back, to head back to Theriso with one or both platoons and Bandouvas' men and to leave Ryan and perhaps Anna in charge of the civilians, then he would surely have discharged his duty to the colonel and still have salved his conscience as a soldier. It would not please Bandouvas, but it would most certainly help him and his men. And the kapitan had told him that he would get them away.

He found Charles Eadie. 'Charles. There's a new plan. You and I are going to head back north with the men. I'm going to leave Ryan here with his own platoon, the King and his party, as originally planned. I'm also leaving the civilians. Bandouvas will want to come with us, but Anna can stay with the women. I'm sure we've come far enough ourselves. Lieutenant Ryan is quite capable of doing the rest, don't you think?'

'I suppose so, sir. Yes. I don't know. But I thought your orders were specific. I thought . . .'

Lamb snapped at him. 'Well, what you thought was obviously wrong. I set out in this war to make a difference, and the best way I know of making a difference is to kill Germans and try to get more of our men off the island, not saving a bloody half-baked German monarch with no kingdom.'

'Yes, sir. Of course.'

Lamb walked away. He found Bandouvas talking quietly to Father Sofronios. 'I've taken a decision. We're leaving the King here, with Lieutenant Ryan. I'm going to take my men back up the mountain. With any luck we'll meet our pursuers on the way. I suppose you'll want to come with us?'

Bandouvas raised his eyebrows. 'This is very sudden, Kapitan. Why the change of heart? Have you become a republican? Has Anna been talking to you?'

'No. I just feel we'd be more useful with our own men doing what we do best.'

'I'm pleased. Yes, of course we will go with you. It's also what we do best, as you know. Do you think Ryan can get the King away?'

'I'm sure of it. I've done what I was ordered to do. I've got him to safety. Getting to the coast from here should be easy. You said it yourself.'

'Whatever you think. Anyway, it's the right decision, if perhaps not exactly what I might have hoped for.' He grinned. 'What about the civilians?'

'They can stay here and take their chances with the King. Besides, I've a feeling that one of them is more than he seems. I'm sure he'll be able to help.'

'Comberwell?'

Lamb nodded.

'Yes, I think you're right. He seems sometimes to behave very differently from the idiot he pretends to be. When do we go?'

'As soon as we can. I've yet to tell the King. Oh, you might want to leave Anna with them. For Mrs Hartley's sake.'

Lamb found Ryan and briefed him, and together they went in search of the King. They found him talking to Prince Peter and Julian Hartley, sitting in the shade of an olive tree, sipping red wine.

'Your Majesty, I have taken the decision, in all our best interests, to return you to the care of Lieutenant Ryan and go back to fight with our army, or what's left of it.'

The King frowned. 'Captain? Are you serious? I thought you had been sent specifically by Section D to escort me to safety.'

'Actually, no, sir. It was somewhat more haphazard than that. But that is what I have done, Your Majesty. This place is as safe as you can be on the island, and Lieutenant Ryan here assures me that he will have no trouble in getting you through the gorge and down to the beach. The attaché has organised a ship which will take you to Egypt.' For once, believing his own reassurances, Lamb felt as if things might have been restored to some semblance of order.

The King shook his head. 'I'm sorry, Captain. I really can't see your reasoning. Surely it is your duty to personally get me to that ship.'

'With respect, sir, my duty is to my men and to my country, and it is my opinion that that obligation is best fulfilled if I now return with my men to the fight. Kapitan Bandouvas and his men will be returning with me, save one of the women who will remain with the British civilians who will accompany you off the island. We intend to confront and destroy the German troops who are on our trail. That should ensure your safety.'

The King nodded. 'Very well, Captain. If that is your

decision I shall respect it. But I must say I am more than a little disappointed and I have to tell you I shall make that clear in my report to London.'

'As you wish, sir. May I say it has been an honour to be of service to you, sir. I wish you luck.'

The King smiled. 'Thank you, Captain. Good luck to you too.'

Lamb was attempting to find Anna when Comberwell came across him. 'I say, is it true? You're leaving us?'

''Fraid so, Comberwell. They can make better use of us in the north, or wherever our front line is now. If there still is one.'

'In that case you must allow me to have a rifle. You've seen I'm pretty useful with one. What harm can it do? If the Jerries find us we'll need every man we can get.'

Lamb stopped and stared at him. 'I doubt very much that the Jerries will find you. And even if they do I'm sure you'll acquit yourself well, Comberwell, or whatever your real name is.'

Comberwell stiffened. 'What? Sorry, Lamb. Don't quite get you.'

'Oh, come off it. I've known ever since Athens that one of you was an agent. A spy. In the pay of London. It has to be you.'

Lamb thought he detected a smile on the man's face. 'Still got me, I'm afraid. Agent? Spy? Sorry.'

'I give up.'

'About that rifle, old man.'

'Oh, take a bloody rifle if you want one. Old man.'

Lamb left him and walked away. In a dark corner of the cloister he found Anna, sitting on her own. She frowned at him.

'Bandouvas told me. Why?'

'You know why.'

'Because you are a soldier. Because you want to fight. Well, so do I.'

'Someone has to stay here with the others. A woman.'

She screamed at him. 'Yes, that's it. You leave me because I am a woman. Because I am weak.'

'No. I'm leaving you precisely because you are *not* weak. You are strong, Anna. Stronger than me, sometimes. If I could do anything to take you with us I would. But I want you to have a chance. And I want you to look after the others.'

She turned away, but he pulled her to him and kissed her. He held her close for as long as he could and then walked away, without looking back. She did not look up.

Standing at the foot of the gigantic staircase in the cliff face, Lamb realised he had known from the moment he had taken the decision what was now all too evident. The only way back north would be the same way they had come down. He stood at the foot of the steps and looked up, and then began to climb.

If coming down the great steps had been difficult, the ascent was doubly gruelling. What had taken an hour to descend took them twice that now, and as he reached the top of the stairs Lamb felt close to collapse. He staggered, and wondered whether the men had noticed. But Bandouvas was at his side. 'Don't worry. We all feel the same. Take time. Rest. You've done it. To be honest I didn't think you would. You impress me again, Kapitan Lamb.'

The rest of the company emerged, one by one, at the top of the steps and flung themselves against the stone wall at the summit. Smart gasped. 'I never want to see another blinking step again, as long as I live.'

Mays nodded and let precious water trickle down his chest from his mouth. 'You're not joking, Smarty, lad.'

Bandouvas had told Lamb they would retrace their steps exactly, but of course going downhill now it would be easier. They would also have the advantage of height and potentially surprise when, as no doubt they would, they came upon the Germans who were tailing them.

'How far behind us do you suppose they can be?' asked Lamb.

'Maybe twenty cigarettes, I would say. They will have had to rest, like us, but we could meet them anywhere from here.'

But nine miles into their route back down the mountain they had still not seen anything of the Germans, and Lamb was growing concerned.

They arrived above Theriso shortly after one in the afternoon and saw the smoke from the chimneys. Bandouvas smiled. 'If we're lucky we might find a bit of lunch. Stewed goat!'

They hurried down the hill, but as they grew closer it was plain to see that it had not been from the chimneys that the smoke had come. The village was smouldering, every house a burnt ruin.

Lamb shuddered. He had seen this before, in France last year, and it brought a hollow feeling to his stomach.

Bandouvas looked at him. 'No.' He shook his head. 'It's not possible. Not here.'

Lamb pulled him down and they lay in the grass and watched. As far as they could see there were no soldiers left in the place. In fact there was no sign of life whatsoever.

Suddenly there was movement on the hill to their left. Lamb cocked his Schmeisser and Bandouvas did the same. They waited and watched as a hunched human form moved towards them through the grass. At ten yards Lamb was ready to fire. Bandouvas whispered, 'No. Wait.'

Then through the grass came a boy. He was perhaps ten years old and his face was a mask of tears. He saw Bandouvas and threw himself at the big man, his arms outstretched. The kapitan gathered him up and enveloped him.

He turned to Lamb, the sobbing child clutched to his chest. 'My nephew.'

Lamb nodded. 'Ask him what happened.'

After a few minutes the boy calmed down and began to talk to Bandouvas, who translated for Lamb and the others.

'The Germans came. On foot, in the dawn. Many of them. Perhaps fifty. There are only two Germans left in the village now. They're going from house to house, to make sure any people who hid are dead. He says his grandparents are still alive. They hid in the cellar.'

There was a commotion down in the village, and peering over the fold in the ground they saw figures moving about in the street before a little house. Two Germans, one an officer in an alpine troopers' *bergmütze* and shorts, the other an NCO, similarly dressed, were shouting at an old woman, presumably the boy's grandmother. Either she didn't understand what was evidently a command or she was just being stubborn, but they kept on shouting. They were laughing now and seemed almost to be playing with her. Neither of them seemed to be armed. Suddenly the woman grabbed a plank of wood from where it lay against the wall and hit one of the men on the head. He crumpled to the ground, reeling from the blow. In an instant the other German had unbuttoned his holster and pulled out a pistol, a Luger. Then, taking careful aim, he shot the woman in the head at point-blank range. The back of her skull exploded and spattered over the wall of her house as she fell. The boy shouted and struggled in Bandouvas' arms, but the men in the village did not hear,

305

for a little dog was barking at them now. At that moment an old man came running round the corner of the house, wielding a sword above his head. As the injured German staggered to his feet the Greek lunged for him, but another shot rang out from the Luger and he too fell dead to the ground. The dog was still barking as the German coolly turned his gun on it and shot it dead too. Then he helped his wounded friend to his feet and, laughing, rubbed at his head as they walked towards a car. Lamb saw that it was a Humber, a captured British staff vehicle, and before the group on the hill could do anything the engine was running and the two men had left the village at speed, heading west.

He turned to Bandouvas. 'Where are they going? What does that mean? Where are all the others? The two platoons?'

Bandouvas looked grave. 'It's not good. What it means is they've got transport. Probably taken from your army. They've taken the road to Meskla and then on to Lakki. It's a good road. Very good. Very fast.'

'And then where?'

'Down through the mountains across the Omalos plateau up to Xyloskalo.'

Lamb froze. 'To the steps.'

Bandouvas nodded. 'It's the way I would have brought you if we had had transport and if we hadn't been hiding. They must control it now. They must have found out where we were heading.'

Lamb turned to the boy, who was weeping uncontrollably in the arms of one of Bandouvas' men. 'Ask him if they made anyone talk before they killed them.'

Bandouvas spoke and the little boy spoke and nodded, and hid his head again.

'They tortured the women in front of the men. Of course someone spoke.'

This was not how he had planned it. He could not blame Bandouvas for not explaining about the other road. He should have guessed at it himself. He had been supposing that because they had mountain troops they would come across the mountains. But why make the effort if you had found transport? And God knew there was enough of that lying abandoned about the island.

How could he have been so stupid? To have left them at the monastery. To have not thought the Germans might take another route.

'How long will it take them? Now that they know?'

Bandouvas gave it some thought. 'It's twenty-five kilometres by road, then a walk of another five down the track to the gorge. For good, fit troops? An hour on the road and then another on foot.'

'I'm going back.'

'What, are you mad? They'll be almost there by now. We're too late. What's the point? The King's as good as dead. We came here to kill Germans. We can't go back now.'

'The King may, as you say, be dead already, but I'm still going back. And if we hurry we can still kill Germans before they kill everyone in the monastery. I've been a fool. I left the King back there, thinking he was safe. I was wrong. And what's more I left good men back there, and women. Don't try to stop me.'

18

In accordance with the best military practice, Lieutenant Ryan had posted his men along the walls and in the belltower of the monastery, using it as much as he could as a fortified position. They stood on improvised fire-steps made from furniture, tea chests, anything that came to hand, keeping their heads down but at the same time trying to keep watch on the valley away to their north. And for every man of Ryan's there was a monk on the walls. All had been armed by Bandouvas with some of the rifles brought to them weeks before from Pendlebury's stock, and each had a bandolier of ammunition and several magazines. They made an incongruous sight. Ryan was glad of their presence, though it seemed to him unlikely he would need them.

Anna too was watching. She was standing on the low wall that surrounded the monastery's well. Part of her, the greater part if she was honest with herself, yearned to see Lamb returning down the pass, regretting his decision, coming back to her, but she knew she would not. He had made up his mind, and she admired him for that quality. She envied him, too, for his chance to kill more Germans, although she realised that she too was playing

308

a role. It was not just to do with the stupid English woman, although she knew that if she had not been there she might have been able to go with Lamb. Bandouvas himself had told her not to come, and the reason for that was reason enough to stay. It was so that someone could keep an eye on what happened to the King. He had said to her before they left that if any opportunity occurred for him to meet with an accident she might somehow encourage it. She knew what was meant. When they left this place they would still have another three kilometres before they came to the gorge itself, and then a further ten at least down to the sea. None of that would be easy. At least they would not have the Germans to worry about. Lamb and Bandouvas would surely see to them. Ryan had spoken of the need to move soon, certainly within the next few hours. There was nothing now to stop them, but Anna hoped they might stay a little longer, just on the slim chance that Lamb and his men would return.

It was as she was watching, looking up the road towards the steps, that something caught her eye. Behind a large outcrop some way up the cliff face to the left of the track she thought she saw something glittering. She rubbed her eyes and looked again, and it was then that she heard the shot that killed the monk who had been standing to her right, tending the monastery's herb garden. One of Ryan's men who had been two feet away from him spun round and fired in the direction of the shot, then he too was felled by the same sniper. Now the whole place was alive with men firing from the walls, bullets flying into the courtyard and ricocheting off the stone. Some of them lodged in the masonry, but others found their home in flesh.

Anna jumped down and grabbed her rifle as a bullet zinged off the wall of the well. Ryan was with her. 'Bloody hell. How did they get here? Come on.'

He ran across to the north wall where one of his men lay slumped over a Bren gun. Pushing the dead man out of the way, he checked the gun and repositioned it on the wall, then, seeing the flash of a rifle, he fired and a stream of bullets shot out. The rocks were alive with rifle and submachine-gun fire now. Anna, who had started to run with Ryan, had stopped herself and gone back to check on the civilians and the King. She found the Hartleys and Comberwell with Tsouderos and the abbot in his chamber. Of the King and Prince Peter there was no sign.

'Where's the King?'

Comberwell said, 'No idea. Hidden by the abbot here at the first shot. Can I borrow your rifle? Meant to get myself one when Lamb left.'

'No, you'll find one out there if you dare go out.'

She turned to the abbot. 'Father, you must tell me where he is.'

'My dear, I'm afraid that would be quite wrong. No one knows but myself, not even the monks, for the very simple reason that if the Nazis take any of you alive His Majesty will still be safe, no matter what they do to you.'

There was more firing outside now. Anna ran out into the courtyard. Three monks lay dead, and two of Ryan's men with them. Others had been wounded, one badly by the look of it, his arm shot clean through and almost severed. Comberwell had made no attempt to follow her. Julian Hartley, however, was at her side. He spoke, and she looked round at him.

'Can you find me a rifle? I dare say I can fire it if you show me how. I was in the OTC at school.'

Anna looked at him and smiled, then she leant down and picked up a rifle that had fallen from the grasp of a dead monk. 'There you are. You just use the bolt, like this.' She pointed to the magazines tucked into the bandolier as she unfastened it from the body and handed it to the writer. 'There are bullets in it. It clips in here. It's very simple. Just point it at a German and squeeze the trigger.'

There was a whoosh and a crash of splintering wood as an anti-tank rifle round hit the entrance gate and made a hole in the centre. Another round crashed in and severed one of the massive brass hinges so that the door swung crazily, hanging on the lower hinge only, creating a yawning gap below it. And then it seemed there were Germans everywhere, pushing madly at the gates as the men on the walls and at the rear of the courtyard poured fire into them. She saw three of them go down, but the men behind just stepped over the bodies and advanced into the yard, their machine-pistols firing. Anna ducked behind the well, dragging Hartley down with her, but not before he was hit. He yelled and she saw that a bullet had gone through his calf muscle. He lay on the ground, holding his leg, as she raised herself on to one knee and fired at a German. The man, from the mountain troops, clutched at his stomach and fell. Looking round she saw Ryan, shouted at him, 'Into the sanctuary.' He nodded, and together they fell back, Ryan waving his men to follow him and Anna dragging the semi-conscious Hartley with her. A dozen of the monks lay dead in the yard now, along with four of Ryan's men and at least ten Germans. Seeing Anna, Ryan ran across to her through a hail of bullets, picked up Hartley and hoisted him on to his back. Then together they pushed through the doors into one of the store-rooms which lay to the rear of the monastery.

As they half fell into the room, there was a strange noise from Ryan. Anna turned to look at him. A bullet had gone through his left eye, and he had died instantly. Hartley was moaning. She tried to lift him, and a heavy boot came down upon her arm. Then she felt the hot metal of a gun barrel pressing against her head. A voice said, in English, 'Don't move. Get up, very slowly.'

Twenty minutes later Anna was standing in the abbot's apartments. The room was lit by the candles which burned all day in the sconces lining three of the walls. She stood between Comberwell and the abbot. Miranda Hartley knelt beside them, holding Julian in her arms. Tsouderos, his cheek bleeding from a ricochet, and the five remaining men from Ryan's platoon stood in a group alongside.

Two German officers stood before them. Behind them a dozen of the Gebirgsjäger and four paratroopers held their machine-pistols level, pointing directly at them.

One of the officers spoke. 'Allow me to introduce myself. I am General Wilhelm Sussmann. I have to say, I'm impressed. You fought well. I did not think I would have to lose so many good men to take you. My lieutenant too. But then you lost your officer, didn't you? What puzzles me, though, is why a lieutenant should have been given such a responsible role. To save the King of Greece.' He paused. 'I'm also perplexed as to why there is only one partisan among you all. Very soon the island will be ours, and then those of you who are military personnel will be sent to prison camps in Italy and Germany. You others, I'm not so sure about. You might be partisans too, of course. You might be innocent civilians. I will make my mind up in due course, and then we will decide. Father abbot, I am disappointed in you. A man of the cloth directing holy men to fire on soldiers of the Reich who were only doing their duty? It doesn't seem a very Christian thing to do. But there again, I suppose your monks are dead too. I must treat you as a *franc-tireur* as well. But it seems to me that there is someone missing here. Someone rather important. Do any of you know where he might be?'

They said nothing.

'No? Are you quite sure?'

He nodded to the men behind him, and two of them stepped forward. Sussmann pointed to Comberwell. 'Him.'

They moved forward and Comberwell took a step back. 'No, don't touch me. What are you going to do?'

'Take him out. To the cell I showed you.'

They grabbed Comberwell and pushed him, still protesting, out of the room and down the corridor.

Sussmann turned to them and walked across to Anna. Standing close enough to her so that she could smell the staleness of his breath, he spoke again. 'I will leave you all to contemplate the state of your memories. Don't worry, your friend will be back soon.'

He turned and walked out of the room, leaving the guards behind but taking the other officer with him. Thirty yards down the corridor they entered one of the cells. Comberwell was inside with one of the guards. He was smoking a cigarette.

He stubbed it out nervously on the floor and spoke. 'You don't know how glad I am to see you, sir. I thought my cover was blown. I was sure that the others, the British officer and the kapitan, had guessed everything about me.'

Sussmann spoke. 'The last report HQ received from you was eight days ago, Comberwell, the day after the invasion. What happened?'

'I tried to keep in touch with the invasion forces but it was useless. I've been working on the inside, though. I knew you would come, of course. I was just biding my time.'

'Biding your time? Listen, Comberwell. I don't like you and I won't try to hide the fact. I am a soldier, but you . . . you are just a Nazi. I fight for my country and for

313

my leader. You have betrayed your country in the name of a doctrine that is not mine. Lieutenant Müller and I are soldiers of the Wehrmacht. That does not mean that we will flinch in our duty or that we will not use every means at our disposal to fulfil our mission, but we are not fanatics like you, Comberwell. It pains me that I have had to rely upon you for the information I need. However, I have had no alternative. Where's the King?'

'I don't know.'

'What? Call yourself a soldier? You're meant to be a secret agent. Berlin said one of the best. Where the hell is he? How don't you know?'

'The monks hid him, sir. I was diverted. Deliberately.'

'Diverted by what?'

'We were having lunch.'

'What? Bloody amateurs. You disgust me. You don't deserve to wear the uniform of the Fatherland. Oh, of course you don't, do you? Well, if you can't tell us we'll just have to find out where he is.'

He turned to Müller. 'Off you go, and make it convincing.'

Comberwell's reply was lost in Müller's first punch, which found his face and sent a tooth flying amid a welter of blood. He staggered back. 'Steady on, Müller.'

Sussmann laughed. 'Did you almost call him "old chap"? Come on, Captain Comberwell, you're beginning to sound like your alter ego. I'm sorry, we just have to make it look as if you've been beaten up.'

Müller waded in again and floored Comberwell with a rabbit punch to the stomach, following it with a chop to the back and a kick in the crotch. Comberwell doubled up with pain.

'All right, Müller, that should look good enough. Thank you, Comberwell. Most convincing. You've done a great service to the Fatherland.' He nodded to the guards.

'Take him back and bring me the civilians and the Greek girl.'

He turned to the blood-covered Comberwell. 'Keep playing along with it. You might still prove of some use and less than a complete waste of time.'

The last few miles of their descent into Samariá seemed interminable. Lamb nurtured the thought that he would soon see Anna again and prayed that she would not have been hurt, or worse. They were certain now that the Germans must have reached the monastery, not least because at the top of the steps at Xyloskalo they had found the transport, abandoned at the point beyond which it was useless: three British Bedford trucks and the staff car they had glimpsed leaving Theriso. Lamb had disabled them, removing the distributors and hurling them into the gorge, then Bandouvas had urged them on, clearly anxious to avenge the deaths of the people in the village. He had changed, thought Lamb. Not obviously, but he was less jovial and inclined to silence. His face too seemed to have set in an expression of determination, and there was something indefinable about his eyes.

They were at the foot of the great steps now and Bandouvas signalled them to spread out as he had directed. Lamb had thought it better Bandouvas took charge at this stage. These were his mountains, his country. If they were to win, it was clear they would do best to fight this battle on his terms. They had agreed on two things: that silence was vital, and that it was madness to try a frontal assault. They would do it by stealth. And for that they would have to wait until nightfall.

Inside the monastery others waited for the night to come, and with quite different expectations. For an hour Sussmann had spoken with Anna and the Hartleys, playing with their minds. He had begun by asking them again the whereabouts of the King, and then with no warning, just as it seemed he might resort to violence, he had left them alone in the cell. Ten minutes later he had returned and so it had continued, until the two women and the half-senseless Hartley had reached a state of mental exhaustion, listening for his footsteps outside. Waiting for the key to turn in the lock. Waiting for what the next visit might bring. Every time he returned his presence seemed more threatening. And now they could hear him coming again – the boots on the stone slabs, the key, the door. But it was not Sussmann who entered, but the other officer, Lieutenant Müller.

'General Sussmann asks me to tell you that he is tired. He will eat, and then he will return to question you once again. If you take my advice you will stop being so stubborn and tell us where we can find the King. I know what the general will do if you do not.'

Anna sneered. 'He'll have to kill us first. Why are you doing this to us? You're cowards, all of you. Call yourself soldiers? Doing this to two women and a wounded man.'

At the word coward Müller stepped forward, and for an instant Anna thought he would strike her. But he stopped. 'Oh, don't worry, we have been questioning the men too. Quite thoroughly. But they are just as foolish as you and they have suffered for it. They have told us nothing. But we will find out soon enough. My general says we will return at nightfall.' He paused and looked down at Julian Hartley, whose leg was clearly causing him pain. 'But perhaps I might have better luck.'

Müller knelt down beside Hartley and gazed into his eyes. 'Tell me where you have hidden the King.'

Hartley stared back, his face a mask of pain, and said nothing. Müller reached down and, taking his pistol from its holster, gently touched the muzzle against Hartley's

316

wound. The writer jerked back and yelped. Müller smiled. 'The King?'

He pushed the barrel of the gun hard against the wound and Hartley stiffened with agony. Miranda screamed at him, 'Stop it, stop it, you bastard. Leave him.'

With his right hand still firmly on the pistol against Hartley's leg, Müller whipped out his left hand and caught her a vicious slap across the face. Then he stood up and, wiping the blood from the barrel of his pistol on Hartley's shirt, replaced it in the holster as Anna comforted Miranda. 'Until nightfall then.' He looked at his watch. 'Not long now.'

Lamb could see the stars quite clearly above him in the sky but, surprisingly, there was only the slimmest crescent of a moon. Bandouvas had taken his men out in front of the rest of them, scattering them among the rocks along the path that led to the monastery. They inched forward, leapfrogging each other so that one man of every pair was always in cover. Lamb had adopted the same tactic and had divided his men into three groups, one under Eadie, one with Bennett and the third with him, each of them numbering some seven men.

They left all that remained of their heavy kit at the foot of the steps and went on only with their small arms, fighting knives and a few grenades, keeping close to the valley floor, hugging any cover they could find – the slightest fold in the ground, every rock and bush. Silence was imperative now. Orders were to be passed by calls, and as few as them as possible: an owl's hoot for danger, a whoop for forward.

He could see the white walls of the monastery now, and the gate, which had clearly been blown in. Shapes at the walls suggested that the Germans had posted sentries where their own men had been. From the

transports and the account sobbed out by Bandouvas'
terrified nephew, they could estimate the force at around
forty men, no more, and they must surely have lost some
men in the fight to take the monastery. Military doctrine
required that an attacking force should outnumber the
defenders of a position by three to one if it were to be
successful. Lamb enjoyed no such luxury. But they did
have surprise on their side. And something else.

The abbot had told Bandouvas of a secret passage out
of the monastery, an old route through which monks had
smuggled freedom fighters during the great Cretan wars
of independence. That was the route Bandouvas intended
to use now, in reverse. He would lead his men through
the tunnel and up into the abbot's quarters while Lamb
and his men waited at the front walls. Then when the
commotion from within signalled that Bandouvas had
attacked, Lamb and his three sections would storm the
distracted guards. As he watched he could just make out
the shapes of Bandouvas' *andartes* as they loped across
the ground to the north of the monastery, walking almost
on all fours to imitate the action of an animal. The last
of them disappeared into the night, and Lamb sat back.
He looked at Smart, Stubbs and Butcher, their faces blackened with mud, as they huddled close beside him among
the rocks. He nodded at them and they smiled back. They
knew, as did all the others, that now there was no going
back.

Sussman stood in the cell and shook his head at Anna.

'What do I have to do? Must I resort to the same sort
of barbaric practices used by your own countrymen?'

She was sitting before him, tied to a chair. Her shirt
was torn and hung from one shoulder, and her right eye
was black and puffy where it had been hit. There was
blood on her cheek and lips. Müller stood in a corner of

318

the room in his shirtsleeves flexing the fingers of his right hand. In another corner were the Hartleys. Julian had passed out from the pain, but Miranda was fully alert, painfully so, for she had no idea what might happen next in what seemed to be a night without end. Sussmann nodded to Müller, who walked across to her and grabbed her by the arm, dragging her across the floor to where Anna was sitting.

'Ladies, what can we do? I do not want to cause either of you any pain or discomfort. I'm an honourable man. But you give me no alternative.' He reached into his boot and drew out a dagger. It was long and thin, and on its grip it bore a swastika grasped in the claws of an eagle. He leant in close to Anna's face.

'You saw the men back there, didn't you? My men. No more than boys. Did you do that? Did you put out their eyes? Or was it your men that did it? How did they do it? Was it like this?'

Jerking away from her, Sussmann suddenly grabbed Miranda by the hair and drew the dagger up to her face. Anna strained against the ropes that held her and shouted something at him, but the general did not hear it, whatever it was, for as she spoke the night was torn by a series of explosions.

Praying that every man on the wall would have momentarily turned to face the sound, Lamb led his section across the valley and ran into the dead ground at the base of the walls. They threw themselves down behind him, and looking along the length of the wall he could see that Eadie and Bennett too had made it. There was not a moment to lose. Carrying on and still leading the way, Lamb moved down the wall towards the gate. The noises of battle from inside were as loud as they could have wished for, masking their own movements from the sentries above, and within moments they were at the shattered entrance. He nodded to Rothman and Grist, and both men pulled the pins on the grenades they were carrying and tossed them lightly through the gap beneath the door. Lamb did the same. There was a shout from above as one of the guards spotted the bombs, but by then it was too late. Three explosions shook the wall and an instant later Lamb and the others were through the doorway and firing up on to the sentries' positions. The Germans did not know what had hit them. Turning, they had barely a chance to squeeze the triggers of their machine-pistols before they were cut down by the hail of fire from Lamb's own captured Schmeissers. There were more Germans opposite them now in the courtyard, and Lamb was conscious of Eadie's men pouring in and throwing grenades at them.

Lamb shouted to Bennett, 'Move left and take the cloister. I'm going to find the King.' Then, signalling his men to follow, he ran across the yard and up the stairs to the cell block. He had no idea where the Germans would have put the King, or even if the man was still alive, but this surely was as good a place as any to start.

The firefight in the abbot's block was as fierce as ever, and Lamb had no doubt that Bandouvas would give them a run for their money. He waved his men past him down the cell block corridor, and as they passed each room they kicked the doors open. All were empty, and then ahead of him in the corridor Lamb saw two mountain troops. They fired, and the bullets hammered into the two men in front of him, Grist and McGrath. One of them hit the wall and ricocheted on to Lamb, slicing into his forearm, but not before he had got off a burst of fire at the two Germans. One man went down and the other stood his ground, but Rothman was at his shoulder now and a bullet from his Enfield took the German in the

320

chest, throwing him back against the wall. Lamb ran on, jumping over the two men, and as he did so another German, an officer in shirtsleeves, ran from one of the cells on the right and, firing a single random shot from his pistol as he went, raced away into the adjoining corridor. A moment later another man appeared at the doorway and paused for a second. His eyes met Lamb's for an instant, and as he turned to follow his comrade Lamb squeezed the trigger and a salvo of bullets hit the wall just inches away from the German, who froze.

Lamb yelled, 'Don't move.' The man hesitated and looked as if he might make a break for it. He began to reach towards his holster, but immediately reconsidered, for six weapons were trained on him now and he realised that he would not have a hope of making it to the end of the corridor.

The German raised his hands and Lamb, waving his men forward to take their prisoner, began to wonder what on earth a German brass-hat was doing in the monastery.

This was not the time to find out, though. Turning, oblivious to his wounded arm, Lamb ran back towards the noise of rifle fire and almost collided with Bandouvas as he charged at the head of his *andartes* out of the great hall and into the courtyard. The Cretan had a fresh wound in his thigh and was bleeding heavily, as he came half hobbling, half running into the light of the burning buildings. He saw Lamb and, smiling, looked his old self again. 'We've done it, my friend. Did you get them?'

'Yes, and we've seen a senior officer too. Where's the King?'

'Safe. The abbot's hidden him. He told me he would. What about Anna and the others?'

'I don't know. Look.'

Lamb pointed across to the gate. The officer he had

321

seen before was pushing his way through it, along with a number of men. He turned to Bandouvas but saw that he was already firing at them and then, as he cocked the Schmeisser again, something hit him on the left arm and he fell backwards. As he recovered and reached up to feel the blood soaking his shirt, he was in time to see the last of the Germans escaping through the open gateway. Bandouvas turned to him. 'They won't get far. The transports are useless, and my men are everywhere. Look, your arm. You're hit.'

Lamb looked at his shoulder. 'It's nothing. Look, so are you.'

Bandouvas laughed. 'I can't feel it.'

'Did you find the others?'

'No, only Comberwell. He killed a German.'

'Then where the hell are they?'

The answer was not long in coming. Bennett found Lamb. 'Sir, you'd better come quick. It's the Greek girl, she needs you.'

'She's hurt?'

'Not bad, sir. Bit upset, though. Mr Hartley's in a bad way too, and I can't get a word of sense out of Mrs Hartley.'

He found Anna in the cell. They had untied her and she was standing now, supported by Mays, rubbing at her wrists. He walked over and put his hand under her chin, raising her face so that he could see it.

'Christ, who did this to you?'

'The Germans. Two of their officers. Honourable men.'

Lamb brushed the hair away from her forehead and touched her swollen eye. She winced. 'Sorry. You need some attention. Perhaps the monks . . .'

'All the monks are dead, Peter. Ryan too, and all his men. They killed the wounded.'

'Where's the King?'

'I don't know. I couldn't have told them anyway. The abbot knows, if he's still alive.'

'Sofronios is dead.' It was Bandouvas. He was standing in the doorway, behind Lamb. 'They killed him. Murdered him. Tied him up and shot him in the head with the others when he wouldn't tell them. My poor, decent, holy friend.' He paused. 'I know where the King is. He told me.'

They found the King and Prince Peter in a tiny room beneath the altar that had been used to shelter fugitives for close on 700 years. Prince Peter spoke. 'Lamb, thank God. We heard shooting and explosions. We couldn't be sure who had won.'

'You're safe with us now, sir. For the time being at least. But now we have to leave this place and get you to the sea.'

He turned to Eadie. 'Charles, I'm putting His Majesty in your care. I think I need to speak to our prisoner.'

19

Lamb always regretted losing his temper. Generally he was able to control himself, in fact he took some pride in it, but at times it just boiled over. As it had half an hour ago when he had confronted Sussmann. The general now bore the evidence.

Bennett laughed. 'Lovely shiner you planted on the general, sir.'

'Thank you, Sarnt-Major. Wish I hadn't in a way. But he more than deserved it. In fact it was his sidekick who did the dirty work. Wish I could do the same to him. Or worse.'

They were walking, as fast they were able, away from the monastery, along the lower reaches of the Samariá gorge which stretched another eight miles down, from the little deserted church of Agios Christos to the sea at Agia Roumeli. At least it was even ground now and, he sensed, getting gradually lower all the time. Despite protests, Lamb had refused to bury the dead. He had known they would have to move fast, trying to use the cover of the night, before dawn came up. It was harder walking by moonlight, but already he could see the sky changing colour and he tried to quicken his pace. Fatigue was beginning to tell and he wondered how the others, particularly the women and the King, must feel. Hartley they had placed on a bier, improvised from half of a door, and he was carried by two of Eadie's platoon. He had been unconscious for some time, and when he did open his eyes it was to mutter something unintelligible before passing out again.

Anna and Smart between them had dealt with both Bandouvas' and Lamb's wounds, well enough for the present, although as far as Lamb was concerned the pain was really beginning to kick in. The second wound was the worse of the two. The bullet had hit him in the upper arm, and although it had not lodged itself it had taken away a piece of flesh the size of his fingernail. The field dressing was rudimentary and without any pain relief. He hoped the adrenalin of the moment would compensate. He was more concerned with the fact that he had left two of his men dead back there and it had fired him with an extra impetus to get the rest of them away.

Bandouvas, he knew, had suffered worse in the fight at the monastery and he could only speculate as to the man's current frame of mind.

It was not long before he found out for certain. Bandouvas drew alongside Lamb at the head of the little column as it snaked between the massive sides of the gorge.

'Are you all right? It looked a nasty wound.'

'I'll live. At least until we get to Alex.'

'Pray God you do, Kapitan.'

'You know the Germans are behind us. Not far off. I don't know how many yet. They won't give up now. They don't just want the King. We have their general.'

'Yes, I know.'

'They will have called in reinforcements, I think. You do know they'll do anything they can to get him back.

325

And they know where we're going now. Your navy will have to be good to get in and out without being bombed out of the water.'

Lamb nodded. 'I know that too. You sent a signal?'

'I sent my runner. If he gets through then we must hope that whoever is left at your headquarters can still send a signal.' He thought for a moment. 'But you don't need to take the general, do you? It's the King you came to rescue. And I know you're determined to save him, whatever I might think.'

Lamb turned to him. 'What do you suggest? The general's a valuable prisoner.'

Bandouvas shook his head. 'He's an animal. You saw what he did at Theriso. And what about Anna and Hartley? And Ryan's men too? And the monks and Sofronios? He deserves to die, Lamb. Right here, right now.'

'That would go against the principles of war and the Geneva Convention.'

'Did he respect the Geneva Convention? I don't think so. He's denied himself any decent treatment. We should kill him and leave his body for the crows, before they have a chance to get him back and he can do the same again, to more innocent people. Think about that.'

Lamb's mind was racing. His code as an officer demanded that a general, any enemy officer, should be treated with respect, but Bandouvas was right. What respect had Sussmann shown to his victims? Besides, over the past few weeks he had seen the old rules being thrown away. It would also make their journey easier to be rid of him.

'Perhaps you're right. Perhaps we should kill him. Who would do it?'

Bandovas shrugged. 'I don't think I'd have any lack of volunteers.'

Lamb bit his lip. 'Give me a few moments.'

Bandouvas nodded and fell back in line, and as he did so Lamb noticed that Comberwell had been walking close behind them and wondered how much he had heard. He walked over to Lamb.

'All right. I'll come clean, Lamb. You were right. I am with Section D.'

'Why did you lie to me? Why keep up the pretence?'

'It's just the way we're taught. No one must ever know who we are, in case they get caught and give us away. But now I have to tell you. I heard what you said to Bandouvas. You can't do it, man. We have to get Sussmann away, back to Alex. He's too great a prize. You have no idea of the information we can get out of him.'

Lamb looked at him. He found it hard enough to believe that the man he had taken for a fool was in fact a British secret agent. And now he was telling him to go against his gut instinct and save the general – to intervene on behalf of a man who had ordered the massacre of a village and the torture of a woman he loved.

'I'm not sure I can do that. It's too late.'

'It can't be. You have to stop it. If my head of section found out he'd chuck you in the Tower and throw away the key. You'd be finished.'

'Why should he find out?'

'Look, old man, I know you must hate the general, after what he did to Anna and the rest of them. But believe me, if we can get Sussmann back to GHQ he will be the biggest prize we've ever had. Think of what it would do for your own career.'

Lamb realised that either way he was compromised. The revenge of executing Sussmann would be sweet but short and ultimately futile. But perhaps to use this sadist as a means of his own advancement might be a sweeter revenge altogether. And there was the undeniable fact that the information he might provide to the intelligence service would almost certainly save hundreds, maybe thousands of Allied lives.

'All right. I'll do what I can.'

Comberwell clapped him on the back. 'Thanks awfully.'

Stalling Bandouvas, Lamb pressed on along the gorge, pushing against the pain. After three miles he called a halt. The sky was quite clear now and the morning sun shone down on them. Lamb knew that the Germans could not be far behind, but they simply had to stop for a few minutes. Crossing a narrow wooden bridge, they found themselves on a wider path where a stream from further up the mountains cut across the valley floor.

'We'll take a rest here, Sarnt-Major. Ten minutes. No more. Post sentries and make sure everyone gets some water. The civilians included. And the general.'

Bandouvas walked across to Lamb.

'We could do it now. I could take him back down the gorge. There's a cave. Did you see?'

Lamb nodded. 'I did, but I'm sorry, I can't allow it.'

'You've changed your mind? Why? That man Comberwell. He is an agent, isn't he?'

'I'm sorry, Kapitan. It would be better to keep him alive. He has valuable information that could save many lives.'

Bandouvas spat. 'He's a killer. A sadist. He deserves to die. Here.'

Lamb turned on him. 'No. I'm in command, and I say he stays alive. That's an order, Kapitan.'

'Why should I take orders from you?'

'Because we came here to help you.'

'You came here because you were driven out of Greece. And when you came you brought only misery and suffering, and the Germanos. I owe you nothing, least of all respect.'

Anna ran towards Lamb. 'Stop. Stop fighting. I know why you are fighting.' She turned on Bandouvas. 'You want to kill the general, don't you? Because he murdered your family in Theriso.' She looked at Lamb. 'And you, Peter. You'd like to kill him too because of what he did to me. And I should want you to do it. I should want you to make him suffer. And if I told you to do that you would, wouldn't you? For me.'

Lamb nodded. 'Yes, I believe I would.'

'Well, I won't. I won't tell you to kill him, or to hurt him until he screams in agony. Oh yes, I'd love to do that. Can't you see that I would?' She paused. 'But I won't.'

She turned back to Bandouvas. 'And I'll tell you, Kapitan, why I won't do that. Because I want Kapitan Lamb to take the general away. To take him to Egypt. I want the general to sit in a cell with people who question him until his head spins, and I want him to suffer, and then I want the British to use everything he tells them. And then he will truly suffer. Yes, he will really suffer very much in his mind once he knows how much he has helped Germany to lose this war.'

Bandouvas shook his head. 'I still say slit his throat and let him bleed like a pig.'

She stared at him. 'No. He lives.' She walked away.

Bandouvas looked at Lamb. 'It is not what I want. But she has suffered. It is her honour too that has been offended, and it is her right to decide what to do with him. You can take him.'

After precisely ten minutes Lamb got them going again. He sent Eadie's section in front now and placed himself with Smart, Stubbs, Bunce and Rothman, all that remained of Wentworth's command, around the King and Prince Peter, followed by the Hartleys. Bennett followed on with his men and Sussmann, whose hands they had tied with the same rope he had used on Anna. After them came Comberwell and Anna, while Bandouvas provided the rearguard, his men strung out for 100 yards behind them, ever watchful. As they walked, the mountain goats scattered before them, scrambling away to left and right.

They crossed another bridge, which could hardly be called that, being no more than two planks of wood across a wider stream. Lamb watched them from the other side until they were all across, including Hartley on his improvised bier.

Last across were Bandouvas and the remaining *andartes*. Lamb waited for him. 'How much longer until we reach the sea?'

'How long now? Four hours, perhaps. It depends on how fast they can go, and you also, Kapitan. You are tired.'

'How far are they behind us?'

Bandouvas shook his head. 'They're getting closer. My men have just come in. They say there are no more than twenty of the Germanos, but they move like wild goats.'

The mountain troops, thought Lamb. 'Four hours? We haven't got that long, have we? Until they catch up.'

'No. I don't think we have. We could wait for them. In ambush.'

Lamb nodded. 'Yes. That was my thinking too. But not here. We need to make some ground. Another two miles? Less?'

'No more. And we'll have to pick the ground with care.'

They had been walking for two hours and already the day was hot. The dry, stony ground shone bright white in the rays of the sun that managed to penetrate down through the crevasse, but Lamb was thankful of the rock-face of the gorge, which offered shelter from the heat. High in the sky, just visible through the gap 2,000 feet up, against the vivid blue sky, a bird of prey soared above them.

They were nearing the narrowest part of the gorge and it seemed that the very earth was closing in on them. It was barely eight feet between the sides.

'The *sideroportes*,' said Bandouvas. 'The iron gates. This is where the fighters of Crete used to hide from the Turks. There is a story of how one Turkish soldier followed them down here. They found him hanging from a pear tree. The *andartes* had taken out his teeth with a bayonet. I don't know if he was still alive. I do know that the Turks never came down here after them again. People used to say of the *portes* that they were the doors of hell.'

Smart shivered. 'Don't like the sound of that, sir. Not at all. Gives me the willies. How much longer, sir?'

'Not long, Smart. Soon be at the sea.'

Lamb could see the light through the end of the great rockface gates now. Eadie's men had gone on a little, and as he picked up some speed to follow them Bandouvas caught up.

'I will say one thing more. You know, Kapitan Lamb, if you get this man away, the general, what the Germans will do? They told my nephew's people that for every German we kill they will kill fifty of us. Fifty for one, eh? Imagine what they will do if you take a general.'

'Nice try, Bandouvas. But my mind is made up. Anna did that for me.'

'We should stop then, once we reach the other side of the *portes*. If you're still of a mind to fight.'

'We have no choice, do we?'

At last they spilled out of the slit in the rocks and the hills opened out into gentle slopes covered in loose rocks. The stream too was wider here, lapping gently under the overhanging banks. But the openness meant no shade, and the heat was overpowering.

'Here,' said Bandouvas.

331

Lamb nodded. 'Yes, this will do. But we'll need cover.'

The slopes to either side of the gorge were filled with poplar and cypress trees and strewn with boulders, and there were a number of low stone walls, almost enclosures, which might at some time have housed sheep.

He called Eadie to him. 'Charles, we're going to make a stand here. It's a good place for an ambush. According to Bandouvas' scouts there are only a score of them following, so with luck we'll catch them when they exit from the gorge. Get your lot in position, in whatever cover you can.' He called to Bennett. 'Sarnt-Major, detail three men to guard the prisoner and the King. We'll put the Hartleys with them too. Oh, and find a rifle for Mr Comberwell. We'll need his help this time.'

For thirty minutes they sat there, waiting, silent. Lamb had told them to do nothing until they heard his signal. They were to sit tight. Bandouvas had agreed, although he had chosen his own positions. As Lamb yawned and wished for a cigarette, two goats bolted from the entrance to the *portes*. He thought that he saw something glistening in the sunlight and waved from his position behind a huge boulder to the others, signalling them to keep down. Then, very slowly, he saw one of the Gebirgsjäger crawl along the valley floor, hugging the rocks, followed by another. The two men made the cover of some rocks directly beside the *portes* and one of them called back with a bird call. Three more mountain troops appeared, and behind them Lieutenant Müller. Emerging into the sunlight and seeing no evidence of any enemy, Müller half straightened up, then called forward the other men behind him. One of them carried an MG34, another its ammunition and a third man an anti-tank rifle. Lamb counted. The *andartes* had not been wrong: exactly twenty men. Taking no chances, Lamb kept low, scanning the hillside for signs of life. They had taken the precaution of gagging Sussmann, but still, as he crouched out of sight, he could not help but think the enemy might see some evidence of their presence. He counted to five, slowly, and on the final count blew the whistle that hung on a lanyard around his neck. From behind the rocks and walls the men opened up. Two of the Gebirgsjäger went down immediately. Another managed to squeeze off a few rounds from his Schmeisser before the bullets took him, ripping into the left side of Partridge, who was with Bennett's section. Valentine hurled a grenade and it exploded among some rocks, killing three of the mountain troops and creating a shower of lethal stone which sent shrapnel into three more. Having sprayed the rocks to his front, Lamb changed clips and was watching Dawlish and Hobdell as they pinned down a group of Germans to his left, when he noticed Comberwell. The man was lying across a rock, resting his rifle upon his arm, as if he might be about to take down a stag. As Lamb looked on, while bullets from both sides ricocheted off the rocks, Comberwell fired, and the round from the rifle smashed into Müller's shoulder. The lieutenant let out a cry, and instants later a second bullet hit him in the thigh. Lamb watched, transfixed, but Comberwell had taken aim again, and his third shot got the lieutenant in the heart. The officer spun round and fell dead on the stones. More grenades found their mark, but the Gebirgsjäger were responding wildly now. The anti-tank gun fired a round and, hitting stone, splintered it into large fragments, one of which flew crazily across the valley and took off a section of Philips' skull.

Lamb moved forward and found a position slightly closer to the enemy. Taking careful aim, he squeezed off a single shot and saw a man go down. Anna was up with him now, firing into the enemy, and the few other

remaining *andartes* had climbed higher up the rocks and were pouring it on from above. Lamb saw more of the Germans fall, and then one of them threw down his gun and raised his hands. He died with a bullet from Bandouvas' gun. When another did the same, Lamb yelled, 'Cease firing. Hold your fire. Stop firing.'

The firing sputtered to a stop, and the remaining Gebirgsjäger stood up, their hands above their heads. There were just six left, four of them wounded, one severely.

Bandouvas yelled at Lamb, something in Greek, and he waved back. 'Sarnt-Major, bring them in.'

Then Lamb turned, and walking back to where the royal party had been placed under guard, he stopped dead.

The guards lay dead on the ground, and above their bodies stood Comberwell. He was holding a knife to the King's throat. He smiled at Lamb. Beside him stood General Sussmann, who also smiled.

'Captain, well done. Good shooting. Although you had a little help, didn't you? From Mr Comberwell.' He nodded at Miranda Hartley. 'You, the Englishwoman. Go to that man there.' He pointed to Valentine. 'Bring me his pistol.'

Miranda walked over to Valentine and went for his holster. Sussmann yelled.

'Not so fast. Turn round, so I can see you. And don't try any funny stuff. Nor you, Sergeant Valentine, or Mr Comberwell here will slice the King from ear to ear.'

Miranda reached into the holster and pulled out the Luger. 'Now bring it here.'

Sussmann rubbed at his wrists as Miranda walked towards him, and for an instant Lamb thought she might try something. But she simply handed it over.

'And now we will take the King. Of course it means nothing to me whether he lives or dies, but right now he's our insurance so we'll keep him alive. For the rest of you, though, I'm afraid time is up.'

Lamb played for time. 'Comberwell, what I don't understand is how you managed to alert the colonel.'

Comberwell smiled and relaxed his hold on the King. 'Oh, it was simple really. Such luck. You see I really am in Section D, but I recognised you from a list in Gestapo HQ. I went straight to Colonel "R", as fast as I could. He was overjoyed to find that his protégé was in Athens. And then I had you. I knew that at some point in our little adventure I would be able to manipulate you and, well, here we are. Not quite as I had planned, but it will do.'

Sussmann spoke again. 'Yes, it will do. You're all finished now.' He called across to the captured Gebirgsjäger and quickly they walked over to Lamb's men and began to disarm them. He called to Lamb, 'Captain. If you please.'

Lamb nodded to Bennett and the men handed over their weapons to the Germans, who moved quickly to join the general. He called a command and the Germans motioned Lamb and his men and those of Bandouvas, with the civilians, to close together into a tighter group. Lamb knew what would come next: the order to open fire.

Valentine, who was beside Lamb, shook his head. 'There you are, sir. I told you we should have killed the King when we still had the chance.'

As one of the Gebirgsjäger poked him back with the muzzle of a rifle, Lamb spoke again. 'Shut up, Valentine. How's your German?'

'Fine, sir.'

'Well then, use it. Tell them Bandouvas has them covered.'

Valentine called to Sussmann, who laughed and shook

335

his head. 'You must think me very stupid, Captain. I know that all the kapitan's men are with you.'

He scanned the group and then looked concerned, for he found himself unable to spot the big kapitan. 'All right, Captain. Where is he?'

Lamb muttered to Valentine, 'Don't say anything, just point up the hill.'

Valentine raised his arm and pointed as Lamb had directed, and from instinct Sussmann shifted his gaze for a moment, to follow the line. It was enough.

Lamb snatched the rifle from the German nearest to him, swung it into his jaw with a thud that sent him to the ground and then, tucking it into his own shoulder, aimed at Comberwell. Moving it ten degrees right, Lamb squeezed the trigger and a bullet hit Sussmann in the shin, knocking him off his feet.

Comberwell turned and loosened his grip for a second, and as he did Lamb moved the rifle. The second shot hit Comberwell in the centre of the forehead and for a moment he seemed to stand there, frozen in time. Then his body fell limp to the ground, his dead fingers dropping the knife.

One of the Germans fired, hitting Bunce in the stomach, but then the rest of Lamb's men and the *andartes* were on the Gebirgsjäger with their fists, snatching rifles away and using them as clubs. It was over quickly, the remaining Gebirgsjäger raising their hands in surrender.

King George put his hands to his throat. 'Thank you. Thank you, Captain.'

As he spoke Lamb was aware of Sussmann rising from the ground, picking up the Luger. He raised his rifle just as the general took aim at the King. Too late. There was a crack, and the gun flew from his hand. As Sussmann yelled in pain, Lamb looked for the smoking gun and saw Anna lower her rifle from her shoulder.

336

He walked over to her. 'You know you could have killed him with that shot.'

'But I wasn't aiming to kill him, Peter.'

'If we take the general to Egypt you know what it'll mean for you? Bandouvas told me.'

'I know there will be more reprisals. More deaths. I know that you are condemning us all to death, but I know too that you must take him. He must go for all of us, as a symbol of our defiance. A message from the people of Crete to the world.'

Lamb shook his head. Messages, symbols, when all he wanted to do was save lives. Her life. Here it was tenfold, twenty times over, that nightmare of his again, of killing innocent people. But there was no choice. 'I can't leave you to that. You can't make me do that.'

She smiled. 'I can, Peter. Because I love you.'

Bandouvas had been watching them. He reached up and put his hand on Lamb's shoulder. 'Now you must leave, but we will carry on the fight till you return, Captain Lamb, "Arni". My friend. May God go with you. Be sure to come back to us soon.'

Anna looked at him, smiled and said nothing. Then she took him by the hand and led him down the hillside and he saw that there, beyond the beach, riding the tide, lay a British destroyer.

Cursing the wound in his arm, Lamb pulled himself up the rope scrambling net that swung against the side of the ship. Above him he was aware of Prince Peter being helped aboard with the Hartleys and below, being helped out of the bobbing launch, Eadie, Bennett and what remained of the men of his company. Then, as he reached the deck he heard the last notes of the boatswain's call, piping aboard the King and the Prince.

Lamb steadied himself on the deck as the ship's captain

saluted him and he returned the gesture. The officer was smiling and speaking to him now, but Lamb, oblivious to the words, turned his head to look back at the coast, trying in vain in the twilight to make out the last remaining traces of the olive groves, the vineyards and the cypresses. Even as he watched, the night grew darker, and soon all he could see of Crete was the great mass of the island rising high above the shimmering water, as immovable and steadfast as the people who were proud to call it their home.

HISTORICAL NOTE

The battle of Crete was without doubt one of the most disastrous debacles engaged in by the British and Commonwealth forces during World War II. It was also a conflict which produced some of the most heroic actions and acts of individual bravery, seen not only in that war, but in all military history.

Poorly provisioned and equipped and suffering from disease and exhaustion, the Allied force which put up such a staunch defence of the island for those few days at the end of May 1941 deserves to be remembered in history in the same breath as Leonidas' Spartans at Thermopylae and Macdonell's Guards at Hougoumont. As a consequence of this tenacious performance, the German Fallschirmjäger suffered incredible and unforeseen casualties and it was as a direct result of what happened in Crete that Hitler declared that never again would the German army undertake a large scale airborne operation.

As before, I have set Lamb's story against a background of real events, following the withdrawal of the Allies from mainland Greece, just as it happened. Most of the characters in the early chapters are invented, although the units are genuine, save for Lamb's own. The civilians encountered in Athens are also an invention, although many British and other foreign nationals did join in the retreat and land up on Crete or in Egypt.

The plot surrounding the King of Greece is based on truth. King George was indeed evacuated from Athens to Crete with his core government and stayed on the island until the German invasion, at which point his bodyguard, led by Lt W H Ryan managed to get him down to the south coast, from where he was evacuated to Egypt.

Naturally I have taken some licence with the actual characters involved in the King's escape, not least that of the great Cretan kapitan Manoli Bandouvas (sometimes spelt Badouvas) whom, as far as I am aware, did not actually take part in the escape. Bandouvas was though one of the most important of the many Cretan kapitans whose actions did so much to confound the German operations in the Mediterranean, ensuring that even after the Allies had been forced to leave the island, the Germans would be compelled to tie up many thousands of men on Crete whom would otherwise have certainly been used to greater effect elsewhere.

The little village of Galatas which saw one of the fiercest battles of the campaign is today a site of pilgrimage for New Zealanders and boasts a wonderful war memorial and a fascinating museum of the battle. By sheer concidence, a café now stands in the exact place in which I put Anna's *kafeneio* in the book and is run by a husband and wife team. Interestingly she is originally from England. Their café is filled with books and mementoes of the battle. Parts of the armour plating from Roy Farran's tank were later made into garden gates by an enterprising villager and are still performing that function today. I have taken more than a little licence with the character of General Wilhelm Sussmann. It is well known that

340

Sussmann perished with all of the occupants including his staff, when his glider crashed on the island of Aegina after exactly the incident described in the book. I have merely allowed him to live and conjectured what might have happened had he indeed had orders from the Führer to find the King.

King George had indeed been declared an enemy of his own people by Hitler and there is some evidence to suggest that the Germans did have orders to find him. We also know that the battle was heavily dependent upon intelligence on both sides. Freyburg was privy to the intelligence gleaned from British enigma decoders and, as he ate breakfast watching the first enemy paratroops descend, he famously looked at his watch and declared that they were 'dead on time'. Comberwell, while an apparently unlikely character, also has his basis in fact and can be seen as a distillation of the many fifth column-ists in Greece at the time. While he may also seem like a caricature, the character of John Pendlebury is entirely real. Of course, I do not know whether Pendlebury would have spoken exactly as he does in my book, but I hope that I have allowed him to live again with some degree of reality. An extraordinary man, he was undoubtedly immensely brave and his death on Crete at the height of the battle was an incalculable loss. While I have used real names for many of the characters, and as ever have endeavoured to be faithful to their memories, I must make two further confessions. Lieutenant Ryan, who commanded the King's bodyguard as he does in the book, did indeed do all that he could to get His Majesty to safety and succeeded triumphantly. Although I have taken the liberty of using his name, his conduct, from the encounter with Lamb to the end of the book, is entirely fictitious.

Secondly, some readers may discern that the character of Hathaway appears to be based on that of Captain (later Major General) Michael Forrester CB, CBE, DSO, MC, who, among his other feats, famously led a charge by Greek soldiers and civilians which forced the Fallschirmjäger to abandon their positions on Pink Hill.

Certainly, Hathaway's character was suggested by Forrester's extraordinarily brave action and his appearance mimics that of the real man. But there the resemblance ends. Hathaway's questionable conduct thereafter is entirely of my own invention and I would hate to think that the descendants of the estimable Captain Forrester might suppose that the two are in any way related. What I wanted to do and what I hope I have succeeded in doing was simply to conjure the flavour of the battle and to deliver some sense of the extraordinary cast of characters who took part in it.

Thus, while I have included the character of Evelyn Waugh, who took part in the battle, he is there not merely as a literary joke, but also because I wished to convey the cosmopolitan nature of the Allied forces, among which not the least bohemian unit was Bob Laycock's commandos. I would refer anyone and everyone who reads my book, not only to the histories of the battle by Anthony Beevor, George Forty and Alan Clark, but also back to Waugh's masterwork on the Cretan debacle, *Officers and Gentlemen*, the second volume of the Sword of Honour trilogy.

One thing which became abundantly clear to me in the course of the writing of this book and during my hugely enjoyable and rewarding visit to Crete to research it, was the extraordinary bravery of the Cretan people. The best and only way in which I can pay tribute to their sacrifice is to dedicate it to them.